DOGGONE

A Story of Loss

Arabella Ark

Doggone is a work of literary fiction. Names, characters, and incidents are the products of the author's imagination and are used fictionally. Any resemblance to actual events, or persons, living or dead, is entirely coincidental.

Doggone © 1995 GAIL BAKUTIS
Doggone © 2014 ARABELLA GAIL ARK

Copyright case 1-1363290751
BOWKER ISBN PRINT: 978-0-9884762-1-9
BOWKER ISBN E-BOOK: 978-0-9884762-2-6
ISBN-13: 9780988476219
ISBN-10: 0988476215
Library of Congress Control Number: 2014938582
ARABELLA ARK, HANA, HI

Published in the United States
ARABELLA ARK
P.O. Box 667
Hana, Maui, Hawai'i

Cover Art: *On the Shore* © by Barbara Perrine Chu

T. S. Eliot, excerpt from *"The Hollow Men"* p. 302, *A Little Treasury of Modern Poetry,* Charles Scribner's Sons, 1950

"Blame It On The Rain," permission of Alfred Publishing, L140521-9005, lyrics Diane Warren

Also by the Author
Pants On Fire! A Tale of Friction

❧

This book is dedicated to
The ones I always have loved and
Those hardy souls trekking high roads

May the way be lit by the twinkle in your eyes
May your thirst be quenched by the water of laughter and tears
And may hearts be opened by the innocence of a smile

❧

Like a lotus flower that grows out of the mud and
blossoms above the muddy water surface, we can rise above
our defilements and sufferings of life.

Buddha

❧

Nothing human cannot be forgiven.
We are not human beings going through spiritual
experiences; we are spiritual beings going through human
experiences, in order to grow.

unknown

Shape without form, shade without colour,
Paralysed force, gesture without motion;

Those who have crossed
With direct eyes, to death's other Kingdom
Remember us--if at all--not as lost
Violent souls, but only
As the hollow men
The stuffed men.

from *"The Hollow Men"*
T.S. Eliot

DOGGONE

A Story of Loss

PART ONE

BREAKAGE

1

APART

She killed a dog. Not any dog; her dog. A chocolate lab, Moses had been her rambunctious joy, full of boisterous, undisciplined enthusiasm. He loved to greet her with a furry embrace, standing his full ninety pounds upright on his hind legs and placing his front paws around her neck to slather her face with kisses.

Lucky and her husband, Bullet, had gotten Moses as a pup before deciding to have a family of their own. As Labs were water dogs, the name Moses had been a natural choice as the Biblical Moses had been found, after all, floating in the bulrushes. They raised their Moses in the freshness of their young love.

Moses had hiked and camped with them in Yosemite and the Cascades, hunted bird and deer in the Trinity Alps, surfed and played with them in the waves of Santa Cruz and Hale'iwa. Most importantly, he had guarded their newborns as they arrived.

Over the years, he had grown deaf and arthritic, hardly able to rise off the ground without a tremendous effort. He favored the cool spot on the grass under Lucky's truck to snooze in a retreat from Hawai'i's midday sun, which beat relentlessly down on their home near the shore on O'ahu's west side. Napping that day, he hadn't heard the truck door shut; he hadn't heard the click of the ignition; nor had he heard the start of the engine.

Lucky had already been crying, loading boxes of clothing and food into her truck before she reversed out of the driveway. Bullet's van partially blocked the drive, adding to her annoyance.

Lucky had been distracted over the summer by sudden and unwanted changes in her life. Like a kaleidoscope of emotions, she was sometimes focused on anger, then turned to sadness, spun in confusion, and generally stopped at longing. Three months earlier in June, on the morning of her twenty-fifth wedding anniversary, Bullet had given her an unexpected gift at the breakfast table.

"Lucky," he said, "I've decided to terminate our marriage. I've given you twenty-five years, and that's enough. I won't spend one more day of my life with you."

She was caught pouring coffee into his cup. She hadn't moved. She had stood there pouring coffee, spilling it onto the table, pouring, still pouring the coffee, spilling it onto the floor. She slid down the wall to sit, legs splayed and wet on the coffee covered floor, mute, weak, disbelieving.

The night before, they had celebrated their anniversary, attending an art opening where she'd won an award. He had given her double *pikake lei* to wear. She had worn double *pikake lei* as his bride. She looked at last night's fragrant and sentimental *lei* as they swam awash and brown in the coffee she had spilled on the breakfast table. After the award ceremony, he had taken her to eat fish at a cheap, Chinatown dive, where they had sat at a *Formica* table under the naked glare of fluorescent bulbs, his choice of restaurant disappointing her. She had felt out of place, dressed as she was in silk and pearls.

Back at home after dinner, she had sat on his lap in the darkened living room, their three children asleep, quietly recounting to him their blessings in life, her commitment still glowing. They had made love on the living room floor not ten feet away from where the spilled coffee now pooled and where nine-year old Nico lay watching Saturday morning cartoons, quite oblivious to his parent's life altering conversation going on at that moment in the adjacent dining area.

Bullet really had to spell it out.

"I don't love you. I haven't loved you for a long, long time. I cannot live with you anymore. I feel like I'm being swallowed up by you. And, I can't breathe."

By the end of September 1989, they had agreed to separate. It was almost two in the afternoon, and she was rushing to get on the freeway to pick up the girls from private school by three thirty and move into their newly rented apartment in Manoa. She was leaving Moses at home, temporarily she thought, as she sorted out this move. She was leaving her little boy, Nico, at home temporarily as well. Their girls attended private high school in Honolulu, and their boy went to a Christian primary school near their beach home. In theory, she and Bullet hoped to trade weeks, one in town forty miles away and the other at home, to accommodate their children's school lives while Bullet enjoyed the separation he desired.

She'd found a ground floor apartment in a large New England missionary style home in Manoa, Honolulu, where she planned to wait out the separation Bullet was demanding. Along with her teenage daughters came one of their little girlfriends, Gigi, whom she loved, a French fourteen year old whose own parents had gone off to a Beverly Hills fertility clinic in a valiant midlife attempt, hoping a fourth child might stitch together their marriage.

Unlike their marriage, Lucky's was ripping apart. She did not want to tell the children there was anything amiss in the marriage. Yet, despite any hope she might have had of reconciliation that fall, she watched her happiness unravel as their estrangement deepened.

In the driveway that fateful afternoon, she had to turn her wheels sharply to the left to avoid hitting Bullet's van. She felt a bump under the passenger tire and figured she'd cut too close and gone over the curb of her flowerbed. She bumped it again with the driver's side tire and cursed under her breath. Once on the street, she got out to check her tires and to close the gate behind her. The truck was fine. The flowerbed was fine. And next to it, she saw Moses, who was not fine.

She rushed back through the gate. Hands over her mouth, she tried to muffle her scream. She ran to her beloved dog, sank to her knees and stroked his flanks. He wasn't breathing. He wasn't moving either and was quite bloody. His skull was crushed.

"Oh, God. What have I done?" she cried. "Moses, Moses, I am so sorry. Oh, I am so sorry. I love you. I love you, Moses, honey dog. Please forgive me," she begged, sobbing, whispering, hoping somehow her love could bring him back to life, which it could not.

She had been too upset to say anything to Bullet. Almost worse than telling him, how could she tell the children that their Moses was dead? How could she appease her guilt or alleviate the horror she felt?

She decided to go without saying anything. To just leave Moses as he was. To get her children. To bring everyone home to bury him together and to mourn.

First, she picked up Nico from his elementary school. Crying every mile of that afternoon's long drive to town past scruffy hills and sugar cane fields, she prayed. *Please, Lord, let this anger go.*

"Oh, damn it. Damn it," she finally cried out in the truck's cab stuck in traffic, tears slipping past her sunglasses, sobs choking the words. Weaving over the painted edges of the asphalt lane, she wondered if the other drivers sensed her crisis. Perhaps they thought she was drunk?

"What's the matter, Mom?" Nico asked, looking up from his *Gameboy* when he heard her swear. Her prayer for the anger to pass hadn't worked. She couldn't answer him. And, she was crying. Her dog was dead. And, her thoughts were tumbling irrationally through her mind.

Bullet hates me, that is real. He wants nothing to do with me, that is real. To think, only this morning I lay naked on my bed looking through redwood lanai slats at that bluest of all tropical oceans, the Pacific, and debated if I should ask him to make love, as though that familiar act would solve our problems and superglue our souls back in place. Her instincts had stopped her: *No, too painful.* If he had said, "Yes," what would that mean? Would they have to talk and look into each other's eyes?

He would say, "No." She knew he would say, "No." Or, "That's not really a good idea." Or, "I'm kinda busy right now." And, she would be visited by that new and uncomfortable acquaintance, humiliation, deep red and burning, at opening up for another wound.

With Nico in tow, she parked at the girls' school and waited for her daughters to come from class. When they got in the truck, she told them about running over Moses. Instead of going to Manoa as planned, they drove home in silence to say goodbye to the family dog. Together, they dug a seaside grave for him in the sand dune in front of their house. Ande wove *lei* of *naupaka* and beach moss to lay over him. Marianna read aloud a poem she wrote. Bullet kept his thoughts to himself. Nico just cried.

Then, after a quiet dinner, Lucky and the girls trekked back to Honolulu to move into the new apartment. But, that night Lucky could not sleep. The full moon looked like a glacier rising above the sultry volcanic peaks of the Ko'olau range. It soared above her heart outlining her new neighborhood, illuminating urban houses abandoned due to rockslides, carpets of weeds overtaking their porches, houses whose chain link fences offered a semblance of protection from intruders. She went out walking, prowling really, gazing at the shadows cast by the night's cold and foreign moon whose light revealed gaping holes in the houses' metal or shingled roofs. She stared through these roof portals at the disintegrating haunts and felt a kinship of soul with them. Her life, she mused, looked abandoned, neglected. It still seemed like her life, its shape was the same, as she was still a wife and mother of three, but there was a hole where the heart of it, her husband, belonged.

Lucky called her brother, Jackie, who lived in Idaho.

"Hey, Em," he answered roused from sleep, "what's up?"

When she told him she'd run over Moses, Jackie said, "Look at it this way, Em: he was a great dog; he was old; you liberated his spirit."

"God, Jackie," she moaned. "I'm having my worst nightmare. I haven't told you, because I hoped the situation would blow over. But, it hasn't. Bullet doesn't want me anymore. He wants a separation."

"The schmuck. Why?" Now Jackie was fully awake. "What's going on?"

"I dunno. What I do know is that I got an apartment in town, in Honolulu, which we really can't afford to do."

"Well, on the up side, Em, now your girls don't have to get up at 4 a.m. for that long drive to school," Jackie remarked.

"I don't want to tell the kids we are separating, Jackie. It was bad enough telling them about Moses. You know how bad it was for us with Mom and Dad," Lucky said. "I don't want to move. I want to stay in my home, be with all my kids."

"Can you?"

"I don't know. Things are changing so fast. But, you know me: who searched for the apartment, who answered the newspaper ads, and who called all her friends for help in locating a place? And, who just moved in? Hmmm. Yours Truly. And, poor Nico has to stay home with Bullet when I am in town with the girls. I don't know how I'll get any work done being away from my studio."

"I'm sorry, Em."

"Why in the world do I, even now, pick up Bullet's ball and run with it? I'm like a well-trained dog. *Oh, here, Lucky. Good girl, get the ball, Lucky. Run with the ball, Lucky. Fetch, heel, catch!*"

"That's typical of your relationship. I've watched that from the beginning," Jackie observed, "that you do all the work, even for the very things you don't want. I think you've never trusted him to do the right thing."

"Yeah, you're probably right. One positive note: anxiety makes a great diet," Lucky told him. "I'm losing weight."

"Should I be jealous?" her health-conscious brother, who lived his life by weights and measures, laughed.

After a day and a half in Manoa, Lucky drove home to Wai'anae, homesick, missing her son, her dog, her house, her routine, her life; angry at being displaced. Anger was her passenger; it was her fuel. It rode shotgun through her days like a sidekick traversing the two worlds.

"How's the apartment in town?" her father-in-law, Rex, asked when she arrived.

"It's bullshit," she muttered. She wasn't prepared to tell the truth; it entered the scene on its own, as uninvited as the humiliation. *Separation, divorce, dead dogs, all bullshit. What happened to our wedding vows, to our commitment?* Her heart pulsated monotonously, "I want my husband back, I want my dog back" in a steady rhythm.

At the same time, she wanted to kick both Bullet and herself. She thought he was spoiled rotten and had grown tired of his selfishness. *He feels he can cast me aside and destroy my life as wife-mother-partner, because he thinks he's fallen out of love with me,* she fumed. She was mad at herself for being so distracted, so dislodged from her life, that she would run over her own dog.

2

FUSION

Lucky had done a porcelain firing that June, opening the cooled kiln before celebrating their anniversary. Though he was a painter, Bullet had made some bowls and put them into the firing alongside her work.

"Well, this firing is like us, all right," she quipped. In the intense heat, his pieces had slumped on top of her pieces, fusing them into unrecognizable forms. When she saw the mess, she began to laugh.

"Maybe this shows we're fused, Bullet, you know, welded together."

"I see nothing but an unmitigated disaster," he remarked, unloading the hardened, deformed globules of glazed clay and throwing them into the dumpster.

The next morning, he had asked for the separation. Lucky wanted to know why.

"Any problems we have are between us, Lucky," he told her.

"What problems?"

He swore many times that there was no other woman, that he wasn't involved in a relationship with anyone else.

"Look, Bullet, I can give you time apart. I just don't understand what is going on. If you leave, the kids will be upset. Why would you want to hurt them?"

"Why don't you take them back east for the summer," he suggested. "Go see my sisters, go to all the theatre you can handle in New York, take the kids to the museums. Give me the summer to sort myself out."

When she returned from the mainland after that summer apart, he was not happy to see her. While away, their phone conversations, when she could reach him, had been the *how are you feeling?* sort. Lucky felt he was in the driver's seat on this one, not she. She was only along for the ride.

He said, "I'm not driving either. This separation is just something that is happening. I'm not controlling it."

Then Miette, an art student of Bullet's, called. Lucky scarcely knew her.

"Bullet is not telling you the truth, Lucky," Miette said. "You should know. He's been having an affair with Francine since last spring. He spent every night of the summer at her apartment at Makaha."

"I should have trusted my instincts," Lucky moaned, hanging up. *Francine. I knew and I knew and I knew.* He had denied it. Yet, every time he cheated, Lucky had felt a chill in her spine, cold water tingling there telling her in her bones that he was deceiving her.

There was no *Richter* scale to measure her anger, no barometer, thermometer, no gauge to indicate her level of pain. Chicken skin all over, chin trembling, the bile crept under her tongue with that feeling of unwanted saliva seconds before barfing. She got sick to her stomach. Then she screamed.

"The *SLIME*." That was the word that came to her mind to describe Bullet, the *SLIME*. He had lied into her soul, into their life, into their years together.

It took an acquaintance to tell her that he was with a woman, a woman who had been divorced, a woman who was twenty-three, who was from the Seychelles, a girl, really, who looked like Jackie Kennedy. Francine. Lucky knew. She knew when he danced with Francine at Miette's party. Lucky saw the lust, felt their heat. That party had been June third, before school was out and before she left for the east coast.

"Dance with anybody else, but don't dance with her anymore," Lucky had told him.

"You're a wet blanket. I'll take you home."

She stayed, but despite her entreaty, he danced with the girl, sat with her on a chaise lounge, whispering into the black curls tucked behind her ear that his wife was envious. And, Lucky was, for the first time in her married life. The girl fell into some emotional hysteria, dwarfed and crying in a high-backed peacock chair. Miette had a son, a Marine, who was now dead, not from a battle but from HIV. In the wee hours of that drunken morning, Lucky heard Miette accuse Francine of infecting him.

"I will never speak to you again if you deny what I know to be true," Lucky warned Bullet on the telephone from her gallery in October. She had to hear the truth from his own lips. She waited in silence for over an hour with the receiver pressed to her ear.

"All right, Lucky," he finally spat, "yes, I have been unfaithful to you."

"A tiny step on the road to truth," she exhaled. "Thank you. It's a beginning."

He galled her by adding, "If we hadn't been having problems, I wouldn't have fooled around; I wouldn't have looked somewhere else."

"We weren't having problems! We were just an ordinary family with growing pains," Lucky countered.

Lucky had met the girl at a few parties and knew she took one of Bullet's art appreciation classes. She had struck Lucky as an airhead, a fruitcake, a raven-haired *Barbie*.

"Puppy love and adoration are one thing, Bullet; mature love is another. You keep retrogressing, going back in time to your mindless parochial school adolescence and the heat of puberty."

"You're crazy," Bullet said. "Your mind isn't right for the way it twists things. What you say is ridiculous." Ridiculous was the word he used when Lucky was suspicious of his affair. He repeated her words of thanks for the good things in their relationship over and over as though she'd forgotten she'd said them.

"I've never, ever endorsed your lack of morality, Bullet. All you've done is hurt me and dragged our marriage through the garbage."

He yelled, "We're different. We're very different. It's our differences that have driven us apart. I'm tired of your brain, of your *knowing all*."

"Well, I hate your half-assed way of doing things: from a half-finished house to a half-finished family. You're *half-assed Pulaski*."

Lucky was dumb, too dumb and trusting to recognize the game Bullet had been playing. She wished she could feel cold and distant from the hurt, free to say, "It's over."

"Are you blaming me for your infidelity?" she gasped. She wondered how she could sit down to a family birthday dinner without gagging? *Damn Bullet and his lies.* Before he could answer, she snarled, "Shall I serve this up to your mother at her birthday dinner, your *sleeping around?*"

She suddenly hated him for sullying what she thought was the beauty and goodness of her life. She had trusted him as her best friend to be faithful, to love their family, to protect and provide for them.

Fannie must be totally the opposite of me, Lucky thought. *Maybe Bullet has been seeking that non-judgmental ability to laugh, sing, dance, and be happy in the moment. No pressure. No goals. No expectations. Just a good time. As a perennial playboy, Bullet might prefer that to his responsibilities of parenthood and marriage.*

After Queenie's birthday, Lucky suffered a night of locked guts without sleep, tossing and turning with an Italian birthday dinner that refused to be digested. She shouldn't have eaten. She knew she would gag. She managed to get through dinner with her in-laws, only at night to have her bowels raging in an uproar.

In dark, après vomit despair, she mumbled aloud, "He's pirated my love. He's stolen my privacy. He's spreading himself everywhere. I thought his body, his erections, his ejaculations were for me; instead, he was playing the single man who just happened to have a wife and three kids."

Dancing, how Bullet loved to dance. Fannie did, too. She was in his arms at Miette's party that night in June, looking so natural, spontaneous, and fun. Lucky caught a glimmer of Bullet's desire and saw he craved this girl. She didn't know he was willing to go to any lengths to get her.

Dancing in front of people, Lucky was plagued by self-consciousness. She felt like she did the dogtrot. Music didn't reach or move her with its rhythm. She could not lose herself in it like other people could. Only in the intimacy of sex could she relax and be free.

Demons of anger and hatred raged untethered in her wakefulness. Her mind got stuck on *them* in bed, on *Francine*, and thoughts of revenge. She wished it wouldn't; she wanted to stop obsessing, imagining their fire-lit bodies and mindless ecstasy versus the cool, rational, backdrop of her organized home, children, and daily routine.

Lucky wrote hate messages in her cruel night mind to Francine: "May you burn in hell for screwing my husband. Don't come near him or me or our children again." *How lame,* she thought.

Crazy for vengeance, she wished she could tear Fannie's head from her body, watch her shrivel, collapse into dust.

Lucky imagined:

- Going to Fannie's apartment manager for a key to sneak into the apartment
- Writing, "Screw you, Bull, Bully, Bullet" on underside of toilet seat, so when he lifted it to pee, he'd read it
- Beating him to the ground and jumping up and down on his torso in high heels
- Scrawling "Slut" across bathroom mirror in Francine's reddest lipstick
- Opening the bed and writing "Filthy Bitch" on the sheets
- Smearing dog poop on rims of their glasses and utensils
- Throwing away all their underwear
- Peeing on the carpet
- Peeing on the bed
- Putting a poisonous snake in the bed
- Sprinkling rat poison on the food in their fridge
- Pulling out Fannie's hair
- Pulling off Fannie's face
- Putting nails in her tires, every day
- Running over Francine with a grocery cart

Oh, God, Lucky laughed at herself, *I really AM a housewife. Running over Fannie with a grocery cart?*

Lucky thought she could sleep then. She turned over and prayed for peace of heart. Nights were like this for Lucky.

Joining an aerobics class, Lucky worked out daily for the next several weeks. She exercised in a strong wind in the dusk, lying outdoors on the concrete on a blue mat with left leg held high, ferociously side kicking. She pictured kicking Fannie's head, hard. Fannie was buried in sand up to her neck, so only her head showed. Lucky's pink running shoe hit Fannie's head repeatedly and rhythmically on her temple, which listed a little more to the side each time it was kicked, and a dark maroon trickle of blood appeared at her mouth.

Fannie was clothed in a blue shirt and caramel tight skirt as the locale changed to open space with no gravity. Lucky was driving a railroad spike vampire-style through Fannie's heart, watching her breast and chest collapse. Her thick blood oozed like vermilion pudding around the stake as Lucky hammered it deeper. She changed weight to the other leg. Her anger was an exorcism, an attempt to drive out the evil she felt by facing it.

Lucky worked out like a madwoman. She visualized punching Francine's smug face over and over like a boxer's bag, as the face bloodied and lolled on her neck. Then, she punched down between her legs, where she punched Bullet's head in the soft imagined earth where it protruded from a newly dug grave. She vigorously pummeled him. She punched to the sides, aiming for bitches and bastards everywhere.

All her muscles, even her legs, felt taut, as she got into the best shape since she was fifteen. She felt fifteen, too, as dumb, emotional, and crazy. She just looked older. The part of class she liked best was when she punched upward toward heaven, where she opened a path to escape the mess of her life.

Working out in late fall next to her former studio assistant, Yoko, Lucky panted over her shoulder, "Did you know that Bullet left me?"

Yoko hugged Lucky several times, wet with workout sweat, saying in her Tokyo English, "I so sorry, so sorry. I shock. Take care, take good care yourserf, Rucky."

One hundred sidekicks completed, Lucky knelt on the mat, hands on ground, and began bent leg lifts.

I don't want to kill Bullet. I want freedom from attachment to him and this anger, this anger, which is eroding a gorge through my heart, creating my own grand canyon of destruction. I need to watch out: I don't want to slip off its edge.

She dreamed as she worked out, too. Dreaming, Lucky was underwater in the sea. The water was electrified like a Japanese furo, and she was immersed in pain. She tried to swim to the surface but could not. All sorts of mysterious dangers moved in the murky deep. She swam in the viscous dark worrying of sharks and eels. She knew the sea was a force of nature, as it had neither emotions nor allegiances.

She surfaced as a snorkeler and emerged with her back to the shore, the water depth at breast level. The skin of the water had changed to a tranquil turquoise. In the dream, she cursed into her mask, "Damn Fannie, such a slut." Lucky the dreamer turned her head and was humiliated to discover the bathers behind her in the shore break had heard her remark. From the balcony of a beach apartment, a young woman watched.

Bullet's mother, Queenie, who lived right down the road, called Lucky, as she had every day for almost twenty years.

"Lucky, dear, I want to tell you what my bad boy, Bullet, said to me. 'Oh, Mom, Fannie's so sweet. I love her, and I like the way she does things. She's just like you.'

"Oh, no, Bullet, I told him, you're very wrong. I would never go with a man who is married with three children. You need to handle the task of loving Lucky, your wife. And remember, Bullet, your Catholic vows."

Queenie was like Fannie, Lucky thought. They were both puppy-like persons living in the moment. Queenie enjoyed shopping for pretty things, entertaining, and silly story telling. She was charming but still adolescent at seventy-two.

Lucky had resolved not to fight with Bullet anymore, as they had been since the separation. She'd do nothing: no panic, no divorce, patience. *I'll give Bullet time, at least until January, before I file,* she thought. *By then I should know if he's taken Queenie's advice.*

"I don't want a separation, a divorce, or a weird living arrangement," Lucky told him. "I want to fulfill our commitment to our children, to maintain our family, to love one another."

"I want those things, too, Lucky. I just feel suffocated by you. I don't love you."

She seemed not to notice and added, "Well, living with you has made me feel constant stress. I let you quit your job to follow your bliss, to be an artist. But, you let us depend on groceries from your mom, rent from your dad, and my hard work in the studio. You've never supported this family with a real income."

"Everything you say is bullshit," Bullet yelled. "What about my paintings? They sell. What about the house I built?"

"The house you built? You mean the house we built, and I paid for?"

She loved the house, particularly its strawberry guava and koa staircase. She recalled how steam rose from a pot of boiling water placed under a turning spit which held the twisted wood Bully and Big Al had harvested from a ravine in the Wai'anae Mountains. Steam was their strategy to straighten it. And, steam had worked its magic. The finished staircase stood rustic, hand-hewn, and original. It, more than anything, was her Bully in the house.

"Yes, you might have built the staircase, but I paid for it, I paid for the whole house with my inheritance," she protested. "And, I did half the work, remember? I was the 'go-fer'? I made the tiles; I laid the floors and counters, and I painted every wall."

"Not loving you has made the soul go out of the house. I don't care about it or the art anymore. I don't want to be with you, Lucky, because you're too much in control. There's no room for me," he complained. "You haven't fostered love in the kids' hearts for me."

"Bullet, you are responsible for your relationship with the kids."

"It's better when I'm alone with them; we all have a great time. I'm a better father without you around."

They hacked and cut each other to the bone, exposing the skeleton of their marriage. If it was dead, truly dead, she thought, they could bury it. If it wasn't, if they could assess where, what, and who they really were, perhaps they could resuscitate their relationship, grow healthier flesh and tone muscles to move forward together as a stronger couple.

"I thought the separation was to give you time and space? I agreed to it for that reason. I didn't know at that time you were involved with Fannie. You failed to tell me that little detail. And, I didn't realize, I mean," Lucky could not control the quiver in her chin, "it never occurred to me, that you didn't love me."

"I want to take a hard look at our marriage," he repeated.

"Counseling?" she asked.

He shook his head no.

"Are you taking a look at trying to make it work?" she asked. "Or, do you intend to break it?"

He continued to shake his head, looking lost.

"Your mother tells me you're having your blood tested for AIDS. Is this true? I know Miette has accused Fannie of giving her son AIDS."

Bullet didn't say anything for a while. Then he said obliquely, "I've done many things I'll never tell you about." He stared at her, and then took a quick jab below the belt. "I hate your face. Your nose gets more and more pointed, your cheeks more sunken and sharp..."

She rejoined, "If you'd lost twenty-two pounds in five weeks, you'd be bony, too. So what? What's my face got to do with our marriage? I'm skinny, because I can't keep food down, because you nauseate me and have turned my stomach and my life inside out..."

"Lucky, you're writing and starring in your own little soap opera. I am waiting to turn the light on in your head. I am waiting for you to feel guilt for what you're doing."

"Guilt? Me? What am I guilty of? Being your wife? Washing your dishes, cooking your meals, being faithful, keeping house, caring for the kids? Am I leaving you? Am I sleeping around? Am I hurting, deeply hurting, the four people who love me the most, not to mention our parents? I thought we got married in the Catholic Church. I thought those vows were supposed to mean something. Am I wrong?"

He stormed out.

Two cups of tea helped her runny nose. Perhaps only time would help the nausea. Her new tight jeans were slipping off. Best diet she'd found: Trauma. *The right ad company ought to be able to package that up and make me a millionaire,* she thought. *Get the New Miracle Diet: 'Trauma': Comes in daily doses. Start with 'Cheater Husband' and then take 'Daily Lies.' Guaranteed to make you lose weight or your money back.*

She changed her mind about patience, deciding to seek legal counsel for a divorce. *How can I have been in this relationship and know him so little?*

3

BABIES

Turning fifteen and a half, Marianna needed her birth certificate to apply for a driver's license. While looking in her first baby album for it, Lucky stumbled across photos of *them*, the golden couple making the golden family, young and in love, *picture-perfect*, living at the beach with baby, Marianna, who was such a beautiful baby.

The interstellar miracle of that birth, Bullet by Lucky's side, together for hours of wonder as they were left on their own in Kaiser's delivery room, watching the slow movement of the midnight clock, holding hands over the sterile green sheets during contractions, smiling into each others eyes after each passed, moving them closer to the pink and lavender arrival of Marianna. Bullet loved his baby girl, whom he dubbed "BeeBee," short for Baby Bullet.

Ande's arrival three years later surprised them coming weeks early one summer's eve, smooth, swift, and relaxed in an atmosphere of laughter during a jazz concert at the Waikiki Shell, Bullet high on *Wild Turkey*. A picnic of spinach quiche and mango turnovers was left for their friends to finish as

Bullet and Lucky ran between sets to their bronze *Porsche 912* in the parking lot. Slung like a hammock above the horizon in the late evening sky next to Venus, a slip of new moon lit their race to Kaiser hospital, where Ande appeared in less than fifteen minutes, pink and perfect.

Delays and false alarms accompanied two eventless trips to the hospital in the weeks prior to Nico's birth, Lucky not knowing if it was another girl or their first boy. Lucky wanted a boy so much; she was over-anxious for him to arrive. The third trip was a frenzied, late night ride to town, during which she gave birth on a futon thrown in the back of the rusted *Plymouth* wagon, a ring of fire burning her loins, as they passed the airport in the fast lane of the freeway. At the hospital, she was rushed up the emergency elevator on a gurney. Bullet was forced to take a different route in the public elevator. On the maternity level, Lucky saw him fly down the hallway from that other elevator to rejoice in the arrival of his new, very red, very fiery baby boy, hanging upside down in the air like a skinned possum, ankles held high by an orderly. As unlikely as it seemed in that moment, held that way, the baby looked to her like the Hanged Man, Tarot card number twelve.

Bullet's whole being was lit up like an electric power plant. Lucky was lying on the gurney swathed in white sheeting looking up and out at the scene, thrilled.

On the way home from the hospital, Bullet pulled into the parking lot of the first surfing beach on the coast. He lifted two day old and as yet unnamed Baby Boy out of Lucky's arms and turned his soft head toward the waves.

"This is Rails. You've gotta watch out for the sharks here. They're attracted to the warm water from the power plant." Two miles further up the coast, he stopped at Keaulana's. "When there's a south swell, there's a good right, and it's usually not too crowded here." Looking through the windshield, he turned the baby by his cheeks toward the break, whispering vital surf statistics through uncomprehending ears onto the virginal gray matter inside. The family zigged and zagged up the coast as Bullet pointed out favorite surf spots to his infant son.

"Bullet, you missed the turn to our house," Lucky cried, surprised. She was feeling very weak from two hours in the car and her exhausting delivery. Her breasts were hurting as the milk was coming in. The little girls were antsy in the back, asking for drinks. And, in the rear of the wagon, pacing on the old futon, their four family dogs were whining to get out.

Three-year-old Ande said, "Daddy, I need to make *shi-shi*."

"You better stop, Bull," Lucky warned.

"She can pee at the bathhouse at Makaha. Okay, Ande Pooh? I've got more beaches to show the baby." Eight miles further at Makaha, he grabbed the baby and carried him up the steps of the orange lifeguard tower to show Boxer.

"Boxer, name my son. Give him one Hawai'ian name."

Boxer considered the infant for half a second and said, "*Ikaika*. Means brave, strong, plenny energy."

Lucky was aghast. She had sorted through hundreds of boys' names and had a long list of her favorites, all of which had been eclipsed by one casually cast out by a beach boy.

"What are you going to name the baby?" asked Lucky's mother, Edna, calling long-distance later from the mainland. "I hope you don't name him for Bullet. It's so hard for a boy to be a junior. Besides, if you name him Richard, he'll be called Dickie. You don't need another little Dick running around. And, please don't name him for Jack or Rex, either."

"No, Mom, I don't seem to have a say in the matter. Bullet's Hawai'ian friend, Boxer, named him: *Ikaika*."

"Ka-ka? Ka-ka? You're naming my grandson, Ka-ka? It sounds like shit."

"It's not Ka-ka, it's *I-kai-ka*. It's a good Hawai'ian name. It's not my choice, but Bullet is keen on it. He says I have to accept it, since it's special to have a *ha'ole* baby named by a Hawai'ian."

Lucky called him Nico.

What a gift he had been. When she married, she hadn't wanted children, at least hadn't wanted children of her own. There were too many orphans in the world. If she were to have a family, she would adopt. But, Catholic Social Services had refused her on the grounds that she was bio-logically able to bear children. There were other applicants who were not and had precedence. Would she like a fam-ily, for example, of five Japanese siblings each afflicted with muscular dystrophy, they inquired?

Bully had no interest in adoption. He wanted his own babies. They were working overtime as journalists: she for television covering the return of prisoners of war from Hanoi, who generally arrived around two in the morning at Hickam Air Force Base. She conducted brief interviews with them and called her reports to CBS in New York, which in those days constituted "live" coverage. Her shift started around one a.m. and ended at noon the following day. Bullet reported for print journalism, writing eloquently on the Hawai'ian Sovereignty movement that was growing in sup-port with protests over the Navy's bombing of the island of Kaho'olawe. He worked the late shift, starting at three p.m. and returning home around midnight.

The only marital time they enjoyed was the midnight hour. It had taken months for her to get pregnant. Bully used to joke, "I wanna see my woman pregnant at the stove and barefoot on the beach." After a few years, she was.

Lucky lay beside Nico. As she put him to sleep, she saw his profile outlined clearly in the moonlight, such a handsome child. His eyelids appeared to be white marshmallows dozing on the sandy, toasted skin surrounding them. They flanked his proud and strong nose. Lips arced in a smile as he drifted into the sweetness of sleep. Her fingers caressed his head as softly as the gentle rustling of a fairy's feathers.

Lucky was grateful to have nine-year-old Nico, her little lamb, to snuggle, to hear prayers, to lightly tickle. He had made some really fine clay fish in her studio after school. Then he had painted a giant aquamarine mega-wave and nailed it to his bedroom wall. She lay with Nico's haystack head by her lap, stroking his hair and telling him over and over how glad she was he was her son. He fell asleep that way.

Nico had brought her joy and goodness every day of his blessed life for almost nine years. She remembered wanting Nico, dreaming of him, her toddler boy, wanting to get pregnant for the four years it took. She wanted him so badly. She had to develop faith and patience, and he came into being, a miracle granted for her to nurture and enjoy.

Lucky couldn't bear to keep Bullet's shirtless photo holding two-week-old Nico in his arms on the bedroom wall any longer. She couldn't continue to see it upon waking each morning. Before she added it to the recently assembled too-painful-framed-memories in a cupboard in her unfinished bathroom, she sat on the cold azure tiles she made years ago, looking at the man who fathered that sweet baby.

Oh, Bullet, my Bullet, my husband, my dear. How I loved you. How we both wanted that son. How precious he was to us. Nico Ikaika Samuel: "asked for from God," our son. She felt Bullet's absence like death's chill.

Lucky looked at his naked torso in the photo, a torso she knew so well, having traced the lines of veins up his arms, taut biceps, here in a tender pose holding his almost weightless son, veins she had caressed with her tongue, felt harden and fill with passion so many times. His nipples. His not so-hairy chest. She remembered examining his armpits after making love, his arms flung relaxed overhead, and remembered the tender primate searching for certain pores which would regularly get clogged or the isolated blackhead she felt compelled to disgorge, as though a little more coming was called for.

Oh, Bullet. I loved you. I loved your vitality, your humor, and your eyes. She felt his presence as co-creator of this space, her house. She looked at the walls, the posts, the beams, the long wall of folding doors, and knew this had been his space. Eighteen of Bullet's paintings lined the walls. Her eyes lingered on the long rows of his paintings, visually caressing each one, even though they weren't very good and had never sold. She cried, only a little.

The insecurity in her relationship with Bullet had begun a day before Marianna's birth. He had told Lucky he "might not be there." He had pulled the rug out from under her, she nine months with child. His irresponsibility had come flying directly into her face that evening in Queenie's kitchen as they cooked dinner.

"You better be prepared to be alone," he warned.

"What are you talking about, Bullet?" his mother had asked. "Are you trying to scare your poor wife?"

"Don't you WANT to be with me, Bully?" Lucky asked quietly.

"You know I hate blood," he answered.

"Are you afraid of the hospital?"

"I'll pass out if I have to go there."

"This baby was your idea. What do you think I can do about it now? I don't get to be squeamish."

The challenge of giving birth frightened her. Worse, Bullet wanted to abandon her. No one else could do it for her. She was venturing, willingly or not, into a dimension of pain and mystery beyond herself with no chance of turning back. At the very moment most crucial for her to live, her own death loomed as a distinct possibility in her mind.

"I mean, maybe I'll be at work or in an accident, or something will come up. I want you to be prepared to be on your own," he said.

"Don't you think I'm aware of those possibilities?" she replied. "Of course something could happen. But don't you want to be with me?"

During the pregnancy, she had read a lot of physics and astronomy during afternoon rest periods. When she did deliver Marianna the next day, Lucky felt sucked into the universe. She cried out in the delivery room during a contraction, "My butt is disappearing into a Black Hole," startling the obstetrician on duty, who didn't understand her Stephen Hawking's connection.

Bullet ended up beside her for that birth and for the others, and shared in the flesh and the miracle, as amazed by the arrival of their children as she. But, she was the one who delivered life. She saw her tiny fleck of time, her mortality. She survived each childbirth, absorbing with it knowledge enriching her heart. As a woman, she'd faced the loneliness and arbitrariness of the universe, flesh, and spirit all at once. She learned to partake in life in a way no man could, perhaps becoming aware of its fragility and preciousness the more so, because pain and birth, life and sorrow were all tied inextricably to joy.

There had been a few key moments in her life when the universe seemed to stand still. Completely detached, she could hear its silence. Birthing, giving birth three times, brought her face to face with herself alone accomplishing a deed. Like mountain climbing where she survived in the thin-aired northern Chilean wilderness, like trekking which created rugged self-confidence. No one else could walk those cliff faces for her, bear her load, or carry her out if she got hurt.

The legacy of her ferocious Wolfeson independence had been transmitted somehow genetically on those Chilean winds, imprinting fetal Ande, who was conceived in a tiny wind-whipped tent, perched atop a Patagonian glacier. Ande, who became the feral mountain goat of the family, climbing the cliffs of the islands in exploration of a swiftly disappearing natural world, in pursuit of her own unexplored nature. Early on, Lucky had dubbed this daughter her *Amazon*.

Romantic love made Lucky feel alone as well. It was a different and wonderful kind of aloneness, as someone special, unique, desirable. But in the wake of that love's departure, she experienced the reverse.

Bullet spent his first night at the Honolulu apartment with the girls. He called it *The Dungeon*, because it had low ceilings, rock walls, and small windows. Lucky took the next Tuesday and Wednesday there. Thursdays and Fridays were to be his.

On Friday, Lucky was working at home in her studio. Bullet arrived from town, loaded his surfboard in the van and crept away, hoping not to be noticed.

"Hold on!" she said. "Where are you going?"

"Surfing."

"Where?"

"Makaha."

"You are supposed to stay with the girls in Honolulu."

"I'm not going to stay at the *dungeon* ever again," he said. His wanderlust surfaced, and he wanted to go to Fannie. He couldn't, just couldn't take care of his daughters.

Lucky called Birdie's mother to ask if the girls could spend the night with her.

He is a cup with a hole in its bottom, she thought. *No matter how much love pours in, there'll never be enough to fill him.*

On Monday back in their studios, Lucky questioned him. "Where were you Friday night?"

"Down the beach."

"What did you eat?"

"Your lasagna."

"Bullet, you weren't at the beach…"

"Yes, I was…"

"No, you weren't."

"How do you know?"

"'Cause I was down at the beach, and you weren't there. And you didn't eat my lasagna."

"I was home. I was in the park with Boxer."

"I wish you would stop lying to me. Don't you get tired of lying?" She removed her apron saying, "We'd better talk to the children, so they will hear from us and not someone else that this separation is real, that it is not just to avoid the school commute like we told them. We need to tell them our family is in big trouble."

The next weekend with the whole family at home, she lay on her bed to gain calm and perspective. *Dear God, Is this the time I am supposed to talk to you? Is this what praying feels like? I need to say a prayer of protection for my children.*

Bullet came in and sat on the bed beside her. They circled words to sort out feelings, trying to sense where they were, what they were about to do.

"I want to talk to kids individually," Bullet said.

"No. I am tired of secrets," she contradicted, insisting on a whole family gathering. Both were uneasy, worried about inflicting hurt.

"Do you still think separation is best?" she asked him.

"I need time apart, Lucky."

"You had the whole summer."

"I need time."

"If you move in with Francine, I'll file for divorce. Immediately," she warned. "In two seconds flat."

"I won't," he promised. "This is a trial separation."

They went downstairs, took the plunge, and called the family meeting. Bullet did well.

"Your Mom and I plan to live apart. We are separating. That's really why we got the apartment. But we will always be there for you." A long silence ensued.

Nico was the first to speak up.

"Be where, Dad? I don't get it. What are we going to do? Are we moving?"

"Not really. Your Mom and I are going to live in different houses. That's why we got the *dungeon*. I'll uphold my responsibilities as your father."

Jumping from her perch on the stairs, Marianna exploded.

"I don't like either one of you right now," she cried. "You're both mean. I worry so much about you and school that I never smile anymore. I knew the apartment wasn't for school. I knew you didn't like us anymore, Dad." She stood in front of her parents, her face cracking open. "I've thought about suicide. I might as well kill myself right now," she threatened. Bullet tried to hold her. She pulled away, sobbing, "I wish I could live with someone else."

Lucky winced; she didn't think she could handle this pain. Bullet began to cry. He hadn't cried for Lucky or the marriage or the family, but Marianna's pain touched him.

"Marianna," he said gently, "you know how scared we feel whenever Hula Girl is missing?" Marianna nodded, glancing at her wrinkled Shar-Pei splayed out on the floor. "You know how much we love her and would miss her if she were gone?"

She nodded again. "Just like Moses, you mean."

"Yes, like Moses. Only I'd miss you a million times more than that if you left us," he said. Marianna cried harder and let him hug her. "I love you so much," he told her, "so much." She'd never seen her father cry. Bullet held each child for a while: Ande, then Nico.

Ande whispered in his ear, "You treat Mom like shit." He looked a little surprised. Then she made rabbit-lips and said, "I love you, Daddy." Laughing through her tears, Ande said to Nico, "Dad is so stupid; he needs a new brain."

Nine-year-old Nico said, "You are the best Dad, and Mom is the Best Mom in the whole wide world." Everyone sat in long-faced silence.

"Where are you going to sleep, Dad?" Ande asked. "I know you won't stay with us in Honolulu."

"Oh, I'll sleep in the van down at the beach, at Keaau's, I guess."

"Isn't that kinda risky?" Marianna asked.

"Maybe I should take my shotgun," Bullet said. "Nico, check if it's under the bed." Nico ran upstairs and reported that it was.

Lucky walked outside, too overwhelmed. She swept the carport. Bullet threw some clothes over his shoulder. She overheard him chastise the children for not hugging him good-bye.

"Where's my kiss?" he asked each one. He ignored Lucky. He got in the van silently and began to back out. She stopped him.

"May I have a hug, too?" she asked.

He held the wheel, pausing.

"Do you want me to stop where I'm going to get out of the van to give you a hug?"

She waited. He reluctantly got out and gave her a stiff hug with little pats of release, almost slaps, before returning to the van and backing out. She closed the gates behind him. Then a long cry of pain like her dog slowly being run over came from inside her. She gripped the gate knowing her world had collapsed.

Lucky was tempted that night to see if Bullet was with Francine, but that temptation passed. *I'm already beyond it,* she thought. She was not.

It was a quiet Sunday night, very black, most lights out, gates shut; everyone asleep, already preparing for a new week, everyone except Lucky, who was driving to check the true whereabouts of Bullet. Boxer's house was dark and silent; the chain link gate was closed. She was sorry. She had hoped her van would be there like in the old days with the two guys drinking and playing *ukulele.*

One pass by Makaha Beach, only one unfamiliar car there, and on by Makaha Shores Apartments. Should she drive out to Keaau's where he claimed he stayed? The children were asleep at home. It would be a long drive and if anything should happen? She made a U-turn and checked the parking lot again at the Shores. Their van was parked on the top deck. She approached it apprehensively, hoping to find Bullet asleep inside. It was empty. She walked the ramp to apartment 203. Miette had told her, apartment 203. Darkness punctuated by the noise of a television.

She knocked. She waited. She knocked. She waited. She knocked louder. She knocked longer and louder. She sensed they knew she was there but would not answer. She walked to the beach side of the apartment looking for lights. Darkness greeted her.

She decided to move the van, so Bullet would think it had been stolen and have to admit where he was. It was locked. She drove home to get the keys. When she got out of her car, the phone was ringing.

She answered, "Hello? Hello? Hello? Hello?" four times. She heard breathing on the line, but Bullet didn't say anything. She searched the house for the other set of keys but could not find them. She could not settle down to sleep. Hours passed. Sleepless. Sleepless. That was the hardest to deal with: her churning brain restlessly seeking answers or plotting revenge as questions of a thousand lonely, paranoid nights from the past rose in her mind. Had he had a sexual relationship with his young model, Fay Landis? Should Lucky ask? Why did it bother her to find her life in doubt?

After three a.m., she drove back up to Makaha Shores to knock and bang on Fannie's door for what seemed like half an hour. Finally, Bullet opened the door, sweaty and stinking terribly of sex, *her* stench. *The sweet smell of sex between us gone,* Lucky realized, *now he smells foul and randy like a goat.* His torso was naked. He'd pulled on a pair of black *T & C* sweat pants before opening the door.

"What do you want?" he asked, perturbed.

"I want to talk to you."

"About what?"

"Come to the truck." He turned to get a shirt, but the door had locked behind him. She wanted to comment on his smell but refrained. At the parking lot, he refused to get in the truck. They sparred. She got in on the driver's side and waited. Sullenly, he got in. She reversed out of the parking lot and then accelerated onto the highway.

"Where are you going?"

"I'm taking you home."

"Oh no, you're not." He leaned over and jerked the emergency brake, spinning the truck around on the deserted highway where it came to a screeching halt near the public bathhouse on the beach. He got out, slamming the door, and walked onto the sand. Slowly, she followed.

They sat by the old riverbed, murky with mud from the recent rains, as disgusting as a pigsty. The bathhouse reeked in the shadows behind them. The night was dark, cool. Time passed with their silence. Suddenly, she began pommeling his bare chest with her fists.

"I am so angry. How can, how dare, you do this to me?"

He grabbed her hands, stilling her. "I'm glad you came and found me. I guess I wanted you to."

"Why, Bullet? What have I ever done to make you hate me so much to want to hurt me like this? You're throwing my heart into the garbage."

"I'm in love with her," he said. Long looks. Time. The night. The few stars. Lucky felt his soul looking at hers, and she knew he was not in love with Fannie. Yet that was somehow okay.

"Lucky. Let me go." He repeated. "Let me go."

She knew this was what he wanted. Francine was a symptom. The name of his need was *freedom*. This truth reached the center of her being. How could she hold on when he begged to be released?

She knew she would let him go. It was not rational or verbal yet, but it was a sense of knowing. They talked till four-thirty, and then he walked back to Francine's apartment. Lucky drove the other way home in the new dawn.

She followed the billowing clouds, reflecting soft pink from the setting sun as she whizzed down to Pokai Bay on a bicycle. She hop scotched across the clouds in a dream of freedom where calm, beauty and nature reigned in her breast, that calm time before and during sunset when the world wore a special blue, tinged on its edge by the sun's peach rays. She was dressed in a tube top and shorts. The wind from biking cooled her face and shoulders. *If I were any creature now I'd be the emerald green Quetzal bird from the Amazon rainforest, elegant, sleek, exotic, flying, soaring above the jungle canopy,* she thought.

Her reality was different. There had been sleepless nights, churning stomach, constant diarrhea, buzzing brain, and fights.

That day, two long fights. All morning. Late afternoon.

"Bullet, do you have a plan? I mean, do you want to keep me and the family at home, maintain your art studio and business, and enjoy the freedom to have a mistress as though you had an independent personal life of your own?" Lucky asked.

"Maybe something like that," he conceded. "I don't want to divorce you. You can still be Mrs. Pulaski."

"Gee. Wow. I get to be Mrs. Pulaski. Should I take a lover, too? Move one into the house?"

He looked at her but didn't say anything.

"You fail to work on our marriage," she said.

"I've tried," he insisted.

"Will you try professional help?"

"No, that won't work for me." As always, he shunned outside advice. "Shrinks don't know a damn thing about me, or the way I live. You're difficult to live with, Lucky. You're too strong. I want a weak woman."

"Like your mom? Too bad you didn't marry her. You married me."

"That was a mistake. It was a piece of paper. Marriage is just a piece of paper, and we can rip it up."

"That was when we were young, Bullet. We have a history now, a twenty-five year history. You can't tear that up and say it's over. We have three beautiful children, three children you insisted on having, remember, and who are only half-raised. You say you don't want a divorce, and you don't think you love me. Well, there's more to marriage than love. There's commitment, responsibility, home, family, work. Can you focus on those things? Love can come and go during a life together. Maybe our love will come back if we try."

"You're re-writing history. I never even wanted to marry you."

"Ha," she laughed, "What about your mother's blue sapphire ring? You gave it to me for our engagement the autumn I got home from Europe."

"I should have divorced you after Diza Feinstein."

"Diza Feinstein? You were lucky not to get locked up in jail for that one, screwing one of your teenage models in our marriage bed four months after the honeymoon. Had it not been for the mood of the Sixties with communes and free love, I would have left you. I was too open. What a fool. I didn't know enough to foresee you were going to become the *Don Juan* of the decade."

"Our relationship was over for me then, you sanctimonious bitch," he said with contempt. "I've never respected you, a Wolfeson from Fruto, of all the godforsaken places, hallowed home of the Wolfeson nutcases," he added, trying to make her feel small by emphasizing her small town roots.

"It should have been over for me, too," she retorted. "Why did you stay with me?"

Why did I stay with him? What a dummy I was she thought. *Damn him and Fannie and all his damned "Fannies" of the past.*

"I want you to stop using the family van to drive Fannie around," Lucky announced. "Not while we're married. Not while I own it."

"Sign it over to me, then. I'll drive her in it anytime I want."

"I don't want her to touch anything I touch or my kids touch. I'll kill you and her and blow out the van tires."

"Like you killed Moses?" he shot back, adding, "I've got to take care of Major before dark."

Lucky turned away to start cooking dinner and said, "Right."

"I'll be camping."

"Right again."

After dinner at the end of a rain-clouded sunset, she stood under a palm tree at the beach away from the kids to cry. *Why did I ever love him?* She felt she was the darkness after sunset when the sky was without color, without light, without flash.

4

THE KENNEL

"I'm building a kennel, a kennel for our dogs."

"But, Bullet, I hate kennels. Who wants a dog if you have to put it in a kennel?" Lucky asked. They were out back in the corner of the house by the little girls' bedroom near the water-runoff ditch six years earlier. Bullet was hammering a crude, recycled-wood fence, corral fashion, calling it a kennel. Lucky was mystified and not a little miffed.

"We just don't see eye to eye on pets," she mused. It was Christmas Eve, though, so she didn't press the question. She threw the kids in the old red *Toyota* pickup along with dozens of gaily wrapped saffron braids, cinnamon rolls, and pottery gifts to deliver to friends in the community, her annual Christmas *Aloha*. Out on the highway a few hours later, Lucky was passed by another truck, this one laden with cases of *Budweiser*, Bullet, his friends, and, in the back, some unidentifiable animal.

What a surprise was in store at home: a really big "dog": a four-month-old donkey, a donkey for the "dog" kennel.

"Merry Christmas, kids!" Bullet chortled. The kids laughed, eager to pet the long velvety rabbit-like ears and feel the rush of donkey breath on their upturned faces. Then, off to bed they went, visions of sugarplums...

All except Mom who stayed up alone, as she did every Christmas Eve, to wrap endless Santa surprises and stocking stuffers. About three a.m. the braying started: endless, loud, heart-rending braying. This donkey was hungry.

"Oh, Lord," Lucky sighed. She ran upstairs to waken beer-besotted Bullet. "What do baby donkeys eat?" she whispered. He was clueless and barely conscious.

"Grass? Milk?" he mumbled.

Then she remembered the *Quick Quaker Oats* in the cupboard. She located an old plastic baby bottle and nipple in the utensil drawer. In the wee hours before Christmas dawn, she stood at the stove cooking oatmeal for a bereft and hungry baby donkey.

Before Lucky could get the food to him, he'd eaten half the railing of the new kennel and cracked the window of the girls' bedroom in his frenzy to find his mother and sustenance. Lucky fed him, dribbling water into his mouth between handfuls of the oatmeal. They bonded, or so she thought.

Outside at Christmas breakfast, which sleep-deprived Lucky served on a beautiful Hawai'ian morning, Bullet brought the donkey round to join them. Interrupted by a long-distance telephone call from Gramma Edna, Lucky left a table filled with three days worth of her annual baking efforts: a French bouche de noel which the kids dubbed *bushy*, Swedish Santa Lucia rolls, and Danish marzipan pastries, not to mention her annual eggs benedict and blueberry blintzes. When she returned, the golden eye of an egg yolk stared up from her plate. The rest of her plate and the entire rest of the table were empty, licked clean.

The children's delighted giggles filled the air as they chanted in unison, "Mom, Major loves your pastries." At that moment, the donkey became her enemy.

She learned a lot about donkeys the hard way. Old Mr. Olafson, a *ha'ole* grease monkey from Tennessee who regularly repaired their third-and fourth-hand cars, warned Lucky.

"The more stripes a male donkey has on its legs, the meaner it gits." And sure enough, week-by-week, Major added more stripes.

When Major pissed, he'd lower his hips and blast at least five gallons of potent urine in one steaming shot. One day he walked through the long living room window to eat the green shag carpet he'd gazed at hungrily for months from where he was tethered in the yard.

"Dear God, please don't let him piss on my carpet before I can get him out of here," Lucky prayed under her breath, moving stealthily toward the beast.

Ande lured him away by shaking an opened box of *Cheerios* under his nose. He laid his ears back, let out a devilish bray and charged out the double doors in hot pursuit of the cereal and Ande.

Bullet felt some indefinable brotherhood with this big *dog*. As the donkey matured, Bullet rode him everyday, cowing him by beating his flanks and head with a stick, which made Lucky cringe. He also made a habit of tying the donkey to a chain rail in the public park across the street. Major would graze on un-mown weeds by the hour. He did his share of re-planting, dropping calling cards all over the parking lot and road.

The local police weren't appreciative of Major's gifts, especially Sergeant Furokawa, who didn't take kindly to *ha'ole* "smart-asses" like Bullet, who had offended the officer once by asking if he was "the donkey patrol." Sergeant Furokawa adamantly refused to allow an "animal in the park" and wrote citations for each violation. Bullet accumulated tickets and court dates not to mention the enmity of the rest of the local force.

Bullet blew marijuana smoke into Major's distended nostrils and force-fed him beer. They became more than brothers; they became alter egos. The donkey, it turned out, even shared Bullet's sexual appetite. In the absence of a jenny, Major began to covet, who else but Lucky.

That donkey almost killed her, twice. He found a way to pin her up against a rock wall when she added water to his bucket or to flatten her to the sand when she changed his grazing stake, his donkey penis extended like a fire hose, flailing with unguided liquid pressure and hormonal urgency, slapping her about the head, shoulders and back. He liked to rear on his hind legs. She had to do a quick body roll, feigning to the right, and suddenly rolling to the left to avoid being stomped as his hooves came down. After the third brush with abuse, she refused to go near him. He could starve as far as she was concerned.

Despite being unable to train or discipline Major, and the fact that none of the kids could safely be around him, Bullet kept him at home in the kennel. He refused to geld him or put a bit in his mouth. The police, however, prevailed. After one court appearance too many, Bullet was ordered to remove the donkey from a residential area. He moved Major to a farm.

That move to the country provided a convenient alibi for what Lucky later would learn were Bullet's sexual trysts. By midafternoon or at dusk, Bullet would say, "Gotta go and take care of my ass." Dinner might just be on the table or the kids just returning from school, but no staying at home with them; his ass came first. Bullet would drag home around midnight, if then.

Lucky took Marianna, Ande, and their friends, Birdie and Gigi to St. Louis Heights for an all day hike up the vertebral ridge topping the the Koolau Mountains rimming the back of Honolulu. Her girls took off like mountain goats. They enjoyed a fabulous day, reminding Lucky of the Patagonia hikes of old which had been taxing, frightening, and challenging. She felt happy to be on the ridge in greenest of all Hawai'i with views of beaches, skyscrapers, valleys, and cliffs spreading below. She loved slogging through mud bogs, mincing single file along narrow trails, hanging from vines, butt sliding down treacherous muddy stretches, muscles trembling and watery.

Lucky felt like the intervening years hadn't happened. *I feel soooo good I feel fiiiiine.* Her hair was a little messy, French-braided and held by a wee red squinchy at the end; she wore a red see-through swimsuit and old green corduroy hiking shorts from summer she was married and hiked through Yosemite. What a thrill to have the shorts fit after twenty some odd years.

They bathed off the mud at the apartment. Lucky called Bullet to fix dinner before her hour-long drive home.

"I can't cook," he complained. "You've had the day off. I'm busy painting."

Cane fires were burning along the freeway in Pearl City and Maili, and smoke filled the air. Lucky picked up Nico from Al-boy's before going home. Once there, she checked the porcelain drying in her studio. She spotted a bowl, not her own, on a shelf. She picked it up. *Fannie* was etched on its bottom. While she was gone, Bullet had let Francine use her studio. Deliberately, Lucky let the bowl fall from her hands onto the bricked floor.

"Ooops" she feinted, as Bullet heard it crash and looked over from his studio. "Accident. It slipped."

"Oh, Lucky. No," Bullet's voice was soft, recoiling like dry sand before the impact of the next wave.

"Oh, pottery breaks all the time..." she started to say.

He was up and coming toward her, a bull in her china shop, his countenance black and menacing. Suddenly frightened, she screamed.

"Don't touch me, Bullet. Don't you touch me. Don't even THINK about it." She turned to escape. He hurled a large glazed *Hula Girl* teapot directly at her. Ande had made it, but he assumed it was one of Lucky's pots. It caught her on the hip before falling to the ground. Not too stunned to pick it up, Lucky threw it back at him. With her usual poor aim, it hit her potter's wheel instead and shattered. She dashed into the kitchen.

"What's happening?" Marianna asked.

"I broke Fannie's pot."

"Gimme five, Mom," Marianna exulted. Nico entered the kitchen and wanted to do a *high five*, too. Bullet stood at the kitchen door and then returned to his work. Lucky cooked. She and the kids were eating when he left.

Sporting a huge bruise and sore, two days later, Lucky called her mother.

"Bullet won't change his patterns of neglect and dishonesty after so many years of practice," Edna told her. "Get out of it now. Listen, Lucky, any future with him as your husband will only rob your soul of strength."

At seven a.m. Monday, Lucky called her lawyer, Thomas Ayck.

"I want to file for divorce," she told him.

Combing the self-help section of *Walden Books* near her gallery, Lucky picked up a book with its title in big red letters, *How To Forgive Your Ex-Husband And Get On With Your Life*. It had a section called the "keys to freedom" about living in the present. It told how to accept the changes in one's mate and self by counting up the opportunities each brought to the relationship and to say thank you, how to forgive in order to let the past settle.

She spoke privately to the children. Golden-haired, nine-year old Nico sat upstairs with her on the edge of her queen-size bed, blue eyes somber.

"Nico, honey, I'm going to divorce your Dad. I'm really sad and sorry about this. I love our family. But, I can't live as his wife knowing he has a girlfriend."

"He's a poor sport, Mom. He just says, 'Naw, I don't wanna play' and never even tries it, even though being with you is the most fun game in the whole world."

"I would divorce him, too," twelve-year-old Ande told her, "if I were you." There was a long silence as they looked at each other. "I know, Mom, you have to."

After a while, Ande added, "I wish he wanted to be with us. I wish Dad would just knock this stuff off and come home and be with us."

"You know what makes me mad, Mom?" Marianna asked. "Dad would just never try. He just never would do things with you. And, you're the most beautiful woman I know."

"Thanks, Marianna," Lucky said, not expecting the compliment. "You know, your lives will be about the same. You can see Dad whenever. We both love you very much and that will be the same."

"What I wanna know is when did Dad get so macho?" Marianna asked. "And, how can you stand that? He is always putting you down. I hate it when he calls you a fat-ass."

"Me, too," Lucky said. "He never used to be macho. I think it started when we moved here, and he stopped writing poetry. He wanted to do these huge paintings of huge Hawai'ians, and he started hanging out with surfers, doing a lot of sketches. But there was a low-life crowd at the beach who drank all afternoon and smoked dope. He never did any drugs in graduate school or when we lived in Europe. He was super straight. But he got sucked into that drug stuff here." Lucky sighed. "The truth is I don't know why your father stopped loving me. I didn't really notice. I was too busy."

"I think your life would be a living hell, Mom," Marianna said, "if you stayed with Dad. I think your marriage looks like this, see: it's a wooden house shaped like a wedding cake. The bottom layer is the kids, the middle layer are the promises, and on the tiny top tier stand the bride and groom. Your groom turned into a termite that is eating away the promises. The wife needs to protect her kids who are down below. Get it?"

Lucky looked at her daughter.

"Let me understand. Are you saying you don't want me to stay with Dad?" Lucky asked her.

"I thought Dad would be tired of being away by now," Marianna sidestepped. "I thought he would be sick of Fannie or had a fight or something by now."

Everyone looked sad.

Standing on new scales, Lucky weighed one hundred and three pounds fully dressed. Could it be? She weighed herself over and over. Something in her had changed. She was very thin and felt wonderful about "shedding her old skin" and becoming the body and the person she used to be.

Bullet noticed, saying, "Lucky, you're looking really good. You're looking tight, like your body is coming together." He actually grabbed her ass when she turned away and squeezed it, eliciting an "ugh" from her, not at all the reaction he had intended.

That afternoon, Lucky overheard Bullet tell the children, "Your Mom and I have been having problems for years."

Bastard, for saying it, Lucky thought.

Perhaps Bullet had found someone with the qualities he loved intuitively in his mother, the same qualities of uncritical adoration he got from Hula Girl and Moses, pure joy, pure love, pure happiness, and no criticism.

The next day in the studio, Lucky said, "Bullet, you really are a mommy's boy."

"Why?" he asked.

"I think you are taking a midlife journey back to the womb with this Fannie girl."

"You have just articulated what I feel," Bully said and started crying. "That is the feeling I've had in my gut but haven't been able to verbalize."

"What a child you are. You just need love and security."

"The most meaningful conversation we've ever had in our years together is what you just shared with me," Bully added.

"Really? You think so? I am saying that you are dumb enough to throw away the love and security you have with our family. You are mistaking Fannie's puppy love for a mature commitment," Lucky said. "You'll get over it, when you grow up."

Some days she saw clearly and with a sense of relief that life was getting easier without his demands. She no longer felt like a kicked dog. *Better alone than being stuck in that miserable relationship,* she thought, *carrying the whole load, including Bullet's dead weight.*

She got stronger. She was not withered and whimpering. Her nails were no longer bitten or picked, and the breaking of that old, nervous pattern felt very, very good.

I am liberated, she thought. *And, I am going to do what I want.*

"Are you ready to divorce?" Thomas Ayck asked her Monday morning.

"Honestly? I'm vacillating. It's the kids."

"I advise doing it swiftly to avoid bitterness since separations rarely work out. By the way, the photo of you in the *Art Calendar* is not nearly as attractive as you are in person. You must have a portrait in the attic somewhere that's doing all the aging," he joked.

Is this like a legal version of a doctor's bedside manner, she wondered? Embarrassed, she mumbled, "I feel like an f-o-o-l," spelling it out.

Thomas countered, "No, you're just a w-i-f-e," spelling it out as well.

Nice man, she thought, grateful.

5

VOWS

She read and reread the vows they had written in the old brown shingled Berkeley house so long ago.

"Love, faith, and hope are the things that last, and of these, love is the greatest. These wedding rings symbolize the unbroken circle of love and peace of mutual life. I promise to pass through the pleasure and pain of life and death with you in a union of body, mind, and soul."

How did that promise get broken, she wondered? *A promise written by us, witnessed by God and our guests? Doesn't a promise stay a promise for all eternity?*

Rotating the gold bands on her finger as she lay flat on her back on the bed, she sobbed seas of water, enough to float an armada, her arms flailing as she released the hopes, years, sorrows, expectations, and joys of the past, of the present. The skylight above let in the light, where the sky was the cool yet sunny blue of a tropical winter morning.

Praise the Lord we left the roof open to the sky, to the light, to the heavens, to God, she thought.

She slow motion dance-stepped through her memories where a dream-like Bullet floated, memories which seemed to be accompanied by the plaintive notes of an imagined oboe underscoring the current of her loneliness.

Image after image of white cloths, sheets, garments flowing: Bullet in white gauze *Nehru* shirt, Lucky in white dress, ends caught in a breeze, *Isadora*-like, trailing them high above their heads, the blue of the sky, true robin's egg blue, like his eyes, like her eyes. They were always someplace airy: Mykonos, Arabia, Morocco, Chile, Hawai'i. The whites of the cloths, the blue of the sky. Jumping, leaping. Then, they'd be back in their bedroom when she was with him, when they loved each other, with all her favorite colors there: the white walls, the white canvas shades still pulled against the morning rays, the soft saffron shadows crossing the windows to light his back, the crack of blue sea rising below the edge of the shade and above the terra cotta threshold of the deck. She really had loved him.

Rolling slowly over, they'd turn to caress, the soft-feathered strokes of lazy morning love, unrushed, rumple-sheeted, and quiet. Bullet. The glowing ivory sheets, skin smooth and soft as she loved it, sunlight illuminating the pink skin behind his ear on the pillow. Ah, how that light penetrated the delicate rosiness of the outer edge, making his ear glow a capillary flamingo. She would trace its rim delicately with her fingers, then moisten their tips with her tongue before retracing their route around his ear. And then, tracing its rim without her fingers, with her tongue alone. Turning him onto his back, his sleep sated face greeting her morning caress out of warm, sea-blue eyes. Kissing his full lips, softly. Their kisses were never perfunctory, each one an exploration, a discovery of more regions of love, maps of possibilities yet to be charted, each a journey of rare delight. They kissed often, liking to travel.

She could not believe he would hurt her. She could not believe he had gone from her life. There had been such goodness to celebrate, every reason to live and to love, to stay best friends. She used to tease him about being like two kids at summer camp. She'd pull the top sheet over their heads and whisper stories to him. She could never stop talking and go to sleep; being in love with him was too exciting. She didn't want to miss a minute in those early years.

When she looked back, she saw how poetic she was, leaving him love notes to discover: in the dishwasher, under his pillow, on the typewriter, ambushing him in the yard or at his easel with ebullient embraces midday, showering and "dressing" for dinner in long gowns and upswept hair, dinners candlelit with soft music playing to the tones of their sensuality, as desire would ignite over the table, heat up with the lighting of his pipe, and not wait for bed. She'd just hoist her skirt up as he flung her over one of the white, slipcovered couches in the living room, and he would thrust himself directly into her as though he was *Ahab* harpooning a great white. They would thrash about fully enmeshed, and he would come in an instant of whitewashed froth.

Lying in bed, she thought about their lilies. They had put in a long lily pond paralleling the entrance to the house. They had purchased three special lilies to grace that pond: a pink for Marianna, a cerise for Ande, and a lavender for Nico. It was her favorite place to sit in meditative quietude on Sunday mornings on the cool Mexican tiles. They also purchased three white lilies to float in the turquoise Chinese ceramic pot they'd set to the side of the lap pool, overlooking the sea. The turquoise glaze of the pot matched the turquoises of the pool and the sea beyond.

She often woke thinking about those lilies. And when she rose in the morning, she'd venture onto the damp tiles, to check on the lilies from the bedroom deck, to see if they had

yet unfurled their petals, and if so, to count how many blossoms they had. Then she would announce happily, as though
she were the delivering obstetrician, "Bullet! We have five lilies
today!" And, as enthusiastically, she would enter the bathroom
to brush her teeth before kissing him with minted breath.

If she could just speak her wishful heart, this is what she
would say: "I want you to love me, Bullet. I want you to drop
everything and love me. I want you to love the children, take
me to Italy, buy me clothes in London, and take me on a life
of adventure. I want you to recognize my beauty, talents, and
uniqueness. I want you to tell me you miss me."

She wanted him to tell her he was sorry for hurting her,
sorry for all the mistakes he'd made, sorry for his moodiness
and ill temper. She wanted him to tell her that after a summer
apart, he realized how special she was and how wonderful her
love was and that he'd do anything to get her back.

None of the betrayals mattered. Only the original love
mattered. She wanted to cut away from memory all the later
shit to solely cherish and celebrate their key instances of love.

One morning in early June, she recalled, when he thought
she wasn't looking, his face wore a mask of hatred. Then, when
he knew she was looking, his gaze remained hateful despite a
feigned smile. Her spinal fluid had run cold. She knew that
he was going to find a way to end the relationship, that he was
going to find some way to outrage her, to kill her love for him.

She asked herself, *Why, why, why? Why did he have to be so
awful, when everything was perfect?* His energy and talent, the
gorgeous house she loved, the gardens, the compatibility, the
travel, the art, not to mention the children. She felt like God
gave her everything she ever asked for in a man, a lover, and a
relationship. Well, almost everything. There were a few excep-
tions, if she was honest. God threw in the twists: the secrets, the
temper, the alcohol and drugs, the laziness, and the macho,

macho attitude that came from left field midway through the marriage, ruining it. Why?

She took off her rings. Queenie's sapphire and two gold bands, which glowed like two halos. She set the sapphire aside on the duvet. She held the wedding band while she rotated the engagement ring, alone, slowly on her finger, the finger deeply etched by years of ring binding, so skinny by wear between its knuckle and joint. This ring meant the most to her as it had marked a beginning. And then, she took it off, kissing it. Side by side in her hands, between her index fingers and thumbs, she held the two rings. She saw their glow, their holy radiance. She felt blessed by them, by the wedded experience they symbolized and witnessed.

She went to the old ceramic jar where years of small treasures no longer in use were stored. A baby tooth of Nico's, a lock of Marianna's flaxen hair, Bullet's canoe paddling medallions. Down at the bottom, she found the tiny *Granat Bros.* box the rings had come in. It was empty. She replaced the rings there.

She saw Bullet's black jewelry box. Yes, inside was his wedding ring, so large, more than twice the circumference of one of her fingers. He had never worn it. She pressed it to her lips. *Aloha,* fond farewell, *Jerk.* She set it back next to his black rosary beads and fraternity pins, closing the lid on the jar. Her hands were naked for the first time in twenty years.

After the big rains on Tuesday, flooding, mud, and debris were strewn over the island. Wednesday had diminishing skies with intermittent showers. The sun appeared a few times in the morning, briefly to dry the land, before the next short squall or drizzle, not safe for Lucky to do a wash yet, but clearing.

Lucky felt unsure of herself, after spending one-and-a-half hours with two lawyers to file the petition of divorce. She went through the motions, disengaged from her emotions, from herself, her old life and values.

I need to take leave of him. He'll probably accept the divorce and be relieved. Please, let there be no fight, she prayed. *In the long run,* she worried, *he's going to want to live in the house and keep the business.*

She had wept the night before at prayers with Nico, even wept over hot chocolate and strawberry tarts from the bakery next to her gallery. She cried again when she told her mother on the phone that she had decided to divorce. She was ashamed.

The next day she went to Bullet's studio where he was painting.

"Bullet, I need to speak to you." He looked up from his palette. "I filed for divorce yesterday," she said and paused. "There are to be no fights." He nodded. He motioned to Lucky to sit on his lap. "I need to thank you, Bullet..."

"Thank me?" he asked.

"Yes, for the good things: most important, our kids, making me a mom, trekking in Patagonia, the years in Paris, sharing art, building this house, bringing me to Hawai'i."

They cried and embraced.

"I'll always be there for you, Lucky," he said.

"I've never experienced a love as deep as the love I have for you, Bullet," she replied. "Please do well. Find what you want. I want the best for you. Be a good father to our children." She numbly hoped he understood that love was why, was how, she could let him go.

"Look on the bright side, Bull," she added, "you can always marry me again."

They cracked up laughing. Blubbering and laughing, they made euphoric parting promises.

"Lucky, I'll give you whatever you want. I won't fight you. What do you want?"

"I want to live in the house and raise the kids in their own home. I want sole custody of the kids."

"Why not joint?"

"Because, if I want to move to the mainland in a few years, I don't want to have to fight you about it."

"Would you, if the children didn't want to go?"

"Probably not. I think I want to stay in Hawai'i."

"What shall we do about our studios?" he asked. "We have show commitments through the end of the year, right? Do you think we can still work together?"

"No," Lucky said.

"Where's our money gonna come from?" he protested. "The invitations have already gone out."

"Oh. Right. I guess we'll just have to do the shows," she sighed.

"I'll make a deal with you. We'll split the show sales fifty/fifty. Okay?" he asked. "Is it a deal?"

"Deal," she agreed. They shook hands.

6

BOXER

" **I** had a fren. His name wuz Bullet. But, he dead to me now. He stay fockin' up his family for some fockin' cunt. He dead to me now."

Boxer and Bullet were sitting under a *hala* tree drinking *Primo* beer, just the two of them in their usual spot at the far end of Makaha Beach. An all-round waterman, Boxer had surfed, smoked dope, and speared fish at Makaha almost every day of his fifty-three years.

"Grow up, Bull. Straighten out," he said.

This was tough advice for Bullet to hear from Boxer, his Hawai'ian mentor and hero. Big Al sauntered over, dripping from the sea, carrying a long board. He helped himself to a *Primo* from Boxer's ice chest, took a deep toke on Bullet's joint, and swung his long legs over the worn wooden plank of the park picnic table bench.

"You're out of your mind, Bull, awash in fantasy land. Boxer and I can't forgive you for hurting your kids." Big Al was a Vietnam era dropout, who discovered the beauty of Hawai'i while engineering bombs for the Navy at Pearl Harbor.

"Stay outta my life. You don't know what you're talking about."

"You've gone over the line," Big Al continued, "gone beyond the unspoken code. You're free falling out in gaga land. There are no rules there, no routes to follow."

"Eh, you focka, Al," Bullet defended himself. "I've seen you. We were together with Lei and your little 'friend,' remember? We've been around the same block. So don't get all high and mighty with me." He swept the beer with his forearm off the table and out of Big Al's grasp. It spilled on Boxer's lap. Both guys jumped up and shoved Bullet into the sand. He rolled over onto his back with his legs and arms limp in the air above him exposing his belly like a defenseless puppy.

Bullet yelled, "Okay, punch me. Give me some licks, if it'll make you feel better." They wanted to punch the guy. Knock his lights out. Bring him to his senses. But, he looked too pathetic.

"Shit," muttered Boxer. "I jes' trying fo' talk to you. No need get mad. You stay crazy. I goin' call you, *Mistah Mix Up*." Bullet was crying as he loaded his boards into the van in the parking lot. Pearl pulled in to pick up Boxer and their grand kids.

"Eh, bruddah, Bull," Pearl called. "Whatsa mattah?"

"Oh, Pearl," he mumbled. "It's tough, you know? Everybody is down on my case. What do people think of me?"

"Not much," she answered. "You're stupid. You won't listen. You're a common punk, leaving your wife and kids for no damn reason. Fucking some cunt, who's nothing and nobody, leaving a good woman who loves you. Nobody respects you, nobody trusts you, nobody knows who you are anymore." She talked to him until past sunset when her grandkids came shivering out of the water ready for dry towels, home and dinner.

"Stay strong, Lucky," Pearl counseled Lucky in her kitchen later that week. Big Al was there, too. "Stop being *Mrs. Goody Two Shoes*. Bullet is hurting the family, and none of the guys can understand it. Throw him out. Pack his things in boxes and put them on the street."

"It's so painful." Lucky cried.

"Lucky, you're not hard enough on him," Big Al told her. "You're playing his game. You're washing his clothes, cooking his food, giving him a place to stay. You love him. You're part of the problem. Nothing will change unless you stop doing what he says and wants." Lucky toyed with her wooden chopsticks on the *Formica* table as Al went on.

"Make him feel what he has done. Give him nothing. Don't let him come home. Don't let him work there. Make the separation real. Make him feel what he's fucked up. The bubble is going to burst. And, protect yourself, Lucky, I'm warning you," he added. "Get a restraining order. Anything could happen as his guilt mounts."

"Hold strong, Lucky," Pearl said. "You are one frail and weak-looking thing, but I know you're one intelligent woman. You've been dignified throughout this mess. But one day, honey, you'll get real mad, and you'll fight fire with fire, dirty with dirty. Stick up for what you want, put yourself number one, and take care of the kids."

"I think Bullet has never seen the 'dark side' divorce brings but I have," Lucky said at last. "He's led such a protected life that the dodo is unaware what the consequences of his actions could be for the kids."

Al nursed his fifth beer. "Bull is not acting like a man, Lucky. He's acting irrationally. I hate to say it because he's my buddy, but a man would make a clean break and get it over. Bullet is just a little kid. He's letting his dick speak for him. We all are afraid to get old; we don't want to. He feels young by fucking a chick seventeen years younger. It feeds his ego. That's okay, maybe. But, hurting your kids is not okay. That's where we have our responsibility, our kids, to keep us in line, to take care of them. Bull's gone over the edge. Midlife crisis I understand. But not going public with it, flaunting it. That's where the Bullet I loved, the Bull I respected and who was my friend, is history."

"Eh, he's da bull in da China shop, ya know?" Pearl quipped. "All you can do is get him outta dere fast. Damage control."

"Remember Donald?" Al asked. "Bullet found his body at my rental unit, flopped on the bed, the guy a fuckin' suicide, with a gun in his hand and a bloody hole in his head."

Yes, Lucky remembered sweet, shy Don.

"My point exactly," Lucky said. "Don was a child of divorce. Don used to tell me that his life had been maimed, stunted when he was eleven, because his dad had abandoned the family, never to be seen again. I even gave Don one of my dogs for company. He seemed so lonely."

7

NICE DOGGIE

Born under the most likable sign in the Chinese zodiac, the Dog, to most people, Lucky was as irresistible as a puppy. The Chinese said a person born in the Dog year sometimes stuck to the object of affection no matter how unworthy the person was. The Dog born did not desert easily. Such persons were said to be loyal, honest, intelligent and affectionate, with a passion for fair play and justice, trained to defend home. Born in the year of the Fire Dog, that described Lucky, all right.

And, she had a natural affinity for dogs. She admired their ferocious, obedient, loyal, intelligent, honest, animated, loveable nature.

There had been many dogs in Lucky's life. Ready to establish island roots, the first thing she needed in Hawai'i to feel like a family was a dog. Moses had to be held in quarantine for four months. A new neighbor, Rod, worked at the airport and knew of two homeless pups left from an orphaned litter. Seemed their mother had gotten in the way of a plane shortly after their birth, so the guys at the hangar had hand-nursed her pups for six weeks.

Although a genuine *"poi"* dog, Champ looked like his Golden Lab dad and nothing like his German Shepherd mom. With gold in his heart, Champ was a jewel. Big cinnamon brown eyes resided in a body that grew to about forty pounds of tawny muscle.

Champ became an all-time great retriever, learning all the right moves from his mentor, Moses. The two dogs entertained picnickers in the park in front of the house while catching the *Frisbee* on the run. Their balletic, mid-air pirouettes earned them nicknames, *Nureyev* and *Bolshoi*. Rarely, if ever, did they miss a toss. As great buddies and rivals, they were equally adept in the water as in the air, vying to be first to get anything tossed to sea.

Bullet would throw two fluorescent chartreuse tennis balls as far in the water as his strength permitted. Moses and Champ would race into the shore break, swimming over waves to fetch and return them, only to bark and yap in impatience if the balls weren't immediately thrown over the pounding waves again.

They suffered a mild depression when Lucky returned home from three days in the hospital with her first "real" child, Marianna. A great sadness entered their eyes, its shadow remaining there for the rest of their years. They knew their place in Lucky's heart had suffered an irreversible eclipse. Days would pass with Lucky too preoccupied with baby to swim or play catch with them. Realizing perhaps that they were just dogs after all, they may have suffered, but at least they still had each other.

Lucky imported from England an eight-week-old Irish Setter as a present for Marianna's second birthday. Hennessey O'Hara was a royal blue blood. Her fur was a deep burgundy, and she was a real beauty. Lucky should have named Colleen, but her incredible energy and deep color led to expensive brandy like Hennessey. Unfortunately, her bounciness as a puppy soon fell into lethargy as the tropical humidity sapped her adult strength under all that long, beautiful red fur. Transplanted like a belle of the sleepy South, O'Hara just dozed the days away, her mind permanently out-to-lunch.

Like most dogs, she lived for treats. Table scraps of any sort: left-over milk from *Cheerios* bowls, bacon fat pulled off the cooked strips, crusts of lunch sandwiches, crunchy lobster shells, tidbits of pasta, steak gristle, potato skins. Three sets of cinnamon eyes from Moses, Champ, and Hennessey, scrutinized every move at mealtime, their bodies held taut in nervous anticipation as the family forks went from plate to mouth and back again. When the first chair scraped backwards on the tiles, signaling the end of the meal, O'Hara would leap up to run for the kitchen, nose held high, tail rapidly fanning the air behind.

Lucky didn't need a garbage disposal. She used the pets. Her only rule was no treats were to be given to the dogs from the table. So, when the meal was finished, remains were scraped into the dogs' bowls outside.

Hennessey was a lanky five-month-old when Lucky celebrated a Fourth of July barbecue. Two legs of lamb lay butterflied on the kitchen counter. The guests drank beer outside, enjoying the sunset from the front yard. When the coals whitened under the grill, Lucky went inside to get the meat. It was no longer on the counter. Nor was it in the fridge.

"Bullet, did you do something with the lamb?"

"No. Why?"

"I can't find it."

Poor Champ cowered in a corner of the studio with *don't blame me, I didn't do it* eyes, tail thumping pathetically beneath his quivering body. Moses glanced pointedly toward puppy O'Hara who lay under the slab roller, rhythmically and tenderly licking two near meatless lamb bones.

To break a dog of stealing food, the dog obedience manual advised tying the bones until completely rotted around the offending dog's neck. Lucky obeyed. Hennessey wandered stinking about the house and yard for three days with a necklace of clanking bones. But, rather than punishing and breaking Hennessey of a bad habit, the bones dangled as a delightful lollipop which she licked with relish.

Then ticks discovered her. Hennessey, Moses, and Champ could be sleeping side by side. Champ, mixed breed that he was, would be flea and tick free, while Hennessey hosted hoards of ticks to a never-ending feast on her aristocratic blood.

Picking ticks became a regular morning chore. Lucky would fill a glass half full of water, sit with the unwilling and whining seventy-pound dog clasped tightly between her knees, and twist out the bloated gray-blue insects. She'd drop them into the glass, and later dump its wriggling contents into the toilet, flushing them away.

Meanwhile, Hennessey fell in love with the neighbor's Irish Setter, Rusty. When his owners moved to the high and cool country of Kamuela on the Big Island, Lucky shipped Hennessey along. There, away from the salt sea and languorous humidity, she flourished, delivering twelve pups a year with her beloved mate, until he passed away of old age, and the good life.

Seal did not fare well. Bullet acquired the new puppy the same day Lucky returned from the hospital with baby Ande. "Seal," so named by Marianna because the pup was black, had the distinction of being the first of a long line of dogs Bullet brought home without Lucky's approval. He claimed he got

Seal to divert Marianna's attention away from any jealousy of her new sibling.

Seal was cute, stupid, and sneaky; maybe obstinate was a better adjective for her. She refused to listen, and she never tried to please. Marianna wasn't the least bit jealous of her baby sister. Seal was.

Seal the voracious, coveted baby Ande's toys, eating them all. Whenever Lucky's attention was elsewhere, Seal bit holes through the playpen screen and tugged out the stuffed animal of choice to demolish it, foam innards and all, in a frenzy of puppy dental ecstasy. Lucky would find the toys she had created and sewn for the babies, routed music boxes, bits and pieces of fabric, gingham and rick-rack, fur and stuffing in various locations through the house or in the yard, the trail winding back to the playpen or Seal's jaws.

It was especially dangerous if Ande was blanketed on a bed or table, because Seal would catch an edge of that little flannel, sweet smelling blanket in her sharp puppy teeth and haul it away at full speed, flipping the unsuspecting babe onto the floor along the way.

Seal ate a hole right through Lucky's patience. Accident after accident, Lucky would scold. Seal would cower and cringe guiltily. She made Lucky feel like a heel for not taking more time to train and play with her. But, obedience training was low on the list of daily tasks. Lucky felt simultaneously that she should be doing more for the poor dog and that she wanted to kick the shit out of it. The pup became more of a pest each day.

Lucky reasoned Seal was Bullet's dog, his to train, and hers to live with. There was no worse pain for her than to live with a pet she detested. It induced a profound sense of guilt. Bullet made her feel like an outsider in her own home. Either the dog or she didn't belong, he'd said. Lucky thought the dog was the intruder. Bullet said Lucky was a bitch.

The part of Seal that was Labrador wanted to catch *Frisbee* like Champ and Moses. While it was a joy for Lucky to play with them, it was not fun with Seal. She ran interference and grabbed the *Frisbee* after either Moses or Champ had caught it, yanking it from his mouth, running away to chew the *Frisbee* into unrecognizable chunks of red or yellow plastic, in some one of her many secret hideaways, spoiling their game. She pulled the same maneuver with the tennis balls in the ocean waves. She'd steal Champ's ball and disappear with it. Not noticing the theft, Champ would swim round and round in circles in the water looking for the "elusive" ball.

One day Seal was out rummaging through some garbage cans. The yard wasn't fenced, and Seal had free reign of the neighborhood, the park, and the beach. Two dopers high on some chemicals were shooting firearms in the park. They decided to use the dog for target practice. Lucky heard shots and startled, looked up from pottery making just in time to see Seal leap over the wall of the studio and collapse at her feet in a pool of blood, shot through the lung.

"Oh, my God. Call the police," Lucky yelled to no one in particular, as she was home alone. She did call. The police arrived in her driveway with the two drugged space cadets in tow.

"I'm gonna kill you, lady. I know where you live, and I'm gonna fuckin' kill you," snarled one of the space cadets. Seal had gotten Lucky in trouble with a couple of black T-shirted, tattooed, metal-bedecked, gun slinging, longhaired, greasy motorcycle-type acidheads.

"Why?" she asked the policeman, mentally calling him an idiot, "have you brought these men to my house? They are armed and dangerous and have just shot my dog. They are threatening to kill me right in front of you. And you, you stand here asking if I'm going to press charges? What do you think? Thanks a lot."

"Well, are you, ma'am?"

"I think I'll pass," she demurred while the druggies continued making their threats.

"We know where you stay!" they leered.

Taking Seal to the vet to extract the bullet and sew up the wound, Lucky added a five hundred dollar bill to her credit card debt. Back home, she dialed the Humane Society to schedule a Sunrise Service for this troublesome beast she could not afford and could not love. Her nerve failed. To have Bullet's dog put to sleep? Would she live to hear the end of it? She hung up as the phone was ringing.

When she told Bullet she wanted to put Seal to sleep, he said, "If you'd done it, I'd have put you to sleep."

"We need to find the dog a different home," she stated. He agreed.

The task of finding Seal a new home, naturally, fell to Lucky. After many false leads, she unearthed a willing farmer. Lucky drove Seal nine miles to his small acreage deep in the Nanakuli Valley, dropped her off, and sped away without regret. By sunset that night, Seal had found her way back home. *If the dog wanted to live with them so much, so be it.* Lucky relented.

Seal fucked every dog for miles around and had many litters of puppies. Moses and Champ had been neutered before Hennessey's arrival as Lucky had hoped to mate her with another Irish setter. With household bills mounting as her family grew, Lucky didn't want to spend another dime on a veterinary fee to have Seal spayed. As it was, Lucky thought she paid more for her unruly mongrel's veterinarian than for her own children's pediatricians. As other priorities commanded the tiny household budget, doggie birth control was not high on the list. Lucky rationalized that it would be good for the little girls to care for the puppies.

Countless puppies did entertain for brief periods, acquiring names concurrent with the children's interests: "Margaret Orchid Flower," "Leafy," "Tree," "Rosie," and "Rocky" were some of Marianna's nature-period favorites. "Chocolate," "Brownie," "Dumpling," "Milkshake," "Gummy Bear" and "Lollipop" arrived during a food phase. After learning to ski with Uncle Jackie whose own nickname was "Uncle Weiner Dog," the kids named a new litter "Powder," "Snowball," "Hot Dogger," "Gondola," "Wedge," "Slalom," and "Chute". They got a "Tuffy" and a "Meathead," along with the pre-adolescent bathroom yuk-yuks with a "Turkey," a "Doodoo," a "Peewee," and a "Shi-shi." Fortunately, the names were short-lived, as the pups found rightful homes and new names.

Lucky raised chickens for a while, until they broke too many teapots roosting on the unfired handles at night, knocking them over when startled awake by marauding cats. Rousted half naked from bed, Lucky would run after the offending hen or cock brandishing a hatchet. With the slathering aid of one of the dogs, she'd corner the terrified fowl and chop off its head.

One morning when Lucky discovered several pots had been broken in the night and her rooster was pecking idly in the yard, she quietly took her hatchet from the hook in her studio. She stalked the bird. Moses mirrored her moves on the left, Champ on the right. She swung the hatchet in an arc over her head and landed a clean blow on the cock's back. Next, with a single whack, she chopped off its head. The cock's headless body hopped around the yard with the dogs following its path for several moments before coming to a halt near Nico. Two-year-old Nico had watched the chicken butchery from a perch on the deck where he sat in silence and in relative safety as his mother rampaged.

"I be good, Mommy. I be good," he promised earnestly when Lucky looked up at him after wiping up the blood and feathers. A couple of nights later the family ate coq-au-vin, and Lucky mourned the passing of some fine clay pots, while savoring every bite.

Every night Lucky read bedtime stories aloud. Nico's favorite was *The Three Little Pigs*. He'd beg for it to be told three times in an evening. He hated *Hansel and Gretel*. It became the forbidden fairy tale. He was terrified by the wicked witch's oven.

Lucky had an even bigger oven, a fire-breathing kiln, in the studio just behind Nico's bedroom. He could hear the roar of hot gases and feel the blast of its heat late into many childhood nights. His imagination already stretched by reality, Nico could not tolerate Hansel's dilemma and screamed in terror if the girls asked for it to be read. Later, years later, Lucky realized his fear might have been prescient of the crematorium.

Lucky kept bunnies and lop-eared rabbits with soft fur, doleful eyes and long, sharp claws. Her forearms got raked red getting the bunnies in or out of the hutch for the children to collar and hip-hop on leashes around the yard. The cage door would inadvertently but inevitably get left open after one of the feeding or petting sessions. At sunset she might spot a jumping motion in the park or down the beach, heralding the escape of one of their dearly beloved lops.

If the dogs hadn't noticed, she would chain them up to prevent them from joining her "rescue" effort. A fish scoop net was kept on a nail in the carport for such rescues. She'd throw it over the rabbit's head in hopes of trapping it. They lost a lot of rabbits.

Stew, their big white buck, lived in a fenced dirt mound in the back yard. Stew. Stew Rabbit. One day he just disappeared. Lucky was reading *Watership Down* at the time and discovered that the bucks are the diggers of the burrows. *Uh-oh*, looked like

Stew had dug a tunnel to freedom. Several neighbors reported sightings. One evening, she discovered his escape hole in the park. That rabbit had burrowed across her lot, under the road and into the public park. She never caught him, and after a time the sightings stopped.

She developed a *que sera sera* attitude toward the animals, abandoning cages altogether. She let the guinea pigs loose in the yard. If the pet was meant to be a family member, it would stay. Sometimes, with the cats, it worked. Other times, with the darling guineas, a sad story of survival-of-the-fittest unfolded.

The guinea family had burrowed into the soft ground near the snowbushes to raise their babies. One day Rod was *talking story* in the carport. Before anyone knew it, his red pit bull, Pokai, charged into the yard, grabbed the daddy guinea in his jaws, snapping its back. Next, Pokai attacked the mommy and all her babies. The children watched in mute horror. Then they began to scream and cry. No cage protected their defenseless little pet fur balls. The freedom Lucky had given them became their undoing.

More dogs took up residence with her family. Chubby, an Australian Heeler, was a repulsive beast, covered in salt and pepper fur with a spattering of brown patches. Just as his parents, Candy, a Heeler, and Koa, a brindled Pit Bull, were unqualified disasters, so was he. Chubby inherited their negative characteristics of pig-headedness, nipping from behind, and general surliness.

He paid no attention to Lucky's commands of: "No" or "Down" or "Knock it off." Instead, he tried to wheedle his forty-five stinking pounds onto Lucky's lap in an attempt to merge, to become One. If she said, "Come here, Chubby" to pet him, in he would move, encroaching on her space, licking obsequiously. He would begin the servile little licks slowly, licking her hand, her arm, her shoulder, more and more, faster and faster, increasing intensity as he inched toward her face, the neediest dog she ever met. His resistance to being shoved was like an army tank: he wouldn't budge an inch. To make him get off, Lucky would have to push, foist, thrust, beat, scold, and shove him out the door, barring him from the house.

And the looks: the long, *I-am-worthless-and-you're-a-shit-for-not-loving-me* looks oozed from his eyes. He wasn't satisfied with whatever was given him. He always wanted more. His defeated eyes were a perpetual reminder of her failure to give him enough.

Chubby got on her nerves and occasionally for some infraction, she would kick him a swift one in the ribs. He'd yipe and cower in a corner, glancing balefully up. She'd be riddled with guilt for hurting an animal and be unable to face him. Yet, she couldn't apologize with an open heart. She'd sort of pat Chubby on the head and say, "Sorry," rushing away before he could feel genuinely forgiven. She grew to hate this unsolicited *Jiminy Cricket*, this unbidden conscience from the dog world.

To make matters worse, he was jealous of anyone she cared for. He ate Moses' food, growling from the side of his mouth; he stole Champ's tennis balls and hid them under the house; he slept in Seal's bed, shoving her late at night onto the cold concrete. He actually nipped or bit Lucky's friends. He'd go at them from behind, a sneak like Candy. Tied up, he'd look at Lucky dolefully, as if to say: *Hey, I love you and was protecting you. That's why I bit.* She feared that karma would engage between them, that her inability to love him would boomerang one day and leave her unloved by someone she adored.

The older Chubby got, the more Lucky resented his presence. He didn't project the warmth, love, and beauty a dog should reflect from its owners. He made her ashamed, ashamed to own such a mean and ugly dog.

Worse, she began to identify with him, growing chubby herself. Bullet didn't seem to like her. They no longer shared similar tastes, opinions, or values. He got into kicking Lucky psychologically, telling her she had a "fat ass" and couldn't cook or clean house, the latter not her most prized skill anyway. Bullet was working less, surfing and smoking marijuana more. She worked hard to please and appease him. To him, being with the boys or in the surf was a lot better than being with his wife. He missed dinners. Baffled and hurt, she'd sit alone at the table late at night, eating a second dinner, the dinner left out for him.

In the middle of remodeling the house, Bullet latched onto *doggie-style*. Maybe it was Lucky's fault, too. She desperately wanted to have a boy, after two beautiful daughters. Her obstetrician told her to eat vegetables, take her temperature, wait four days after ovulation for intercourse, and make love *doggie-style* to conceive a boy. It worked; they got a son.

But, Bully got addicted to *doggie-style*, a demeaning pose Lucky hated. To have her hips held in a vice grip and be relentlessly, forcefully, and rhythmically pummeled from the rear while on her hands and knees? No, thank you very much.

She didn't know how to escape her husband who was turning into a vulgarian.

One evening late for dinner, Bullet brought home the ugliest-looking, most bedraggled rat of a puppy Lucky'd ever seen. She thought it was a joke. He was going to show the kids the ugliest puppy in the world and return it wherever he found it. Wrong. It was a gift, daddy's little gift to the kids. Marianna immediately named it "Candy," for no apparent reason. And, despite Lucky's refusal to accept it, her disgust, disdain, tears, and displeasure amounted to nothing. The pup was there to stay.

Candy was born at *Paniolo* Ranch in an unspoiled valley on the far western shores of Oʻahu. Mana Gomes, the ranch's Hawaiʻian caretaker, was a dear man, revered by everyone in the community. If Mana gave you a dog, Bullet insisted, you kept it. At the same time they received Candy from Mana, Boxer gave them Koa, a brindled bundle of mangy pit bull. There was a sanctity in Bullet's eyes surrounding these dogs because of their breeders.

Candy was an Australian Heeler, bred to nip the heels of sheep on the range and herd them into disciplined groups. Candy's response to motion was intense. True to her breeding, any body part below the hip, she targeted as fair game. Skating around that heeler was sheer masochism. Try bicycling, running, skate boarding. Bullet, the kids, Lucky: none were spared. Every time Lucky's back was turned, Candy would take a nip of heel, ankle, or Achilles' tendon with neat, sharp, electrical shocks of pain. Lucky's legs became punctured like the perforations of a bloodied sieve.

How many times did Lucky have to take an unwary passerby to the clinic for a tetanus shot and stitches after one of Candy's swift attacks? Seeing movement, her beady eyes would light up and out the gate she'd dart. Her attacks cost Lucky ninety bucks a crack plus threatened lawsuits.

Lucky prayed for the pound master to pick Candy up, give her a Sunrise Service on the taxpayers' dime. He did pick her up once, but to Lucky's dismay, brought her back, charging a twenty-five dollar fine for letting Candy run loose in the first place.

Koa, the brindled pit bull, had been born in a tiny cement and chain link kennel in Boxer's treeless backyard, which bordered a befouled county drainage canal. Koa's father was a vicious, massively muscled, pugnacious pit bull, his mother, a surly German Shepherd. In appearance, Koa pulled toward his father, the brindled pit bull. Unfortunately, in behavior, he favored the father as well: he was pig-headed and offensive.

Lucky was visiting Pearl shortly after the pups had been born. They were untended, filthy, covered in fleas and feces. Koa was not only as repulsive as his littermates; he also had a herniated belly, which needed surgery. Bull did not ask Lucky if she'd like another dog. He simply dumped the puppy on her like he did most domestic chores, saying, "Deal with it."

As Koa was male and Candy was female, it wasn't long before Koa grew old enough to get stuck on Candy.

"I'm a real success at breeding," Lucky sighed. "All the worst dog traits and behaviors are getting genetically blended in my home lab." Endless litters of pups began to stink up her carport. Lucky tried to keep her humor and be a good sport, as the kids loved the puppies so much. When they begged to keep Chubby, the fattest pup in one of the litters, she gave in. Moses, Champ, and Seal still lived with them. Hennessey had moved with friends to the Big Island.

By this time, both Koa and Candy had to be kept chained on dog runs in the front or back yards, which made them crazier than normal and very hyper. But Lucky couldn't spend her life protecting the neighborhood from their bites.

At night, she allowed Koa to sleep on the upstairs deck outside her bedroom. He developed heartworms from mosquito bites, long spaghetti-like parasitic worms common in the tropics, which bore holes through his heart. He had begun to lose weight and pep, and finally, totally emaciated despite large daily meals, had a heart attack and died.

On the particular night he died, Lucky was awakened several times by the sound of his legs scratching, rattling her bedroom door.

Irritated, she'd yelled out, "Koa, knock it off," imagining him relentlessly scratching his fleabites. The next day when she opened the door to let in the air and morning light, she found his body stiffened by rigor mortis: it had been death, not fleas, visiting him.

She gave Candy to their single friend, Donald, who needed companionship. Unfortunately, he abandoned Candy altogether when he blew his brains out in his bedroom. Lucky didn't take Candy back.

8

THE STARS

C herry owned an astrology business called Star Search next to Lucky's art gallery. One rainy night when the gallery was quiet due to the bad weather, Lucky decided to get a psychic reading.

"Within last ten years of life, you've been hurt, wounded, but you are now wakening," Cherry interpreted when Lucky drew a black tarot card pierced by nine swords, picturing a person holding head in hands waking from bad dream, as her Past Self card.

Lucky then picked her True Nature card upside down: a woman surrounded by stars, filling and pouring water by pitcher from a pool and back into a pool, onto the earth, surrounded by guardian angels, nurturing and replenishing all that's around her, the Star.

"Reverse it to get your life in proper perspective and see your blessings. You are always watched over by guardians, and if you seek their guidance, they will help you."

For her Present Self, she drew the Queen of Wands, sitting on a throne with a harvest of sunflowers. Cherry said it indicated Lucky was very strong, at the pinnacle of her career, reaping rewards, holding new potential in the other hand.

"You can continue as you are and reap harvest from its seeds. In your other hand is a young sapling. You can plant and reap a new crop and gain larger rewards. The black cat in front means you can tap into spirituality for guidance."

The Significant Other in Life, representing Bullet, was a sad, worried, and angry man, who held a sapling in his hand.

"Do not seek help or guidance or support from this person," Cherry warned her. "He has spent his life planting many trees and doing much for others. Now he seeks to do for himself. He is confused. He has no power or energy to help you. He can only help himself right now. He will pull you down.

Lucky pulled the Death card. Death wore a black cape and was riding a horse, a tiny religious figure stood at the horse's muzzle next to a child and in the distance the sun shone behind a golden castle.

"Something is ending in your life," Cherry said. "Let it go. Do not hold on to Death. No hurt or harm will come from this card, if you let go."

"Are these cards always right?" Lucky asked.

"Pretty much so, in my experience."

Cherry told her the central card overlooking her life was The Lovers. It had a bright yellow sun in a blue sky. Happy and harmonious, a man and woman stood in equal positions with a stream flowing down the center between them.

"You will always need or have a lover in life. You will not be alone. Your life is in balance and harmony. Equilibrium is central to this picture. Your life needs love for balance and will always have it."

Her Future Outlook card depicted several wands suspended in the sky above a castle.

"The way is clear for you to reach your heart's desire and goals."

Out of seventy-eight cards, she had blindly picked up the Star, the Queen, the Lovers, and Death.

꩜

She fixed dinner for the old Pulaski tribe: Aunt Patti, Gramma, Grampa, Bullet, and the kids. She barbecued shish kebabs of chicken and tiger prawns, mushrooms, tomatoes, green peppers, and onions, made garlic bread, steamed rice, and chilled chocolate mousse. Lucky's passion for food and cooking had taken her to observe classes at the *Cordon Bleu* in Paris, when she aspired to be a gourmet. She adored food: its preparation, presentation, and, of course, taste; the pleasure it gave her guests, the vitality it gave her family. Home after *hula* and soccer practice, Ande and Nico had a great time in the kitchen helping her prepare everything. Ande cut a comic book jack-o-lantern and set it on the dining table where it glowed with waxy orange light.

Marianna came in and asked, "Do I have to eat dinner? I ate earlier at school, Mom. I've got so much homework."

"Okay, honey," Lucky assented.

"Fannie stole your yellow surfing hat from the van, Mom," Ande reported. "She has really ugly hair, Mom, and pinched kind of face."

"Yeah, Mom. Who does she think she is, anyway? She just stared bug-eyed at us," Marianna put in. "I was in the Makaha parking lot stretching after my run."

Bullet arrived to frame a new painting. *He's probably been surfing and sleeping all day with his twat,* Lucky thought. Bullet acted 'cute' and happy, ignoring Lucky, kissing Queenie and Patti who had already arrived and were waiting to eat. It made Lucky mad to see him happy and healthy when she was suffering.

"Hey, Lucky, come over here and help me stretch this canvas."

"I'm busy with dinner now. It's too late to work. I thought you were coming over to help me load my kiln?" Getting no response, she said, "Anyway, if loading my kiln is a hassle, forget it. I'll do it myself."

She didn't seat him at the head of the table at dinner.

"You are a guest," she told him, "and not the host anymore." She sat in his customary place.

He complained, "The prawns are burned."

"Only yours. I gave you the burned pieces," she retorted.

"Where's Marianna?" he asked.

"She's in her room. She already ate at school."

"Hey, Marianna. Come out here and join the family. Gramma and Grampa are here." Marianna kissed Aunt Patti and her grandparents before taking a seat at the table.

"Eat some shish kebob," Bullet ordered.

"No thanks, Dad. I don't eat chicken anymore."

"Well, you better eat it, girl, because you're growing and doing all that running cross country."

"I really don't want it, Dad."

"I said to eat it. So, eat it. You can sit here till hell freezes over for all I care. But you will eat it."

Marianna politely complied, forcing the shish kebob down. Then she excused herself to go to the bathroom, staying there during dessert. Bullet refused the mousse, but took bites of everyone else's. He offered Lucky no thanks for dinner.

Bullet seemed to hate the good dinner with his whole family there and the conversation of old times in Norway and Yosemite. He acted like a grouch, maybe because he'd lost this life. He saw his wife do family things right. So, Bullet fought, bouncing his anger off her. He seemed panicked that Lucky'd detached, removed herself. He tried desperately to annoy her. Bait and charge. Fire away.

The kids played a game of baseball in park after dinner. Lucky wanted to play after washing the dishes and joined as catcher. No one wanted to let her hit. She grabbed the bat anyway, imagined Bullet's head, and whacked a homer.

"Lucky, you're a jerk for having your out-laws to dinner," Edna told her. Edna called Queenie and Rex the "out-laws" now, Edna the punster.

"Mom, I want to tell you how much your support means. I have been lost for a long time. I must have thought I was Penelope, you know, the faithful wife waiting twenty years for Odysseus to come home. Only in my case, he doesn't. Bully had potential, don't you think?"

"All I ever saw," said Edna, "was irresponsibility, and all you've ever gotten from him is disrespect."

"I am amazed by how passive you've gotten," Edna said. "I mean you are very passive with Bullet. You just let him do anything."

On hanging up, Edna's closing remarks ate at Lucky.

Me, passive? I never thought of myself that way.

"Nico, tell her I'm sleeping," Lucky said when Miette called. Bullet took the phone from Nico, telling Miette he'd bring her some mangoes, then handed the phone to Lucky.

"Lucky, I'm having a party Friday at the beach in front of your house. Please come. Fannie is not invited, nor is Bullet, unless you want to bring him."

"I'll have to check my calendar," Lucky hedged. Lucky got the uncomfortable feeling Miette was a troublemaker.

Miette remarked confidentially, "You know, my son, Randy dated Fannie in the Seychelles when he was in the service. She'd had a failed relationship with a married man in Thailand, who had two kids. Randy went to California; she followed him, claiming to be wildly in love. Randy says she's an easy lay, so easy he fooled around on her for the six months they dated and treated her badly. He heard she screwed two other men after him, then Bullet this summer. Randy even accused her of giving him AIDS. That's why Fannie went hysterical at my party last June. I tell you, Lucky, this girl's been around the block and up and down it several times, too."

Memory of the odor from Fannie on Bullet assailed Lucky like a fetid stench. *How can Bullet put himself in that public cavity,* she wondered? *Fannie is like a ship that sailing from port to port, rotting through the seas.*

Miette went on, "Bullet says she makes him feel like a god. She says she does everything the way he likes it." Lucky was getting a stomachache. "Of course Fannie is sweet to Bullet," Miette meowed. "You bait a man with sugar, not with poison. But, she'll become herself soon enough. She'll have to. She can't play sweet forever." Lucky listened silently. "You know, Lucky, Fannie gloats over getting Bullet from you. She always has a self-satisfied smirk on her lips. Don't divorce Bullet, Lucky. Don't hand him over to her. Don't make it easy for her. Let her have a baby; let it be a bastard."

Was Fannie pregnant? Lucky wondered.

Miette prattled on, "She told Bitsy, 'Everything is going smoothly, just as I planned. Lucky is getting a divorce, and Bullet and I have set a wedding date'."

"No," Lucky interrupted, suddenly grabbing at a life preserver. "We're not divorcing." *I haven't signed anything,* she rationalized her fib. "There's no way I'd ever divorce Bullet. He must be lying to Francine."

Miette went on, "Last spring, Bitsy told Bullet her apartment was not a brothel, and he was a married man and not allowed to go into the bedroom with Fannie. He said he could do what he wanted. She said not in her house. Fannie didn't speak to Bitsy for a month and then she moved to Makaha Shores this summer when you left and that's where Bullet stays now."

"Perhaps, Miette, you should tell Bullet what a whore Fannie is. You're the one source he would believe. If you care about me, if you care about Bullet, for friendship's sake, go ahead and tell him what you've just told me."

"I told Bullet he was being very bad. 'How could you hurt Lucky so, when she loves you so profoundly? And the children? Fannie will leave you, Bullet. She'll tire of you and leave you. What will you do then'?"

"What did he say?" Lucky asked.

"'Miette, he said, I thought you were my friend.'"

It was time for Lucky to stop, to say and do nothing, to rest. She regretted talking to Miette, ashamed to have gossiped. But, it was done. She had to live with herself as best she could. *Stay away from the Pain Zone,* Lucky counseled herself. At least she didn't dream of Bullet any longer, nights ruptured by sleeplessness and imagined sexual entwining. *Don't get sucked back into that destruction derby.*

"Lay down with pigs and you'll get muddy," Cherry commented. "When you're pushed up against the wall and people are firing at you, it's natural to fire back, not to turn the other cheek. If you want, you can tell Bullet you're sorry for succumbing to that sort of mudslinging."

Talking, talking, talking. Lucky was talking. She needed people. Needed to hear people. Needed to talk. She needed to hear herself talk. She talked too much: constantly, repetitiously. Why did she need to tell the same little anecdotes over and over? Why did she seek people out? She felt blind, biased, nervous and neurotic. Too willing to talk ugly talk. Forgetting to get on, get over. *Slow down, Lucky. Slow down,* she thought.

Lucky's face crumpled in the midst of glazing or making beds. It collapsed when she least expected it. Some days she escaped the sorrow. Those days were filled with town activities, phone calls, business, and kids.

She remembered being alone in Paris when Bullet had gone fishing in Norway to earn some money. Her back had ached from not being held and hugged by him. How it had ached. She knew the ache would go away when she saw him again, because they were in love and married, and the separation would end in a few weeks or months. It was a terrible pain that she'd never forgotten.

This time was different. There was no date for the pain to end. The pain was jagged as an arrow being wrenched from the flesh it had neatly pierced. There was no lover; there was no holding; there was no telling what the future would bring. It required a great leap of faith for her to stay alive.

9

JOLTS

Squabbles. Marianna was vacuuming the house. Lucky was working on the accounts upstairs in her office. Bullet shouted from the painting studio for Marianna.

Instead of coming inside to talk to her, he shouted over the din of the vacuum, "Marianna, Marianna." Marianna couldn't hear him at all. "God damn it, Marianna, I'm calling you. Come here." Suddenly, a knee assaulted Marianna on her backside. Bullet jerked the vacuum out of her hand and pulled the cord out of the socket. In the ensuing quiet, Lucky heard Marianna burst into tearful screams.

"Dad, Dad, stop it. What're ya doing?"

"You answer me when I call you, girl. I don't want to have to interrupt my work to come and get you."

"Dad," she cried, "I couldn't hear you. I couldn't hear you, Dad. You're hurting me." Bullet, who was six three and weighed two-twenty, had her thin arm twisted behind her back and was pulling it painfully upwards. In this position, he lectured fifteen-year-old, five-eight, one hundred and seven pound Marianna on how she should 'respect' him.

"I don't always respect what you say, Dad," she whispered.

"Why not?" he asked, finally letting go of her arm.

"Because, you're a doper. Would you trust what a woman cocaine user says?" He looked blankly at her. "I wrote a paper about drugs for science. Marijuana kills brain cells. I felt so ashamed when I presented it in class," she cried almost hysterically, "because I learned that my dad has all the same symptoms as a drug addict or an alcoholic."

"Lucky," Bullet roared. "You. You're responsible for this. You set this kid up to study drugs and make judgments about her dad. I otta kill you for sending her to that fancy-ass school."

Lucky went into Marianna's room later to console her out of earshot.

"Honey, don't make a mountain out of a molehill. Your dad is under a lot of pressure right now. We're getting ready for our big sale. It's a tough day. I'm sure he didn't really mean to hurt you."

"Mom, you always take Dad's side. He kicked me and tried to break my arm. Are you blind? Don't you care? That's child abuse."

"Oh, it is not. He was just frustrated," Lucky said.

"You should call the cops."

"I'm not calling the cops into our family life, Marianna. We can solve our own problems. It's no big deal. You'll get over it."

"You just don't want to see what's going on, Mom, do you?" she asked as Lucky walked out of the room.

A letter from the University of California Office of Admissions arrived in the morning mail for Marianna. Lucky walked into the girls' room to place it on Marianna's top bunk bed and gasped. The walls of the room were no longer white. They were covered in row upon row of red, marking-penned graffiti.

I hate you, Mom. I hate you, Dad. Losers. Fuckers. I hate you. You only care about yourselves. I hate you. I wish I wasn't your daughter. I wish you'd die. Die, Mom. Die, Dad. Fuckers. I hate you. I hate you. I hate you.

Lucky sat down on the floor, pulled there by the weight of the shock. She got up after a while and walked slowly to Bullet's painting studio.

Bullet asked what she was doing.

"I need some white gesso, a pan, and roller. Take a look at Marianna's room."

She didn't want Ande or Nico to see this mess. She repainted two walls. Despite her efforts, the angry red words bled through.

The kids bathed that night, ate Chinese take-out rainbow tofu soup in front of the TV, and went to bed. Nico came upstairs, coughing and miserable, wanting to sleep in Lucky's bed. He was sick with a cold and sore muscles. She'd picked him up early from school. He had been parked most of the day in front of the boob tube.

"Is this leukemia, Mom? Am I going to die?"

"Of course not, honey."

"I don't get it, Mom. Dad told me today he loves me, that I'm his first son. So, I asked, 'First son'? Are you going to have more sons, Dad?'"

"And what did your dad say?"

"I dunno. I turned up the TV, 'cause I didn't want Dad to see me cry." He fell asleep in her bed propped up by three pillows for his chest cough.

"I hate our family not having its father," Ande blurted when she came upstairs.

Pulaski's Annual Holiday Studio Sale was long over; everything was cleaned up, put away, back in order. Lucky watched Bullet drive away, his van going down the street. All she could see were its red taillights and its black spare tire. The retreating van became another reality jolt. She got lots of them. Everything seemed so normal, even their fight.

Despite the garbage of the last six months, Lucky continued to find it hard to imagine life-without-Bullet. Her marriage was such a physical thing, losing it was like life without her leg. She went through all the legal motions of putting him out of her life, but she still felt they were a family, a unit; the head was just gone for a while. She had thought his love was permanent.

Instead, Lucky's rock, she used to call Bullet her rock, had crumbled into sand and washed away. Gone: gone love, gone youth, gone freshness, never to be again, except in memory. Bullet had been her Apollo: this man with a physique of sunshine and Dionysian laughter. But, he held a devil inside, she realized, who was destroying all she held sacred.

Their annual art show of beautiful work proved to be a day filled with clients, sales, and conversations. Good friends came to the sale, good friends. She announced to each of them that the *All American Family* was no more; its bubble had burst; the picture had shattered; the dream had ended. She sold every one of her pieces. Bullet sold two small watercolors. It looked like he would be the beneficiary of their fifty/fifty deal.

Bitsy and Miette had come.

"What are you getting Fannie for Christmas?" Lucky overheard Bitsy ask Bullet. Lucky froze like she'd seen Judas in the flesh, her world suddenly violated. She roamed around the courtyard inwardly raving under her big lauhala hat in anger and hurt. She finally locked herself to have a good cry in the stinking plastic outdoor portable john she had rented for the event. Had Fannie come, Lucky'd have flown screaming at her, in public or not.

Little words of truth played back to her: "I'm choking," Bullet had given as his reason for leaving his home, his kids. "I'm choking, suffocating, drowning." *Is he breathing better in his new house with Francine,* Lucky wondered? *Is he free and happy?*

In this time of assessing, she realized she loved the shape of her life, not the content. *Con*tent. Con*tent.* Interesting word. She thought about faith and hope: the ability of people to change and adapt. In those years of marital discontent and self-abnegation, she had built a career, built a family, built a lifestyle.

She really shouldn't have wrung her hands and acted like the separation was a shock and the end of the world when yes, the subterfuge was a shock, but not the inevitable dissolution of the relationship. She had somewhere along the line decided to stay in the marriage, to find satisfaction, if not as a beloved wife, then within other corners of the marriage, as the mother and homemaker.

Lucky had put her soul in the closet of her marriage, letting it get musty on a shelf, quite forgotten. There, dulled by disuse, stiffened by age, it napped. Now she felt it waking. Anything was possible. She would sign the papers. The divorce would become fact. No turning back.

10

ANNIVERSARY OF LINNEY'S DEATH

"You think your kids can get out of this unscathed?" Cherry asked Lucky over a leisurely morning coffee.

"Absolutely. Or, at least I hope they can. The truth is Marianna is having a hard time. She's pretty angry. I don't want to set up camps of hatred like my parents did, so I have been letting Bullet be at the house whenever he wants to." Lucky sipped her espresso.

"I never imagined I'd get divorced, Cherry. My brother, Jackie, and my sisters, Laura and Linney, and I vowed that if we ever got married, which we highly doubted, we would never divorce. We would never, ever put our kids through the hell our parents put us through when they divorced. So, now that Bullet has broken the marriage, I am doing my best to maintain a semblance of normalcy. I want the kids' world to look the same. Same house, same town, same school, same friends."

"That's probably a good idea. They'd be pretty traumatized if they had to enter a whole new world like moving to the mainland."

"Right," Lucky agreed. "They adore Queenie and Rex. I still invite them over for birthdays and holidays. It wouldn't be fair to cut them off just because of the divorce. I sure don't want to get hit by the same troubles my Mom had with Linney and Jack."

"What were those?" Cherry asked, refilling their cups with decaf and milk.

"Oh, God, you don't want to know."

Cherry looked at her quizzically.

"Okay," Lucky went on, "so when my Mom divorced my Dad, they engaged in a battle over money and custody. Their fighting lasted three years in the courts. It was really vicious. During that time, my Dad broke into the house, took furniture, and beat my Mom and Laura, if they were there. Anticipating trouble, my Mom made me keep the number of the police department written on my wrist like a holocaust tattoo. If I was home, I'd call the police. I never got hurt. I was *the lucky one*. Lucky. That's how I got my nickname. Didn't I tell you, everybody called me Emily, my real name, before their divorce?"

Groaning, Cherry shook her head, black curls corkscrewing from her scalp like slinkies down a staircase.

"Linney was my sister. Actually, I had two sisters, Laura, the elder, you've met her, and Linney, the younger. The one I am going to tell you about is dead. She was Linney.

"She was younger than me and unwanted. That is, I didn't want her. That was when I was four. My father didn't want her. That's when he was thirty and about to become a millionaire and very important. My Nana told me that. He told my mother to abort the baby, but instead, my very Catholic mother had a nervous breakdown along with my new little sister.

"Nana didn't want her either, 'because', she said, 'babies are a lot of trouble.' And, Nana had to come live with us to take care of all the trouble, because my mother was staying in the hospital a long, long time."

Lucky was not sure when the tragic coincidences started: had it been the day her sister, Linney, died? Perhaps. Or, had it been four minutes after midnight on November 29th, dead Linney's birthday, when Lucky's own daughter, Marianna, had been born in 1973? Then again, maybe it had been the April day in 1945 when Lucky's mother, Edna, had killed her own mother? Sister Laura had been named for Edna's mother, Laura, a grandmother who died shortly before Lucky had been born. Lucky's birth had triggered the first of Edna's postpartum blues. Blues or grief, whichever, colored the rest of Edna's days.

What had started was pure generational hell. Lucky knew that for sure. As far as she had traveled, as many people as she had met, as much distance as she had put between herself and her family of origin, the losses had caught up to her, held her in their grip, rattled her inside out, and proceeded to dine upon themselves at her very table, eating her children and her soul.

Her Nana had a ping-pong paddle with lots of holes drilled in it. She said "it would sting a lot harder with holes in it when I catch you, if you're naughty." She hung it in the broom closet. Because Emily had to pass that closet each time she entered the kitchen; she skirted as close to the opposite wall as she could.

Then the baby came home and cried a lot and was generally weird. Babies seemed weird to most four year olds, and she didn't like her mother's much.

When the baby could walk, she got in the way. Got in the way of the wooden plank swing, and it wasn't Emily's fault the baby got hit on the noggin. That swing knocked that baby flat down on the ground. A big purple plum grew out of its forehead. The baby screamed a lot, and her Nana screamed a lot, and Emily wasn't allowed to play with the neighbors or the swing for a full week. And, she had a fierce encounter with that paddle.

Baby Linney would grab Emily's dollies, which she told Linney over and over was a "No-no." The baby would grab them anyway. None of Emily's things were safe.

Emily remembered finding the baby in the living room with a real hammer, banging the mahogany coffee table.

"No-no," Emily yelled. The baby, still holding the hammer, toddled over to the side table and banged it.

"No-no," Emily yelled again and tried to wrest the hammer away. The baby wouldn't let go of it. Emily took the baby's arm with the hammer still in its grip and hit the baby on the top of the head with that hammer.

"When I say, 'No-no', I mean, 'No-no'. So, you better listen." The baby started crying, and here came Nana and out came the holey Ping-Pong paddle and who got hit? The bad baby? No! You know who. The one who was trying to protect the house and mom's furniture. Emily never liked that sister, especially not after that.

"By the time I did like Linney," Lucky told Cherry, "she was a funny little poet girl, all grown up and yet so vulnerable. And, she didn't like me. Linney had gotten too sad from all the years of wishing she was liked. And, then, she died."

Lucky sobbed; her grief and guilt, unadulterated, years overdue, for Melinda. Dead by suicide, sweet Linney, who devoted her life to trying to reconcile their warring parents and to be loved. Her death was a direct, albeit ten years later, casualty of Jack and Edna's selfish, emotionally explosive battleground, where they recklessly laid minefield after minefield on the landscape that was their children's playground.

Linney lived for their reconciliation. It was her fantasy. It was as if, in her schizophrenic mind, her parents could get together again, then she, Linney, could get her heart, soul, and rationality together. That, of course, never happened. Linney's mind had divided against itself. It assumed the shape of the violent divorce, each side hating the other with no chance of reconciliation. It housed no mental or emotional safety zone for her crushed spirit.

When her parents' big custody case came up, it looked like Jack might get Linney and Jackie permanently or, at the very least, every other weekend and a month in the summer. Laura and Linney grew worried over Linney being left alone with Big Jack after what he had done to Laura. Before the custody hearing, they shared with their mother and her attorneys a carefully sequestered little "secret," the secret that Jack had molested Laura a few summers earlier.

Laura's secret became the ultimate weapon in Edna's arsenal. How Edna chortled in her joy. With this secret in her hand, she knew she would gain control. She gave no thought to Laura's humiliation and need for therapy. She had gotten a "secret" weapon to destroy Jack. She could hit him back for the years of violence she had endured. She could hit him back for the women he had seduced. She could hit him back for the money he had withheld. Hit him back she did. But, she also hit each of her children in the process.

Edna went public with the *secret* in the courtroom of their small town. Sex abuse in the Fifties was looked upon as the girl's fault. Laura suffered after the custody hearing more than she'd suffered with the original abuse. In the courtroom, her secret exploded, a scandalous bombshell, ripping the family forever asunder and casting them out of their small town's society.

Laura's friends from childhood cut her out of their world as being "tainted and dirty," a *bad* girl. Miserable at home and shamed, deeply shamed, at school by gossip leaked from the courtroom, Laura begged Edna to send her away to boarding school. Edna had no money. And, she was blind to Laura's pain, feeling her own so acutely. Denied the option to leave, Laura's only recourse was rebellion, which she took in the greasy arms of her after school *pachuco*.

11

STORY OF THE BIG BAD WOLFE

Lucky fell into a reflective time warp. She fell backwards to her ten-year-old self, Emily. She was sleeping. Her back was curled in the fetal position on a single bed. It was dark, quiet. The sound of covers rustling, and the pressure of someone getting into the bed woke her. As Lucky remembered, she saw a close-up of her child face waking in fear.

That young Emily slipped out of the bed on its other side, ran in four a.m. darkness to the bathroom, carefully locked the door, and turned on the light. The bathroom was old-fashioned, for it was in an old San Francisco Sutter Street hotel, its style from the nineteen twenties was white and cold. Tiny octagonal mosaic tiles on the floor resembled old oyster crackers. White subway tiles traveled up the walls as wainscoting. There was a pedestal sink with chrome fittings and faucets, each reading hot and cold, and above, a wall mirror. She was cold, so very cold.

Emily sat on the toilet, her legs dangling, not tall enough to touch her bare toes to the floor. She did not need to pee. She sat and waited, listening, watching. The glass doorknob twisted, its cut crystal facets turned slowly back and forth. She was sure she'd locked it. Still, she gripped the sides of the toilet seat. She was so afraid.

Two sisters, Laura and Emily, lay in twin beds on a summer night in 1956 under a roofed *lanai*, where heat stored there from the day wafted into the still light air filled with wet, rice paddy humidity and the faint smell of shrimp, which the Mexican-bound ducks from Canada devoured as they flew south.

The covers and sheets were neatly folded up to each chin as though the beds had been made with the girls inside them; their little faces paralleling each other as they looked straight up at the opaque *filon* sky, not looking at each other, whispering. The elder, Laura, was twelve with dark auburn hair shadowing her round head and metal braces on her buckteeth. She described the hunting trip she had just returned from with their father, Jack Wolfeson.

"His thing, Emily, his pee-pee. Dad pushed his pee-pee in me."

"What?"

"Dad and I had to share the double sleeping bag, you know, the one he and Mom always use at the lake? He didn't want me to bring my new *Spin and Marty* one. And, I woke up, because I was sleeping on my side, and I felt this thing behind me in my legs. I started kicking like crazy, but I couldn't get it away. I screamed bloody murder, I was so scared. I thought it was a bug or a snake. But, it wasn't. It was Dad."

"Dad? What do you mean, Dad?"

Laura didn't say any more. And, ten-year-old Emily didn't ask anything more. She lay puzzled at first under the thick blanket of secrecy, which would co-join the sisters like Siamese twins in a bond thicker even than their blood. Emily lay silent, fearful of what she did not know but sensed she somehow comprehended. She let the implied warning sink in. She could not know what really had happened to Laura; Emily was too young. But, she understood Laura's fear, outrage, and, was it shame?

"Does anybody know?" Emily finally whispered.

"I don't think so."

"Didn't anybody hear you scream?"

"I don't know. The paying hunters were sleeping right near us in camp. But, they were in tents. Maybe they couldn't hear. George, Poole, and Ernie slept out by the fire near the horses. They all drank a lot. Dad and I slept in the open, too. We set up further over closer to the trees where the provisions were hung. Dad had me keep my mess pack and a hatchet under the pillow in case bears came around. You know, to bang on the metal to scare 'em away and wake the camp. The dogs were tied up by us."

Emily remained silent.

"When I woke up and felt this thing, I screamed and reached for my hatchet. I had it under my pillow in case those bears or coyotes came 'round. Dad grabbed my arm. He was whispering, 'Don't make any noise. It's all right. It's just me. Shhhhhh.' It hurt a lot."

"Huh?" Emily interjected. "What? What hurt a lot?"

"Dad's thing, dummy. It hurt me a lot. I got up to pee, and I was bleeding and sticky. Nobody said anything in the morning. I couldn't even wash 'cause we had to break camp."

More silence from Emily.

Then, Laura asked, "You believe me, don't you?"

After a long pause, Emily said, "If Mom knew Dad hurt you, she'd divorce him, don't you think?"

"Yep. She would. So, don't tell Mom, okay?" pled Laura. "We have to keep it a secret, our 'little secret,' okay?"

Emily felt a searing heat like that of a branding iron burn into...where? Not her brain, not her heart, but rather into her soul. It was her soul that was torched, where this new knowledge incinerated her innocence in one incandescent burst.

"What about Linney?" Emily worried. "What if Dad tries it on her? You know how Dad loves to snuggle her on the couch during *Gunsmoke*, or *Maverick*, or *Wagon Train?*"

"She's too little to tell. She wouldn't understand anyway. But, *you* better watch out."

"Okay."

Emily remembered the morning just weeks before when she had sat alone in the cold hotel bathroom scared of her own father. She had wondered since then if it had been a dream.

The summer night was hot, bearing reminders of the one hundred and ten degree heat of the afternoon. But, Emily felt a chill skitter across the surface of her skin. It was a strange chill, carrying revulsion and seduction like twin passengers. Her skin was moist from the heat, from the chill, from her fear.

Nine-year-old Linney played her game of "Pretend Mommy" nearly every morning on those same twin beds, where she liked to feed, diaper, and sing to her dollies, something their real mother never did.

Jack and Edna ate and breathed ambition for the material wealth America in the Fifties promised to its educated middle class, fresh home from World War II and newly distended with babies and bills. They dreamed of careers in business, memberships in country clubs, vacations, large houses with garages to house big boats and big cars surrounded by big front and back yards. They wanted it all. And, they knew they could have it, if they used their brains and ingenuity.

They made Phi Beta Kappa, dean's list, attended business and law schools. They strove tirelessly. There were not too many hours in any day to work or too many hands to shake as they ascended the ladder of material success.

Borrowing from everyone they knew and obtaining loans from the government, they started a hunting lodge and wilderness outfitting business. They invested wisely in raw land, buying and leasing huge tracts of wilderness in Alaska, the Olympic peninsula, the California and Oregon coasts, the Cascades, the Sierras.

After college, Jack moved Edna and his ambitions to Fruto where he had been born, to base their burgeoning hunting business in the heart of Northern California. There, with its spongy overlay of small town sky, its rice paddy humidity, its endless breeds of mosquitoes, where wetness oozed from the intricately canalled land where thousands of wild ducks and geese fattened off shrimp before taking their seasonal aerial migrations to Canada or Mexico, there, with its adjacent sheep roaming foothills, there where deer and elk roamed the coastal range, Jack and Edna raised their family.

Edna felt suffocated, stifled, oppressed by the heat, the small town gossip, and the loss of her intellectual circle. Her mother had just died of uterine cancer, the "c" word in those days, when Jack moved Edna with him to the country. There was no time for Edna to grieve. She was too busy. She had a two year old and was seven months pregnant with Emily.

Laura had begged Edna to kill her.

"Please, Edna, please. Get the morphine."

"Mother, it's only been an hour since your last injection," Edna protested.

"Edna, Edna, please," Laura implored. "I can't take the pain any longer. Please. All the morphine. Let me go."

"Let you go?" then twenty-three year old Edna asked, not sure what her mother meant.

"Let me go to God. Let me be finished here."

"But, Mother…"

"Just do it."

As Edna's own babies started piling up, Edna's system couldn't hold up to the added demands. She collapsed with post-partum blues, spending months in bed, showing interest in neither the babies nor the business. By her thirtieth year, Edna had popped out four live ones and suffered three miscarriages. She lost herself in closets of depression, hung herself with medications, and wore headaches like veiled and feathered cloches. Abortion lived far distant from her Catholic mind and loins. To avoid more babies, she began a silent withdrawal from Jack.

Jack resented what he saw as her weakness as a woman. He resented the loss of his partner. And, he most certainly resented her departure from his bed.

"Snap out of it," he commanded, month after month, year after year, wanting his svelte and brilliant bride to return. When she couldn't, he took her on the ride of her life: electroshock therapy, the emotional clearinghouse of the Fifties.

She came out of that all right, the light in her mind snapping on and off at random intervals for years to come. Quieter, she was much quieter for a little while, walking with only a slight limp in her left leg from the violent twists her spine took on those infamous sanitarium rides.

Their skirmishes began as Edna regained her strength, and they escalated over the years. She had bounced out four Catholic kids in ten years and used her economics degree working past midnight to turn Wolfeson Wilderness Outfitters into a multi-million dollar empire. Despite accumulating wealth, their material success had little effect on their malignant, if not quite aborted, hearts.

Jack was very smart and became very rich, very powerful, and very attractive. He was a consummate outdoorsman with better rugged good looks than the *Marlboro* man. As arrogant as he was big, he often behaved like a jerk in public, liking nothing better than pinching waitresses on the rear after placing his order. He relished cracking crude jokes. It didn't matter if he was in front of his family or business associates, Jack liked a dirty laugh.

The family court judge denied Jack rights of visitation following Laura's testimony and ruled that Jack could never be alone with any of his three daughters. The physical violence wrought in Jack's house had hit all the females living there. But, since Jackie was a boy, the judge did not consider Jack a threat to him and granted Jack visitation rights with the only son.

Edna happily sold the family home and immediately moved to the Bay Area. Hating men, she donned the badge of an ultra-feminist. She reentered the work force and devoted her incredible energy to humanitarian causes like UNESCO and Save the Children. She succeeded on a global scale at what she couldn't accomplish in her own backyard.

Indeed, her "backyard" was a mess. Edna did not come out of family court the "winner" she wanted and deserved to be. Abused, victimized, and humiliated, she felt outraged. She became vindictive. Surviving seventeen violent years under Jack's rule, arduous years for which she never gained a cent of recognition after her divorce, a divorce which cost her more than money, a divorce which cost her the life of one child, the heart of another, the companionship of a third, and more, she became a staunch feminist standing with the likes of Bella Abzug and Gloria Steinem.

The emotional abuse in Edna's new house after the divorce kept its residents staggering. She forbade the children referring to Jack as "Dad" or by his name, Jack, and instead forced them to call him, "The Ripper." All the good and positive things he had ever done were conveniently "forgotten" as he was demonized into an object of fear and loathing. The party line was that "The Ripper" was evil, had ruined their lives, and was dangerous.

Young Jackie was treated a bit as a traitor for visiting him. On return from his weekend away, Edna would sit Jackie down on the kitchen counter and begin an interrogation, noting every word, every nuance, every gesture. She wanted to know about Jack's lady friends, his associates, and his finances. She wanted to know where they went, whom they saw.

Nine-year old Linney listened, missing her daddy, suffering what she thought was his rejection in ignorance. She didn't know why Edna suddenly thought her daddy was so bad. Edna told Linney "The Ripper" had divorced her too, along with Edna, and didn't want her anymore. As the marriage was broken, Edna broke Linney.

Linney loved the stories Jackie whispered to her late at night about what he had really done on the weekend. He related a trip hunting for elk in the Cascades one weekend, a flight to the Aleutians to seek Kodiak bears another. Linney made up her mind to live with her father as soon as she reached fourteen, when the courts would hear her appeal.

Just before that fateful birthday, she told Edna she no longer wanted to live at home. Edna flew into high gear. She knew Linney was free to choose to live with Jack. But, if Linney were ill and under a doctor's care, Edna would remain her custodian. Linney was a physically healthy adolescent. Edna was more than familiar with mental illness, having spent months after each pregnancy in sanatoriums for post-partum blues and other forms of depression. She knew what the signs of psychosis were.

Edna called her most recent psychiatrist and told him her daughter was having a mental breakdown. She said Linney was seeing snakes coming out of mirrors, had run in her night-gown onto the freeway entrance, had taken the kitchen knives and hidden them under her pillow, and had lit the curtains of her bedroom on fire.

Away at university, Laura and Emily were summoned home to help Edna face this crisis. The psychiatrist, at Edna's request, admitted Linney to a local hospital's psychiatric ward. On her first night there, an orderly raped her. When the family arrived for a consultation on her condition and treatment, Jack came, too.

Linney was brought into the room unable to talk, her tongue swollen by the Librium salts administered to her by the staff. The doctors recommended keeping her there under observation for two weeks. Her roommate was a fifty-two year old nymphomaniac. Emily visited every day. Linney begged her help to get out. But Edna had convinced Emily and Laura that Linney was dangerous not only to herself but also to others. The sisters never doubted Edna, never questioned whether Linney was actually ill or not.

Linney was too terrified to speak up for herself. She wasn't safe. Look where her family had thrown her when all she wanted was to be with her dad.

Months later, she was released from the psychiatric unit. By then, Jack had petitioned the court to allow him to take care of her. The court reasoned that Linney had become ill living with Edna and ruled in his favor; it was time to give Jack a chance.

He had remarried an attractive woman Edna termed "an airhead" and become involved in the society circles of San Francisco. In reality, he had no time to spend with an emo-tionally unstable adolescent. He enrolled Melinda in a hoity-toity private school he could brag about to his friends. And, the "airhead" let their Hispanic help look after Linney for the most part.

The first time they left home after Melinda had moved in, Constancia was cleaning up. She went to the basement to make sure the lights were turned out and to store some leftovers in the walk-in freezer. Opening its doors, she found Melinda huddled in a ball on the floor, unconscious. She had left a note, something to the effect that nobody wanted her. She was fifteen. She had written it in perfect French. And in perfect Spanish. And in Latin. And in Japanese. She was brilliant, if unappreciated.

Melinda moved in and out of mental hospitals from pre-adolescence to her early adulthood, sometimes living with Edna and "hating" Jack; other times living with Jack and "hating" Edna. Jack paid for the best psychiatric care available. Emily realized too late that the truth about their father's sexual molestation of Laura and a few genuinely loving hugs for Linney might have been cheaper and more effective therapy than hospitals and drugs.

Failing to reconcile the broken parts of her life, at twenty-one, Linney leapt from the Golden Gate Bridge, not into oblivion in the San Francisco Bay's gray waters as she had intended, but rather onto a cement piling far below. A passing motorist spotted her crumpled form. Brother Jackie ID'd her at the morgue.

"Her cerebrum was shattered," he told Lucky on the phone. Lucky and Bullet had moved to Hawai'i only a few weeks earlier. "She looked so fragile and sweet. I thought she was going to wake up, Em," he choked. "But, the skin on her forehead was translucent where she hit, and underneath, it looked like a spider's web, only the web was red, etched by her blood."

Emerging from her reverie into the past, Lucky whispered, "Oh, Linney, please forgive me, forgive me. You loved me so much, and I was insensitive at that time. At every time," she admitted. At critical moments. In fact, Lucky had been out of sync with Melinda most of her shortened life.

"I want to come to Hawai'i with you, Lucky," Linney had begged in her odd, Lithium-slurred speech on the phone from the sanitarium where she was kept in isolation. "Let me live with you. Please," she pleaded the night before Lucky was to depart.

Just back to the U.S. after a year in Paris and flying to Hawai'i in the morning, Lucky could not imagine taking along her damaged sister.

"Oh, Linney, you can't. Bully and I don't even have a place to live yet." Lucky made a natural excuse, but it masked her terror of having to take care of Linney. Linney, after all, was safely taken care of in the sanitarium, which turned out to be not so safe, since she escaped on a forged medical pass to self-destruct off the bridge a week later.

Linney's death, she remembered, didn't affect Bullet at all. Minutes after she received the tragic news from Jackie, Bullet's parents had arrived for dinner at the new house. Lucky was weeping in the bedroom. Rex knocked loudly at her door.

"Lucky. We're here for dinner. Where the hell is it?"

So long ago. It had all happened so long ago. Yet, it was still painfully alive in Lucky. Atop the coral reef, Lucky walked and mourned. She walked her too-short beach, walked through the years, hopelessly etching the grief of her tracks onto its shifting sands.

Well past midnight, Lucky's body was quiet; there was not even the sound of her heartbeat. She was aware of her pulse drumming in her eyeballs, temples, heart, stomach, and limbs, aware of its steadiness, its slowness. The night air was viscous and laden with salt, damp with north swells' chill. Huge surf pounded on the shore a few yards outside, a constant thundering tremor in the outer world, then each wave diminished crawling into shore like thick green spittle.

Yet, it was quiet, too, so quiet she heard echoes from the past, sounds of her father leaving the autumn she turned thirteen.

"Give this to your mother," he had said, handing Emily, not yet known as Lucky, an envelope bloated with divorce papers. She heard his heavy home office door close with finality, the rasp of the pink *Imperial*'s ignition, the cumbersome groan of the axle as it lurched into the rounded curb gutter clearing the driveway, the powerful thrust of the engine as it accelerated onto the road.

She had liked the things the family had done together: the kids hanging out at the country airport on weekends learning to drive while Jack tinkered with his plane engine, learning to co-pilot when they flew to remote Indian reservations for Sunday picnics, learning to shoot at the grange, fly fishing in rivers, camping on glaciers, and rock-climbing just about anywhere. The kids simply could not get enough of the outdoors.

As a girl, Emily loved Big Jack. He taught her skills of self-sufficiency, how to survive and to take care of herself in the wild. She felt most alive exploring the wilderness or the sea with him. He also taught her how to taxi and land the *Cessna*, how to drive the *Imperial* with its classy panel of push buttons. She drove a stick shift at age twelve, worked in his personnel office after school, joined the National Rifle Association to be like the boys, and won blue ribbons on the town's swim team.

If he asked for straight A's on her report card, she earned them. She would hand him the card still wearing her white *buckskin* shoes from school, expecting praise. Looking it over, he would casually ask, tossing the card on the floor, "Why aren't these *A pluses?*" She would try harder the next term, far surpassing her classmates. Yet, no matter how well she performed at school, she could never please him.

She groomed herself carefully, sewing her own clothes based on the sophisticated fashions she saw in *Vogue* and *Bazaar.* Edna had lost interest in her own appearance. The children heard Jack criticize her for losing her figure and "going to fat." Lucky just had to look beautiful, to be noticed. At ten, she even went to a modeling school in San Francisco, The House of Charm. She wanted desperately to be attractive. In addition to weekly ballet classes, she stretched her back nightly on a bar in hopes of growing taller, as Jack equated height with power and the accumulation of wealth with intelligence.

She hoped he was proud of her. Perhaps he was. He bought her lots of extravagant presents: a *Schwinn* bicycle, her own *Zenith* television, *I. Magnin* and *Ransahoff* dresses. He even bought Emily an airplane, a *Cessna 172.*

He drove the whole family out to an empty sugar beet field on the edge of the Poole's ranch in the early evening hours of Emily's seventh birthday. There sat his new plane. It was his, after all, not really hers, though he pretended it was, claiming it was her birthday gift. That way Edna couldn't scold him. He did teach Lucky to fly. As the years passed, Jack acquired several private planes, squiring clients up and down the Pacific coast from Baja to the Aleutians in the same path those wild geese flew.

What Jack lavished on Emily, he withheld from his wife. Edna grew jealous and called Emily a little gold-digger. Jack had found another way to control them both.

Edna had to beg permission from him to drive the *Imperial* to the grocery store or to pick up their four kids from school. Yet, Edna worked. She worked as secretary and accountant for Wolfeson Outfitters in a home office. And, she worked for no reward that Emily ever saw. Jack held the purse strings and refused to buy Edna a car or a washing machine. "Your mother can go without," he told the children. If she wouldn't put out for him, he wouldn't put out for her. He'd show her who was boss in the family, even though they both wore the pants in the business, a business that sparkled brightly with success while their domestic life dimmed.

The Wolfesons were members of the Porpoise Club. Summers in Fruto could only be survived outside of air-conditioned interiors by full-bodied submersion in the cool of swimming pools. By May, the whole town seemed to move into pools. Kids competed on swim teams, taking long morning lessons, synchronized swimming, water ballet, diving, or Red Cross junior life saving. Parents, bodies coated in the foreign luxuriance of *Bain de Soleil* tanning gel, lounged in the water with inflatable platters of wheat thins coated with cheese whip, green olives stuffed with red pimentos, and the perennial martinis with tiny white onions speared on colorful toothpicks.

Emily liked the high dive best; cannonballing was her specialty. If she executed an especially good one, the splash and wake would drench the adults, send their inflatable appetizers adrift, and considerably dilute the alcohol content of their drinks. Jack would lunge into the deep end, chasing her through the water. If he was quick enough to catch her, he would dig his long fingers under her armpits or into her ribcage in a ferocious tickle attack. Emily would do her best to skitter away, laughing and screaming.

But, if Jack caught hold, which he usually did just at the ladder or as she was pulling herself up the side of the pool, she was doomed to a long and tortuous session of feigned "fun," which was what Jack called his relentless tickling. It was painful. She would be paralyzed, unable to scream or cry out.

Sometimes, she would swallow so much water, she would choke and fear she was going to drown.

"It's so gross," ten-year-old Emily told Laura, "how Dad tickles me in the pool. I told Mom, but she just pooh-poohs it. She says, 'Dad is rough housing, just having some fun, playing with you.' I didn't bother to tell her how sometimes he pushes up on me, too, right in the pool in front of everybody."

"Yeah. He does that to me all the time. You know, presses into me, between my legs? I hate it. I wonder if he tries it on our friends? Like when we play ball tag?"

Both girls fell silent at that mortifying thought.

Because of Jack's thwarted sexuality, Emily could not trust him. Like a rabbit or a deer stalked in the woods that has caught the scent of danger in the air, she became alert and cautious to the signs of Jack's approach. She curtailed her movements, carefully avoiding being caught alone with him, not wanting to get trapped.

Emily knew Jack loved her the best of the three girls. But, she was not able to stop his rages. When Edna and Jack's divorce ground to a halt in the sludge of legalese, the ensuing violent outbursts were especially bad.

"Write the number of the police down on your hand," Edna told Emily, when she knew Jack was coming over. "And, if your father hits me, call the police and say, 'There are acts of violence being committed at 986 South Normal Street,'" a mantra she made Emily chant by rote.

Emily's thirteenth autumn found her pert from acrobatics class, hair shorn in a pixie cut, standing in the kids' bathroom staring blindly at the salmon-pink, bordered-in-blue bathtub tiles and blue *W* monogrammed terry cloth towels hanging on the white porcelain rack. Frozen in paralyzed silence, she intently listened to the scrapes, grunts, and scuffles echoing down the length of the house, where at the far end, Jack was trying to move the king-size bed he and her mother shared out of their bedroom.

"No, no. You can't take that," Edna cried.

"Get out of my way. Just get the hell out of my way."

Slap, grunt, scream, scuffle, scrape, scuffle, then, a million decibels of her mother's anguished screams, as her father's open-handed slaps-on-flesh reached Emily's ears. She hated their warring, the sounds of their fighting. Big Jack dealt his attacks with full frontal blows, breaking noses, ribs, arms, rupturing eardrums, blackening eyes. Edna, like a defending general, lashed with her tongue, wounding psyches, hearts, and souls. When words failed her, she marched out the troops, marshaled their hapless children sometimes behind her as backup weapons, other times turning on them herself, objects of her emotional wrath.

Emily chose not to engage in the family battles. She silently cried instead, locked in the relative safety of the bathroom, body shuddering, helpless to stop them. She was a child of eight, nine, ten, eleven, twelve, and finally thirteen during those beatings. Publicly, Emily adopted a "show must go on" attitude. Her parents' problems loomed above her young life like a leaky circus canopy. She was a professional clown, managing to perform well enough while pretending to ignore the family's tragedy as it raged as unpredictably over her as weather.

What could she do? She knew she'd get hurt herself if she interfered. It was her parents' fight, not hers. Many days after school that autumn of their divorce, Emily cried in frustration, privately pounding the salmon tiles of the bathroom or the floral plastered walls of her bedroom. Day after day, she beat a painful rhythm to their fights. She believed anyone moving into their house when it was sold after the divorce would be infected and sicken and die from the pain drummed and cried into the walls.

The family home was a battlefield. The most devastating wars of Emily's life were fought out on that emotional no-man's land, her *home*, a never to be forgotten wasteland each of their spirits continued to haunt. *Home is where the heart is*, she thought, unable to understand the cruelty of her parents in hurting their children, in viciously using them as pawns in their attempt to destroy one another.

Laura came to Edna's rescue countless times, a dutiful soldier, Laura who dared run interference for Edna, Laura who was brave and wouldn't stand for Jack's bullying. Emily saw Big Jack strike Laura many times. Linney, ripped apart psychologically, became the most obvious casualty, dying as she did, although all the children were wounded; they couldn't help but be. And, Jackie, little five-year-old Jackie, was prized as the spoils of war.

When Edna and Jack's divorce was final, Lucky buried her sadness like waste from an abandoned campsite. She never allowed herself to grieve for the breakup of her parents. There was no time for it as the broken family moved from crisis to crisis. She vowed that she would never marry, never have children. She never wanted the pain she experienced passed to another generation. Lucky attended Sunday school every Sunday without a miss in seven years, but that fall she lost her faith in God.

That was how it had gone living in her family. After Big Jack left, Lucky never felt she could trust anyone to love her, not as faithfully or deeply or silently as she loved them. Insecurity and distrust burrowed graves in the fertile ground of her soul, where they took up permanent residence.

Edna had been married to a man who not only beat her, but also sexually abused her daughters. When she found out the latter, she tried to kill him in every way she could, except physically. She tried the legal system, but it backfired on her with machismo. She got custody of her kids. But, Jack saw to it through his clever lawyer pals that she got no money, no alimony, and no child support.

Jack Wolfeson denied all allegations of misconduct made against him. He took as his second wife a model, who climbed social circles, not mountains, and loved spending the fortune Jack had amassed through Edna's expert accounting. The macho mountain man remained highly regarded in his business. He suffered no social stigma from his acts of incest and violence. Jack never paid for his crimes against his daughters or ex-wife. Jack cut Laura, Linney and Emily out of his business, as though his three daughters never existed. No financial legacy would be passed on through the females, he determined. He never expressed remorse; he never asked their forgiveness.

After Lucky and Bullet moved back from France, Laura asked Lucky if she had any contact with Big Jack.

"Why would I?" Lucky asked. "Do you?"

"Yeah," Laura said. "I see him sometimes. He's still a control freak. Even though he's married, I don't think he really likes women."

"Laura, don't you get it? Of course he doesn't like women. He's all about control. We weren't people to him. That's how he could treat us like he did. To him we were like objects he thought he owned."

The only bad thing that happened to him was to see his innocent, blue-eyed, strawberry pig-tailed Linney die. Of course, he crippled Laura emotionally, but after the rape, he no longer cared about her.

When Edna sold the country house and moved the kids to San Francisco, Lucky didn't cry or express sadness at leaving her small town home and her friends. Out of self-preservation, she threw all her energy into a stage career and new friendships. Greek tragedy stood at the top of her list. She played *Antigone* and *Electra.* She memorized Shakespeare, loving the role of *Portia* with her famous "quality of mercy is not strained" speech and the half-mad *Ophelia*. Lucky wandered the gravel road in front of the house on cool October mornings reciting lines from August Strindberg's *Miss Julie*, lashing the autumn air with Julie's sadism. Lucky languished in the hammock on late afternoons pretending to be each of Tennessee Williams' debauched and decadent heroines. She volunteered at the San Francisco Actor's Workshop, doing odd Girl Friday chores, even bringing coffee to Tennessee Williams during rehearsals for a production of *The Glass Menagerie* there.

By the time her parents' divorce was final at the end of her junior year, she had developed into an ardent young actress. She wore theatrical characters' lives like a colorful Joseph's coat instead of dealing with her own pain, pain that she was becoming quite adept at ignoring.

Edna was alternately controlling and smothering. After Jack left, she lived and breathed life through the children, as though unable to function on her own any longer, like a patient hooked to a respirator.

"Our family is like a tire," Edna would tell them repeatedly. "I am the hub, and you children are the spokes. You're each an extension of my personality." The kids would groan, knowing another of her diatribes was starting, and look for an escape. Edna grew so difficult and emotional that for Lucky the strain of living with her mother was almost a worse prospect than living with her father. But Edna held the trump card, threatening to kill herself if any of the children left. Lucky had to stay.

12

FOOD FOR THOUGHT

L aura turned to food for comfort and protection. Chocolate became her "raison d'etre," coating her shame with calories. Her torso assumed the shape of a thousand *Almond Joys*, profusely sculpted into gleeful *Mounds* of feminine delight. *Hershey* bars and *Milky Ways* boarded short-term in the fridge. She gained a thick layer of fleshy protection from ever being violated against her will again. She got fat. She got asthma. She got pregnant. But, she didn't get happy.

Lying flat on her back on the living room floor, Lucky was awash in memories of a summer when she was eleven or twelve in a lakeside cabin, lying upstairs on cots with Laura, where perspiration dripped from Laura's fourteen-year-old flesh. As a fat teenager, she suffered a near death sentence in figure-conscious America.

Lucky loved Laura, how close she felt to her; Laura wasn't angry or judgmental then. She was riding the brink of abuse, walking the edge of her pain, like an unlikely tightrope walker, a crippling crash possible at any second.

It was easy for Laura, with the biggest calves and boobs in town, to get noticed. But, it was hard for her to get asked out on a date. For all their years in elementary school, Lucky, Laura, and Linney practiced five-positioned plies in Saturday ballet and tap classes. But, even the regular exercise couldn't control Laura's girth.

Lucky learned sewing in a mandatory home economics class. Shirtdresses were longer in those days, below the knee but high enough to show girls' calves. Lucky sewed for Laura the most basic of gathered skirts and hemmed them just below mid-calf in a well-intentioned effort to hide her legs. Eventually, the rest of Laura's body caught up in size, and there was no hiding that.

At that lakeside cabin so many summers ago, both girls were lying on cots, looking up at the ceiling, then lowering their gazes to their knees. Lucky could see hers clearly, where she had a *Mad* magazine propped open. Laura couldn't see her knees. Her breasts blocked her view, large watermelon lobes rose out of her fourteen-year-old chest. Lucky wondered if melons, too, would be her destiny.

At forty-three, she knew they were not to be, for her chest was as flat as it had been that summer afternoon. It swelled briefly in the promise of youth, flourished in nursing three babies, and shrank back into skeletal repose with middle age.

Lucky occasionally regurgitated her own private memories of Big Jack from the dark well of her past. *Oh.* Like poking her from behind, catching her unaware. She was six years old and had just memorized the *Hail Mary's*. As she climbed up the rungs of the ladder to sleep in her top bunk, Daddy shocked her. He pressed his stiff member against her tiny back, holding it parallel to her spine, rolling it back and forth over the vertebrae. Another night, he grasped her little buttocks and pretended to give her a boost.

"Let's get right up there, Emily. Up you go," he huskily whispered.

Some nights back then he caught her with a probing finger, pushing an unpleasant piece of the rough-washed flannel from her *Lanz* nightie into the folds of her warmly bathed tushy. In bed at prayer time, wet probes from his thickened tongue met her wee mouth instead of chaste goodnight, paternal kisses on the proffered cheek. She deliberately slept in the top bunk, where crawling in with her was nigh impossible for a man with his large frame. Her prayers and formative relationship with God were co-flavored by sexual arousal and revulsion. Two things she couldn't bear after that childhood were gratuitous, wet, sloppy kisses or anal stimulation.

Her *little girl* craved *daddy's approval* not his sexual attention. Her ego knew that was 'wrong,' 'taboo.' But, her libido absorbed it, storing it in a hidden corner, where it remained to haunt her like a twisted "love dowry" popping out unexpectedly in adulthood.

Emily vowed to live a good life, to be decent, kind, and fair to people. When she married Bullet, it was because she felt he would love her unconditionally, like a rock. He wasn't ambitious like her father; he wasn't anything like her father, except he enjoyed the outdoors. He was a hippie, a creature of the fine arts, poetry and painting. She thought she would be safe with him.

Just as Laura looked to food for comfort and for protection from her parents, Lucky used food to attract attention, to please men, to serve them, for a challenge, for a chance at perfection, for visual and visceral presentation. She became a gourmet, a model chef, and a social cook.

Edna had taken no interest in domestic chores, hiring a cleaning woman, and spending her days in the office as Jack's paralegal and long nights at her desk as his company accountant. Emily took over the kitchen. She baked her father Boston and chocolate cream pies, chocolate chip cookies, and devil's food layer cakes from packaged mixes. It was a start. She learned to serve a man. She made the dining room beautiful, picking flowers and lighting candles. She called herself *Emily Post* and practiced impeccable manners on his clients, employees, and brother Jackie.

Being the youngest of the children, he needed help cutting his food and holding his utensils. Emily took over. She carefully sliced the cutlet away from the bone and cubed his meat into tiny, half-inch bites. He didn't want the bone left on his plate.

If she accidentally pushed the meat into the potatoes, Jackie's legs began an agitated swinging under the table. If she put more than two peas on his fork at a time, he would begin shaking his head from side to side, mouth tightly shut. He carefully segregated the meat from the potatoes, the potatoes from the peas, the peas from the cubed meat. If she dropped a morsel of food back onto his plate, he screamed, hating his food to be mixed. Nothing could touch, or he'd cry, even the butter was not allowed to melt out, but was kept dammed in by the crested peaks of his mashed potatoes.

He grew up tired of being the spoils of war, the prize fought over by Jack and Edna. Jackie looked to food for control. When adult, he took command of his body as a microcosm of his world. He ran seven miles a day five days a week, walking, skiing or mountain biking the other two days. He developed into an athlete and fitness guru. He worked out with weights with a personal trainer for forty-five minutes each morning before breakfasting. He fasted one day a week and assiduously drank sixty-four ounces of pure spring water a day. He scheduled two physicals a year. He carefully counted calories, checked cholesterol levels, and weighed portions.

Once, he had a new refrigerator delivered from *Sears*. He observed that the rate at which it turned on and off was too frequent for maximum efficiency. He hooked a tape recorder up to the refrigerator along with an alarm clock and monitored it for a twenty-four hour period. Proving his assumption, he returned the refrigerator with the tape recording as proof to *Sears* that it was inefficient and ordered a more energy efficient model, which he also subjected to the tape recorder test before finalizing the purchase.

His dogs had to be obedience trained. As the ultimate controller, he wouldn't tolerate being embarrassed or inconvenienced by them. He took pride in showing guests that his pets would "heel," "sit," "lie down," "come," or "stay" at his command. He didn't tussle his dogs fondly or speak in sweet, soothing tones. His dogs didn't rush up to him, tails wagging, noses sniffing, tongues slathering with kisses. They understood their job was to serve their master's will, to stand at attention, alert, keep their tails low, ears back, and eyes up.

He expected people to be trained and efficient as well. He measured his potential girlfriends' heart rates, heights, and weights. He demanded handwriting analyses, polygraphs, and letters of recommendation. He read their resumes and checked their financial backgrounds just as he would review a potential employee's, only these young women were auditioning for a personal and romantic role in his life, so desperate was he to have his relationships run smoothly.

As a child of five, the court had divided his time and attention into equal portions between each parent for visitation. As an adult, he devised a similar system, which parceled out his time and affection into neat rations, given to carefully pre-screened recipients. He didn't want to risk making a mistake. This highly efficient and regulated man had learned to mince his way through love.

13

THE PRIVATE EYE

"**I** want to stop thinking about this divorce. It feels like a punishment or a nightmare," Lucky told Cherry. "I feel scarred by the constant rehashing of wrongs, like trenches are being dug in my soul."

"Nyah," Cherry contradicted. "You're just a masochist. End your dealings with Bullet right now."

"Why didn't I think of that?" Lucky joked. "I need money. I thought I could put my life and feelings on hold until December 31st, thought I could work and earn money as usual until then."

"Well, it's obvious you can't."

"*Can we work together, can we work together* has been our constant refrain. My answer should have been an emphatic, *No.* I thought he would want me back and end the separation. Silly me."

"Look, Lucky, you don't want to do the Christmas sales. You're asking me if you should keep the commitment? I can't answer that. It's hell if you do, and hell if you don't. You're in a situation where you can't win."

Bullet and Lucky agreed to divide Pulaski's Painting and Pottery equipment and studio supplies. Sitting across from one another at the green marble table in the painting studio, Bullet said, "I'm sorry, Lucky, sorry for hurting you."

"Bullet, this is the first time, the first time in all this mess, you've told me you're sorry."

Tears, his red eyes were filled with tears. Tears rolled down her face, too.

"I've told you lots of times," he said.

"No, this is the first."

"Lucky, I am so sorry for this mess. I've done wrong, for hurting you, for the kids, for losing our kids and the home. I miss it, and I feel so guilty. I love you, and I'll always love you deeply."

"Are you saying you want me?" she asked.

Bullet looked away and slowly shook his head no.

"Okay," Lucky said. "You've burned your bridges. There's no turning back. Look at what you're doing to Marianna. You've made going back impossible. You cannot turn back your actions like returning borrowed books to the library. The kids remember. They are part of this divorce, and they are suffering as well."

"Lucky, let's be friends," Bullet suggested. "Come on. We're friends. I'm your friend. I want to be your friend."

"No, Bullet, you're not my friend. You're my worst enemy. No one has hurt me like you; no one has ever been as cruel to me as you. You're NOT my friend."

"Lucky, I am asking you if my classes could come paint here as usual?"

"Bullet, are you kidding me? We're getting divorced, because you are fucking one of your students. I'm irrational on this issue. I have no good feelings about your art classes. You've been screwing your students, not to mention your models, for years apparently. I feel no responsibility toward any of those people. What's important here is how I feel. This is my house, and I don't want your classes here. They will distract me from the little work I'm able or trying to do in my own studio."

"But, they're just getting used to the painting... " He trailed off, upset, then tried a new tack. "You've already thrown me out of the house. I know you're planning to throw me out of my studio in January. 'Bye Bye Bullet.' Your hatred is really coming out, Lucky. You're bitter."

"Bullet, I am acting in good faith. I've had you and your family here for dinners, never denied you time with the kids. I told you I'd divorce you if you moved in with Fannie, which you did. I wanted no fighting, and you agreed. But, fighting is all you've done."

"I've had a chance to think about it," he justified.

"If you don't give me those three things we've agreed on, I'm not asking alimony and I'm giving you half of a business which I own, then we will fight and litigate and spend all kinds of money we don't have. Think about it. I'm the loser. I've lost the one thing I wanted: you. So, what's a house? A house for a husband?"

"I can't give up the house. I put my heart and soul into it. If I sign it over, I'll be out. I wouldn't want to come fix things like the roof leaking or to pick up doodoo. By the way, I want one of Hula Girl's pups."

"Look, Bullet, Hula Girl is Marianna's dog. I paid four hundred dollars for her, gave her to Marianna last Christmas, and registered her in Marianna's name. She is Marianna's dog. Besides, Hula Girl is not pregnant."

"I am telling you, Lucky, Hula Girl is not Marianna's dog. If Marianna took care of her, Hula Girl'd be dead like Moses. Hula Girl's my dog like Moses was. I pick up her shit, I take care of her. Let's look at what's real, not what you say is legal."

"You like to deny facts when you want to assert your skewed reality. You've blown it all. That's what's real. And maybe that little fact is just starting to hit you."

Lucky had come home from the Manoa coffee date with Cherry dressed in Ande's white, child's size twelve pedal pushers and red tank top, thin, svelte, and looking good, hair long and sleek and Lauren Bacall. Bullet, working at his easel, had emitted a low whistle.

"Lucky, would you look at these paintings?" She had ignored him.

"Hey, Lucky," he demanded, "what do you think? It's probably my greatest work. The lines are stronger than in the *Boki Series*." She glanced over her shoulder.

"They look like your mind," she answered. "Confused." She put on her studio apron and rolled out some thin slabs of porcelain. He continued to interrupt her concentration, wanting to talk.

"When are the papers coming?" She stopped what she was doing, called her lawyer, who said he was waiting for property info.

"Thomas, just sign Bullet's portion of the house to me."

"You want all I've worked for on a silver platter," Bullet protested.

"You have three children to work for."

"I've changed my mind, you know," Bullet informed her. "I want half the business and joint custody of the kids."

"By the way, I seem to remember you promised not to fight."

"I'm through with you," he yelled, changing moods. "I want more."

"It's not you who wants more. It is Fannie. She is the one who wants more. I've seen her looking at my house. She came in here as your art student. She looked at everything I had. She wanted my husband, my home, and my art. That's what she's trying to take. Everything that is mine. You're just mouthing her words."

"You're spiteful and full of hatred."

Lucky wished she wasn't embroiled in this nonsense. It was wearing. She felt like too much time had passed, and she hadn't acted quickly enough for an amicable settlement while good will was in the air.

She overheard Bullet telephone Fannie from the kitchen, whispering, "Lucky wants me to be her slave. Well, I won't do it."

"I know all about your little conversations," Lucky goaded when Bullet started to paint again.

"So, what? You have a private detective?"

The idea of spying grabbed hold of her.

She borrowed Bullet's keys to the van to run errands. Before grocery shopping, she snuck quickly over to *Woolworth's* to have a copy of Fannie's apartment key made. After dropping the children off at school the next morning, she dressed herself in a long, loose *mu'u mu'u*, dark glasses, and a floppy brimmed beach hat which obscured most of her face and hair.

Parking at the condominium complex and skulking between cars and corridors trying to pass undetected, she was quite unnerved by the time she got safely into Fannie's apartment, ready to see for herself the new life Bullet was choosing. A plastic *Love Is* magnet held a party invitation from Bitsy on the fridge, which was stuffed like a cholesterol nightmare with cuts of beef, ice cream, milk, eggs, and coffee. On the counter were stacked paper plates and plastic spoons and forks. There were no cooking pots, pans, or utensils. *The Good Housekeeping Mini Cookbook* in red and white plaid cover sat next to a microwave. Two TVs flanked one of Bullet's watercolors, which was hung on a wall next to a recent portrait he must have done of Fannie. Lucky stared at the close-up of her rival. Oh my god, she had a harelip. Fannie had a harelip, and Lucky had not noticed.

The hollow tile apartment was tiny: a bath and a kitchen that doubled as the entry to a single room. The only personal artifacts Lucky found were two photo albums of Fannie. A bed doubled as a sofa, arranged with purple and blue *Smurf* stuffed animals and assorted carnival prizes. A tape deck. Bullet's clothes were folded in piles with suitcases layered beneath.

Lucky looked for birth control pills or contraceptives of any kind. In the bathroom under the sink, she only found two big bags of makeup and cheap costume jewelry. In a bureau drawer in the living room under some clothing, she found an unopened package of *Ortho Novum* birth control pills. She also found an envelope containing Fannie's birth certificate, marriage, divorce, and settlement papers, passport, and resume. There was a map drawn by Bullet to Big Al's office. Lucky read every word. She discovered Big Al had arranged for Fannie's job at his bank, where she earned more each month as a rookie teller than Lucky did as an established artist. Fannie finished Catholic school at seventeen, married at nineteen, divorced at twenty-four. She was born in 1962 when Bullet was a sophomore in high school. *Fannie was four years old at the time Bullet and I met,* Lucky calculated. Fannie's father was French, a ferryman, and her mother was an African/Indian, who worked as a maid.

A photo of Bullet in green *Shore Line* rain-gear in Japan taken by Ande earlier that summer sat atop a pile of laundry. Japan was supposed to have been Lucky's twentieth anniversary trip. She remembered feeling left out, sad that Bullet wanted a separation rather than a celebration and didn't want to take her on his second trip to Japan. Lucky had suggested he use her ticket to take Ande, which he did.

At Kamakura where the Golden Buddha resided, Ande said Bullet purchased a roof tile to have a monk read his fortune.

"Kenji, translate. What does this mean?" Bullet had asked the guide, pointing to the character the monk had inked on his tile.

"There is a fork in the road. You are taking the wrong path; you must turn around and take the other fork, or your life will be havoc. That sign is the character for havoc."

Pearl was on the trip with some other friends from Hawaii, listening.

"Bullet, what chu doing? What's goin' on in your life?"

A year before in May when Bullet was going to go on his first surf-sponsored trip to Japan, Lucky had told him to keep on going, if he wasn't going to be a good father, a decent husband, and provider. She was fed up with many months of his not working, surfing instead and partying. She had told him to take a good look at what he wanted in life, because she didn't want him back the way he was acting.

The night before he was to leave, they had made love very carefully, Lucky silently weeping beneath him, a negligee of tears sliding down her body, where he was touching her very tenderly. She felt ashamed that she told him to go when she knew he was her life's blood. They were wedded, one and the same. Being without him would be like losing an arm, a leg, or a vital organ.

They had taken leave of one another at the airport, Lucky standing firm, letting him go to make his own decision, Bullet kissing her, keeping her near, holding her. Five days later, lonely, he had returned.

He hadn't decided to stay away that time. He had come home. What a good year had followed. She had felt encouraged. They were getting older and used to their different ways and needs; settling in, maturing, ripening. When their twenty-fifth anniversary rolled around the following June, she was self-congratulatory. She thought they had made it.

The kids unpacked his suitcase excitedly when he and Ande returned. Marianna held up a tiny package and said, "Look, Mom. Dad got you a ring."

"You better put it back, honey, and let Dad give it to me when he's ready." But he hadn't. The ring sat atop Fannie's basket of costume jewelry.

The apartment had only enough space to eat, screw, listen to music, and use the john. Bullet said he 'liked Fannie's style', 'the way she did things', 'how she kept house', 'her cooking'. It was the apartment of a nobody, of a nothing, a foolish adolescent girl with stuffed animals and plastic love messages. No class. No style. No history. No taste. *And she probably can't cook. Bullet caught his brain in his fly over this little nothing.*

Lucky found a morning note he left for Fannie. "Sweetie, I absolutely, devotedly, without a doubt, indisputably, beyond reason love you, your honey, Bull."

Lucky carefully let herself out.

14

REMNANTS

Bullet got a speeding ticket driving Marianna to an interscholastic varsity cross-country meet in Hawai'i Kai. She had a good run, made good time, placed twelfth, but no medal, not in the top ten. Marianna invited her dad in for a steamed *opakapaka* dinner, which she knew was his favorite and asked him to stay for videos.

"No thanks, honey. I have to take care of Major." Lucky knew which ass he was going to take care of.

Ande asked no one in particular, "Why does Dad go to *her*?"

"I can't answer that," Lucky said. "Just accept your dad's love. Accept what he offers you."

The thought that he had to rush away to *her*, instead of being with the kids on a weekend when they were all home and available made her burn. His bullshit sentimentality, "I miss you guys and love to be with you," sounded as soppy as his frequent refrain, "I'll make a better daddy when I'm divorced."

Lucky rented *Rainman* and *American Dream* and borrowed Rex's VCR. Her father-in-law looked older, tired, and worn. He was worried about their property settlement, which included Lucky's home, which Rex co-owned with her.

"Lucky, drop the divorce," he commanded. "And stay married. Can't you cast a blind eye on Bullet's indiscretions? In the service and at *Pan Am*, lots of pilots were indiscreet, and their wives never asked a word. Keep up appearances. Nobody gives a damn about what's happening inside your four walls as long as you keep the house looking good. Grow up. Stop seeing the world in black and white. Believe me, Lucky, life is very gray."

"I like to think life is in living color," she murmured.

"If you stay in the marriage, you'll legally inherit half of everything Bullet will get from my estate when I die."

Lucky shook her head.

"You can always leave half of Bully's share for the kids or for me, whether I'm married to him or not," she suggested.

"Not on your life. You have to stay married to get my money. Queenie and I have to hold our heads up in the community here and at the club with all our friends. Can't you play your part?" Not receiving an answer, Rex again broke the silence between them.

"Queenie keeps her feelings bottled up inside," he said. "She's too embarrassed to tell anyone about the divorce. You'll keep quiet for her sake, won't you? She's going to Mass every morning now. I take her in the evenings as well on Wednesdays and Fridays. I know she's praying that you'll stop this divorce nonsense."

"I thought she was praying that God would cure her cancer."

Lucky's anger ignited. She was irked at being trapped by her father in-law. Suddenly, she felt compelled to get Bullet's things out of the house. Out. She seethed. She refused to live like a hypocrite any longer. *Bullet's wife keeping the home fires burning while he's out with his girlfriend. He dresses here, naps here, showers here, gets ready for her here in my house, and*

I put up with this? No more. If he's with her, then he's not staying here nor is his stuff.

She sped up the two-lane highway to Makaha to tell Bullet to move out of the house. She drove, pressing urgently on the accelerator, gripping the wheel, venting.

She saw his van in the lot but not *her* car and thought perhaps he was not there. Light seeped through open jalousies of the apartment. She spied Bullet through the slats cooking in his *Hang Loose* shirt. Fannie stood beside him. *A couple, they look like a couple.*

"Bullet," Lucky yelled. He looked out the jalousies and saw his wife in one of the kid's *Walt Disney Goofy* shirts, ponytail, and dangle earrings, ready to kill.

"Come out here," she screamed.

"Why?"

"Come Out Here Now," she commanded. Fannie peered out the jalousies, wearing

an apron and big, dumb-looking, square glasses on her pinched face. Bullet opened the door.

"I want you to go home and pack all your things and get out. Now."

"Why? I thought we had an agreement," Bullet argued. "I could live in the house till our last art show? Why are you flipping out? I thought you said, 'Bullet, do what you like.'"

"You are flaunting that f-ing cunt's stink in my face. You are rubbing my nose in garbage," she hissed, letting sins of the sewer spew from her mouth in the current of her rage. "Your kids are at home, they invite you to dinner, and you don't stay with them. You come to this f-ing cunt to cook dinner. Either you pack or I will, and if I do, you'll find your crap thrown off the balcony all over the street."

"But, Lucky, I don't understand."

"Look Bullet, you've chosen her. We're divorcing. I don't want to have to wonder where you are or look at your stuff in my bedroom. Get it out. Let me live my life. If you want to work, call. If you want to see the kids, call. But, you, you get out."

He came home. Lucky gave him a trash bag for his belongings. He packed and said goodnight to the kids.

"You'd better tell them where you're staying."

"I'm staying with a good friend," he said reluctantly.

Nico piped up, "Fannie?"

"Yes." Bullet turned to Lucky and asked, "Do you want a family party for your birthday?"

"Dad's scared," Ande told her. "He's lost you, Mom, and he's left the family. Maybe he'll lose the house. Maybe Fannie will leave him. Maybe he doesn't really like her, but if you get divorced, he'll have to marry her, and he's scared. He's done a lot of bad things, and people don't like him anymore. And, he's got a lot of hurt inside. So, he just blames you for everything."

Lucky's mind was a Laundromat: her thoughts set on soak, rinse, or heavy wash; finally all spun out, her watery tub of regrets, a cacophony of varied cycles and temperatures. She knew that sometimes her mind spun at too fast a cycle; she needed deliberately to decelerate. *Can I emerge from being a wife, tied to a sophomoric idiot, backsliding in this island ghetto-welfare community, where everyone is either retired, semi-comatose, drugged-out, or brain-dead; OD'd from drugs, surf, or ignorance, and emerge into single adulthood?* She prized the peace this community had afforded, precisely because it was such a backwater. But, she didn't belong there. Despite clocking in twenty years, she remained an outsider.

"Why do you always have to look so New York?" Bullet would ask before they'd go out to a get together, which passed in Hawai'i for a dinner party. "Why don't you just wear a *mu'u mu'u* and relax?"

"You two are feuding," her neighbor, Rod, commented over coffee in her studio. "Bullet has found the ultimate way to hurt you, to take this woman and say, 'I give it all up' to everything you two have built together. And, he'll blame you: 'My wife kicked me out.' Wait and see." Lucky quietly paddled the clay sides of the small square containers she was assembling.

"Think about it, Lucky. I never saw Bullet take care of your family first. With him, it was always friends first. And, none of his buddies could possibly be your friends. They're all his *real people, the little people,* the local jobless, under-educated parolees. He chose those people to alienate you, to drive you away, to make his world separate from yours.

"I remember him asking why can't you be like Pearl? Put a pot on the stove and feed everybody? Pearl, whose daughter is in prison for armed robbery, is not my idea of a role model. And you said, 'Because I'm NOT Pearl; I'm me.'

"Do you want me to get some guys to teach Bullet a lesson? Local style, you know? Break the guy's knees? Whatever you like, you say the word, Lucky. I'll help you out."

Lucky must have been healing a little, because she was tired and actually needed sleep. She still suffered from wakefulness but was not insomnia ridden as before. She was gaining an appetite and eating more. The emotional edge was wearing off.

Piles of Bullet's clothes she'd thrown out of the house still lay strewn and dirty on the floor of his studio. His wedding jacket was dusty with clay and pitted by bug holes. Dabs of paint spotted a shirt. Tie. Clothes Lucky'd sewn him years ago: the Cossack shirt, suede vest, leather jacket, corduroy shorts, even Viennese Lederhosen, discarded, remnants from the fabric of their life. She recognized how impossible he made their relationship, tying her hands with so many cords, cutting her out of his life, and patterning a life to suit only himself.

She started reorganizing the house, transforming it into the kids' and her house. No traces of Bullet, except in the gallery and the occasional photo.

Lucky focused her thoughts on singleness and an open future. Thoughts of new friends tended to push the old uglies away. Sneaking images of his dick and balls served up to him on a turkey platter still flashed in her mind, but less frequently.

Little things took her aback yet pleased her, too. Bullet took Ande and Nico to the movies, while Marianna attended her school carnival with her pals. Lucky joined some neighbors having a potluck. Rod had been doing cocaine and had that funny faced, lopsided smile, and numbed *Novocain* look. He accompanied her to the Peter Moon Band concert.

Dancing, not her usual little dogtrot, either. She boogied like she had never danced in all the years of luaus and parties, inhibited and self-conscious being Bully's wife or her kids' mother or not pretty enough. She was letting it all out, feeling totally free and happy. Rod and she danced three slow ones, which felt very nice, not tight, but very comfortable. Rod reminded her of a party years ago at Cherry's when Bully and she danced.

"You were the wildest people there; people you'd want to know," he said.

15

BLAME IT ON THE RAIN

T he incessant rain obscured the light. In that autumn of pain, clouds had stormed the sun, taking away its yellow light forcefully like militant, unstoppable warriors. They moved across the sky, filling Lucky's horizons with darkness and dread, dropping their rain so fiercely it invaded windows, penetrated jambs, and soaked walls.

You said you didn't need her
You told her good-bye
You sacrificed a good love
You let her walk away
And it just don't feel the same
Gotta blame it on something

Should have told her you were sorry sorry
Could have said you were wrong
But no you couldn't do that
Had to prove you were strong
But you want her back again

Oh oh if you hadn't been
So blinded she could
Still be with you

Got to blame it on something
Blame it on the rain that's falling
Blame it on the stars (shine at night)
Whatever you do don't put the blame on you

Blame it on the rain yeah yeah yeah
The rain don't lie
The rain don't care
Got to blame it on something
Blame it on the rain

Whatever you do don't blame the thing on you
Blame it on the rain
Blame it on the rain yeah yeah
Blame it on the rain yeah yeah
Blame it on the rain
Blame it on the stars at night

Milli Vanilli

Lucky's life trickled away as the rain fell continuously. Vog and haze filled the air, volcanic debris blew to mix with local humidity. It washed, drained, bled down upon roof, studio, home, and the land. She was under a blanket of many kinds of rain. Some days it drenched her, others it rinsed. If she was lucky, the rain would float like a drifting of sunlit showers, gently moistening and cleansing. She felt quite naked, not ready to emerge, not ready for the sun.

Lucky walked Hula Girl along sand and reef feeling alone, the beginning gold and scarlet rays promising a late, peach blooming sunset. The large wall of blue light above them was intersected by rows of scudding marshmallow like clouds, yet a dark corner of the sky stood like galoshes, portending more rain.

Big waves had sculpted the beach into a steep slope, leaving rubble and shells behind. Hula Girl peed in all sorts of inappropriate places, once almost on Lucky's foot. She didn't expect that constant pissing from a female. They sat at the far end of the beach before the dying embers of the sun, the end where she had mourned her father. She wept frustrated, tired tears. *Oh, God, let me be divorced. Let this be over. Let it be over.*

She was a woman alone with her dog at sunset roaming a familiar stretch of beach that had witnessed grief over a sister's suicide, a father's implosion in mid-air, a husband's betrayal. The same stretch of beach had witnessed joy at three children's' christenings, infants swimming like blennies in tide pools while puppies buried bones in the sand. She was the sole mourner at the funeral of a love once blessed in her student days by an old, black-garbed crone at a Florentine train stop.

The crone had faced them, sitting inside their first class compartment on the four-hour trip from Milan to Florence. Lucky and Bullet were playing cards, madcap, rummy, and whist, laughing and cheating and yelling vociferously, oblivious to the observant eyes behind the elegant black veil. As she rose to leave the train, she spoke slowly, smiling at them, in a deliberate and careful English, and commanded, "Stay together." Then, like an apparition, she disappeared from view.

Lucky's face was drawn; the muscles pulled heavily down around the edges of her mouth. She felt aloneness engulfing her for all the neighborhood to see. Felt a tear creep down a cheek from the left eye. Later one rapidly rolled from the right eye; even her tears were discordant.

She walked the beach, Hula Girl straining at the leash and hardly felt the tropical waters engulf her feet or noticed stepping into the rocky tide pools on sharp-crusted points of lava. The waves offered a fascination in their rhythmical lapping; the delicate white of their froth glided sensuously inland up the legs and thighs of the sand. She watched the changing sky as it witnessed her separate from herself.

Lucky was tired of herself. She no longer felt like the Lucky who was so soft and loving, the *Mom* in the family, the wife. Her heart was out of place. Partly it was the foul weather. Partly, it was the diminished family.

She was slipping into a quiet depression where loneliness charley horsed her spirit in cramping bands of pain.

She kept silent, not wanting to worry her boy. At home, Nico was the only child with her, and he was so dear. Marianna and Ande were staying with Cherry, at least for ten more days prior to Thanksgiving vacation. Cherry had taken in the girls, no questions asked, when Lucky gave up the *dungeon* to return to her new single parent life at home. The *dungeon* had been a time apart from Bullet, a respite, she realized.

When she got home, she would call the girls. Nico practiced bouncing-on-arm muscle tricks as they played catch in the park. Her crazy kid raced across the grass, tackling Hula Girl for the ball with marvelous energy. Nico faked biting Hula Girl to Lucky's amusement as he squatted on the dog's back. Then he ran home to watch cartoons before dinner.

Instead of cooking, Lucky decided to take Nico on a special date to a local beachside restaurant where he ordered five cherries in his *Shirley Temple.* Lucky ordered something stronger. They sipped colorful drinks festooned with paper parasols, holding hands.

At prayers, Lucky asked Nico if he was okay.

"Yeah. I miss my sisters."

"Me, too," Lucky said.

"And Dad," Nico added.

Later Lucky called her daughters. "How're you doing?" Lucky asked.

"All right," Ande said.

"Cherry's nice, Mom," Marianna replied, "not like you. You're mostly a bitch."

Bullet was smoking dope. Half-used joints, bags of buds, rolling papers appeared in the studio, and then disappeared. Lucky noticed his eyes were very red; he stayed late, the first time in almost two months. He was up to something. He left new dope and rolling papers in the paint cupboard. Nico said his dad got the dope from Kalani. Lucky trashed it.

Lucky sat alone at a restaurant in Kailua, waiting for a steak she didn't want to eat, waiting for a film she didn't want to see, killing time, waiting to pick up Ande who attended her eighth grade boyfriend's birthday dinner.

16

SHRINKING

O n her slick slide downhill, she made a call for help. Therapy. Her appointment was for November 8th. *Hold on till then.* At Kaiser, a very sympathetic Dr. Chandler screened her request.

"Are you feeling suicidal?"

"Yes."

"Are you feeling homicidal?"

"Yes," she answered, "but, it's nothing too serious. I have three kids to take care of.... I am feeling definitely distracted and rather accident-prone right now.... I've been not-quite-with-it. I sideswiped my truck door in the gallery parking lot, got a bad dent and scrape on it. I knocked out the electrical switch in my carport with the van side mirror. I've had two car accidents in two days."

She suffered diarrhea, unless she remembered to take iron pills. She was happy at her changing figure, glad to have lost weight, but she also felt like she was dying, shrinking, withering, being absorbed in a black hole of despair, a void of gloom, sliding into nowhere.

She had become preoccupied with her body. Looking in the mirror, she noticed her face is aging with long vertical lines down each side just outside the laugh lines. *Could easily benefit from a face-lift.*

Ande and Nico told her, "Oh, Mom, you're so old."

She looked in the mirror and wondered how long it might take to mend her heart. A pregnancy lasted nine months. Tolerable, because there was a termination date. School terms lasted nine months as well. College, four years, on average. But a marriage? With the idea she had bought of a lifetime sold short, the marriage ended, how long before she healed? She was scared she'd be stuck in this crying mode forever, her needle catching, endlessly repeating like Beckett's *Krapp's Last Tape.*

She tried to reshape her saddlebag hips, even scheduled liposuction surgery. If the surgery turned out as big a disappointment as the beauty parlor did on Friday, Lord help her. As it was, the hair frosting was a disaster. She looked like Richard Widmark, the washed-out blond actor of Fifties' westerns. Her hair was gray by the temples and ears, yellow as hot buttered popcorn on top. *Thin, leathery, aged, a tough old ha'ole, about-to-be divorcee,* she thought. Superstitious about her bad luck, she canceled the liposuction, which she couldn't afford anyway.

After filling out forms in the clinic waiting room, Lucky sat nervously for her appointment to see a shrink. *Check all screws to see if any are loose and put me back on track.* Twenty minutes elapsed before a man pranced out wearing cinched, above the waist, tight polyester pants below a cascade of gold jewelry, and a swish, hair-sprayed coif.

He called, "Mttthhh Pulantthhhki," lisping the name. *Geez.*

"I am here due to a divorce," she told him, ensconced in the prancing therapist's office. This announcement was met with silence. "I want someone who can understand a marital breakup." Silence. "After twenty years." More silence. "I have three children." Silence. "Still to be raised." More silence. He nodded, waiting for her monologue to continue through the pricey hour. But, she didn't want her time wasted. She turned the interview around and grilled him.

"Have you ever been married?" she asked.

"No," he answered, looking startled.

"Any children?"

"No."

"I want someone who can relate to what I'm going through," she said slightly apologetic.

"Perhapths you'd like to see a different therapithst?"

"Why, yes, that sounds like a very good idea" A couple of inter-office calls later, he introduced her to a Dr. Dousch, who'd been successfully married for twenty-eight years and raised two children. He agreed to take her on.

"Your instincts are good, Lucky. Follow them," he advised her. "You're too hard on yourself. Why beat yourself up? You are not responsible for this mess and someone else's breach of faith. Relax. It's not your fault. Quit hurting yourself. Feel your anger, feel your feelings. It's okay. Trust your instincts." He was looking appreciatively at her stockings and added, "You're a very attractive woman."

It was not a flirtation; it was an acknowledgment. Lucky blushed, pleased to be complimented by a stranger when she hadn't felt appreciated or attractive in so long. She had dressed carefully in the morning, wanting to look well.

"Let the facts speak for themselves. Don't bad mouth anybody; it will come back to haunt you. Speak the truth. You didn't have an affair with anybody; you didn't lie to anybody. So you couldn't recognize the signs in your husband. You were acting on trust, and he wasn't."

Dr. Dousch pointed out, "At this midlife age, many men 'act out' what was earlier suppressed or denied. This infatuation with Fannie will last a year or more, but as soon as Bullet is cut off from your life, things may change with her. But don't care or worry about that, because it's nothing to do with you or your new life.

"Do not enter into power plays. If your husband tries to engage you in fights, ignore him. Realize you've decided to divorce," he continued. "Try to keep him out of the house, so your life can be freed. No food, no bathroom, no shower.

"Listen to the kids. Listen well. Speak sparingly and listen well. Let the children have their feelings. Don't tell them what to feel.

"And, Lucky," Dr. Dousch added, "you must mourn, must grieve, a death. Pretend Bullet is dead. Give yourself a year. Buy flowers. Cry. Recognize that it's over. It's gone, through, done. Your lover is dead."

Rain. The rain was clearing her thoughts, washing her brain. A night sky melted down; she knew it from the noise, a pelting on the roof, a heavy, steady dripping from the lack of gutters, a crunching and splish-splashing on the cobblestones. Sounds of water puddling, pooling, separate sounds, separate rhythms intensified and subsided. Lucky sat huddled under the Swedish blanket in the living room listening to the intermittent swoosh of traffic on the wet night highway.

The sudden downpour brought with it flash flooding. Just as suddenly, but perhaps not unexpectedly, her soul of gray drizzled unleashing a torrent, drenching her face and clothes. *Why doesn't he care?* Thunder boomed, lightning flashed, and the roof leaked. She scurried about placing towels and buckets under its drips. The rain came down in thick mourning shrouds eroding her world. She wished she could place a bucket under the leak from her eyes.

It occurred to her that all of life transpired in watery surrounds. Creation flowed in saliva, secretions, ejaculations and watery saps, juicy liquids that propelled love and lust and life. Birthing unleashed an aquatic bag of blood and vernix. Even sorrows were drenched by tears and drowned. Tears from the living bathed the dying. Fluids, circulating on the life-death cycle, cleansed, loosened, released, and finally even grief could be washed away.

Lucky had backtracked and begged, done everything to save her family and woo Bullet back. The love she gave had become a burden rather than a gift to him.

She was disappointed in the change of mood as hatred was clearly between them. Warfare. Blatant animosity. She was angry. So was he. She never would have left him, never, even though he pummeled her emotionally like one of those plastic, inflatable *Bozos*. She had revived to say, "I love you." Bullet would strike and down she'd go again only to bounce back up for another punch. What a clown. She wondered who she'd been for so many lost years?

She felt alone. Really on her own, all ninety-eight pounds of her rappelling without a rope.

17

MANY RETURNS OF THE DAY

*H*ey, Em. *Your little brother here. Many returns of the day, old girl. Ha ha. I am sitting at the lake at Dad's old place. It's chilly but the sky is crystal clear. It was a wonderful day to fly. His place always brings me peace. I hope you plan something nice for your birthday and that your divorce continues with a minimum of animosity. Keep moving forward. Take care of yourself. No one else will, Birthday Girl.*

OOO Jackie

Forty-third birthday found Lucky taking care of herself: sunbaths, afternoon tub baths, dancing, lotions, oils and pretty clothes. She shopped with Queenie and got a *Putumayo* shirt and pants. Lucky didn't want to cry on her birthday, but she already was before she realized it, hiding her face behind the lunch menu at the art museum where they ordered a delicious pate followed by mussels in saffron.

Queenie said, eyeing Lucky judgmentally, "Wives who feel superior to their husbands always have their marriages fail."

Recovering, Lucky asked, "Have you met Fannie yet?"

"Oh, horrors. Heavens, no. Why would I?" Queenie exclaimed with a sound of scandal in her voice, adding in a dramatic undertone, "I told him not to bring *her* around the family. Bullet came to me. He wanted to talk about that girl. 'Oh Mom,' he said, 'Fannie's so sweet. I love her, and I like the way she does things. She's just like you.' Oh, no, Bullet, I said, you're very wrong. I would never go with a man who is married and has three young children. You need to handle the task of loving Lucky, your wife."

On Nico's tenth birthday, the children had a balanced day. Nico was entered in a Keiki Surf Meet at Makaha. He caught great rides to cheering from the beach and won a new board.

But, when Bullet brought Nico home along with Jacob, Ben, and Al Boy who wanted to go to the carnival, Nico was in tears. He had lost his birthday twenty-dollar bill in the water. Lucky replaced it. Then the boys rode their bikes to the carnival.

Lucky grocery shopped. She made crepes and blintzes for a late birthday brunch. Bullet ate them. Then he ate the *poke* she was saving and stayed through dinner of barbecued steak and ice cream cake.

"So, Marianna," he asked, "don't you want some steak?"

"Nope. Mom's fixed me a yam."

"Lucky, do you fix special food for this girl?" Lucky didn't acknowledge his question.

"Look, that's wrong," he continued. "She's a member of a family. She eats what everybody eats. You can't afford to feed her something special."

"Bullet, it's no problem for me. Sweet potatoes are cheaper than steak anyway. Marianna's concerned about her health.

She doesn't want to eat mayonnaise anymore, either. No foods high in cholesterol. No animal products. Marianna is becoming a vegetarian, which is fine by me. Anyway, it's part of her program for track."

"You're making a big mistake. You're spoiling her. She has to learn to fit in, to get along," he said.

During the "family" style dinner, Lucky burst out before anyone had even taken a bite of the steak, "This is the saddest goddamned birthday party ever." She scraped her chair away from the table and raced out the back door. She stood sobbing in the banana grove at the far corner of the lot near the laundry room. After a time, Bullet found her.

"I love this family. I love this family," she said, tear-stained under the clothesline in the dusk.

He looked back sadly at her, "I do too, Lucky, I do too." And, he left.

"Best birthday I ever had, Ma," Nico said, thanking her at bedtime, happy with his *GT* bike and new body board. He was full of beans and ten years old.

Lucky bought Marianna a car, a 1979 Mustang, giving her a big step toward independence, both hers and Lucky's. They fixed it up, oiled the door hinges, mended the ceiling fabric, put a new cover on the steering wheel, glued on a rear view mirror. Nico labeled it "a piece of shit." Marianna named it, "Pale Rider," after her father's first horse, a horse she had never known.

18

BARKING UP THE WRONG TREE

"**O**h Lucky, dear, this is Dottie. I am sad, so sad for you; everyone has known you're divorcing, except you, since July. Boxer told the Deales."

"Gee, Dottie, I only decided to divorce this fall."

"The Deales are staying friends with you, Lucky, because you are such a lovely girl and the children are so beautiful, not because of Bullet or his parents at all. He's never been worthy of you." Lucky was surprised to hear old friends held such a low opinion of Bullet.

"Don't spoil your little Nico, Lucky," Dottie warned. "You spoiled Bullet terribly. You're a smart girl, and you'll be all right. But, now is the time to be mercenary. Get everything in black and white. Get that house for your children. Get what Bullet may inherit."

"We'll see," Lucky said. Then Dottie remembered the purpose for her call.

"Rex and Queenie are missing."

"What?"

"They didn't come to my dinner party in Honolulu tonight at the *Golden Dragon*. And, they're not at home. I've been calling all evening. I thought I should let someone know. I don't know how to reach Bullet. I'm sorry to trouble you, Lucky dear."

Lucky phoned Kaiser's emergency room, then Bullet at Francine's. After she left a message on an answering machine for him to go look for his parents, he called. *Screening calls*, Lucky thought.

At the same time, the radio announced an earthquake in San Francisco. Sinking anxiety landed in Lucky's stomach. *Mom? Laura?* In the five o'clock rush hour traffic, part of the Bay Bridge had collapsed, and Laura was ten cars behind the fallen section; she was safe; rerouted. Edna was okay; the perennial survivor was in her office parking lot when the quake hit. She was knocked around a little in her car. Then, she stayed up till midnight organizing rescue efforts; she was safe. Lucky's loved ones were safe.

Queenie explained in her pre-Alzheimerese, they hadn't been able to find the Golden Dragon, had eaten at *Horatio's* instead, and just gotten home. "Sorry that Dottie's call panicked you, Lucky."

When Bullet stopped by, Lucky had slipped into her worn-out dream, the dream that brings her midnight tears, the melancholia, the longing for the past, wanting the old life, wondering, *when will this be over?* wanting her golden family, golden home, golden career, and golden lifestyle.

"Please stay the night," she whispered to him as if in that dream.

"Do you mind if I go eat dinner first?" Bullet answered, disrupting her reverie.

"There's food here, if you're hungry," she snapped, angry with herself. "If you have to go eat with that girl and then come here, forget it. Just forget it."

"Wait. Let's try and work this out..."

"I don't want you, and I don't need you." She was furious with herself for falling into the past. She locked the doors and turned out the lights.

Whenever I hope or soften, she realized, *I open myself to humiliation. I keep thinking we have a relationship, a friendship I can rely on. After twenty-five years, I have NOTHING.*

Barking up the wrong tree. That's what I'm doing. Wanting Bullet and trying to resuscitate his love is putting my energy in the wrong place. I'll never get going, get better this way. I have to take the reality dose, swallow the unpalatable pill of who he is, what he does, who I am, and what I do, and let that medicine, pleasant or not, take effect on my mind.

The unhappiness had been there for both of them for a long time. She had been unhappy enough to leave when Lei, not just Lei but Bullet as well, shattered her trust. The girls had been so young. Lucky thought they needed their father. But, she no longer felt secure in her marriage after that tryst.

19

AN UNFAITHFUL LEI

I t was late at night. Lucky and the little girls were in bed. Nico had not yet been born. Lucky looked at the clock, the empty driveway, back at the clock. She got up and called the *Columbia Inn* where Bullet usually had a drink before driving home from the late shift at *Sandwich Isle Graphics*, but Bullet was not there. She went back to bed. She got up and called police dispatch to ask if there had been any accidents on the freeway. Three a.m. She called several hospitals. Four a.m. Bullet arrived home. Lucky heated leftovers, relieved and happy to see him.

"What happened? Where were you? I was so worried, I called all the hospitals to see if you'd been hurt."

"I was tired, too tired to keep driving. I thought I'd pass out. So, I stopped and fell asleep in the cane fields."

"You fell asleep in the cane fields?" Like a little monkey, she may as well have put her hands over her ears, her hands over her eyes, and her hands over her lips, for she "believed" this story.

Then her brother, Jackie, called from California.

"Dad's dead. Dad's dead, Lucky."

"What happened?" were her only words. Her mind spun. Her father was dead. A packet of Ande's baby photos sat on the bureau waiting to be mailed to him.

"He was burned up in mid-air. Some bozo in a small jet plowed into him just after takeoff from the lake. The *Cessna* exploded. Everybody was killed. I saw it. I drove him to the airport and was just pulling out of the parking lot when it happened. There was a big boom and a fireball. The wreckage started a forest fire."

"Oh, Jackie. Oh, Jackie. I'm sorry."

She took the little girls to Jack's funeral, which was held at his mountain headquarters in Idaho. There wasn't a body. Just a commemorative urn. There wasn't a will. There wasn't any need for the airhead widow to seek comfort from her step-daughters, since they had not grown up with her, and she was not interested in their attention or lives. Jackie had a new girl-friend whose arms had opened wide to comfort him. No one in that broken family needed Lucky or Laura to stay.

After the service, Lucky drove with the children and Laura to Los Angeles, where Laura lived. To take their minds off their father's horrible death, they visited Disneyland. Lucky wanted to stay with her sister longer, wanting comic relief, relief of any kind.

"Bully, I'm at a phone booth near the airport. I need some more time with Laura. Would it be okay if the girls and I didn't catch our flight today and came home instead in a week?"

"Sure. That's okay. Do what you like." What did she hear? What did she sense over the telephone line that was wrong? *Uh-oh.* The plan to stay did not seem okay. She raced in Laura's red *Austin Healy*, blonde babies' hair flying, to LAX to catch their scheduled flight home as planned.

Bully and she immediately embarked on a month long binge of the most erotic lovemaking of their marriage, high on a bed held up by logs. After one particularly torrid morning, Bully turned pensive. She asked what was wrong.

"Nothing, nothing. Nothing's wrong."

"Bully, I know something's wrong. Is it the job? Do you hate it so much? You can quit, you know. It's okay with me. The money doesn't matter. I just want you to be happy."

"Lucky, there's nothing wrong." He paused. "There's nothing wrong at work." They stood naked in one another's arms next to the bed.

She pressed. "What's wrong, then, tell me what's wrong?" she whispered as she held her face against the soft buffer of hair on his chest.

After ten minutes standing silently in their embrace, he said very quietly, "I'm in love with another woman."

There was no time. There was no air. Lucky had no legs.

"What?"

"A *hula* dancer. Lei."

Lucky pulled away.

"I won't put up with this, Bull. Not now, not again, not with two babies. I'm too valuable for this. Make a choice," she stuttered, surprised at the strength in her voice. "It's me, or it's her. But, it's not both. You choose. And choose now. I'm not Hawai'ian, if that's what you want, and I never will be. Neither will you. I don't want to be dragged over the coals on this. Make it clean. Either way. But, make it clean."

The ensuing nights left alone increased her paranoia. She lay crumpled like a pair of discarded pantyhose on the cheap, spattered black linoleum tiles on the cold bedroom floor, or leaned her head and shoulders against the white wooden doorjamb, crying with a Charlie Chaplin woebegone mouth, drooping in the *Waaaa* drone of a wee baby. She never knew where Bully was. He wavered for an agonizing month until finally telling her he'd broken off with Lei.

But her trust dissolved, and their marriage became a shell. Not a calcium hardened seashell, but rather a delicate eggshell, imperceptibly cracked, its substance evaporating over time, leaving a perfect, if empty, shell behind. She balanced precariously, a regular *Humpty Dumpty,* on the thin wall of her life.

Lucky attempted to rebuild her faith in Bullet against the tide of her despair. She spent a lot of time at a different beach from her regular favorite, healing, gathering shells, helping her toddlers float on surfboards in flat tidal pools that lay cratered in the blackened lava moonscape. She called it her edge-of-the-world beach.

She and the girls spent hours building sand castles, proud of their tall architectural wonders. Once, as a castle rose in the morning light amid sounds of her children's chatter, her neighbor Rod witnessed their careful sculpting. A few days later she found a fifty-pound bag of white porcelain clay on her doorstep.

"You ought to build castles that don't float away on the tide," Rod had written on the bag.

She took his advice and began to build castles out of clay, albeit Asian rather than European in style.

And a keloid scar from Bullet's betrayal thickened palpably across her heart. She thought the stitches of its mend wouldn't show after awhile. And, she had another baby.

Maybe the memory of Lei calmed her enough to let her see the length and breadth of the problem of infidelity. Bullet's lies and betrayals had clouded their recent separation with charged emotions. Lucky realized she had lived for years feeling unsure of her husband's love, only to have him run away, proving she should not have hoped and kept faith.

Maybe she couldn't trust, because she was being tricked. Maybe she couldn't trust, because her father, Big Jack, had left the family when she was young, didn't love her enough to stay, to see her grow. She had been left by Jack. Marianna and Ande were being left by Bullet.

It was not just Bullet who wanted out, who felt trapped, and suffocated. Lucky wanted out when her degradation began.

Shortly after they had built their beach house, Lucky had asked Bullet to play a game she had read about in the morning paper. The game was supposed to make people aware of who they were in life and what they really wanted to accomplish. It would bring greater self-awareness and perhaps, her hope, greater intimacy to a couple. Following the instructions, they sat on the floor, closed their eyes, and began the questionnaire.

"If you could be anyone at all, at any time in the history or future of the world," the first question posed, "who would you be?" Her own answer, "Shakespeare," was at the ready.

Not missing a beat, Bullet replied first. "I'd be a Spanish conquistador, exploring, pillaging and conquering the new world."

"Bullet," she interjected, slightly aghast, "they were rapists."

"So what?"

The second question she asked was, "In the best of all possible worlds, how or who would you like your partner to be?"

Again, without hesitating, he said, "I'd like to see you with a can of *Ajax*, on your hands and knees, scrubbing my floors."

She opened her eyes and said, "You've got to be kidding."

"I'm not."

"Bullet, do you really want to see me cleaning your house, or do you want a clean house? If you want a cleaner house, I have the solution: I'll hire a cleaning woman. If you want to see me cleaning, you've got a problem. Because, that's not what I'm here for."

There sat two Berkeley-educated M.A.'s, flower children of the Sixties, veterans of free speech, peace, and love movements, yet Women's Lib was more than an ocean away from their front door, a door on a home on a Pacific island far from her chosen career, close to diminishing any dreams she might have entertained of performance and production.

She had trained as an actress, always feeling other people's feelings, always 'out there'. She empathized with other people before she became aware of her own feelings and reactions to a situation. She was a slow respondent in her own life. Maybe it was leftover from childhood; Jack invalidating her, trying to violate her. She had avoided his seduction in order to survive, putting in the closet the painful truth of his abuse.

Her life wasn't being lived the way she wanted, and she was imprisoned by its inescapable weight. Her university acting class comrades and theatre associates had become regulars on television series or were making movies, winning *Emmys* and garnishing *Oscars*. They'd put in their obligatory ten years of work and were attaining success. She watched their shows in her mid-Pacific isolation. One year's *Oscar* presentation left her so frustrated, she roamed the aisles of the local *7-Eleven* store during the wee hours past midnight looking for chocolate, wine, beer, ice cream, anything to substitute for her loss.

Her girlhood dream to be the world's Greatest Actress had focused her life. She had put all her attention on it. As a child, she had acted in community theatre; she had won talent shows. She got a scholarship to study theatre in college; on graduation, she joined a regional theatre company. She went to Hollywood where she assisted a major studio director and script consulted for *Twentieth Century*, so in love was she with theatre and film.

But, she also fell in love with a man who wasn't interested in her dream. Bullet didn't support her career, refusing to live in Hollywood or New York where she had to be. He disavowed the role of house/husband. Yet, she married him, left the film world, left the theatre, followed his whims, and bore his children.

Lucky did try directing community dinner theatre using the local veterinarian and lifeguards as actors with local *hula* dancers as pre-show performers. She tried making films but the market from a tiny island in the Pacific was for sea turtles and monk seals, not Greek drama, and filming soon bored her and became untenable. She did work briefly in journalism as a reporter and drama critic. But the only plays to review were college productions, of which she tired. She had babies to tend, a husband to feed, and a role as wife and mother to fulfill. Her primary theatrical dream became crippled and remained in the end only as a memory, its clippings destined for a scrapbook.

Somehow, she had opted for that secondary dream, for love and promises of forever, a dream like the first that was mutating and dying, her two dreams shattered by the same Bullet.

Bullet accused her of being a bitch and treated her like an unwanted mutt. Disliked, desperate for love and companionship, no longer a "Lassie," Lucky had felt like a kicked cur, like old, abused, unloved Chubby. She thought she'd never smile again.

The feared boomerang came full circle. As a terrible Kona storm blew in off the sea one year, rain fell heavily all night. In the gray morning as Lucky dashed out to the mailbox to get the newspaper, she spotted Chubby in the front yard. He was as close to the rock wall as he could get, sort of nestled in the wet shrubs there, tied to his lead. *Tied to his lead?* She'd forgotten to untie him. He'd been left out in the storm overnight, forgotten, and quite dead.

Never a dull moment, her phone rang.

"Is Bullet there?"

"Who is this?"

"Hi, Lucky. This is Dave."

"Oh. Dave. No. Didn't Yoko tell you? He doesn't live here anymore? Bullet and I are divorcing."

"Ah shit. That fucker. No, no. Yoko didn't tell me anything."

"What do you need him for?"

"I want to kill him."

Lucky gasped.

"That fucker's ruined my life, killed my marriage. I wasn't going to tell you, Lucky. I didn't want to hurt you. I wanted to find out if he was home, so I could come over and blow his fuckin' head off." Lucky could hear the liquor in his voice.

"Dave, what's happened?"

"Ahhhh, I came home one morning and found Yoko and Bullet butt-fucking in my bed."

Yoko? Yoko, my assistant? Lucky had never suspected. She remembered how sexy Yoko looked at aerobics. Lucky even mentioned what great shape she was in to Bullet. He was always solicitous of Yoko, full of compliments and jokes when she came to work in Lucky's studio.

"Before and after painting class," Dave told her, "I'd find Bullet 'just leaving' with some excuse or other about dropping off paint. I threw Yoko out of the house. I started looking for Bullet about a year ago when I'd pass your house or the guys down at the beach. I'd throw my shotgun in the truck, grab a six-pack, and drive."

"A year ago? My god. I remember the kids told me you called several times. I thought you wanted Bullet to help build a studio or something for Yoko." Lucky had thought she'd reached the end, coping, recovering. Then, wham. The rope on the pulley up from the abyss was cut, and down she fell at another betrayal, this time by her assistant, who took her husband for his friendship, his talent, and his dick.

"Yoko, this is Lucky Pulaski. Dave told me about you and Bullet. I need to hear about it from you." Yoko had been crying in the bathroom since Dave had hung up from his conversation with Lucky. She was snuffling as she answered.

"I ferr in ruv Burret. He my good friend, best art teacher I ever have. He so nice to everyone. I stirr ruv him. I never want hurt you, Rucky, or your bootifur chiren or Burret's parents. I so afraid causing divorce."

"Oh, right. Why did it end?"

"I don' know. He stop coming over. Maybe because Dave catch us. Dave hit Burret in face, and Burret push Dave down steps. You know, Dave have bad back..."

"How long?"

"Christmas. Not this Christmas. Two years before."

"Jesus," Lucky spat.

"I shock, hurt, you terr me about divorce. Burret find other woman. Not me. This time not mind rooz house, wife, famirree, friend. I hurt he not pick me. But Burret never terr me he ruv me. He always say, 'I ruv Rucky, my famirree, my kids.'"

When Lucky confronted Bullet, he defended himself, saying, "I'd never have made love to Yoko if I'd loved you. I quit the affair with Yoko, because Dave was trying to kill me. Remember the hit-and-run accident I told you I had at the parking lot at the beach?" She nodded. "I really got sideswiped by Dave on the highway by Maili Point. He was trying to run me off the road in his big rig. I decided to leave you to protect the family. If I left, at least our family wouldn't get hurt."

"I'm not buying that cheap explanation," Lucky said. "If that was true, why did you start up with Fannie?"

"Because of you again."

Just the other day, Lucky thought, Bullet had accused her of rewriting history, of creating a soap opera, of writing her own melodrama. *Wow, I don't think I could have thought this up.* Lost pieces of the puzzle of her marriage were surfacing one by one.

"Don't tell anyone, Lucky," Bully begged. "Please don't hurt my parents and family by telling them about Dave and Yoko. And, don't hurt Yoko."

Lucky's chest, her flat and bony chest, heaved and shuddered as she'd never imagined such pain could visit her heart, the humiliation of Yoko coming to her house, her studio, using her designs and her glazes, exercising and smiling in aerobics, all the while screwing her husband.

Bull wondered why Lucky wouldn't respond to him the next day as she glazed in the studio.

She snapped, "I have nothing ever to say to a shit like you except 'get out of my life'. You can at least apologize for spoiling it. You make me feel soiled and dirty, so terribly dirty."

"Shut up, shut up, shut up," Bullet ordered.

Lucky saw her sister-in-law, Patti, walking past the house without stopping. Lucky ran to the gate and called Patti back.

"You pass right by and can't even yell, 'hello?'"

"Don't make me feel like a crumb. Mommy and Daddy are waiting for me to eat breakfast." Patti was fifty-two years old.

Coming in reluctantly, Patti said, "You'll have to sell the house."

"Patti," Lucky blurted, "You can talk a person to death with your saccharin 'concern', but you aren't doing a thing to help me."

They walked into Bullet's studio where he was cleaning brushes, and an argument ensued.

"Fannie is not the first," Bully boasted to Patti. "I've had hundreds of women."

"That's disgusting. Why are you bragging about chasing women?" Patti asked.

"I thought you'd like to know."

"You're a sex addict, Bullet," Patti said.

"A what?" he asked.

"A sex addict. Usually men who have low self-esteem are the *Don Juans*. By the way, where is Marianna? I want to ask her to go for a run with me after breakfast."

"Marianna is not here. She is quite angry," Lucky told Patti. "Her feelings are volatile. She is upset with Bullet. She's living in town during the week with friends. Our home has become torment for her."

After Patti left, Bullet took Lucky's truck to Fannie's, leaving Lucky without a vehicle to pick up the kids. Angry as she usually was, Lucky broke a teapot spout loading her kiln. As it preheated, she cleaned the glaze studio. The washing machine broke for third time, spewing water all over the floor. Lots of things were breaking.

Lucky raku fired. She was unsure of how to measure the gas pressure, repaired a leaking pipe with plumber's tape, called Teddy Bear Ha for advice, clipped banana leaves and loaded them into metal reduction cans, and, taking her time, fired one large load. She felt peaceful. There was no pressure; no tension; no exhaustion; only Lucky, her pots, and nature, which was beneficent. Every piece came out a jewel, beautifully glazed, and beautifully fired. Every color worked: from glowing corals and bronzes to lustrous blues and crackled whites.

Sunday morning was mildly voggy. After eating donut centers and cranberry juice with Ande and Nico, Lucky sat knees up absorbing the morning blues and random wave patterns. She was startled when Bullet intruded.

"Did you turn on the blowers to give the burners air?" he asked about her kiln.

"My firing's over."

"Oh. You fired already? When did you do that?"

"Last night. And, I really don't want to converse with you, because last night when I was firing, I opened the kiln manual and out fell several pictures of you and Yoko. So, if you don't want this coffee cup smashed on your head, you'll leave."

"Okay. See you," he said, going out.

"Really nice, Mom," said Ande.

"Well, that's the way it is," Lucky said.

20

CUTTING THE DILL

You come to me
You come
To my bed
A shadow
Stale smelling and tired
You have become memory
Distant
My tears though fresh
Linger on my lids
Pooling
Slowly
Sluggish
Before descending my cheeks
To dampen our old rose stained sheets

Silken cords, you called them,
The silken cords binding us

Torn asunder
Sometimes I have forgotten you
And then there is the night
Darkness and shadow
Longing
Sliced by the sharp memory of your lies

It is not that I want you
It is not that I love you
I am weary
A reluctant soldier
Not missing the battlefield, never that
Having seen too much
To ever return to who I was
Before
You
No longer quite fitting
Not fitting the old life
Even if I wanted it

But your stale odor
Clings to my nights
And sickens the air of my dreams

She awakened with aching back muscles, aching to be loved, to be hugged, to be held, to be wanted. To awaken that needy, that desperate, to awaken in that state, resentful and cold turkey celibate frustrated her.

She'd forgotten what it was like to kiss. She kissed her arm. There was hardly any sensation. She focused on her lips touching her skin letting her tongue flicker at the muscle, where she kissed it. Her lips carried no feeling back. Her tongue did, though. It told her the arm was old, its skin loose over taut muscle, old and disgusting.

Her feelings laid dormant; she felt like an unearthed mummy, motionless under an archeologist's mirror, able to watch herself age and decay in the air.

She began chewing her hand, gnawing it with her teeth, biting it hard, on the side of the palm, on its heel. Starving for love, for contact, she fed on herself.

Lucky had always held a self-image of freshness. She liked daisies, bold blue and white stripes, yellow sunshine, crisp breezes, and scudding clouds in a bright sky. She liked Hawai'i. She liked clean, raw, erotic sex. She liked making beautiful children. She liked her simple, open house and big yard fronting the sea. No curtains in her life; she kept her windows flung wide open.

She thought masturbation was an ugly word. The way it sounded. As an adolescent, she used to wonder what in the world it meant, gathering it mostly had to do with horny boys or loners playing with themselves. It had nothing to do with girls or women or with her initiation to sexuality. She'd had less than ten wet dreams in her life. Not until her thirties did she begin to have orgasms during intercourse. Prior to that, she'd had them while thinking about someone she really admired, or while driving a car, or wearing tight jeans, or riding horseback. Later, it was after intercourse, when her arousal was complete. She'd come on hot dates as a freshman in college from making-out and petting but never directly from intercourse.

Bullet proved very athletic at making love. An untiring gymnast, rambunctious and energetic, he liked to make love two or three times a day. Lucky pleasured him. He didn't pleasure her. In fact, he rarely even tried to "turn her on." He never could locate her clitoris, if he knew what one was, and his fingers had all the sensitivity of bear paws. *Slam, bam, thank you ma'am* was his motto. She calculated that they had been together for twenty-three years or more, and, at the minimal rate of twice a day, she'd had intercourse with him over sixteen thousand, seven hundred and ninety times. Lucky had believed that doing it frequently underscored his love and need of her.

When he came, he never shouted, "Oh, Mama," or "Baby," or "I love you, Lucky." Instead, he'd roar at the top of his voice, his body shuddering like an idling bulldozer, letting the decibels of sound taper off into gasping grunts. He would yell from the depths of his chest, like someone had slammed the door of a heavy American-made car on his hand, "Aaaauuuuuurrrrrgggghhh." Occasionally, his Catholic schooling caught up with him, and he'd moan, "Oh, Christ, oooh, sweet Jesus." Or, "Holy Mary, Mother of God." Usually, he'd just cry, "Suuuueeee," like a farmer summoning pigs.

If Bullet was high on cocaine, time would pool languidly into an extended, erotic float. He would drift down and eat her pussy without muttering his stock complaint, "it's too fishy." He liked to see how long he could last, not to see if he could bring Lucky to orgasm, but rather to see how long he could sustain his own anticipated pleasure.

Because of his monumental selfishness and her naiveté, Lucky had borne two children before reaching an orgasm under his helm. The *Kegels* she used to strengthen the birth canal for easier delivery introduced her to orgasmic control. With concentrated effort and exercise, she contracted her vaginal walls to a count of ten, in sequences of fifty. Once she learned the trick, the reward was worth it. She caught the ring on the carousel. Managing orgasms lent a sense of control over her own pleasure and made her feel independent. She could be the aggressor in sexuality, if she chose, not the supplicant.

In her clay studio, she practiced *Kegels*, grabbing her crotch Michael Jackson style as she danced to radio rock 'n roll. She stopped glazing, ran upstairs, stripped naked, and rubbed in #6 sunscreen. Everywhere. She wanted a big, lively dick and arms and hugs. She wanted to lift her pelvis high and hard to receive her lover's thrusts.

She sunbathed on the deck, her body smeared with sun tanning oils, risking being seen naked through the open slats of the deck, naughty, delicious fun, letting the breeze flutter through her thighs to flit about her clitoris. She had *Orgasms-by-the-Weather*, sunning her old nipples and white ass, evening out the tan lines.

Some nights, dark and quiet and solitary, she crept around the house, finally standing on the upper deck in the wind and half moonlight, stretching on the railing, wired. Days of juiciness. Ripe. *Rotting on the vine?* Lucky thought of Rod and imagined his thickness, wondering if he would be kind in bed. Immediately, she was discouraged by thoughts of sex leading to real relationships and their complications.

She cultivated an *I don't need you attitude*, relieved that she could help herself and not have to involve anyone else, feeling smug about her orgasms like the cat that swallowed the canary. Some days, she couldn't get the smile off her face or the feathers out of her teeth.

After Nico went to bed in her room, she wrapped in a towel and tiptoed barefoot downstairs. She laid out the towel on the living room floor behind the couch where she wouldn't be seen. She got a pillow and a new bottle of coconut oil.

She touched herself carefully. Her arms were muscular and trim, belly flat, legs and hips thinner, but not yet satisfied with them. She held her crotch. It was warm, soft, and squishy. She was happy for that. She massaged her clitoris with oil; petted and played and got reacquainted. Her whole body, her whole self needed love, needed to move and writhe, do the old bump and grind. She turned onto her stomach, lifted up off floor so her pubic bone wouldn't scrape, as she was so thin.

She went to the refrigerator and opened the door. There, on a backlit shelf, sat a jar of well-chilled kosher dills from *Safeway's* deli, small crippled forms suspended in brine. She selected one with the same thick, rubbery quality of Bullet's erect, somewhat flabby penis, closed the lid, drying off the vinegar with a paper towel. And, pickle curled in palm, she walked in darkness back to the living room.

She took the plunge. Or, rather, the pickle did. It felt good and somewhat familiar. *Moby Pickle*, cold and rubbery, stretched her vaginal walls. It almost got swallowed in that dank cavern. She had to pinch its slippery, doused with *astroglide*, end tightly, fearing it might disappear in a drowned sea of memories, pre-menopausal periods, sheddings and slakings. She got so carried away with the thrusting rhythm of the pickle, that her mind swam away, flowing on the ebb tide of her pleasure and urgency.

Bullet was not on her mind. Instead, a phantom appeared. She dreamed of a kind, gray-haired fantasy lover as she laid in the dark. She entertained fantasies of this phantom lick-lick-licking her into sweet frenzy. Her loins were fluid with oil. She stayed very still, slowly embraced by quiet moments of longing and desire. She imagined him filling her, anticipated his full, slow entry, her muscle walls swallowing and contracting hard as her whole pelvis swiftly swung upward in his grip, holding on for a fast, up-down, carnival ride. He was as large as a Macy's Thanksgiving Day parade balloon, emitting huge wet clouds of white ice-creamy steamy sperm to her delight, plowing her into oblivion.

The dill did the trick. She came in an enormous orgasm, her fingers feeling each pulsation of her furrowed walls, as she got self-inflicted rug burns.

She put her left hand like a protective umbrella over her eyes to cover her shame. A tear fell from one eye. Stillness. One hand, the right, clapped tightly between her legs, the left, the other, over her mouth, stifled the tidal cry of her loneliness. Tears and sobs put a strangle-hold on her heart, asphyxiating her, because she had come to this, alone on the living room carpet, masturbating with a pickle.

Choking and coughing, she slung her other arm over her face with the used dill clenched angrily in her fist. She slowly rose to her feet, wrapped the towel around her body, and walked into the bathroom. Turning on the light, she took hair-trimming scissors from her make-up drawer.

She cut the dill carefully into three parts, letting them fall ceremonially, part by part, into the toilet and flushed them away. She washed the scissors and dried them. *What an image,* Lucky thought, *cutting the dill.* She felt like getting drunk. She regretted not returning the dill, used, to the jar and watching Bullet eat it for lunch one day with a tuna fish sandwich.

Sexual energy electrified the household. The kids spouted graphic remarks. Nico played with his shark puppet, letting it eat his crotch.

"Nico, stop acting gross," Ande complained. "Mom, do you know Nico flipped the bird to Fannie? Dad warned Nico, 'If you flick people off, you'll get your fingers broken.'"

Marianna said, "Fannie's a tattletale."

The girls were changing fast. Marianna got phone calls from two boys, John and Darryl.

"Mom," Marianna blurted, "Birdie slept with a boy this summer."

"She did? Who?"

"What is orgasm, anyway?" Marianna wanted to know, standing in kitchen in *Gap* blue jeans and *Esprit* navy tank top, golden hair long and glistening, blue eyes shining, teeth straight and white since the braces came off, smile young and full.

"Mom, if you weren't my mom, would you find me attractive?"

"You're a very pretty girl, Marianna. You remind me of a prized filly. You've got the most gorgeous, racehorse legs in the world. Running track and cross-country is your thing. Lord knows, your dad and I have never been runners. Look at you, number one in the state for the sixteen hundred and your photo with Coach Rohlberg in the newspaper as this year's most promising athlete. I am so amazed by you."

"Well, I like running and being really good at something. Tennis and ballet were such washouts. Not to mention piano."

"You know, your running can get you into Berkeley on an athletic scholarship. I called the athletic office at Harmon Gym. They said for you to send a copy of your U.C. application directly to them. Do you want to do that?"

Marianna looked excited as Lucky went on, "The Wolfesons have gone to Berkeley for three generations: Great Granddad, Grampa Jack, Gramma Edna, Great Uncle Wooley, Uncle Jackie, Auntie Laura and Linney, all my cousins, then me plus your dad. They're looking for women who are athletic and smart."

"Sure, I'll apply. My grades are no problem, but I don't know about my SAT scores."

"That's why the Athletic Department wants your application. If for any reason Admissions turns you down, the Athletic Department can red-flag your application for their own review."

"I guess I'll go for it, Mom. Just don't get fixed on it, 'cause I don't want to disappoint you, okay? I'm not as smart as you were; I don't do as well in school or have as many activities. And, coming from Hawai'i, I don't know if I can take the pressure of a huge school like Berkeley."

"You'll do well no matter where you go. And to answer your question, yes, you are a beautiful girl."

"I'm not as pretty as you."

"Be quiet. You're smart and friendly. I like how you share the happiness inside you. That's the true beauty I see."

"I like people, Mom. I want to be friendly, be more like Birdie and Gigi and my other friends."

21

HOLDING THE MIRROR

Guilt was painful, and Lucky suspected Bullet felt condemnation from several sources: certainly from her, but also from the children, his parents, his friends, and maybe from his Catholic God.

Bullet told Lucky, "I know that what I'm doing is difficult for you, but someday you will understand that it is for the best. This separation is really YOUR fault. Your drove me to it. I never really loved you, even when we were young. In fact, we should never have gotten married in the first place. We're too different. It's better if I let you go now than when you're fifty. This marriage is just a piece of paper."

"Wow, Bullet. How marvelous you are at rewriting our history."

"No, I'm not. I'm really doing this for your good."

"By saying that we never should have married are you saying that our union is just an unfortunate mistake rather than a relationship that God ordained and our vows cemented?"

Bullet continued, "Look, Lucky: I'll be a much better dad when we're divorced. The kids and I have a great time when you're not around. I'd love to raise my kids. I'd love to shop and cook and feed them. I take care of all their medical needs."

Lucky translated, "You mean you fix aloe as a cure-all for any ailment and force the kids to drink it. You generally refuse to take them to the doctors' as it disrupts your day. You never drive them to school or pick them up from sports or their friends' houses. And, when, may I ask, have you ever grocery shopped or cooked a full meal for us?"

During their eight months of separation, he had cooked breakfast for the children once, taken two of them to a movie, taken them all to the beach a handful of times, picked up Nico before and after school twice when he couldn't find anyone else to do it, driven Marianna to one race, and called to talk to the kids only occasionally.

"Do you believe your escapade with Fannie is actually a constructive thing?" Lucky asked. "Never mind what our kids see, Bullet. What conclusions do they draw about why you left, and why you don't seem to love them anymore, and why the divorce might be their fault, and why life has become so painful and scary?"

"I love the kids, Lucky."

"They are going through hell, Bullet," Lucky told him. "They are really, really sad. Have you thought about what Marianna said when you told her we were breaking up? Remember? She said she wanted to die?"

"Really," Bullet huffed, "what kid commits suicide when the parents get divorced?"

"My sister, Linney, for one."

"Oh, yeah. I forgot. I can hardly wait to hear what your mother will have to say," Bullet added. "I've prayed about this decision, Lucky. I've gone to confession. I feel certain that God approves of my love for Fannie."

"God approves? You heard from God?"

22

THE TRAIN

Bully was left far behind. Lucky was like a train, and he was left on the station platform, as she moved toward the frontier on a track to freedom.

She reran the first scene of their journey back in 1966 over and over. Steam hissed up from a train on the tracks in Lisbon just behind her. She was dressed in a multi-colored mohair coat at the railway station in late December. She imagined a swelling John Williams' score surrounding her youthful European romance. Most students of her generation saw Europe on a Eurail pass. She was no exception.

For Lucky, a rich country girl from California growing up used to small planes, train rides had not been part of her small town experience. Trains carried freight. Tracks had a social implication, delineating whether someone lived on the "wrong" side of them or not. To go any distance, Jack Wolfeson flew his young family in his *Piper Cub, Cessna 172* or *195*. If he drove the super-highways of the late nineteen-fifties, it was in his spanking new, long-finned, bathtub pink *Chrysler Imperial* with traffic post tail lights.

The Wolfeson's left-handed cleaning lady had lived on the wrong side of the tracks, Lucky remembered, in one of those unpainted wooden houses where dark attics hid beneath the gables. The wooden floorboards of her house had grown so skinny over the years that they had wide gaps in between, barely held together by lackluster nails. Dust crept up from the three-foot crawl space below, incubating progeny like spiders in a fuzzy mantle, which dispersed over the boards and under the carpet.

Dust suffocated that carpet, where some afternoons, the Wolfeson kids played, babysat by the cleaning lady in addition to her own brood. Every sad shade of brown ever seen was in that carpet. Emily, Lucky was Emily then, didn't think it had ever been young.

Conceived as pseudo-Persian, it was rectangular with intricate borders and a viney floral motif, probably born in some *Sears* or *Montgomery Ward* mail-order catalog before the Depression had sent it way out to California. But, not before generations of families had tread on it, rolled it up and heaved it atop old jalopies on the move downhill, from one worse job to another, into the dry dirtiness of poverty on their way West.

In the ravages of old age and decrepitude, it almost begged not to be walked on, as it was quite worn out, a barely skeletal form, wheezing its last from dried and shriveled lungs. The phlegmatic cleaning lady was too tired to take care of her own house after cleaning places like the Wolfeson's all day. And, her greasy bunch of kids got it dirtier by their cavorting. What a greasy bunch of kids she had.

Greasy wasn't good, at least not in Emily's book. At high school, greasy haired guys were not knowable; they came from mysterious, mongrelized backgrounds. They weren't Chinese like the Fongs, or Italian like the Ferraras, or Episcopalian like the Frosts. They were from the "wrong side of the tracks," from out of town, from one of the little gas stops along the canal or from one of the little farms down by the river. Or, maybe from Artois, where drifters found work picking turkey feathers off the Thanksgiving would-be center pieces at one of the many poultry farms there.

The kids at school called them *pachucos. Pachucos* didn't have parents a nice girl ever met and didn't live in houses a nice girl ever saw. They sort of emerged on the scene, appeared in hallways at school, acne on their faces, grease in their hair, T-shirt sleeves rolled twice, their jeans sporting a cocky teenage bulge. They usually had suped-up racing cars or hot rods and hung out at the drive-in after school, drinking *Coca Colas.* In fact, most nice girls imagined if they even touched the door handle of a *pachuco's* hotrod, they'd get knocked up. Nice girls didn't look at *pachucos.*

One freshman day outside the cafeteria before lunch, Emily recognized the cleaning lady's oldest son, idle under a sycamore tree. He had grown into a greasy and hormonal, cigarette-smoking *pachuco* with lazy lidded eyes. Oooh, he was a greasy one, Emily thought, and she did not say hello. This *pachuco's* black hair was so heavily greased he could have changed the oil of his mother's worn-out *Studebaker* with it.

One week later that fall before Big Jack had left the family in tatters, Laura hadn't gotten home yet from school. Edna sent Emily over to the cleaning lady's house to pick up Jackie, who was being babysat. Entering the dusty darkness of the house, Emily avoided the familiar carpet on her way through the unlit living room. She always walked around its threadbare woof anyway; its loose strands that reached out like stiffened spidery legs or squid tentacles scared her. She didn't want responsibility for knocking out the last of its wind.

She was headed to the dining room and into the cracked linoleum kitchen beyond to find Jackie and a glass of *Kool-Aid,* when she stumbled, rather, she bumped into something big that was rolling on the old carpet. She heard a sneeze. Dust billowed up followed by more sneezes.

"Huh?" she muttered and reached for the light. There, beneath its glare, rolled big sister, Laura, the dateless, in a rough legged embrace, wrestling crinolines up to her armpits with whom else, but the *pachuco,* whose blue jeans were dropped around his ankles.

Emily couldn't figure out what Laura could see in him. But, sight wasn't Laura's dominant sense in those bitter, rebellious years. The sensuous power and providence of the dank attic above her legs, the bulk of her blossoming womanhood, and the desperation of her damaged ego ruled supreme.

Emily kept silent, going home on foot each afternoon alone, while asthmatic Laura grew accustomed to rolling an alternate route after school on her backside, locked in that clandestine, dust ball embrace before returning home, her allergies be damned.

Lucky's own romantic adventure had begun in the cold winter of 1966 in Lisbon, Portugal. Hardly anyone was traveling, as it was the holiday between Christmas and the New Year. She had the train station almost to herself. She bought some oranges and alone boarded the first class car bound for Sevilla, Spain.

She was wearing the designer coat purchased on a splurge earlier that winter in Goteborg, Sweden, where she was spending a year studying the dramaturgy of Scandinavia's sons, Strindberg and Ibsen. Her legs were wrapped up to the kneecaps in chartreuse suede, *"Barbarella"* boots, and her head was bare, her *Miss Clairol* blonde locks flashing straight down her back. Attracted by the beacon of her hair, several Portuguese soldiers stopped outside Lucky's train window to flirt. Her train wasn't scheduled to depart for two more hours. On the next track sat a train leaving for Madrid in a matter of minutes.

To escape the soldiers, she switched trains, found another empty compartment, and settled in. As the train began pulling out, several people rushed on board, hurrying past her door and speaking excitedly in English. *English? Americans? Company?* Lucky was cold and lonely, bored as well, after losing her latest boyfriend over the holidays to a gay theatre director in Paris, who manufactured LSD on the side, and then losing her luggage in her escape to Lisbon.

She had spent three days guzzling robust Portuguese wine, passing out drunkenly in a cheap pensione on Rossio square adjacent to the beautiful national theatre and Column to Pedro IV, waiting and hoping for both luggage and boyfriend to arrive, so she could get on with both sightseeing and her love life. The baggage had finally shown up, but the boyfriend had not. A pattern, perhaps, destined to repeat.

She quickly opened her window. Then she innocently knocked at the door of the next compartment.

"Does anyone here speak English?" she asked.

The brown-bearded American, she preferred the taller redhead, answered demurely, "A little."

"My window is stuck," she lied, "and I was wondering if you could help me close it?"

And that is how, twenty-five years before, she had met Richard Elliot Pulaski, known affectionately as "Bullet."

The redhead was his traveling companion, Billy-Bob Hackerby. There was a female student on board whose name Lucky couldn't remember. Lucky did recall her grunts, however. They still resounded in her ears. That girl had crazy sex with Hackerby to pass the time that night, doing her best to heat up that freezing midwinter first-class compartment.

There was also on board an elderly tour group escapee, a white-haired secretary who worked at the San Quentin penitentiary. She drank whiskey from a red, Scotch plaid lunch thermos and told prison stories all night, oblivious to the rollicking human furnace next to her, as over the icy bed rails to Spain they chugged.

By the next morning Lucky had developed a great liking for her future husband due to her tremendous relief he hadn't tried to rape her on that ride. *My kinda guy,* she thought.

Weeks later they met again at a youth hostel north of Barcelona. After a night freezing cold and sleepless under a greasy horse blanket on a raw, aged mattress without sheets, she'd risen early, hoping not to miss Bullet in case he was staying there during his Mediterranean surf safari. She wasn't quite sure of his itinerary. She was eating a dreary breakfast, when he found her at one of the tedious cafeteria tables surrounded by dozens of other youthful travelers. Seeing her, he pressed a kiss, the sweetest kiss she'd ever tasted, on her upturned, oatmeal-encrusted lips.

23

FUJIMURA'S

Lucky vacillated over Thanksgiving. Queenie called several times a day, opening the conversation with her usual question, "Well, what's my bad boy been up to?" followed by her customary titter. She adored gossip and fed off Bullet's "naughty" behavior. Her military life with Rex had been strictly regimented, and she craved misbehavior in others, openly encouraging it in her son, to get a mindless, vicarious thrill.

Queenie asked if Rex and she could come over to eat. Lucky wasn't sure if she would invite Bullet, as she was taking things one day at a time. He practically demanded to come when he heard his parents would be there.

That made her so mad that she definitely didn't want him to come. The problem was the kids; it would be good to have all three kids home for Thanksgiving vacation. They were funny and bubbly and dear.

She shopped for groceries at Fujimura's. The most remarkable thing about Fujimura's Super was not the store but the people who went into it. Locals. The Leeward locals. Always a big crowd there. Prices were rock bottom compared to most of Hawai'i's stores, which had exorbitant markups due to overseas shipping, warehouse storage, and trucking. Welfare days there were a nightmare when checking out could take over an hour to get through the line.

The parking lot at Fujimura's alone was quite a colorful scene, its asphalt hot in the Hawai'ian sun, long lines of cars inching off the highway to commandeer one of the prize stalls. *Huli-huli* chickens, sold by local canoe clubs for annual fundraisers, roasted on spits over *kiawe* wood fires to the side of the parking lot, charcoal smoke adding to the heat of the day.

And the cars: big, old, American, moved slowly. *Buicks, Chevrolet* wagons, at least fifteen years old and rusted out, filled the parking lot. Samoans loved big American cars. Heavy from the giant passengers within, car bellies scraped the pavement, grating mufflers loosened as they slumped under their unwieldy loads.

Men emerged in lava lavas, women in pareaus, children astride one hip, all lumbering toward the entry. The local farmers and pig raisers came into Fujimura's muddy and tired from work, wearing black galoshes damp with fetid spatters from taro patches or pigsties. Lucky often entered with paint or clay swashed on her skin and her perennial workaday swimsuit, oblivious to any need for propriety. Construction workers, sun-burned and dusty, stood in the liquor line armed with their nightly twelve-packs of *Bud*.

There were some *Astro* wagons and *Mazda* or *Ranger* pickups. The local elementary school teachers, second and third generation Japanese, clearly belonged to the middle class, as did the bank clerks and secretaries. Not too many professionals lived in Wai'anae though: two lawyers, four dentists, a few commuting doctors, one veterinarian.

Fujimura Super (pronounced Sue-pah) smacked of pidgin. It stood for Super Market or Suprette, but its first generation Japanese founders, newly emancipated from labor in the cane fields, knew just enough English to get the message across: Super, along with their proprietorship. Fujimura's was not a big chain. They didn't have warehouses. Their employees were not unionized. And, it was cheap, the cheapest store in the islands. That's why everybody shopped there. At the other grocery stores, Lucky had to pay $2.69 for four rolls of toilet paper; at Fujimura's they cost $1.09.

"How come?" she asked Norbert once.

"Only 4% mark-up," he said. "We store all our merchandise here and pick it up from the dock in our own truck. So, cheapah," he said as he blazed a gold-capped smile, wrinkles relaxed and warm around his eyes.

Best, Fujimura's was a family store, taken over by old O-San Fujimura's two grown sons and three grandsons. Sometimes she saw O-San checking the shelves in the store, supporting his crippled knees on a shopping cart, unable to play his life long passion, golf, since his seventy-fifth birthday. He waited, as did all his employees, for his toothless, spinster-sister, Mitsui's, daily hot lunch of fried lettuce and *Spam* doused wetly with shoyu or a mixed vegetable platter made for the old timers.

Fujimura loved golf. He even paid for the local links to be built. He passed out free golf balls to any player who showed up. He walked the course for years, until his knees could no longer support him. Then he got a deluxe electric cart. Finally, scooting around the course in the cart, he'd park next to his ball. While sitting stock still at the wheel, he'd swing his club, still alive in the game. In old age, he sat in the cart, filled with loyal friends, *talking story*, content to watch others play.

Afternoons, he'd sit on the stacked dog food bags in Oshiro's Farm Store, passing the time with old Mr. Oshiro, rows of purple dendrobium orchids bobbing behind his head and yellow baby chicks cheeping in incubators to his left. When Oshiro's son took over, and Oshiro retired to raise orchids at home, O-San's visits stopped.

Certain customers entering Fujimura's emitted blatant hostility as locals sometimes did in many of the poorer neighborhoods in the islands. *Locals Only* tank tops abounded, emblazoned with airbrushed images of pit bulls sporting heavy metal spike collars, braless breasts bulged undulant and lazy beneath the thin cotton. Both men and women needed bras. Bellies protruded: some pregnant and full of life, others "calorically enhanced" by three scoops of rice at every meal, *plenny poi*, too much salt, and too little exercise. Shirts pulled tight above belly buttons, revealing the brown flesh below, scarred by purple stretch lines of human gristle. Tattoos abounded on both sexes from teenagers to seniors, glimpsed on any body part left unclothed: *kapa* designs, intricate florals, love oaths, gang affiliations, elaborate yakuza drawings.

Men, easily weighing three hundred and fifty to four hundred pounds, slowly swaggered into the store, the *rubbah slippahs* they wore on their feet squished flat on the inner edges from their load. Cigarettes dangled smoldering from loose lips, mouths toothless or with gaping holes where teeth once lodged.

Loud, angry voices from cranky mothers and aunties, assaulted their half-dressed, crying, dirty children, "Eh, you like I slap yo head? Like I punch yo face?"

If you happened to be *ha'ole*, white or foreign, watch out, you were doubly suspect. *Locals Only* was not only a brand of clothing. It was also an attitude in Wai'anae.

There was another loudness made of the happy sound of whooping laughter: greetings of friends, shouts of *aloha* and shrill screams of laughter, wet smacks of cheek kisses or claps of high-five, followed by, "How you stay?" and more laughter.

When Lucky arrived on the Leeward Side, it had the highest concentration of native Hawai'ians and part-Hawai'ians in the state. It was also a welfare community. As such, it had all the problems accompanying a fading race of once-proud people, many now on the dole. Ignorance, lack of Puritan work ethic, poverty, prejudice, obesity, cancer, mental illness, and the highest level of parolee-ism in the state, plagued its residents. A tough place, the entire west side of O'ahu from Nanakuli to Kaena Point stretched like a corridor in purgatory where troubled souls awaited salvation.

Historically, Nanakuli was remembered in history books for its lack of friendliness. It was an arid land, never having enough water to share with outsiders and where bandits hid in the caves above Makaha to waylay travelers. Modern day tourists got the traditional "rip-off" treatment. Enter Nanakuli with a rental car and guaranteed its contents would disappear the instant the car was parked. Rental agencies didn't even put it on the map.

Some tourists from Boston rented the vacation beach bungalow next to Queenie and Rex's for a month. An hour after their arrival, they decided the beach was "too sandy." Go figure, and they wanted to depart. They put their bags back into the rental car and started the engine. The engine turned over. But, the car wouldn't move. On getting out to look for the problem, they saw that the car was sitting on hollow tiles. Its four tires had already been stolen.

The rental car agency representative said, "Oh, don't worry. We get several calls a week like yours from the Wai'anae area."

Fujimura's was a wonder. It had rows of exclusively Chinese foods, Japanese, Filipino: fish sauce, nori, shiitake, sweet rice, and mirin. The fish department offered Oka's own *poke*, raw chunks of tuna mixed with *limu*: seaweed, many varieties available; green onions, ground *kukui* nut *inamona*, anjinomoto: a known killer of brain cells but soooo *onolicious*, chili peppers, Hawai'ian rock salt and shoyu.

There was always chicken or pork *laulau*, *kalua* pig, and *lomi* salmon. That was at the local cholesterol counter. Its fish department offered fake crab and shark paste shaped like a jellyroll, spiraled in bright red dye to be sliced onto steaming noodles in saimin bowls. Everybody snacked on raw fish, *mochi* crunch, crack seed, sugary Portuguese *malasadas*, and colorful, multi-flavored shave-ice.

Plate lunch from the deli consisted of an entrée: chicken *katsu* or shoyu chicken, teri beef, butterfish or curry stew accompanied by two scoops of rice and one of macaroni salad, served in a white lidded Styrofoam box, rubber band around it holding a napkin, plastic fork or chopsticks on top.

Babies lost the enamel on their teeth from the *Malolo* fruit syrups their mothers bought here and diluted as sugar water into their bottles. Infants were left in plastic infant carriers to fall asleep with a bottle of *Enfamil* propped in their mouths, their heads flattened slightly from lying too long in one position, neglected. Silver caps gleamed behind toddlers' chattering lips in place of white baby teeth. Infant girls' pierced ear lobes sported glittery red or crystal studs from *Woolworth*. Tiny hands were mittened to prevent nails from scratching faces in their first fumbling attempts to touch themselves.

As unfamiliar as Lucky was when she first came to Hawai'i with some of the ethnic foods, so the clerks were unfamiliar with her purchases.

Maizie, Hermie, or Oka would hold up a loaf of San Francisco *Columbo* sour-dough bread and ask, "Whatchu eat dis fo?" Her purchases of romaine lettuce, yogurt, strudel dough, cannelloni noodles, artichoke hearts, endives, leeks, red onions, Greek olives, marzipan, saffron, cardamom, and pistachio ice cream were novelties to them.

In 1979 at Lucky's request, Fujimura's began stocking wine other than *Spumonti*, the usual hit of the brown bag beach bums. O-San brought in *Gallo* and *Christian Brothers*; *Andre* champagne at $2.99 a bottle for Christmas and New Year's, although most locals preferred the sweetness of *Cold Duck* for the holidays.

The available fresh fruits and vegetables were glorious, produce being plentiful all year round. Mangoes of every variety, flavor and color, lychees, apple-williams-bluefield-and-cooking bananas, papaya, star fruit, breadfruit, yams, sweet potatoes, garlic, ginger, lotus root, Manoa lettuce, taro, local green onions, watermelons, corn, sweet Maui onions, tomatoes, Japanese cucumbers so crisp and crunchy that eating any other would be unthinkable, radish, alfalfa, *daikon*, and mung sprouts.

Next to nobody paid for groceries with cash. Food stamps reigned supreme: food stamps for cigarettes, *Budweiser*, *Coca-Cola*, chips, cereal, *tempura, teriyaki,* tuna, *poke*, pork, steak, frozen shoestring fries, *Oreos*, saltines, *Spam*, rice, *poi*, shoyu.

On a visit once, Lucky's brother, Jackie, wanted to shop. He stood in wonder at the checkout counter, watching the vast quantity of groceries, cart after cart, exchanged for food stamps. Lucky could see his anger and amazement growing.

Jackie had become a multimillionaire at thirty-six, inheriting Wolfeson Wilderness Outfitters when their father died and expanding it into Wolfeson Outfitters, Wilderness Management and Expeditions. Embodiment of the very work ethic absent from Wai'anae, he owned forty-four retail stores on several resort sites, thirty restaurants, a chain of health food stores, a fleet of tour buses, charter aircraft, helicopters, jets, camera rentals and processing, reservation and travel services.

He took hunting and trapping out of Jack's business in the spirit of the environmental consciousness of the Eighties.

In~their place, he instituted camera safaris and ecology tours for the new generation where yuppie values replaced machismo, where grains and soy subbed for red meat. He had over eight-thousand employees worldwide; he was a big time taxpayer, health nut, fitness freak, politically correct environmentalist, self-styled *granola-head* Nazi, political conservative, and social elitist. Ayn Rand was his goddess of the written word.

Here in Lucky's backyard grocery store in the middle of the tropical Pacific, he watched his tax dollar burning. It smoldered as the ash on the end of a cigarette between a welfare recipient's lips. It dripped empty calories of diet soda into children's mouths, whose families might not have worked in generations. Lucky was terrified he'd say something to provoke a fight. She wanted to get out of that store alive. After all, she shopped there every other day and was one of their only cash paying, check-writing customers.

She whispered, nudging him, "Don't say anything."

One of the hardest things Lucky had left to do as a family was to live through this Thanksgiving meal. Somehow the anticipation was worse than the actual event. Ande stayed busy-busy all day with place cards, candles, crepe paper streamers, and table setting.

"I want it to be special like always, Mom," she said.

Gramma Queenie offered to cook the turkey and make her traditional apple-sausage-cornbread stuffing. Nico and Marianna peeled apples for pie; Ande rolled the crusts. Lucky made yams, mashed potatoes, rolls, shredded red cabbage with apples, beans, Brussels sprouts, cranberry conserve, mushroom giblet gravy. For dessert were the kids' pies a la mode, pecan, cherry, and apple, followed by pumpkin cheesecake mousse.

Rex mumbled the usual Catholic grace. Bullet *pax vobiscum*'d everyone. Queenie held up her champagne glass for a toast. Then, Lucky broke tradition and chimed in with a reading of her own choice from "Amazing Grace" by Davey Newton:

Amazing grace
How sweet the sound
That saved a wretch like me
I once was lost, but now am found,
Was blind, but now I see.

No one acknowledged the rift in their lives. Queenie beamed all evening. The kids enjoyed the family being together and provided entertainment as they ritually destroyed the holiday turkey and Indian wax candles Queenie had brought to decorate each place setting. A flame and wax mess melted over the white damask cloth. Under the table, Hula Girl and Suds, their white Persian cat, vied for treats, Suds strafing their calves with his lean body and hungry tail.

Looking at the stars after dinner, Lucky felt aware through their visibility of her own smallness in relation to the vastness of the universe. Pettiness and small grievances faded in the scope of the larger cosmos. *But during the day,* she thought, *the sun's brightness obscures the stars and makes my problems appear deceptively important.*

24

EYE FOR AN EYE

"Come watch me surf," Bullet invited, calling the kids three times before breakfast. It was only two weeks before the studio and Christmas sales were slated to begin. It was a gray day, humid and overcast. Lucky felt weighted down by the thick air, sluggish and sad. Sudsy rolled over, pure white beside her, letting her stroke him while Bullet told her he had his "priorities" and instead of painting, he'd entered a surfing contest.

"Dad, we are uncomfortable coming to the beach," Marianna admitted to him. "Fannie ruins it. She comes down to within a few yards of us, lies there and taunts us. We won't come, if she's going to be there."

"I'm alone. I want time with you," he promised.

Lucky remembered when he used to hate her bringing the kids to the beach. Marianna was four, and Ande was about two. Both happy digging sand, loving to crawl into a large hole they'd dug into the shore-break to await filling by a wave. They were blonde-haired, blue-eyed, chubby cheeked cherubim.

Bullet had watched them playing one morning and sighed to Lucky, "If only they had black hair."

"What?"

"I wish they looked more Hawai'ian. They stand out too much. They really look like little *ha'ole*s."

His words stung her.

"They are little *ha'ole*s, Bullet. And, we're big *ha'ole*s. Surprise."

"Don't bring them down to Makaha any more," he ordered as though embarrassed he'd fathered these little white girls. "Let 'em swim at Pokai Bay. It's safer for them to learn there anyway."

Ande started dancing *hula* when she was five. She begged Lucky for two years to take ballet lessons with Marianna at Madame Roche's studio. She coveted the pink netted tufts of Marianna's tutu and the obligatory soft pink *Capezio* slippers worn to class. Lucky had bought Ande the same tiny outfit along with a rosebud pink leotard and tights. She excitedly pirouetted out to the dinner table one night to show off her finery.

"Oh, not again," groaned Bullet. "I don't want another ballerina in this house. If my kid wants to dance, she can dance *hula*." Ande's face fell into dark rebellion.

"I don't want to dance *hula*, Daddy. I want to be a ballerina like Marianna and dance at Madame Roche's."

"Let's get this straight, Lucky. We live in Hawai'i. You're making our kids little Europeans. You drag them forty miles to gymnastics, soccer, piano, and ballet. Look around you, woman. There's a big ocean out there. Let them surf; let them swim. Go down to Fujimura's and get them some bamboo fishing poles. Teach 'em to snorkel and dive. Forget all that mainland crap. Let them play *ukulele*, and dance *hula*. Get with the program, huh? And, teach them to love this place while you're at it."

"Why don't you, Bullet? You're their dad. You teach them what you like, and I'll teach what I like."

"Just do what I say," Bullet ordered.

On Saturday, Lucky accompanied a resistant Ande to *hula* class. Ande spent the hour crying, refusing to set foot in the *halau*. The next Saturday, Bullet took her to class. She spent the hour crying. The following Saturday, Bullet and Lucky took Ande to class. Again, she cried and refused to participate.

"Ande, you can cry all you want," Bullet said. "If you don't at least stand inside the *halau* with the other kids, your mother and I will leave you here with Auntie Pearl until next Saturday. You can't come home until you dance."

As the clock wound through the hour to twelve, Ande, body shaking with sobs, both nostrils running like waterfalls, barely able to breathe, finally inched her kindergarten toes to the edge of the *lauhala* mat and launched herself painfully into what would later become a love affair with the Hawai'ian culture.

Marianna planned to run to Makaha with her best friend, Birdie. Marianna was becoming as big a fitness nut as her Uncle Jackie. The deck was littered with her sports equipment: a sit-up slant board, a *Stairmaster*, a rowing machine, and a treadmill. She asked if Lucky would pick her up. Lucky needed to work but agreed.

"Ande and Nico, do you want to go for a short time to watch Dad surf when I pick up Marianna?"

"Yeah."

They drove up, passing Birdie and Marianna on road. The highway was over-crowded due to the surf meet. Lucky pulled over in a lot on the *mauka* side of highway but there was no place to park.

"Mom," Marianna panted, breathless from the run, "can you drive Birdie down to her father's house in Maili? I want to jump in the water." Meanwhile, Ande and Nico headed across the highway with towels and boogie boards.

Marianna suddenly returned to the car to report, "Mom, Dad is down there with Fannie. He said he wouldn't bring her. What are you gonna do about it, Mom?"

"Nothing."

"You ought to deck her."

Before Lucky could respond, Marianna ran back down to the beach. Lucky had to wait a long while in traffic before she could make a U-turn. By the time she did, she spotted Marianna near the shoreline, pulling Francine by the hair and kicking her in the stomach. Fannie threw sand at Marianna. Marianna pushed Fannie's face, kicked her back, and pulled her hair with renewed vigor. Fannie ripped Marianna's shorts right off her.

Bullet in cobalt *Kanaka Clothing* shorts with a white T-shirt wrapped like a turban on his head charged up to Marianna and Fannie. Lucky feared for her daughter but could do nothing, stuck as she was in traffic. Marianna ran from Bullet, but he grabbed her arm. She kneed him in the groin and broke free. *Had I known twenty years ago I'd watch my fifteen-year-old daughter beating my husband's girlfriend on a beach in Hawai'i...*

Birdie grabbed Lucky's arm, saying, "I never thought Marianna would do that! Don't you want go to her? I can sit in the car for you."

Lucky was actually afraid to get involved, as paralyzed in this moment by pending violence as she had been in childhood. "No, she can handle it," she told Birdie.

Seeing the color drain from Lucky's face, Birdie added, "Oh. You're all shook up, too."

Lucky sat stalled in the traffic when she saw Big Al.

"Al, can you go over and help Marianna?" she yelled. "See that she's all right for me, please?"

After driving Birdie home, Lucky returned to the beach. Marianna, Ande and Nico were very excited to tell her about the fight. Marianna stretched her legs against the side of the truck. Her face was flushed.

"Fannie called me a 'son of a bitch.' She can't even swear right in English, Mom. She said, 'This is between your father and your mother. I am not a part of it.' But, she hit me anyway."

"We hid in the bushes, Mom," Nico exclaimed.

"Nico was so scared. Me, too," Ande admitted.

"Dad tried to protect Fannie, Mom," Marianna added. "He pushed me out of the way like he didn't know me, like I wasn't his kid."

"But then, Uncle Boxer and everybody started cheering for Marianna, calling her 'Da Champ,'" Ande said. "So, we came out from hiding. Marianna wasn't crying or anything. Fannie was, till Dad took her home."

"Oh. Your dad took Fannie home? What did he do for Marianna?"

"Nothing. Dad only cares about his girlfriend. Not me at all. Look, Mom, she ripped my shorts," Marianna added, part triumphantly, part mournfully.

"Dad surfed his heat," Nico told Lucky. "He caught a couple of big glassy waves and slid down the backwash."

"Yeah," Ande said. "We saw him surf like he wanted, but I'm not proud of him."

Lucky was not proud of herself. She had let Marianna usurp her role, exactly as Edna had let Laura defend her. Lucky should have been there for her daughter. She wished Bullet's board would crack him in the head and kill him, even on such a beautiful day with the turquoise sea, clean sun and air.

Rex and Queenie came by the house after golf, all smiling and excited. They'd been to the beach where everyone was talking about Marianna beating up Bullet's "*f.c.*" girlfriend, the gossip of the year. Boxer had told Rex that Marianna had gone after Fannie, and everyone on shore was cheering. Rex and Queenie were neither angry nor disapproving.

"Marianna cleared the air," they exulted. "She did what everyone else has wanted to do." Then they handed Marianna a one hundred dollar bill. "It's an early birthday present," they claimed, not a payment or a reward. They, too, were cowardly, willing to pay their granddaughter to defend the family but unwilling to confront their son.

25

SKELETONS

Like a child counting the days until its birthday or Christmas, Lucky counted the days until she would be free of Bullet. *Only nine days until our Christmas shows are over, then no more working together.* Three days of thick walled silence had grown between them since Marianna and Fannie's fight. Trying to get through a divorce, while working together, unscathed had proved impossible.

Ande stayed with Marianna in town at Cherry's during the school week.

Lucky's house was cluttered with laundry, which had been thrown on the couch for five days, unfolded and unsorted; her desk was piled with bills and books, so high and deep Lucky could barely wedge herself in. Rugs lounged on the bathroom sink not put away. Poor Hula Girl laid neglected, itching with mange, patches of her fur totally bitten away. The dog needed to see the vet and needed to be exercised. The birds were treading guano in their cages up to their ankles. All was neglected because Lucky was working for the Christmas show trying to make money to support her broken family.

Lucky laughed when she finally washed the sink full of dishes at the thought of introducing a line of women's wear for divorcees: year-round horror clothes from her *Halloween Collection*. She asked Cherry if the line might sell.

"Did you hear the joke about divorce?" Cherry responded. "If it doesn't kill you?"

"What?"

"You've survived!"

"Ha, ha," Lucky said. "Very funny. You could draw some of my blood to make a serum. Then anyone about to go through a divorce could get a vaccine. Maybe I'd win the Nobel peace prize for that and get rich."

"Yeah. By the way, you're looking good!"

"Thanks! I feel two hundred and twenty-two pounds lighter: two hundred pounds of Bullet are off my back and twenty-two pounds of my own are lost."

"I remember when you and Bullet arrived from Paris. You remember that Rex arranged for Bullet's *Sandwich Isle Graphics* job through me?"

"Right. Funny, Bullet was not pleased or displeased to be doing graphic design instead of painting. He just went along with his dad. Rex told him, 'You can't support a family selling paintings. You need a real job.' Bullet didn't initiate anything. Rex talked you into giving Bullet the chance, didn't he?"

"Yes. Rex and Queenie used to complain about how loose you were as artists when you lived in France," Cherry recalled. "They didn't approve. I thought Bullet had real talent."

"I remember meeting you in 1972," Lucky said, "for that first company picnic on the beach."

"Bullet was talking about how much he adored you. He was so much in love," Cherry reminded her, adding, "I was jealous. I wished a man would talk about me that way."

"I don't know why he stopped loving me. You know, Cherry, I am so angry. He says and does things that enrage me."

"Lucky, you have to turn the situation around. You have to be you. You are kind, be kind. You want to work, do your work. You want to be you and enjoy life, enjoy it. This is a special time for you and your children. At least you have them, and they love you. I like having your girls with me. They are so good. You need to focus on them. Bullet has to find himself. Find his own path. Do things for himself. I don't care about him. I care about you. Remember what Tom Robbins wrote in *Jitterbug Perfume*? 'Lighten up.'"

26

CHRISTMAS CARDS FROM
THE FAR SIDE

Oddly, the conical shape of Christmas trees reminded Lucky of silly upside-down ice cream cones from her childhood birthday parties: a scoop of ice cream with chocolate chips or jelly babies for eyes and a sugar cone for a hat, ice cream clowns.

Nico turned off the television and sat looking at the tree. Its clear yellow glow of light, tiny warm glimmers on a green mass, so charming, every Christmas just the same, timeless. The tree inspired the same joy of *warm wishes* and *season's greetings* as always. He wound the Santa sleigh music box, listened to its carol, tree watching. The wonder of Christmas was etching a special time on his little boy heart.

Lucky spent an early evening Christmas shopping at Ala Moana Center with Marianna and Ande for little gifts for their classmates and for family. On entering one of their favorite stores, she saw several shirts she'd like to give to Bullet were they still married. At *The Gap* she saw a leather coat for Bullet, which added to her sadness, because she refused to Christmas shop for him. Marianna refused to buy him anything as well.

"I don't want to give him a present," she insisted.

"You need to give your dad a Christmas gift," Lucky stressed.

Ande announced, "I'm gonna get Dad a jillion presents, so Christmas won't be sad for him." She purchased everything Hawai'ian: a buttery *koa* lidded box, a highly polished *kukui* nut lei, a woven *lauhala* mat, two bags of spicy hard ginger candies, a jar of his favorite *poha* berry jam, *ling hi mui* seeds, *mochi* crunch, and dried mango slices for stocking stuffers.

"Mom, can I borrow thirty-five dollars?" Ande asked. "I don't have enough money to pay for all Dad's presents. I'll pay you back by working in your studio."

"Okay, sounds like a good deal to me."

"We've got to go over to the dive shop," Ande said. "Nico wants me to pick up a mask, snorkel, and spear for his present to Dad." She picked out a very high quality *Jacques Cousteau* mask, overspending, wanting to indulge Nico and please Bullet.

They continued to shop. Lucky was captivated by the Mango Tea at *Crabtree and Evelyn*, the Maile soaps, wonderfully packaged in old paintings of the Sandwich Isles. Lime scented aftershave; she loved the smell of lime on his face, on his skin, on his freshly shaven cheek. Wouldn't buy it, though. *Fannie would be the one to smell it.* Bullet had slipped away from his wife down a drain hole in a quest for the fountain of his eternal youth.

Lucky bought boxes of Gary Larsen cartoon Christmas cards. Two goldfish swam in a bowl of water, which held a Christmas tree. The husband fish was about to plug the tree lights into an electrical outlet when the wife fish warned, "Bob, you fool! Don't plug that thing in!" Lucky wrote to their friends:

*Well, "Bob" did and shocked us all. Bullet has left the
kids and me. He is living at the beach with a young
bimbo and won't come home. This is a Boo Hoo Hoo
rather than a Ho Ho Ho Christmas for us.*

She found a roll of "Anti-Bullshit" tablets at *Neon Leon*'s to put
in Bullet's Christmas stocking. Lucky got an idea in the mall
for a sophomoric prank to play after the divorce papers were
signed. She bought three "I Love My Wife" and one "I'm Not
Hawai'ian But I Can Never Pass Up A Good Lei" bumper stick-
ers to paste on the bumpers of Bullet's van, her modern version of *The Scarlet Letter* and laughed herself silly over it. She
bought a golf hat for Rex, a basket for Queenie, and clothes for
the kids. She could not find anything special for Ande, who'd
requested a horse. Fat chance of that with Major still around.
She got Nico an electronic game, as he was fast becoming a
Nintendo game lunatic.

She arrived home to find a lovely package of cookies and
cakes on the counter.

"Yoko brought these over," Bullet informed her as he
walked in from his painting studio.

"Here, Bullet, you take them. I'd choke on them."

"No, no," he said, escaping out the kitchen door.

"Take them and give them to your girlfriend," she dared
him. "You know, share them from one fuck buddy to the other."

"Shut-up," he muttered, "the kids can hear you." She dropped
the package of delectables into the trash.

She got an idea to have the kids help her make a scrapbook
of memorabilia. In it she would include love letters and photos
from her student life in Europe, her wedding, teaching, years
in Paris, art, travels, the arrivals of Marianna, Ande, Nico, various pets, the visits of relatives, trips, and the surfing world they
all enjoyed. They could give the scrapbook to their dad for

Christmas. *If he doesn't appreciate the album now, maybe he will as an old man, and he'll see how badly he blew it,* she mused.

She cleaned ants and rat shit from an upper closet where she stored the boxes of memorabilia. After getting them down, she read the old love letters and early poetry, including *Mea Culpa,* from files nearly mummified up there. She found a black and white postcard of old Stockholm.

27

SWEDEN

Deep in the old city within Stockholm, in a cheap and aged hotel room, under a colorless eiderdown quilt, laid her winter memory of Bullet.

Everything in Sweden had been a tone of gray that winter. The stark, cold, northern light reflected off the snow lining interior landscapes as well, while spirits dozed, docile in dim incubation. Their room was dark, yet it was morning. A large bed next to deep gray walls flanked by heavy velvet curtains was the only relevant thing in that room, shrouded in a shadowy entombment.

The only light, pale ochre from a street lamp, intruded through the edges of that curtained window. Bullet was on his back, propped on pillows, naked.

They'd made love moments before. Within that frozen, drifting, tender zone, Lucky lifted up on her hands and looked across his chest into his face.

Bullet softly stroked her, saying, "I love you" over and over.

She longed for his love that way she'd first known it: young, intense, poetic, sexual. He was enamored of the Romantics:

Keats, Shelley, Byron, and the French rococo painter of veiled eroticism, Jean-Honore Fragonard.

But back then in that bedroom, Lucky had remained silent. She sensed a mounting pressure through the insistence of his fingers, drumming a beat as they swept her back. He wanted to hear her words of love echo his. But, she was not sure she felt them. The simplest of words, but they were so heavy. And, she was so young. She was not sure of her strength to bear them. They loomed like a granite boulder she would have to hoist above herself like some professional weight lifter.

After a time, surprising herself, she managed to pick them up.

"I love you, too," she said and fell irrevocably into his life. She was only nineteen.

Over the next three years, he worked on a graduate degree in English and Art History at Berkeley. She had already finished a Ph.D. in Theatre and was acting professionally. Bullet decided to move to Paris to write his thesis. She quit her job and moved with him to France. He stood at a desk in the sixth arrondissmont garret on the left bank near Saint Germain de Pres, writing; she started a theatre company of ex-pats. She got a few of his earliest poems published in the *Paris Review* and convinced a small gallery on the Rue Bonaparte to exhibit *Behind,* a series of nude pen and ink sketches he had done of her when he had audited a class in line drawing at the Musee des Beaux Arts.

Bullet has forgotten, she thought, *his promises of love, promises of a young poet and painter, the promises that brought me with him to Hawai'i.*

"I can't paint the women of the monarchy if I don't actually live there," he told her. "I need to see Hawai'ian faces and bodies."

"Bullet, I love living in Paris. The art world here is everything you could want. It's vibrant. There is no art scene in

Hawai'i. And, I've got my contract with the theatre for the next two seasons. I already quit one equity job in San Francisco to come here with you."

"I promise we'll stay in Hawai'i only until the series is sketched. Six months tops. We'll sublet the apartment here. I can do the actual painting when we return to Paris." And, so she had agreed to shade herself in the middle of the Pacific under a palm tree or two, not knowing the return to Paris would fall off their calendar.

She got out their wedding vows from an old cardboard box. She read and reread the vows they had written in their shared old brown-shingle Berkeley house. The cover of their invitation was inscribed with William Blake's "Auguries of Innocence":

To see a world in a grain of sand
And a Heaven in a wild flower,
Hold Infinity in the palm of your hand
And eternity in an hour

Below the vows in the box, she found a snapshot taken of them on the Isle of Capri where they swam and made love in the water beyond the moored boats. Another of his yellow bicycle parked on the Spanish steps in Rome. A third diapering newborn Marianna. She loved the photo she took of him crouching in their bedroom recently next to his painting of an ancient Hawai'ian chief, *Boki*, behind her blue porcelain temple. It was a glossy 8x10 black and white photo for publicity. He looked like a movie star, a Paul Newman, but better, those blue eyes and masculine face radiating health and maleness.

Right after she had snapped the photo, she recalled, he tried to break the porcelain temple over her head, yelling, "Fuck you," because she had failed to take the photo from the angle he wanted. Of course, he had refused to take the photo she needed for publicity of herself. Yet, for some reason, that remained her favorite photo of him.

She stared at a Waikiki restaurant photo for a long time of the family dining out with friends. Everyone looked radiant. Boxer and Pearl were seated next to Big Al. On the other side of their table at Sy's Steak House sat a beaming Bullet, arm around Lucky's neck and shoulders, Lucky was smiling happily, as were Marianna, Ande and Nico with sun bleached hair glowing like orbs around their dear heads.

"Ande, when was this taken?"

"Last May." A month before the breakup, the last family photo before Lucky's world fell apart. This picture meant little to her at the time, and now it was a bona fide relic. Her face withered beneath a fresh cascade of tears, her cheeks accordions of damp wrinkles sagging toward the ground.

That night Ande's prayer ended predictably with, "Don't make my Mom so sad. Make everybody happy."

Whoever has described the near-tears-for-no-apparent reason feeling, which overwhelmed women like a wave, a blanket, a shadow of sadness. Tears prickled the eyes; the nose began to run. It was inexplicable, borderline sorrow, like PMS but not so crazy or manic or schizophrenic. It was a wafting into one's soul, like an aroma on the wind, of melancholy.

It began to rain, the day turning from mist to rain, a rain, which came down across the island in thick blankets as if mourning the slow and excruciating expiration of Lucky's marriage. Her soul of gray also unleashed in a sudden downpour of its own unexpected flash flooding.

She had gone to town to read the divorce papers at last. She had left the kids at home, prone, watching TV: sick, not wanting the *Eggo* breakfast she left for them. She nervously drove to town to read and sign the divorce documents, praying along the way, *Dear God, Please let me keep my dignity and please don't let me get too sad,* wishing she had a big glass of happy juice to drink.

She walked in red lizard high heels down King Street in the financial district of Honolulu wearing a sequined paisley vest, mohair sweater, red *Liz Claiborne* shirt, black leather pencil skirt, *Guess* watch, *Polo* tortoise shell glasses, panty-hose, braid, make up, prim and slim and fortyish. Down the street she minced, as the slim leather skirt constricted her steps. Her spattering of *Worth* cologne added to her million-dollar feeling. She was keenly aware of the absence of a wedding band on her left finger. She was alone and out there. *Christ.*

She wondered how she would ever meet a man, assessing the men she passed as potential partners, even the Greek gnome with blackened teeth selling newspapers by the bank.

Her lawyer gave her a nice dose of flattery. Thomas said some word like "smashing" admiring her sweater, saying if he touched her silk shirt the way he was touching her mohair sweater, he could get arrested. He sat too close on the waiting-room couch before they went into the office to discuss the papers. Thomas offered her coffee.

"Don't you have a hit of whiskey?" Lucky asked.

Surprised, he mumbled, "Oh, sure..."

"Naw, naw, naw. I don't drink. That's okay. I'm nervous. It's not everyday I get divorced. It's a big day for me." Thomas got ice in coffee mugs, and they did drink morning whiskey as they read the decree. Everything seemed okay except the financials.

When she finished making modifications, Thomas asked, "Do you want to reconcile?"

"No. I can't live with dishonesty. But, I know I'll always love him."

"Lucky, in six months or a year, you may be head over heels in love with someone else, and you'll look back and know you don't love Bullet. He's in a downward spiral. If he'd cheat on an attractive woman like you, he'd cheat on his girlfriend, if he hasn't already."

Thomas Ayck made her feel like an adult. It was amazing she hadn't been around anyone like him in years.

By Christmas Eve Lucky was worn out. She surveyed the packages wrapped in bunny paper arranged around the living room, bunnies in red stocking caps holding green trees. *Too many presents,* she thought, *as always, too much spending, too much spoiling.* The table was set with a green plaid cloth topped by a special Christmas crèche scene with candles to turn its blades around with their heat.

Before going to bed, Marianna read them a poem she'd written and then tacked it to the tree:

I'd like to recite this poem tonight.
You all have brought me great delight.
It's Christmas.
It's a time of happiness and joy,
There are now four of us not five.
We are tighter than a hive.
We must remember love and respect,
And not fight with our mother.
We will have the merriest Christmas ever,
For we are together.

Outside the sea pounded, as huge winter waves washed in, sounding their arrival like *taiko* drums. Lucky baked an

apple pie then flipped crepes for Christmas breakfast blueberry blintzes. She sat down in the darkened living room to
nibble the food left out for Santa and to read the children's
notes.

From Ande, Lucky read:
*merry christmas and a happy new year this christmas i don't
really want any toys, clothes and stuff like that this christmas
all i want is for my family to be happy i don't want my mom
being sad any more, my sister to understand and be kind to my
dad, my brother to be nicer and more helpful to everyone my dad
to use his brains more often my dog hula girl if you could make
hula girl's skin better also to have my friend gigi move back to
hawaii and that i be nice and happy all the time but most of
all i would like everyone to love everyone and to have a merry
christmas okay santa?*

From Marianna:
*Merry Christmas. We hope you are not having trouble pad-
dling across those giant waves. Don't let the toys sink. Okay?
Thanks a lot. Give our luv to Mrs. Claus and da elves, da
reindeers too.*
PS: don't get too fat, Santa

From Nico:
YO Santa Claus
I want for Christmas a genesis or a gameboy
Please Santi

Lucky penned a note back to the children and placed it on
the empty food tray:
*HO HO HO, PULASKIS. The baklava was TERRIFIC. Best
'lava in Hawai'i. (Joke) HO HO HO Love you all. S. CLAUS*

Christmas morning in Lucky's stocking nestled a tiny package from Marianna and Ande with a note:

Merry X-Mas Mom. We decided to make this puka shell necklace for you, because we remembered all of the special puka shell necklaces you made for us.

After all the gifts had been opened and breakfast eaten, they dressed for Mass. Ande felt let down. She put on the new Christmas *mu'u mu'u* Lucky had sewn her and the gold heirloom Hawai'ian bracelet with her name engraved on it, which she'd really wanted. Gramma and Grampa gave her clothes, which were sort of okay; Uncle Jackie sent the latest *Swatch* watch, which was cool; Gramma Edna sent a round trip ticket to visit her on the mainland; Auntie Laura sent chocolates and a doll, which Ande had outgrown. Nico gave her a silver turtle *honu* pendant and a cool CD, and Marianna gave her a carved bone fishhook necklace from the Bishop Museum and an *ipu* for *hula* chanting.

But Dad. There hadn't been a present from Dad. He had given Lucky a new kitchen garbage can; what was he thinking? He had given Marianna new running shoes. He had given Nico a new boogie board and fins. Ande had asked him for fins. But, he hadn't given any to her. He hadn't given her anything. Marianna found her crying in their closet.

"Oh, Ande. Dad is such a jerk. I told you not to give him anything. And, you got him a *jillion* presents and spent all your money on him."

"I don't care about getting anything," Ande lied through her tears. "It's Christmas, remember? It's all about giving, not receiving. It's made me happy to be able to give to Dad."

"Yeah. You look real happy right now, Ande, crying. Are you happy about bankrupting yourself? Does that feel good? Does it feel good that you go to breakfast with him and listen to all his guilt trips and play *the good kid* and have him forget you at Christmas?"

Marianna climbed up the stairs to Lucky's room.

"Mom, Ande is really sad. Did you notice that Dad didn't give her anything for Christmas?"

"I know. I don't know how he could forget Ande. She's so good to him." Lucky put on lipstick. *Please, God,* she whispered in a quick prayer, *Help me be both mother and father to the kids.*

Downstairs, she took Ande aside.

"Merry Christmas, honey," Lucky consoled. "You know I love you so much?"

"I know, Mom. You're always thinking about us, making things nice and fun. Where do you think I get my generosity from, anyway?" Ande laughed. "You give us so much." Then she cried again. "I'm hurt, Mom, not so much about Christmas, but that Marianna is so angry with Dad. I can't confide in her anymore. She might tell you things. And, then you'll get madder or more hurt. All you do is cry and talk about Dad, anyway. I wish you'd get a life."

Twice Lucky almost bolted from Mass where they sat dressed in Christmas finery at Queenie's behest: Rex, Marianna, Ande, Nico, Lucky, and Bullet in their pew at Sacred Heart Church. They were ruined yet looked liked the ideal family.

Lucky had left religion far behind when she turned thirteen and Big Jack had left the family. Her disillusion deepened on reading William Shirer's *The Rise and Fall of the Third Reich.* Raised in a tiny California farm town as Baptist by her Nana and sometime Catholic by her lapsed mother, Lucky had never heard of Jews nor, consequently, of their persecution. Shirer's holocaust book deeply shocked her.

"Mom," she had asked, "do we know any Jews?"

"Yes. I think Brian Arbogast's father is Jewish." Brian was an attractive boy two years ahead of Lucky in school.

"Why didn't the Allies bomb the train tracks that took the Jews to the concentration camps?" Lucky had asked. "Roosevelt knew what the Nazi's were doing, right? God knew what the Nazi's were doing. I don't get it. The Allies could have saved so many people, but they didn't. And God could have stopped the whole war, but He didn't. I think maybe there is no God, at least not for me."

With Bullet's departure, faith had begun a slow crawl back into Lucky's heart after a thirty-year absence. She had soothed herself by calling DIAL-A-PRAYER almost every day.

"*Aloha*, my friend. Thank you for calling 'Dial-a-Prayer'. Today's message..." was what she heard.

She had also gotten into the habit of mentally stopping several times a day to summon strength, to calm down, to listen to her instincts, and to pray.

At the Christmas mass, the elderly Filipino priest intoned, "... and when days are darkest and one's feeling one's worst, remember you are clay in the potter's hand, and He is molding you, and perhaps you haven't taken shape yet, or He's changing you, and He's not through. He's still working on you."

Lucky was startled by the image of clay. She was a clay artist, after all. The priest made her think of dirt, the real dirt in everyone's backyard. It seemed to be a question of what they chose to do with it, wasn't it? Maybe dirt was fertilizer for the soul helping it to grow. When Lucky's mother, Edna divorced, she had studied Zen Buddhism by watching Alan Watts on the public television station. She had kept a sign posted in the bathroom which Lucky saw every day of her senior year in high school: "Out of the mud, grows the lotus."

Maybe that's what all the dirt in my life has been for, Lucky thought, *to make something beautiful out of it. Oh Lord, guide me. I lost You when my parents divorced, now as I divorce, I kneel before You, humbled. Tell me, am I finding You again?*

Suddenly, Nico lurched forward off his pew, projectile vomiting onto the bench ahead. Lucky grabbed him around the waist and lifted him up. She carried him down the aisle as he continued to wretch and vomit. She ran with him in her arms across the asphalt parking lot, warm in the morning light, to the bathrooms.

Lucky washed him off from the basin tap. She didn't know what had hit him. They had eaten the same food for breakfast, and he was not feverish. Just as suddenly, he recovered. They began to laugh. They didn't say anything. They stood in the ladies' lavatory of the church laughing and laughing.

Lucky was late for lunch.

"What's the occasion?" Bullet asked, waiting for her in the golf course clubhouse. The waitress came. He ordered tomato juice. Lucky ordered white wine and bean soup. She tried to toast him.

"It's our anniversary."

"Anniversary of what?

"December 26th was the day we met on that train in..."

"Wait..." He held up his hand to silence her and to pepper his tomato juice. She tried to toast again.

"Wait..." He took a sip of it, deliberately not remembering or cooperating. Finally, he said, "Cheers."

"To twenty-something years," she said.

"How're you doing?" he smiled.

She felt her eyes sting; she didn't want to cry. Slowly she said, "I'm still in shock. Is this really the way you want it?"

Bullet looked her in the eye and said, like he was Prince Charming, "Well, since you don't want to live with the situation the way it is, I guess we're getting divorced. Isn't that why the kids say you're going to your lawyer's every other minute?"

"This break-up has come about from you. I only want one thing from you same as ever."

"And what may I ask is that?"

"Your love."

He screwed up his face and leaned over the table to get as close to her as he could. "And that's one thing you'll never get," he said.

From her purse, she pulled out the divorce papers ready for his signature. Glancing through them, he got upset over supporting the kids for the state minimum of five hundred dollars a month. He got more upset over supporting them until age twenty-three or college graduation.

"I've signed everything I'm going to sign, and I won't sign anything else. You're getting it all. I'm letting you live in the house. Look at me, I ride around in a junk van."

"You never seemed to mind letting me ride around in it."

He flipped out next over paying the kids' medical and dental insurance, calling it her *trick*.

"Why don't you have a set monthly figure to pay for the kids?" he whined.

"Bullet, the kids live with me. I bear the majority of their support."

"But, what about me? What am I supposed to live on? Doesn't the court know I'm an artist? That I might not have five hundred a month to give my kids?"

"Bullet, the court doesn't care what you do. They just require that you support your kids. Besides, I'm an artist, too."

"How am I going to do that?"

"That's YOUR problem. You figure it out."

"Well, I can't be an artist any more."

"Try being a man," Lucky said. "Just be a man, you know, a grown up, and pay the costs and shut up about it. Read the papers. It's all for the kids. It's not about me. I'm not asking for alimony, just my share of the house." Bullet threw down the papers.

"Do you have money for the tip?" he asked, standing up to leave.

"Bullet, I've spent two thousand five hundred dollars on a lawyer. Get a lawyer; it's your right. It'll cost you two thousand five hundred dollars. If you litigate, it'll cost us each another eight to ten thousand dollars. For what? We don't have any money. I don't; you don't. So, read the papers. They're fair. They're the law. Sign in black ink in front of a notary. Give them back to me, and I'll send them to my lawyer. Then we're divorced."

"I'm not signing anything"

Why did Lucky have to act like bamboo, bending here, bending there, negotiating with an intransigent about to be ex?

"Are you getting your own place?" she asked him.

"No."

"Do you want the apartment in town? You could be with the girls every day and save money on the commute."

"Lucky, with all the expenses I'm going to encounter, I can't afford it."

"Aren't you going to get your own place?"

"I told you, I can't afford it."

"You mean, you're going to keep living with your girlfriend?"

"You don't give me any choice."

Bullet got his old job back at *Sandwich Isle Graphics* on a part-time basis on the drafting desk, starting at half of what he was paid eighteen years earlier. Bullet continued to go back on his word: he did not pay child support, and he fought over custody.

Lucky stormed around her bedroom. She needed to vent steam. She was nowhere, absolutely nowhere, nearer to getting divorced than she'd been in October, yet she held in her hand a bill for over three thousand dollars in legal fees.

She resented being charged for every phone call. *I have such a hard time reaching Thomas, and then I'm charged two hundred dollars an hour, including chitchat and niceties. Shit. No wonder people hate lawyers.*

Thomas failed to address several of her concerns such as back child-support payment and division of the business assets. He told Lucky to make an accounting of income and expenses. Thomas had never mentioned accounting until this letter, and it certainly smacked of Bullet's fanatical niggardliness. Thomas actually sounded like Bullet's best advocate, not hers. Bullet was getting away without cooperating one bit.

Help me, Thomas. What do I do, Thomas? Protect me; secure my assets. But he hadn't.

Was this called reality testing, getting sober on the cold hard facts of life, a big, liberal *Betty Ford* Treatment Center of the real world, where no eyeglasses, blinders, or shades were allowed? Was this legal mire what had made Edna so bitter when she divorced Big Jack? *Where was justice,* Lucky wondered.

28

NEW YEAR

Lucky's assistant, Frankie, caught three large *onaga* off Penguin Banks near Moloka'i during a four-day fishing trip and brought them for her traditional New Year's party when the neighbors gathered to burn their Christmas trees with fireworks at the beach.

She remembered how those nights went: she would steam a prized *onaga*, tail curving gracefully up to touch its head, the kids would drink sparkling grape juice, the bonfire burning dried trees at the beach with fireworks exploding into the cool winter sky and the singing, the fun, the friendships, the family. But, that was what was. She ended the year instead weeping for her broken family, her face a swollen river.

Ande comforted and held her, "Don't be sad, Mommy."

New Year's day was raining and no good for a beach party. She took the kids to a fancy/schmancy hotel in Waikiki instead for a brunch extravaganza. The children made all sorts of resolutions for the Nineties and set a date for brunch in the year 2000 to see if any of their predictions would have come true.

Marianna said she would be twenty-six. She predicted she'd have a nice boyfriend, be finished with college, have a nice, very nice body, and run a string of fitness centers called Celestial Shapes after competing in the Olympics, adding "I'm gonna have plenny-of-sex."

Ande said, "I'll be on my fifth marriage." Typical Ande. She would be finishing college in California or Boston at twenty-three. She had no idea how graceful she was becoming.

Nico predicted he would "invent a boogie board that was faster than any surfboard. I'm tired of getting run over. And, I won't be in college." He would be dead. But, of course, none of them knew that.

Lucky contradicted, "You'll be a junior in college, age twenty."

The kids told Lucky she would be living in California producing movies, and she would be rich and famous. Nico added that he wanted to produce a show, *Lifestyles of the Poor and Unknown* or a *Garfield* spin-off, *Lifestyles of the Fat & Furry*. They all agreed that Lucky would be married.

"To whom?" Lucky asked.

"To Dad," Ande answered.

Marianna and Nico said, "No way. To a rich guy."

"Hula Girl will have gray hair and ten puppies," Nico put in. "Suds will have all his legs broken from jumping off the deck too many times and white fur."

"He has white fur, dummy. That's why he's called Suds," corrected Marianna.

"I know," Nico giggled.

That night they watched *Christmas Vacation* with Chevy Chase, who played a character who headed his household full of romantic dreams of Christmas and ways to share loving family time*s*. *How foreign,* Lucky thought. *Bullet never acted like that.* She wanted a man like Chevy Chase.

She got the blues. She pictured her heart held in her hands. One ventricle was a "crying room," a wet closet where she mourned her mistakes. There were two auricles and one more ventricle pumping like crazy. They thumped on the screen door of her loneliness, sliding it half off its hinges.

The children kept her alive, doing their best to boost her spirits. Marianna drove Ande to school three out of four mornings. Lucky was thankful to be released from the hell of seven prior years imprisoned behind the steering wheel in the daily school commute before Marianna had gotten her license.

Brother Jackie had made private school possible, paying the yearly tuitions. If the family was stuck living out in the country among impoverished locals, Lucky had wanted her kids to experience a good academic life, mixing with kids from higher economic strata. Lucky had to get the children there every morning by seven forty-five and pick them up every afternoon after music and sports. Each trip put her smack dab in the middle of Honolulu's worst commuter traffic.

She had gotten up for years at four in the morning, fed the girls breakfast of a smoothie and croissantwich in the car. The girls would read or doze, listening to French language tapes as the car inched in first gear along the freeway into the city.

Lucky would arrive back in Wai'anae by nine to fix Nico and Bullet their breakfasts. Then she'd do morning office business, arrange playgroup for Nico and get into her studio after lunch. Then at three, she'd strap Nico into his car seat, put the cooler filled with snacks and cold drinks into the car, and drive back into town to pick up the girls. Home by six-thirty, she'd cook dinner, help with homework, and get the kids to bed. Back in her studio, she'd get some clay time from nine till past midnight.

It was the same relentless routine every day. It took a toll on her health. Seven bouts of a pneumonia-like illness from nocardia in her lungs brought on by years of clay dust ingestion collapsed them from the strain and hospitalized her for days at a time.

Bullet refused to drive. "I don't want my kids to go to some private *snob* school. I want them to grow up like real people. I want them to get along, fit in. They need to know how most of the people in the world live: poor."

"Bullet," Lucky responded, "we are poor. You went to an east coast prep school. You led a privileged life. Your family is well off. You went to Berkeley and worked on a graduate degree. Why don't you want the same, if not better, opportunities for our kids?"

"I don't think college does anything for anybody."

"You're talking slop."

"Do what you want, Lucky. You always do. But don't try to involve me," he said.

She started taking the kids on ice-skating dates. Nico opened her car door, took her by the arm, both going in and out of the Ice Palace, acting like such a gentleman on their "dates." Ben, Nico, Marianna, and Ande speed skated around the rink. The visits were exhilarating, and they often had the place almost to themselves. Lucky noticed she was usually the oldest person there except for one gray-haired dad, who didn't look her way.

At first, she fell hard on the ice on her tailbone where there was not an ounce of fat. After getting over the awkward stage of imbalance, she fell into stride, learning to navigate the oval rink. By the end of the evenings, Lucky would have picked up speed, heart beating, breathing deeply, repetitiously circumventing.

She liked the monotony of skating the rink. And the rhythm. Over and over, like a captive porpoise in a tank, making countless passes on the same course. If she lost concentration, she stumbled and fell.

The rock music was deafening. She'd lost her hearing. There was no sense in talking. She didn't look at anything, because the world of other skaters was always moving and changing. She relied on her peripheral vision, a constant but unfocused scanning of all visual data.

Her legs kept gliding, slipping, pushing, and gliding. Every so often her arms jerked to maintain balance as round and round she swirled. The other porpoise-skaters looked proficient skating fast, backwards, putting one fin in front of the other, and laughing. She focused on balance, intent on 'getting round the course,' her face frozen in a fierce frown of concentrated anxiety.

But skate she did, getting pleasure from the monotony, this mindless skating. Nico and she became regulars.

Residue washed over Lucky periodically, missing the old life. She managed to make eight-not-so-inspired pots during Ande's fourteenth birthday slumber party while the girls played games and talked about boys.

Ande brought it home again when she asked for a family birthday dinner the following week.

"Ande," Lucky protested, surprised, "do you really want that? You just had a boy-girl bonfire and a slumber party. Isn't that enough? You're not even going to be home on your own birthday."

"No, Mom. I really want a family birthday with Gramma and Grampa and Dad and us. I miss that. I used to really like 'em, and I miss 'em, and I want one, okay? And, it might be the last one I get with Gramma. It would mean a lot to her, too."

What could Lucky say when Ande's despondent face disintegrated for times and people lost through no fault of her own?

"Of course, honey," Lucky agreed, touched by the saltiness and heat of Ande's tears.

Next thing Lucky knew, Bullet had palmed Nico off on Pearl again.

"I have to take Fannie to eat and to art class. I don't have time to take Nico home." But instead of going to class, he drank beer and got a massage, while his students worked untutored. Lucky charged back and forth to Makaha looking for Nico. She finally found him at Pearl's. Nico was unfed and unbathed. Pearl tended to her own grandkids.

"*Fahquim Z. Ahzhol,*" Lucky hissed, inventing a new Mideast moniker for Bullet.

29

A COFFIN

"**M**rs. Pulaski, your pap smear shows you have 'abnormal cell growth' in your uterus. Dr. Yoni would like you to come in for a biopsy." The nurse from Kaiser told her on the phone.

"What did you find?"

"This type of growth looks like fifth stage cervical cancer."

If this breakup gives me cancer, uterine cancer, that's the last straw. Lucky hoped it was age or IUD irritation. *Here I wish Francine dead, I wish Bullet dead, and I'm the one who might die.*

Bullet stopped over with a carton. Lucky presumed it was saimin for Nico's cold.

"I hope you don't have cancer," Bullet remarked. "Here's some ice cream for you."

"Am I a kid who gets ice cream after being 'good' at the doctor's office?" she snapped, not pleased. "The good news is I don't have AIDS."

"Why? Did you get tested?

"Why did I get tested? Because you said you thought YOU might have AIDS, why else? AIDS creeps up. You better get tested every six months. You could be a carrier. Fannie probably is."

"Oh Lucky, I don't think that's true."

"Well, Miette's son was in the army, and he screwed her. He says Fannie is a carrier," Lucky replied hotly.

"In my judgment," Bullet responded, "she's not."

"Well, you know what I think of your judgment," Lucky snorted.

"Shove it. Just shove it," he said.

"Come," she motioned, crying. They walked behind the house to the painting studio, out of earshot of the kids. "I'm exhausted, Bullet. I need help. I beg you, stop fighting me." He turned to leave.

"I need to talk to you soul to soul," she implored quietly. "Forget the divorce business for a moment. Forget our current battles and grievances. Let your soul listen to mine. This isn't a perfect divorce. But, let's be done with it. If the stress of this situation is leading me to sicken with cancer, it has to stop. Settle this divorce now. Stop fighting me and settle."

"No." Bullet said, refusing to bow out gracefully. "No. No. It's not right," he yelled, shaking his head, when suddenly, he demanded an accounting.

"Did you ever demand an accounting or a budget in our years together? Did we ever save, buy, or invest?" Lucky asked sarcastically.

"I never knew where the money went. You spent it all. You handled the accounts."

"It went from hand," she gestured, "to mouth. Direct deposit."

"Bullshit."

"I'm scared, Bullet. They say I have cancer. My grandmother died of uterine cancer, you know. And, I need help to raise our kids."

"I care about you, Lucky. I wanna help. And, I care about the kids. But, I don't like the terms of the divorce. I don't want you to have sole custody of the kids. I don't think living with one parent is good."

"Living with an immoral one isn't good either," she whispered under her breath, fatigued.

"I'm moral. I'm very moral."

"Bullet, you're a lot of things, but moral isn't one of them. Moral men don't leave their families, commit adultery, lie and cheat."

"And, you're the high priestess of morality, up there on your high horse. You've sinned, my dear; you're not so pure yourself."

"Your meanness is killing me. You might as well get out a hammer and nail my coffin shut, because I'm dying." She began whimpering in a gulping, pathetic rhythm.

Ande ran outside, half-hysterical from eavesdropping, her conciliatory skills hard pressed.

"Why don't you guys quit fighting? Mom, you're a crybaby. Dad, you're a jerk."

Marianna yelled through the window, "Dad, you're an asshole. You're mean to Mom. You hear me? You're an asshole."

Lucky felt her head would explode.

Edna told Lucky she was crazy to tell Bullet about the cancer.

"I had to, Ma. I'm glad I did it. I had to know if he knew I might be dying, if he'd be there for me. That was my bottom line. I had to know. And, you know what he said? 'Shove it, Lucky. Just shove it. Fuck you, fuck you, and fuck you.'"

"Oh, Lucky," Edna said, aghast.

Lucky felt twenty-five shades of blue. *Deja-vu* visions of yesteryear paraded in somber navy pea coats through her mind as her face rested on a Prussian striped beach towel damp with her tears in the two o'clock sun watching Nico from the side of her face who was boogie boarding the crisp azure waves.

"We saw da kine, Fannie," Boxer and Pearl said, sitting down on the sand next to her. "I wuz thinking, 'Oh, Bullet, you stupid: you left your wife and children for THAT?' Hey, Lucky, I don't say this to make you feel good," Pearl confided, "but that chick's ugly. I gave her the evil eye. Bullet went for introduce her, and I stopped him. I said, 'Don't even think about it.' I tol Bullet, 'Eat humble pie. Cut the bullshit and be sincere. Maybe Lucky will take you back.' You believe in miracles, don't you, Lucky?"

Boxer added, "Lucky, when your marriage broke up, I stay shock."

"Boxer, you were shocked, think about me," Lucky replied. "I was most shocked of all."

Pearl said, "Bull took Fannie to the Surfing Banquet, too, you know, instead of Nico. Bullet and Nico were supposed to be awarded a trophy for winning tandem surfing. I talked to Big Al's wife all night real loud so Fannie could hear me about Lucky and the kids and how they ought to be there instead of her."

Nico overheard Pearl as he toweled off. He was hurt and angry to learn his dad hadn't taken him to receive his award. Nico hid from Bullet. He didn't want to listen to his dad's lame excuses for taking Fannie instead of him to the banquet.

The day started with the sale of a single teapot for two thousand dollars. Lucky's phone rang continuously with unsolicited orders: the Group on Maui, the Gallery on Hawai'i, and the Galaxy Gallery on Kaua'i, making an inter-island celebration of sorts. Checks came in the mail for three teapots sold on O'ahu, as well as invitations to sell at a Minneapolis gallery and to show in Washington, D. C.

Then came the humdinger of a return-to-the-crapola: Bullet asked if he could forfeit child support payments, since Lucky had so much money.

"Are you going to pay me half?" he asked.

"I'll never pay you money from the sale of my pottery. That money is needed to support the children and myself. Our only deal was for Christmas and you got paid very well from my work. No more money from my creative efforts is going to support you and that woman."

He muttered "that woman" under his breath, half laughing and disbelieving. Lucky ignored him. Nico couldn't believe his dad kept asking Lucky for money.

"Why doesn't he take care of us, Mom?"

Ande whispered, "Oh Mom, don't worry, you always get what you want with Dad."

Lucky cut Bull in mid-sentence. "Until the day we're divorced, I owe you nothing."

"Circumstances change," Bullet replied. "I need money this month; so there's no money to give you. It's spent."

"Chameleon" she snarled. "You're constantly changing. There's nothing to rely on. Every time I see you, the situation is different."

"Yeah, that's right, Lucky. And, that's the way it's gonna be." Bullet practically frothed at the mouth, reviling her in the car as she drove him to the notary where they planned to dissolve their joint bank accounts. He pushed his face into hers calling her "Wolfeson" in an effort to push her hot button.

She remained unflappable.

"I'm not going to pay you any money," he taunted.

"I am not asking you for alimony."

"You wouldn't get it from me even if you did ask for it," he exulted.

"Are you going to give me the child support payment which is due today?"

"No. You are trying to get everything I have. I'm not signing over the house to the kids in your trust either. If your lawyer had sent the papers four weeks ago, I'd have signed. But, not now." Then Bullet handed her a check for one-hundred-seventy-five dollars.

"What this for?" she asked.

"Child support, less the amount for a pot you sold." She tore it up.

"You owe me two-hundred-and-fifty dollars twice a month for the kids. My pottery sales do not enter into it."

"I never agreed to pay you for the kids."

"You like to forget agreements at your convenience."

"I don't have any money and need it."

"I need money, too. I mailed you an accounting of what you owe me for Ande's bed. You promised to pay for her box spring and mattress for her birthday, remember? I put it on my credit card."

"You'll have to spring for it, because I don't have the money."

Lucky saw he hated her. She also saw he hated his daily tread to town on the freeway, losing hours of his life behind the wheel, working at the spiritless job he used to call his *coffin*. She wondered if a globule of guilt filled his throat like bile, strangling him. The bile, the commute, the job, shame and guilt combined to eviscerate him like they had his nemesis, *The Man in the Gray Flannel Suit*.

She took the kids to see "War of the Roses," Hollywood's depiction of divorce. Its moral: there was no such thing as a civilized divorce. *Tame, compared to what we live through on any one afternoon,* Lucky thought. In the film, the wife stopped loving the husband. That was all it took for disaster: one party wanting out. Oliver, the rejected spouse, wanted to resume the marriage right up to the end. Rejected ones tended to need reconciliation. Barbara, the wife, adamantly refused, unable to stand the sight of him.

"Mom, he was such a jerk," Marianna said. "He was never considerate of her."

"But, he didn't do anything wrong, like squander money, do drugs, or get women..."

"He did everything wrong," Marianna rejoined.

"How'd your biopsy turn out?" Bullet asked but he already knew, because Queenie had told him, and he had talked about it with the girls on the phone: "Isn't it great, your Mom doesn't have cancer?" But to Lucky, he feigned ignorance.

"There's no cancer. It turns out to be a sexually transmitted virus that you gave me that requires surgery," Lucky said. "Thanks a lot."

"Well, who's your doctor? I want to talk to your doctor."

"You can't."

"Why not?"

"It's my private business and none of yours."

"Quit playing games. Tell me your doctor's name."

"I'm not playing games. You're the one who gave this to me. I'm the one who's hurt."

"Fuck you."

"How dare you raise your voice?"

"Fuck you."

"You're a piece of trash."

He retorted, "You're a piece of shit"

"You're a piece of crap," she snapped back. "Don't you come over here. Don't you pick up Nico. You stay away from here." Lucky wished she could float out of her body and wing her way free. She wanted to laugh at their ridiculous exchange.

Pouring, pouring, pouring rain. 1989, 1990, 1991 had come and gone with wet air, surf meets, arguments, irritations, and no divorce. Lucky had treaded water waiting for it. Bullet had continued to circle her home and studio becoming ever more belligerent. Her children grew, her income dwindled, her depression deepened.

Yet another surf banquet was held under tents and awnings. Ande helped Bullet pass out prizes as though she was his right arm. Marianna looked happy and full of herself as she emerged into hormones and young womanhood. Nico won fins for team surfing with Bullet.

Although the kids loved being at the party, getting prizes and gifts, they came home saying, "Dad's a jerk."

"Why?"

"Because he drinks beer when we get in the car to drive home," Marianna said. "I tell him, 'Dad, don't drink beer when you drive me' and he yells 'aaah, shuddap, I've worked hard, and I'm tired, and I want this beer, so shut the fock up'."

"Dad just decides to take us home," Nico added, "and we're not ready, and we're still having fun, but he says, 'Come on, we're going. Get in the fockin' car'."

Bullet had left the tiny beach apartment to rent a house with Fannie, embarking on a new life. He also bought a new, wide-assed suburban luxury van. He looked healthy, happy, affluent, and in love.

Lucky had screamed her throat raw as his expenditures were at her and the children's expense. Emotions she had thought quelled, reared out of control. She cried epithets to the wind, pounded walls and floors.

She imagined Bullet naked, standing sideways, facing a screenless fan, its propeller spinning at a tilt. It sheared off mini slices of his head, his neck, and then turned perpendicular to slice his penis into little flesh-pennies. Next she imagined his head like a watermelon hit by a deer rifle, exploding in juices, pulp, seed, and rind. Then his stomach was hit and exploded the same way, its fleshy fragments falling to the ground, crawling away like inchworms.

She knew she was sick to fantasize this way, but she did it anyway, gaining perverse satisfaction. *Why do I get angry? My veins explode, and I shoot steam and sparks from my ears, nose, toes, simply bursting.*

Lucky had a commission to install tiles in a mural at Nico's elementary school. The scaffolding the janitors put up for her to climb was unsafe. One ladder was set in mud and the other on concrete. The plank straddling the two ladders was termite riddled and not level, a copy of the *Yellow Pages* has been stuck under it. Was she expected to stand six feet above ground to install a heavy ceramic mural on this jury-rigged setup and interact with two thousand precious elementary school kids who swarmed below?

She climbed up nevertheless, garbed in a specialized zootsuit: scarf, respirator, iridium John Lennon glasses, apron. Wielding a diamond bladed grinder, she cut abrasive slashes in the painted hollow tile wall and imagined the wall was Bullet. Concrete and paint chips flew amid high-pitched grinder whir as the aforesaid two thousand little darlins' below shouted questions in pidgin.

"Whatchu doin'? What makin'? What dat?"

Lucky couldn't answer, much less hear, when a murderous, too-much-TV, too much anger, gleam entered her mind, thinking the worst, she imagined some chain saw disaster, headlines screaming, *Divorcing Artist Goes Berserk In School Yard While Installing Tile Mural.* She realized she needed help.

Lucky sat at the beach contemplating revenge, actually conjuring without knowing it. She sensed an unusual energy hovering over the gray ocean, which shimmered in the late afternoon light like smooth aluminum foil. The eerily metallic energy field began far out where the flat edges of sky and sea met at the horizon. She detected a ripple flowing inland.

She did not know, as she had never heard of the Undines, that it was their approach, they who were bid to do vengeance, evil forces believed by the ancient Greeks to live as The Furies in the ocean's depths. They served no one. But, Lucky had unwittingly summoned them. They were a power unto themselves. As they neared, Lucky realized something more was about to unleash than she had bargained for, afraid she had opened Pandora's jar.

Frightened and slightly repulsed by the closeness of this dark power, Lucky whispered, "No, no, no. I do not call for revenge. I do not call for harm. Go back, whatever you are," she begged. Almost imperceptibly, the energy force began to recede, dissipating slowly over the calm sea, leaving her shaken in the graying dusk.

Miette told her Saturday night had been wild at Bullet's rented house. He had thrown a party like he used to, cooking big stockpots of stew and rice for his friends, loading a canoe full of ice and beer. Big Ted and Kalani, especially wasted from dope and drink, had turned nasty. They set off Roman Candles inside the house.

Fannie had screamed at them. "Stop, stop. What are you doing? Are you crazy? Arrete, arrete," she screamed in her native French. "Au secours. Bullet, Bullet. Stop them. The house is burning. Get them out. Out."

She pulled at Big Ted, who belched and laughed, motionless on the couch. Kalani backed away as she lunged for the smoking punk in his hand. He teased her, letting her snatch at it as he lifted his arms above his head out of reach. She turned in circles, screaming and crying, clawing at his back.

Big Al and Boxer heard the commotion inside but stayed outside in the yard. Bullet was pissed; but Big Ted and Kalani were much bigger than he, and he couldn't stop them. The curtains caught fire, and the carpet got burned.

Big Ted slurred, "Eh, if you no more respeck your wife and kids; we no mo' respeck you or your new house or your lady-fren. Thaz why we make any kine."

Boxer took Bullet aside, saying, "Eh, I not trying fo' tell you how fo' live. You got your own life. But as far as I concern', you got one wife, and she fo' life, and three kids, and they fo' life. And nobody likes what fo' you do. Lucky and the kids don' deserve dis treatment."

"My new house doesn't deserve this treatment, either," Bullet retorted.

"Eh, it was good your kids came to the banquet. To be wit' you. Why don' you go home where you belong?"

Bullet shook his head. He was a man in a chasm. Fannie and desire on one cliff, kids and Lucky on another. There was no bridge, no catwalk, no foothold. He could only slip down.

"Don't blame me. You don't know," Bullet said. "So, don't judge me. I'm making a new life. Sorry you don't approve. But, it's my life. So, my advice to you is: keep your trap shut." They could hear Fannie through the jalousies, crying in the bathroom.

"Where wuz the girl fren' night of the banquet?" Boxer asked.

Bullet answered, "Pearl told me not to bring her to another one. Not to embarrass the kids by bringing her down. She said there'd be big trouble from her if I did, that Fannie wasn't welcome."

Boxer looked shocked. "Oh, wow, Pearl, you tol you that?"

Miette seemed pleased to have overheard so much to share with Lucky. "Remember, Lucky, if you want to trap a man, do it with honey."

All Lucky could do was shake her head and hope Miette would go away. She didn't want to hear this rubbish.

"Mom, Fannie had an accident a few days ago in her new black *Blazer*," Marianna announced coming home from the beach.

"Was she hurt?"

"Her car got totaled."

Stunned, Lucky counted back the days to when she had sat on the shore summoning the Undines, reflecting on the power of thought.

The accident proved not to be serious for Fannie, who had walked away with mild whiplash. Lucky felt detached, irresponsible, and somehow satisfied for the glimpse of karma.

She needed a way out, an escape from her life, from the anger, the pain. A plane, a boat, a train? Vehicles of transport: sampans, chariots, carriages, magic carpets began to appear in her work as a series of ceramic vessels, which carried her imagination as well as the body, history as well as future hopes. She fashioned beautiful clay vehicles to travel unknown trails of romance; Pegasus-like winged horses, white bridled swans, rafts, swings, Japanese kago, the paneled, curtained palanquins of the past.

She glazed, preparing wholesale orders. She grocery shopped, banked, and paid first quarter taxes. She hadn't earned as much as a single mother as she had hoped in last three months. *No wonder I'm in constant debt.* She was working hard, long hours.

She blessed her kiln, toasted God, and gave thanks from an old wine glass, sprinkling some sour white wine on the kiln. *Oh, dear God, be aware of my humble and perpetual gratitude.* She downed the rest of the wine in one swallow and flung her glass against the kiln as a christening. It didn't break when it hit the steel kiln door, but did shatter when it fell onto the cobblestone floor. She left the broken glass there to prolong the moment.

A few days later, she packed her newly fired ware to sell at the first craft fair she'd ever done on her own. She piled the truck with heavy crates and set off for town, reminded of a primer story she'd read in first grade about people in foreign lands:

"In Mexico on Saturdays, Pedro and Maria pack pottery on a donkey and walk to the marketplace to sell their ware."

Here drives Maria without her Pedro. Part scared. *Will I sell anything on my own? In a park?* No tent. No donkey. No paintings.

She made more money at this art event alone than Bullet and she had ever made together. Thrilled, she believed God was speaking loud and clear. Every time she had asked a question, He had sent a quick reply, "Lucky, you can do it. You don't need this man. Life is easier without him."

Marianna came home from an overnight with Birdie, upset. She found Lucky still sleeping, lying in bed next to Ande, who was snoring open-mouthed with a nose full of mucous.

"Mom, I waited for Dad to pick me up at Makaha. He didn't show up, so I walked to his house. All the guys were in the yard cooking, still partying from last night. Kalani was there. Birdie says he's the biggest drug dealer on the Wai'anae Coast. So, I ask, what's he doing at my dad's house? There were beer cans and rubbish everywhere. It was degenerate."

Marianna went onto the deck to ride Lucky's *Precor* mountain climbing machine. "I'm gonna work out for an hour, and I don't want anybody to stop me."

The weather became very cold. Lucky was chilled, shivering in her bones. She didn't want to catch Ande's cold. She held her muscles taut and clenched her teeth. Her lips narrowed under the sternness cloaking her face. Yet, she didn't feel this serious, this somber, this old, or this skeletal inside.

DOGGONE

Wearing wool vests and ski hats, Nico and Lucky went for a blustery evening beach walk, under a fleet of navy clouds overlaid with flowery fuchsia and gray ash tones. Nico ran his remote control car on the park grass. Hula Girl strained on her leash.

"Nico, how're ya doing these days?" Lucky asked, "without Dad at home?"

"Mmmm... Okay, I guess. Well, I'm still pretty mad at him. I don't want him to live with us. But, it's lonely, too."

"Yeah. I feel that way, too." Hula Girl ran in the darkened grassy stretches of park. Lucky walked alone a little while at the dwindling edge of day. Black palms specked the pink slash of sunset like flies on a forgotten can of guava nectar.

"Mom," Nico said coming up to her with the dog, "I can't remember what our family dinners used to be like." It had been several months, maybe years, since they stopped, yet to ten-year-old Nico that was forever.

Lucky thought of all the thousands of meals she had prepared. She had initiated the dining routine, replete with grace, the lessons in etiquette, "Girls, Prince Charles will never ask you out, if you burp like that." But, Nico didn't remember.

She invited Rex over. She didn't think he would come because of being caught up in his taxes and the heavy rains. She wanted him to come. Like Ande, she missed the family, too. Lucky spread out a clean tablecloth, lit the koa lantern, which made her feel festive. Spaghetti, adult conversation, kid-humor, and strawberry shakes. Nico practiced cartwheels and Ninja star shooting.

"Queenie's not feeling too well, Lucky," Rex told her. "She's worried all the time about your divorce. She's staying overnight at Kaiser for a series of tests. The doctors' preliminary report is cancer."

"I'm so sorry, Rex," Lucky said, always reserved, father and daughter-in-law. She wanted him to know she cared. She held her head in her hands at the cleared dining table, blue napkin pressed to her eyes, and blew her nose, which had begun dripping like the sky outside.

Its little gray drizzle continued for weeks, permeating her soul. She made beds, did the laundry, hung it on the line under somber skies, cooked dinners at eight in the morning simply for something to do. Daily life was different. Loneliness was seeping into her being with a relentless pervasiveness. She was bored, finding time on her hands at odd hours like when the kids were in bed at night or at midday before school pick-up or dinner activities.

It took Lucky a long while to get started in the morning. Coffee, breakfasts, lunches, newspaper, toilet, errands, phone calls. Then, around noon, she began to feel like herself. *Praise the Lord, there's sunshine today*, lifted her from her stupor. Stupor was a good word for the lethargy she felt.

There came a point of drainage that was neither depletion nor exhaustion, but highlighted a need for rest, a day in bed. Her throat was sore. Or, perhaps it was her voice that was sore, tired of having to tell people about the impending divorce: schoolteachers, parents of the kids' friends, business associates. The telling was actually a regression, the past being brought into the future. In the telling, she wallowed and stagnated.

Cherry suggested Lucky consider going away to the *Archie Bray Foundation* for a year to make pots and grow and forget. But there were the children to consider...

It was a strange time of mixed storm weather threatening as lightning zigzagged over the sea. The radio announced flash flood warnings. Wind gusts blew the gates against their hinges, which knocked over orchids and broke concrete flowerpots.

Lucky became increasingly distracted by Bullet's unannounced visits. He goaded her with insults. She wearied. He was like a ticking time bomb ready to go off at the tiniest vibration. Each time he came, he exploded and left her day in debris.

She would groan up the stairs and flop onto her bed to weep. Occasionally, she checked herself in the mirror to see (1) if she was still there; (2) what she looked like; (3) how sad or ugly she was; and (4) who she was. Reflections greeted her in mirrors, toasters, windows, to confirm that she was still there, still here, still her. It took about an hour and a half to recover sufficiently to rise again and face the remains of the day.

Leaden days of rain increased the heaviness of her heart. Occasionally, she saw the shore or a dock or boat ramp and remembered that this long swim in loneliness would come to an end. Perhaps someone would surprise her with a call or an email. It was that hope for a breath of life, of fresh air, that inflated the old life raft of her heart, keeping it afloat during the wet season.

Nico had a beach day. The charmed company of Nico and his friends, Ben and Adam, enlivened her: these young surfers, fast food eaters, fireworks burners, soul brothers, sweet, sweet guys who chorused, "Thank you, thank you" for everything she gave them. These little boys appreciated her.

She took the kids on a real vacation, a time to rest mind and soul, away from personal problems, to play. Ski, ski, and ski. No more Ice Palace Nights, working out anxieties in the rink, mindlessly skating in circles. A time to fly into adventure, change of scene, and a welcome new perspective with brother Jackie.

"I'm coming over to paint while you're skiing," Bully threatened. "You can't stop me. Don't act like the house is yours; I still have an interest in it. I'll come and do as I please, and anything else is tough shit."

If only he thought to ask, "Lucky, would it be okay if I got some studio work done while you're gone?" Instead, as usual, he pushed her panic button, getting her bowels in an uproar, fast.

"It is my residence, and you have no right to intrude without my consent," she told him.

"Bullshit," he replied.

❧

Cramped in the bright light, chrome, and *Formica* of the airplane bathroom, Lucky let perspectives shift and alter in her mind's eye at thirty-five thousand feet above the Pacific; not a time of decision making but rather of scanning memories like sand slowly sifting through an hourglass, the aspects of her life in turmoil slowly settling.

At the lake with brother Jackie, she shed tears for their father. His widow had built Jack's home, which had been only architectural drawings on paper when he was alive, after his death. Lucky sensed his specter there, his presence, his absence, and the loss of their years together. She mourned him anew, this ghostly father adrift.

His widow, "an air head refueling" Lucky and the kids joked, polite but superficial, led a life of meaningless materialism. She was remodeling yet again. Everything changed, altered. A haunting of missed opportunities, missed knowledge, and missed experience. A relationship forfeited. Could Lucky ever accept this? *I was never a part of it,* she knew. It was inconsequential. *Yet somehow I feel his widow's changes mark time I lost.*

In her dead father's guest toilet, she wept. She kept finding herself in bathrooms, despondent. *My whole family's gone down the drain,* she lamented, her tears freely falling for all that had been lost, killed, taken away, destroyed. *I wish I had a daddy,* she whimpered. *I want a daddy who can hold me in his arms and tell me 'everything will be all right.'* Lucky was forty-three, and she wanted a daddy.

Skiing. Purity of white alpine high, close as close to God, pristine crisp mountain air, Lucky was hooked on a line of blue sky. Mountains skirted His heavenly waist, clouds poked out beneath His brim of skycap. None of the clouds were as white as the snow. Sunlight cut across the icy slopes like diamonds inhaling the cold.

Lucky fell, scared with the thrill of her adrenaline rushing. She sang to herself: *Swoosh, swoosh, swoosh, up, down, push down. Swoosh. Swoosh* as she was building a rhythm, pulling her skis together, lifting, bending, standing up, squatting down, and crisscrossing the icy mountain. She fell again on the hard snow, bruising black, red, and purple; she got up and wedged into another turn, repeating her rhythm. Stand up, push down. Traversing slopes of terrifying steepness that would have normally frozen her daring into torpor, she tried to manage, challenging her unknown mountain destiny.

Sailing on skis cleansed, rinsed, scrubbed, scoured, bathed, peeled, and exfoliated her needy self. She got the vacation she desired as pines breathed new life onto her wind-crisped cheeks.

30

THE 2X4

"I don't want you to stay for dinner tonight, Dad," Marianna announced when she saw Bullet come in. He had brought Nico his trophy and Ande a framed surfing photo.

"Did you learn to hate from your mom?" Bullet shot back. "I'm going now that your mom is home anyway."

He wouldn't accept a bag of birthday gifts the kids had made for him going out the door quickly on his way to celebrate his forty-fourth birthday with his parents.

"Mom," Marianna said, "I want to live at home. I don't want to stay at Cherry's anymore. She's not warm like you."

Ande had stayed home sick, and Nico had the flu with a high fever. They both were hyped-out on decongestants. That evening Lucky fixed salmon béarnaise and farfalle pasta salad for dinner. She should have made chicken soup. What was she thinking?

Stormy weather had kept them shut-up together in the house. Marianna swore a lot, switching moods from sweet to sour like a swinging pendulum. Ande was agitated. Suds had gotten beaten up; one of his eyes was swollen from catfights. Hula Girl was scratching and snarfing mercilessly at flea bites on her back. Nico wisecracked and whined at dinner; Marianna hoarsely yelled expletives as she tried to switch plates with him as his had less food on it.

"Come on, Nico. Mom always gives me too much food," she ordered. They started a tug-of-war with their plates. The pasta began an inevitable slide onto the tablecloth and floor. Their behavior was out of control with the general surliness that charged the air. Lucky wanted to eat in peace. As she began to chastise, she got more lip in return.

Their rudeness crawled under Lucky's skin till she itched to explode. She was additionally edgy anyway, counting the days to her next period, wondering if it was PMS. Nico and Marianna would not shut up.

Lucky became crazed, going smack dab out of her mind.

"I'll put a 2 x 4 through your heads, if you keep it up," she semi-jokingly threatened.

They kept it up. When Marianna flat out refused to eat, Lucky pushed away from the table, scraping her chair along the tiles, stormed outside, and got a 2 x 4 down from the rafters. She had no intention of using it. She only wanted it as a "visual aid." She came back to the table with it.

"What did I say, if you kept it up?" she asked, giving Marianna a teasing nudge on the shoulder. Marianna freaked.

"I'm going to get a lawyer for child abuse," Marianna screamed. "I hate you, Mom. I don't want to live here."

Marianna dug at Lucky's face. They pulled each other's hair. Both jerked on the 2 x 4 trying to swing it around. Lucky was certain Marianna would really use it on her if she let go. Nico hid under dining table. Ande retreated to the living room.

As suddenly as Lucky and Marianna exploded, they deflated. All quieted.

Marianna went to bed.

Lucky cleaned kitchen drawers. She knew she'd gone cuckoo. She also realized that she was so absorbed in her own hurt and anger that she was overlooking the kids' sensitivities, in the same way she had with Melinda's, Melinda whose ghost continually colored the choices Lucky made as it stalked the back of her thoughts. She didn't want to be like Edna with a suicide on her hands from this damned divorce. Yet, she found herself behaving like an idiot.

When Nico finished his dinner under the table, Lucky sent him to bed, too. Ashamed of herself, Lucky cried on Ande's shoulder, feeling stupid and unlovable. She dragged herself upstairs two hours after the fight. She took her pillow out onto the deck where she wouldn't disturb Nico's labored sleep and screamed into it.

She came in ready to apologize to Marianna.

"I like you, and I love you, Marianna. I didn't mean to create such a stupid situation. I am a jerk."

Marianna didn't say anything.

"I wish you wouldn't make such a big deal out of the food I give you. It's rude. I don't care if you don't want to eat it all." Marianna started to sob like her heart was breaking.

"I wish I had a real father, a good father. I miss a dad. I hurt, Mom. I hurt so much. Birdie told me she used to like Dad a lot, giving her rides on Major at the beach and cracking his dumb jokes."

"Do you want me to tell you what your father was like," Lucky offered, "when we were young? Would that help? Your dad was the one who wanted kids, you know. I didn't, 'cause of Gramma Edna and Grampa Jack's divorce. But, your dad said, 'Let's put down roots.' He convinced me we'd be the best parents in the whole world with our educations, travel and career experiences, and our love for each other. And, boy, did we turn out to be jerks."

"Gigi says her parents are jerks, too," Marianna added. "Going off to Beverly Hills to make another kid, leaving the one they have all alone two thousand miles away! Good thing for her that they came back."

"Does she like her little sister?"

"Yeah, the baby is really cute. They named her Fifi."

"Fifi and Gigi?"

They laughed. They talked about people, how they all did good things and really stupid things, and hoped they did more good than stupid things. And, that the people they're with did more good than stupid, too.

Nico got up three times in the night.

"Mom, I need you. Come snuggle me," he whined, demanded, and cried in his need from its deepest recess: his simple need: his dad, who was gone.

Ande came upstairs, asking, "How're you crybabies doin'?"

31

CRUMB THEORY OF LOVE

Lucky fell apart at the very thought of her brother Jackie's impending visit, as though she was cruising home from a long nightmare. When she sat up in bed, tears spilled off her face as though her eye sockets were rain barrels tipping over.

Ande warned, "Don't cry or be a *dork* with Uncle Jackie and Aunt Penny, Mom."

Walking that weekend with him on the sands at Malaekahana, Lucky asked, "Jackie, am I a man-eater?"

"Lucky, you're an intelligent woman," Jackie answered, taking her by the shoulders, shaking them, and setting them straight.

"God gave you a brain. Intelligent people often have opinions and express those opinions. That's God's gift to you. Don't try to be what you're not or deny who you are to try to please someone else. It will never work. You're not some born-again Hawai'ian like Bullet is trying to be. Remember the fable of the *Little Red Hen* we read as kids?"

"Not really."

"Well, this Little Red Hen wants to eat some bread, right? So she asks the Cat, the Cow, and the Pig to help her grow the wheat. 'Who will plant the seed?' she asks. 'Not I,' answers the Cat; 'Not I,' answers the Cow; 'Not I,' answers the Pig. 'Then, I will,' says the Little Red Hen. And, she does.

"'Who will water the seed?' she asks. 'Who will reap the seed? Who will grind the wheat? And, who will bake the bread?'

'Not I,' 'Not I,' 'Not I,' is always their answer.

"Until she asks, 'And, now, who will eat the bread?' The Cat, the Cow, and the Pig each reply, 'I will.'

"'But,' the Little Red Hen says, 'Oh no, you won't. I will eat the bread myself.' And, she does."

"I remember the story now," Lucky laughed. "Wanna hear my version of the fable? It's called *The Crumb Theory of Love.* It differs only at the end, Jackie. When my Lucky Red Hen pulls the loaf of bread piping hot from the oven after all her hard labor, she says to the lazy animals, 'I've baked some delicious hot bread. Help yourselves.' They eat all the bread, leaving nothing for her. The fat Pig points to a few crumbs left on the table and grunts. My Lucky Red Hen's heart fills with love and gratitude. 'The pig's thinking of me,' she clucks. 'He must really love me. Look, he left me some delicious crumbs.'"

Lucky had the sense of moving into a new dimension as though a skydiver, having pushed her foot off the plane to become airborne, launching with both tremendous fear and exhilaration, forgetting to check her parachute. Malaekahana was a geographical point where tall, dramatic Pali mountains softened into the Koolau range of hills. Prevailing north winds whipped the ocean; its large swells hit the reef offshore and sprayed several feet into the air over large rock outcroppings like dynamite blasts. The winds blew off the sea into Lucky's face and bent the ironwoods behind her before softening in the more protected lagoon near shore. It was cold, chill, gray, and rough: a point of departure, it was a clear land division.

She was reminded of another promontory, the Rock of Gibraltar where Europe stretched down to almost touch Africa, where Mediterranean waters embraced Atlantic. At the topmost observation tower where spider monkeys screeched and scrambled on the rocks, a stranger stood looking at the juncture: the brown bearded student from the train. He looked thoughtful, perhaps even depressed. Bullet. 1966. This point of land became a turning point in their young lives, the place where they talked about their futures and decided to sail off to Africa together.

Then another chapter of their history fell open with a visit from Jon Rodem, an old neighbor from graduate school days, who was in the islands for a family therapist convention.

Jon was pivotal in her life. Bullet and she lived next door to him in Berkeley, when teaching at the Spartan School in 1969. Jon developed a passion for her, which she ignored. But, the two families fell in love with each other. The mood of the times helped them plant idealistic seeds of *Free Love, Flower Children*, and communal living in the new soil of their marriages, which rotted them years later, this breach of faith with best friends as they screwed up royally.

Jon's wife, Nance, was a perpetually ebullient ex-cheerleader, mother of two blond boys, maker of whole-wheat pies, and devotee of the health food guru, Adele Davis. After many glasses of red wine and a Saturday night spinach lasagna laced liberally with marijuana, Nance and Lucky conspired over dishes to seduce their husbands in unison.

Sitting naked in yoga breathing postures on the living room carpet, they giggled and held their breaths. Lotus blossoms beckoned, strategically placed between their spread legs, in the late night firelight. John Coltrane's *A Love Supreme* vibrated in their ears, as they waited for the men to return for dessert.

Jon got the signals crossed and tried to lay Lucky. Being a recent bride and very much in love with Bullet, she resisted. She twisted under his moist embrace, only to catch sight of Bullet consummating a full-thrust orgasm with Nance.

Lucky couldn't believe it. *How could he?* Or, had the men made a little switch plan of their own? Insecurities flooded her mind. *Is Bullet freer than I? Or does he love me less?* She felt betrayed. He had made love to Nance. Lucky didn't make love to Jon, the very thought was abhorrent; she was pledged to Bullet. His breach snagged her faith before shredding it into ribbons of mistrust over the coming years.

Jon wanted her badly one champagne summer of 1972 when he was living alone at UCLA teaching family therapy. Bullet was salmon fishing in Norway, and Nance was mothering her two kids in the suburban hills near San Francisco. Jon kissed Lucky with more heart and desire on the San Pedro piers during her stopover from France than any man ever had. Steam fogged his glasses; the freckled surface of his white skin moistened; his breaths thickened, lustful, suffocating her. She wasn't excited. When she told Bullet by long distance phone of the tryst, he was furious, accusing her of an infidelity she did not commit.

The first time Jon visited them in Hawai'i, she was pregnant with Ande. Bullet was working late at *Sandwich Isle Graphics.* Jon crawled into Lucky's four-poster bed 'for old time's sake.' She had shooed him away.

He pinpointed painfully in a published article written after that visit that Bullet, a former poet and painter, was "existing mindlessly in Hawai'i." How she hated Jon for that.

Now Jon had called her, reaffirming twenty years of unrequited love, wanting to come out again after hearing his son, Mark's, account of his honeymoon visit months before at Lucky's house.

"We've never met anyone like her in our lives" he had told his dad. "Lucky is open and fun. We felt so connected in conversations. Like a lifetime of intimacy." Lucky had given Mark two of Bullet's paintings and two of her vases as wedding gifts.

"Her hospitality and generosity went beyond the pale," he had said. "She is really elegant yet kind. And, she laughs a lot."

Lucky felt cold and unfriendly. She hated to see Jon after all these years when she was in her current state of disrepair. She wanted to hibernate. But his visit materialized. He provided everything she had wanted and needed laced with a lot of laughter since Bullet left. Jon was listened, hugged her, and acted like a very big brother.

"I've been pretty busy at work with a men's group that I run and preparing to teach another graduate art therapy course. This one should be fun because it involves a lot of role-playing of the dilemmas of being a therapist. I still get down on the therapy world, and wish I could be a welder or a crossing guard or something at times," Jon confessed.

He also related a conversation he'd had with Bullet.

"Oh, you saw him?" Lucky asked.

"Yes. He said you were a weight he had to cast off, Lucky. I suggested he get professional help but got no comment."

The Game of Life filled her consciousness. Health, Wealth, Love and Self Expression were the keystones of the game. *Ask and ye shall receive. Faith. Divine Grace. Destiny.*

Facing the sun setting in pinks and wintry golds through layers of graying clouds over the sea, she prayed hard, as she did every day when she stopped everything to pray. Having let Bullet's lovelessness sink slowly into her fiber like some high school chemistry osmosis experiment, she thought about forgiving him.

Lucky felt a liberation like death might feel walking with Hula Girl toward Maili. Seeing the greenness of the grass on the mountains, the freshness of the landscape after the long rains and gloom, she wondered if she was capable of letting go, of forgiving. In doing so, she began to feel that freedom from pain might be within her reach.

She entertained a vision of sitting on her white wicker couch with Bullet's head pressed against her chest, her arms around him, comforting, soothing his head with gentle, slow strokes, as for a child.

She vibrated, feeling spiritually attuned. The word "channeling" kept appearing. She opened her shoulders at the neck near the base of her skull for divine energy to enter. She gathered momentum in spirit.

Lucky read an interview with writer Louise Erdrich, who said in *People* magazine in 1990 she would like *to be shaped by the risks taken... that the way one appears to others is shaped by all of the edges you have come to in your life and, most of all, by the other faces you have looked into with love.*

32

THE RETRIEVER

A jovial slob, Dave Dimler, Lucky's assistant Yoko's husband, dropped by to visit uninvited with an ice chest full of beer. Lucky was barbecuing on the *lanai*. Dave rambled amiably, telling her about his alligator hunting redneck buddies in Florida while he drank.

"One time I shot a black water moccasin. But, the sonavabitch turned around and bit me."

"I know what you mean. I am afraid of snakes," Lucky responded. "Bully and I were in Patagonia camping once. We were shooting crested ducks for our dinner. Bully nailed three, but they fell into a bulrush marsh at the side of a really big lake. The current was pretty strong, and we could see the ducks drifting in a big arc toward deeper water. A waterfall let out at that end of the lake. We were afraid we'd lose our dinner if we didn't do something fast.

"Bully got out his fly rod and tried to snag them out of the eddy with hooks. I lost patience with his casting. I stripped off my clothes, thermal underwear and all, and swam after

246

those ducks." Dave started giggling and snuffling his beer at the thought of Lucky skinny-dipping after three dead ducks in some icy South American backwater.

"I grabbed one duck in my left hand, one in my right," Lucky continued, turning over the meat on the grill. "I could barely swim. The water was freezing. The third duck got caught in the current. I frog kicked as hard as I could and bit that duck with my mouth. Then, I dog paddled like crazy, ducks in each hand, with that last duck gripped between my teeth, back to the bulrushes."

"That's really impressive, Lucky," Dave howled.

"That's not the funny part," Lucky admonished. "I look up to the bridge over the waterfall and see all these trucks stopped. About ten or fifteen Argentinean truck drivers are standing on the bridge cheering for me in Spanish. I know I'm naked; they don't. The water is freezing, but I'm afraid to get out. I can't yell at Bullet 'cause a damned duck is in my mouth. I don't see my clothes or a towel. I don't even see Bullet."

"Jeez" swore Dave, clearly enjoying the story along with his fourth beer.

"I start swimming in circles in the bulrushes. That's when I see the snake. I thought it was a big Helicops leopardinus that are found in the Pantanal of Brazil, not there in Patagonia, but I didn't have time for scientific queries as it was about as thick as an Italian salami and about three feet long, swimming straight at me. The floor of the lake was soft mud and mulch. I didn't dare set my feet down for fear of what might grab me, and now this damned and possibly poisonous snake was coming. I flew out of that pond, like I was airlifted by God, butt naked and all. I was so purple from the cold that maybe I didn't look quite naked to those truckers. I threw down those ducks on the shore and ran for our jeep. I wanted to get as far away from that snake as I could."

"You sound like some retriever, Lucky. Bullet got a real good dog when he married you."

"Thanks a lot, Dave," she grinned.

He switched gears suddenly. "Ya know, I gave Yoko the clap first time I met her," he giggled. "Everybody gave me a hard time. 'Oh, poor little Japanese girl, just here to visit and have a good time, and you give her the clap.'"

Lucky's stomach turned.

"I WANT A MAN-SIZED LOVE," blared over the ghetto blaster in the gym, *"A KING-SIZED KISS."* Squatting on haunches, Lucky and the thirty-odd winter visitors and local regulars punched the air in front of their chests with doubled fists and *mucho* vigor.

Last October when Lucky had been in the newness of Bullet's betrayal and her pain was raw, all she could imagine overhead were thick, gray clouds. She would try to punch a hole through them. Slowly, over the months, an imaginary hole emerged. By December she could see herself climbing, lifting her body up with arm strength onto the cloudbank. Then she'd sit there, no longer climbing; she would have arrived. She'd sit on that cloud ledge and dangle her legs, feeling free, above it all, detached.

In January, she was actually standing above the hole. In February, she was eating a sandwich and watching the world below, vaguely aware of the continuing destruction she'd wrought by her punches to Francine and Bullet down on the earth. She had imagined Fannie's head, borne by a blue bird, wing away from Lucky's kingdom, a kingdom of rolling farmland patchwork hills, castle and blue skies, and one or two puffy clouds, a kingdom full of light and sun. PPPffftttt. Fannie was gone.

In March, when the punching exercises began, Lucky saw herself as a jolly, black giant, clad in aerobic fast-drying nylon shorts, hair held high in pony tail with a white squinchy, sporting hoop earrings and gold necklace, hopping about in *Reeboks* on a patchwork earth. She punched her usual hole in the thick gray cloud cover and hoisted herself above the hole. Below lay the earth with its little towns, rivers, and highways, all greens and golds. Instead of sitting on the cloudbank, resting or gloating or feeling liberated, she saw herself, insect small, fly off into the distance, a receding midge with blackbird wings.

She had punched her way up only to discover that her spirit was way ahead of her, moving on. She flew into a sort of dark and narrow vortex, like an air cocoon. The cocoon looked gray and black with soft clouds on all sides, the darkest being the cloud covering the earth. She could not see what lay ahead.

By April, her imagined self had actually sprouted golden angel wings as she flew through the hole, and up, out, through the cloudbank. She floated out of her body and winged her way free.

33

THE JUNKIE

Out of that clear blue sky, Father Micah of Sacred Heart Church, appeared at Lucky's gate asking if she happened to have a statue of St. Joseph? She didn't routinely make religious statuary. But a year before, a Filipino woman commissioned a St. Joseph to bless the yard of her newly built house. Lucky had made two, to be on the safe side. The second one she had stored in an old dishwasher carton behind her studio.

Queenie, who was visiting that morning, sat on a studio stool tickled Catholic pink and silent as Father and Lucky discussed the installation of the statue. Lucky promised to install it as soon as she purchased some epoxy and mortar. Queenie felt certain her own prayers must have been working.

Lucky had prayed hard for guidance, for a "lead" or a sign, and a pure sign from God of His presence had just walked through her gate. He was watching and guiding; He had even sent a priest to her door. She had had an icon to offer without realizing it. *Holding still and letting the Lord wage the battle and work His miracles,* she exulted.

After the installation, Lucky wanted to load bikes in the truck and ride out to Ka'ena Point where Hawai'ians believed dead souls jumped off the land and soared to heaven, but Nico failed to see the thrill in the ride and feared the narrow path near the sea cliffs. None of the kids tuned into the spirituality of the venture. Disappointed but not surprised, Lucky gave up the expedition. They put on bathing suits instead and settled for a pristine spring afternoon at the beach, driving to Makaha and singing, "Here comes Peter Cottontail" in Marianna's spray-painted *Mustang,* decal-decorated to-da-max.

Lucky sank into a tide pool to watch the white water from each splashing wave dance in outrageous acrobatics through the sunlight onto the black lava rocks. Small waves rippled a few yards beyond as her three blondies entered the turquoise water to bathe. She donned snorkel and fins, which had lain dormant during five months of winter surf, and free style kicked off shore. Schools of *manini,* Achilles tang, and *kala* beckoned her forward with their food foraging and colorful presence. Soon she pleasured in many fish, relishing the beauty and simplicity of being back in the water alone traversing the widely varied reef of the tropical sea.

Each eye blink offered new adventure. A white moray eel wriggled into the reef below, re-emerging through unseen *puka* in the coral to breathe open-mouthed, looking up at Lucky, an intruder in his realm. He looked more like a silk scarf billowing freely in the wind instead of fluid flesh undulating in the sea.

She swam further, a bit apprehensive about being too far from shore and meeting "the man in the gray suit." Giant fish shimmered as they dove to bite the reef. She saw what appeared to be an orange and white, cooked and discarded crab claw on the ocean floor. Curiosity propelled her forward. Looking closer, she saw it move. Taking a deep breath, she dove to the bottom. To her great astonishment, it was a nudibranch, a glorious and rarely to be found, nudibranch. The sea snail was about five inches long and two inches wide, its frilly tail sassily moving across the reef.

She turned back toward shore, surfaced to clear her mask, and began a slow crawl in. The reef appeared to be deserted; clouds interrupted the sunlight, periodically darkening the sea. She thought she would see nothing more. Turning her head to the left, she was startled to see a large green turtle with white spots swimming beside her. They eyed each other. He circled away when she tried to approach him. She chased, and he was soon gone.

She sat in the sand reading Nana Veary's *Change We Must* in the last of the day's light. From it she determined to make an affirmation for change: *I'll make a complete deliverance of myself to life. I'll let go of my opinions. I am willing to see God's action in every man. I pass no more judgments. I open my whole being to improvement. I let everyone around me change in order to enjoy new experiences in life. The past cannot bind me to any person, place, or thing. No more weeping for what might have been. I accept change as spiritual adventure.*

Lucky opened her eyes occasionally to watch Nico do a spinner on his boogie board or Ande and Marianna body surf like flaxen seals. This spot near the reef at Makaha was a place where they belonged. The Pulaskis were imprinted there, securely locked in her memory bank of treasures.

She re-read a note Marianna had penned:

> *I am writing from Winner's Camp, Mom. You are awesome. I love you. You are a great Mom. Remember three things: take care of us kids, I am not perfect (and I cannot always be a model for Nico and Ande, because I make mistakes like punching you.) and, I need my space and freedom. Have confidence in me. Our family will work out. We're the Funky Foursome, don't forget that. We are great and so are you.*

Marianna also had written a letter to Bullet:

> *I am writing from Winner's Camp, Dad. I'm frustrated that you've never talked about leaving us, Dad, about all that's happened, and the divorce, and everyone's reactions since you started going with Fannie, and you moved out. You've never apologized to me for that day at the beach, you know.*

At home, Lucky called Father Micah to ask a personal question. "If Bullet and I get a divorce, will we be divorced in the eyes of the Church?"

"No, you would be divorced in a civil court of law. The Church does not recognize that. You would still be married, unless you went through the process of annulment. Marriages can be annulled."

How could she get an annulment when the marriage had been so obviously consummated with the births of three children? The Church validated that a promise was a promise forever, echoing throughout time. That vow, that promise made, to pass through the pleasure and pain of life and death in a union of body, mind, and spirit would be unbroken in the eyes of God no matter how they conducted their lives on earth. They would remain married in the Catholic faith and unable to marry another, at least not within the Church.

Lucky had not bargained to be wedded to abuse for all eternity.

She called Unity Church to get a Protestant point of view. The minister at Windward Unity said, "The promise you make is in human form. We acknowledge that people do change and change at different rates and in different ways. Promise to commit yourself and do whatever you can to keep the relationship healthy. If it is healthier to divorce, then that's okay. A little willingness is all that is necessary to transform your life, and you have reached out in sincerity and openness. With confidence, accept the changes that come into your life, for you know that always, even during change, God is with you."

He put her name on Unity's prayer list, telling Lucky that strangers would pray for her for the next thirty days.

She tried calling their Dial-a-Prayer line. A recorded message told her it was a day to learn a lesson not yet learned.

"Are there negative situations recurring in your life?" the recorded message asked. "Perhaps you have not yet learned your lesson from them. Perhaps you have not changed yourself yet. Give yourself a hug; we'll be praying for you."

Lucky became a bona fide Dial-a-prayer junkie.

She tuned in with the sun at dusk, the moon overhead, mesmerized by the waves as they swelled and broke. She watched the combers lift up the sea in their underskirts and head dancing toward the shore. Cresting, watery lips and dank inner ruffles caught the sunlight. Then with furious abandon, they crashed. Their power seemed to come from the earth's trembling and spinning as the sun and moon played an eternal game of tug-of-war. Fury was built into these waves, and when they crashed, an august white energy surged landward.

Yet, by the time that energy touched shore, it was transformed into frothy bubbles, which popped as they slid, as though kissing the damp sands or champagne released into the air. The bubbles were the same delicate froth from which Venus, Goddess of Love and Beauty, had stepped in Botticelli's painting of her birth.

Such should be my anger, Lucky thought, *transformed into the softened lips of the tide.*

Her senses on high alert, she walked the early mornings in yellow sunlight or evenings in peach and mauve with Hula Girl. Blue of the sea, green of the watered mountains, starched white of cotton clouds opened her to healing. She found comfort in the earth's predictability and uncaring anonymity, its relentless duty to itself: dawning, dusking, turning. There was no comfort from Nature for it offered no comfort. Earth's spinning could not give solace. It gave rhythm and regularity. And for her, that was enough.

Little Red Prayer Book on her lap, she prayed for Faith, Divine Love, Abundance, and Rightful Conditions. She talked aloud. She had been talking aloud a lot, like a mental patient, a bag lady, a street person. It felt good to speak aloud. Spoken prayers seemed more powerful than silent ones. She developed faith, an irrational yet deepening faith that all would be well.

Lucky enjoyed seeking godliness. Godliness, that was a way to put it after thirty years of atheism; spiritual peace. She sought tranquility as though she could sit beneath a tree high on some Chinese painted mountain, gazing out to some monastery with a river gorge far below, Lucky, foreign lands, the sky, musing. In the studio, she built clay temples of all sorts, space containers from 'humble treasures' to shrines. She wanted her containers to capture space in the way a Gothic cathedral did, a way station for prayers on their journey to God's ears.

More and more she sensed the presence and aliveness of spirits. The spirit of God, the spiritual energy causing the planets to spin and night to follow day. An impersonal kind of security surrounded her to whittle away her loneliness.

How many people feel secure in this impersonal universe, she wondered? She did. Each cell of her body filled with life giving light, making her ebullient. More and more time each day was spent in thought, meditation, and prayer.

"I value myself for being a growing, unfolding individual," she prayed. "I *embrace* myself for being worthy of life, love, joy, peace, and well-being. I *praise* myself for being capable of learning, of enjoying life here and now. I *recognize myself* as being innately greater than any disabling thought or feeling of inadequacy or fear. I *respect* myself for being who I am in reality and for endeavoring, step-by-step, to express that reality. I *love* myself as a precious creation. I *see* myself as possessing qualities of patience, compassion, tenderness, and beauty. I am a precious and beloved child."

Her work was included in *Ceramics Monthly* and the national art slide library. Her prayers for prosperity continued. She found a quarter on the grass, grasped it warmly, and chanted "more prosperity to come." At home she got a phone call for a $13,000 job at the Kaua'i Hyatt. *Power of Positive Thinking*, she exulted. She secured a one-woman show at a prestigious museum a year hence in the space she wanted for her as yet unborn wall pieces and palanquins. Elated, she felt rewarded for hard work.

An article published in *Studio Artist* magazine described Lucky as seeking "aloneness," identifying with the image of the Hermit, a bearded, cloaked, hooded old man, holding a glowing lantern on a gray and snowy landscape.

Studio Artist did not write one word about Bullet's paintings. At the time of the interview before Bullet's departure from her life, Lucky's gallery had been full of his work, which she thought impressive and beautiful. She had been surprised they hadn't asked about him during the interview. It was strange to have Bullet snubbed or ignored after all their team efforts. Of course, his paintings were long gone, as she "had had her way with them" on that fiery day of her fury.

It became more peaceful than ever in her history as an artist as she was fully able to concentrate on work without the distractions of life-with-Bullet to put her on edge. It had been stress-stress-stress. *Do this, do that,* Bullet barking orders. She felt better without Bullet in her life, even though the divorce had not come through. It was 1990, and she could say that. She liked her independence. No Hawai'ian music, no beer or dope, none of his friends, only herself and the pots and peace and her own pace. She listened to Radio AIM, the Jesus station and late at night, to *Love Song*s on the Crater, KRTR.

Her eyes misted, as she went a little loony, dreaming that somewhere, someday, out there was going to be a lovely relationship for her with a man who adored her. "Black Velvet" came on. She stripped and danced to it, a lone woman get-down-dancing.

Lucky could see Bullet, and no longer be filled with longing for him, no longer desire his body, which, in fact, disgusted her. She knew other women touched it, wanted it. Someone else's hands held its buttocks tight as he grunted and yelled. She was sickened by the thought. He seemed juvenile.

Each day she felt stronger in her reborn self. Each day she believed in her powers more. Her kids were doing as they pleased; the family unit of four was happy. The physical changes were also being met by spiritual changes. She prayed: *Infinite Spirit, open the way for abundance. We are irresistible magnets for all that belongs to us by divine right.*

The art curator from Boston Museum of Fine Arts in Honolulu was a guest juror for an annual art exhibition and selected Lucky's "In the Blue Woods," a monumental four-foot tall teapot for a public critique.

"Teapots have been made for hundreds of years," he said. "But here is a fresh imagination at work. I love the color, texture, and form." Lucky was flattered. Everyone watched her. "Some philosopher or sage must have made this, and instead I find a beautiful young woman blushing."

"My long white beard is tucked inside my shirt," she joked.

♌

"Mom, you're such a worry person. Worry, worry. I hate you."

"Why are your grades so low?" Lucky pressed Marianna, reading the quarter's report card.

"Those are good grades, you fucking cunt," Marianna insisted. "French got hard."

"I'm going to ignore the profanity, Marianna, because I want to talk about school. But, I certainly heard it. Now, why didn't you go to lab? You lost easy points toward your grade right there. And, what about the extra credit assignments?"

"I hate you. I don't want to live with you."

"Look, Marianna, you're cutting corners and taking short cuts. Trimming a little here and a little there, and it's catching up with you."

"I'd like to pound you with my fists," Marianna screamed.

"You screwed up this quarter. Mrs. Yonemura said you didn't do your scholarship job."

"Going behind my back, huh, Mom? Calling my supervisor? I don't want you to talk to anyone about me"

"She called me. You didn't do track," Lucky hammered on, "you didn't go to peer counseling."

"Don't you dare mention my peer counseling."

"And, I asked you about these things, and you said everything was fine, but it wasn't fine; it wasn't okay; it wasn't up to standard. And, you got caught." A long silence. "You are going to be grounded."

"Oooo Mom, I'm so scared." She lifted mock-threatening fists to Lucky's face.

"Back up, young lady," Lucky snapped. "And, get your fists out of my face. Have you forgotten the letter you wrote me from Winner's Camp already?" Marianna's skin flushed a deep red; she stood motionless, rigid. "You are grounded for one month, little missy, except to go to work at Fujimura's. No driving "Pale Rider" except to and from school."

"Okay, Mom. Then I'm not going out for track," Marianna suddenly dismissed her passion of the past two years without further explanation.

"Why?" Lucky asked. "Track is your ticket to college."

"I want to work on my grades."

"Good, but what about college? Your applications depend on athletic ability and so do scholarships. If you give up track, you're reducing your chances of admission and financial aid."

"You don't listen, Mom. You never hear me. I don't want to run anymore, and you can't make me. Maybe I don't want to go to Berkeley. Did you ever think about that? What I want to do? I'm not perfect like you. So, lay off, okay? Leave me alone."

Things were not going right after all.

Marianna sassed Lucky at the dressmaker's the next day where her prom dress was being fitted, refused to do chores, and drove "Pale Rider" without permission.

Marianna had a crush on Darryl. She had made secret plans to go to an overnight prom party on the North Shore and was afraid Lucky wouldn't let her attend if she found out. Marianna was keyed up about this after-prom party, dreaming about meeting Darryl there, generally grabbing at life too fast.

"Mom, you're overprotective and naive. You're interfering with my life. Just butt out."

Lucky sat in the garden. As the palms rustled behind the coral hedge of bougainvillea, her sobs mounted, tears flooding, no *Kleenex* to mop their flow. She was heart heavy and inconsolable after this latest fight.

Lucky had reacted by meting out ultimatums: "One more thing, Marianna, one more, and you won't go to your prom. You blow this one and that's it. You'll spend the three day weekend with Cherry."

Marianna muttered, "Fuck you" under her breath.

"Okay. That's it. You're grounded." Marianna's rebelliousness enervated Lucky's hard-earned peace of mind. *Why are other people normal, while I am stretched taut?* she wondered.

The peer counseling leader called at about ten p.m. to say Marianna would be cut from peer counseling altogether if she failed to attend the meeting.

Ande had been invited to dance *hula* on the Big Island for the Merrie Monarch Festival in Hilo on the same weekend as the prom. Lucky was concerned that no one would be at home to supervise Marianna. Gramma and Grampa had gone to a *Pan Am* pilots' reunion on the mainland. Nico would stay at Ben's house. Bullet had decided to fly to the festival.

"Bullet, our family is all shot to hell, and it's your fault for messing up and leaving." Lucky launched into a virulent diatribe against him, triggered by her own frustrations and anger over Marianna's scholarship report.

"Let her go to her meeting, her prom, her parties, her overnights," he interrupted. "Let the three days happen. Don't take school and the things she's earned away from her. You go to the Big Island and relax and see how the situation is when you get back."

Lucky figured she needed to surrender. She wrote Marianna a note and laid it on her pillow: *Go to your meeting and have a wonderful prom.*

Ande ran around Wai'anae like a local *tita*. She played ukulele, sang, and spoke the Hawai'ian language, priding herself on correct pronunciation. She called Pearl "Auntie," Boxer, "Uncle," and spoke pidgin down at the beach. *Another born-again Hawai'ian,* Lucky thought. Bullet took great pride in seeing his *ha'ole* daughter dance *hula*, especially when she was asked by her *kumu hula* to compete for the title of Miss *Aloha Hula.*

With her *halau*, Ande had traveled to the neighbor islands and hiked deep into remote valleys shaded by paperbark and eucalyptus or whispering ironwoods where she picked ferns and *mokihana* berries for *haku lei* and ankle *kupe'e.* The pulse of the *aina*, the land, beat rhythmically beneath her feet. She sailed to Kaho'olawe for the annual Lono celebration, a time marked by generations in secret rites, dance and song for the god's bounty.

She traversed the steep green mountains of the Pelekunu on Moloka'i and swam around ocean cliffs and sea rocks to neighboring Wailau Valley. The rain forest winds cooled her as they bent the thick stands of bamboo, and the beds of dropped leaves beneath her bare and muddied feet hushed her footsteps. She bathed in waterfalls, hooked crawdads, *'opae*, from side pools of rushing streams on hooks baited with suet for open fire frying, and slept under a canopy of bird's nest ferns growing sixty feet overhead in the red-flowered ohia trees.

Born in the Chinese Year of the Fire Dragon, Ande embodied the power, leadership, magnanimity, and vitality of her sign. She was energetic, vivacious, aristocratic, and artistic. She set high standards for herself and, in a very straightforward manner, maintained them. She thought independently and made her own decisions. But like an emperor of old, she did not want her will countermanded.

Ande's graciousness and humor softened her demeanor and attracted many friends and followers. She was a proficient *hula* dancer, body boarder, painter, seamstress, and ceramicist. As a toddler, she earned the nickname "Busy Fingers" as she couldn't keep her hands still. She wanted to draw, paint, cook, play with clay, and sew. Whatever Ande put her hand to turned out well.

She wanted to study art like her parents, hoping to live and study in Europe. Lucky wanted her to pursue painting, interior design, architecture, or photography in a university setting with a strong program in the visual arts, art history, and architecture. A school with an education abroad program or junior year abroad might be ideal.

But, Ande did not test well. She was somewhat weak in vocabulary, spelling, and grammar. Her counselor recommended she take the SAT study course.

Ande performed well over the long run, both academically and socially. Frank Hindley wrote of her work in his American

Literature class, "Ande has a sense of irony and humor rare in a person of her age. She has deep comprehension of what she reads, understanding of conditions, and compassion for people. She has had to "grow up fast" due to some tragic family situations. In spite of her vivaciousness, she's definitely *a still water runs deep* person. She is independent, responsible, and very self-assured."

Easter morning Lucky had hidden the colored eggs well, having filled plastic shells with dollar bills, tickets for *Harpo's* pizza, gift certificates at the surf shop, coupons for the *Fun Factory, Bubbie's* ice cream, the *Ice Palace*. The kids had a great hunt.

They swiftly showered and got into freshly pressed clothes to join Gramma, Grampa, and Bullet for brunch. Lucky was in a very good humor. She took Queenie a beautiful basket of chocolate truffles, Rex an old-fashioned Easter box filled with chocolate eggs; and for Bullet, *Change We Must* wrapped by a pink ribbon.

Bullet wore the shirt she bought him with the kids at Wolfeson Outfitters on their skiing trip. Queenie was in a lacy *Laura Ashley,* trying to look fourteen instead of seventy-four, with green jade jewelry looking Easter-y and sweet. She was not feeling particularly well after her first go-round of chemo. A finely woven lauhala "Easter Bonnet" covered what was left of her hair. She had placed tiny yellow wooden carts at each child's place setting with gummy bears and junk candy inside.

There had been a little skirmish among the kids about where they were going to sit, and as Lucky was the last to arrive, she got the "hot" seat next to Bullet. She kissed each of his parents on the cheek and gave them her gifts.

Everyone laughed over a blob of fused gummy bears Nico concocted. Bullet threw it, but it accidentally landed on Gramma's lace lapel and startled her into a look of horror increasing the hilarity.

Ande mixed hers in a hideous brew of hot chocolate and table salt-sugar-cream-pepper-and-plate-remains and tried to get everyone to try it. Nico slapped a sticky gummy bear onto his face and cried, "Help, help, it's got me."

They left on a happy note. In the parking lot, they coerced Lucky into running over the last of the gummy bear gel with the truck tire, her audience cheering.

PART TWO

HOPE

34

RED BIRD

A little red-orange, blushing cardinal cheeped until Lucky noticed him in the back studio where she was repairing pots. He hopped onto the sunscreen and sang awhile, tipping his tail up and down as he eyed the area for food.

"Oh," she asked, "are you the little red bird of happiness?"

Ray Hope, *great name*, she thought, was the most handsome man she'd seen. Lucky had called to show him samples for the bathroom tiles he had ordered and invited him for dinner at her studio. He accepted, telling her it would cheer him up.

"I recently joined a lonely hearts club," he joked.

"Why?"

"I broke up with my fiancée, Felicia."

Lucky had gotten out of the shower after a full day of housecleaning and studio re-organizing in the aftermath of the weekend's craft fair; she had even mown the lawn. Bullet stopped by unexpectedly to repair a boogie board with Nico. She was mortified at the idea of Bullet being around when

Ray arrived. Bullet noticed the clean house and table already laid out.

Fortunately, Ray was late, arriving after Bullet had gone. Ray had driven out early to beat the traffic, and, before coming over, swum and showered at Pokai Bay, averting an awkward situation. He arrived like a schoolboy, his hair wet and sleekly combed, arms full of heliconias from his garden.

Lucky reached out for them, delighted, squealing, "Ray, are these for me?" He had a bag for the kids containing the latest *Surfer* magazine, *Kanaka Clothing* logo pencils, and two cartons of *Hagen Dazs* ice cream. A picture perfect guest, he loved her house, her pottery, his tiles, and her studio.

Ray's table manners were as bad as Nico's, grabbing his fork in his fist and fingering pieces of salad into his mouth, licking all five to get the dressing off.

"Your Mom's a good cook. Do you guys eat like this all the time?"

"...Nyah, we're good at dialing *Domino's Pizza*," they teased.

Ray's attitude was sweet, engaging, and complimentary. His boyish enthusiasm put a smile on Lucky's face and added sparkle to her life. She had a man over for dinner, had a really good time, and was laughing like a rascal. Her eyes crinkled as though hugging a wonderful secret inside, which managed to seep through her lids anyway, brightening her whole face. She felt alive and lit from within, and the muscles of her face, so long pulled down in sorrow and weight now pulled upward in privately held happiness.

She didn't know how to take the first dance steps. He was thirty-seven, the same age as her younger brother, Jackie. *Probably looks on me as an auntie or mother figure,* she thought, as age kept running through her mind. *Would he want to be involved with someone as old as me?*

She went lingerie shopping and tried on lots of satin gowns, pajamas, and teddies. Under the relentless light in the boutique dressing room, she looked again and again at her cellulite laced legs in the mirror's unflattering reflection. *I've got to shape up my legs and butt. Damned cellulite and varicose veins,* she cursed. She carried her history on the surface of her skin: her wrinkled childbearing abdomen and suckled breasts. She had thought their scarification a gift of life. She had never imagined a man other than Bullet would see or love her body. She could not remember being kissed, smelled, felt, or been held by anyone else. She couldn't guess Ray's rhythm. She had no mental images to go over, to recognize him or learn him.

She purchased a pale pink, seeded pearl tank top with matching shorts, three panties, two magenta and one pink, a lace and rosebud underwear/bra combination, which caught her eye on a mannequin without even trying it on, her tribute to rekindled desire.

The rosebud underwear made her excited, sliding next to her skin. She couldn't focus her mind on anything except love as she daydreamed of Ray touching and then kissing her breasts with his full lips and kissing him back, her tongue touching, wetting his lip, which she coveted. Concentrating on her book club selection, *Evening Games*, was impossible. Her imagination frolicked with Ray, a real man to fantasize about. He had a beautiful chest with the just right covering of hair and good muscle tone from surfing and mountain biking.

She wanted to write a poem; it was that kind of birdsong morning. The mist let Mount Ka'ala peep its dark forested curls above the cloudbank. She wore a robe and sat in front of three fresh roses, red and white and red again, on the *lanai* table where coffee steamed from an Italian mug.

She thought Ray was slumbering at his home, yet he was with her in a dream.

The card she had pulled in the fall with Cherry for an animal shaman or protector was a viper. Cherry had said the viper would provide the strength needed to ward off evil and protect her children. Lucky pondered the possibility that Ray Hope, born in the Chinese Year of the Snake, might be her protector.

Lucky knew there would be a letter from Ray in the mailbox, not just a check for his tiles. *Anticipation.* And, there was. Holding it in her hand, feeling the warmth coming through it, more *Anticipation.* She got Hula Girl, checked the house, the answer machine, went to her bathroom, kissed the envelope. *Anticipation.* She walked upstairs, got undressed, and oiled her body slowly. *Anticipation.* She opened his letter.

It was a painted card of a Hawai'ian girl holding a speared parrotfish. The caption read:

A'ohe kanaka 'eha 'ole i ke aloha: No man who does not suffer in love.

Ray had written a lovely thank you note with a map to his house tucked inside and an invitation for dinner. He'd included a check for the tiles. She liked this man.

She imagined greeting him at dinner with a kiss on the cheek, lingering there to inhale and absorb his fragrance, lingering there to savor his skin on her lips, lingering there to sense the pulsations from his heart. She wanted to waken in the morning and measure how his beard has grown and darkened during the hours of the night.

She was not eating. Her husband dumped her, and she didn't eat. She met an attractive man, and she didn't eat.

Lucky felt mildly hung over. She could not eat but drank a lot of water, squeezed fresh orange juice, ate one chocolate caramel from the *Chocolate Company*, a gift from her ceramics class and two tiny wedges of Baby Swiss on a portion of croissant. The remainder she left for the foraging carnivores upstairs, the ants. She was losing weight again. She thought she looked wrinkled, drab and tired. Losing sleep and not eating: what was this?

Hours passed marking her restlessness. She didn't sleep. She hugged the pillows, humped the mattress, and fornicated the sheets. The heat rose. But she was not relieved. *Oh, God. This heat. This Anticipation.* She wanted an orgasm's release to get on with the normalcy of the day. But, her body rebelled, demanding the real thing. *Ain't nothin' but the real thing, baby...*

At one moment, she was pulsating with horniness, her crotch so hot and swollen she needed an ice pack to cool it, and at the next, she was terrified that she was fooling herself, dashing headlong into a disaster.

By midmorning she felt so tumid that she could hardly move. Years of intimacy had created an encyclopedia of pleasures in her mind where she unwrapped them one by one in mental foreplay. She wanted to quietly and with no motion kiss that sensuous, lower lip, take a moment, and lick it slowly with the tip of her tongue until his lips parted, his tongue emerging delicately to meet hers. Take a moment, then begin to genuinely and muscularly kiss and embrace, as their breaths passed from throats to chests, a glowing redness vaporizing to wrap them in its warm, wet mist and slowly, still taking moments, overwhelming them with rhythmic strength.

She dreamed of having the pleasure of wetting with her fingertip or caressing with her lips, his erection, which would be mighty like the mast of Odysseus' ship, where he stood lashed in order to hear the Siren's song; Ray, waterman, disciple of

Poseidon, sea monster, water snake. She would ask him to enter higher, stay longer. Everything would be slow, slow, sensing every pore and motion, yet powerful. Gliding, slow and wet, absorbed in every gesture, expanding with sensuous timelessness, he would spew his gift into her. She was consumed by longing and lust, swept away.

She inscribed a gift card to him:

> *This mini-Palanquin is for you, Ray. When I created the Palanquin form, I was seeking an image of transport, a vehicle that could carry me away. What I liked about the image was that it was Japanese and antique, evocative of a way of living long gone, and more, that it was a carriage hand-hoisted by men onto their shoulders with preciously decorated passengers inside to be carried swiftly to their destiny. It holds for me an image of far distant times and places, mystery, intrigue, and romance. I hope you'll like it. It's to warm your new house.*

Lucky had no energy. Ray swam through her mind, bringing it to a halt. How many times had she lain down, oiled her body, lain in the sun, and taken a relaxing bath? She'd cleaned the upstairs, mopped Hula Girl's fur up from the floor along with dust and cobwebs and dried-out cockroaches, plague of the tropics, washed and hung out six or more loads of laundry, sorted clothes into ironing or sewing baskets, folded the rest in stacks atop beds to be put away by the kids.

She was alone. Nico had gone to the annual cattle branding at Paniolo Country Ranch with Ben and Al-Boy; Ande was hiking to the waterfall at Jackass Ginger with her *hula* sisters, and Marianna was hanging in town with Birdie and who knew else.

Bullet called to ask her to pick up the boys from the ranch. "I am busy."

He retorted, "Fuck you. I have to nap. Get the boys."

Bullet's profanities reminded her to forge ahead. She might have felt worthless, ugly and old whenever he contacted her, because that was how he saw her. She didn't want him to come near her at all.

Ray's place perched like a bird's nest high above Honolulu, nestled between two steep mountain ridges. It was quite a special place at the very back of a valley, sided by high ridges of mango, jack, bamboo, *kukui*, many types of trees in what seemed like hundreds of hues of green. Misted by clouds like a Chinese brush painting, it was borne on spiritual air. It made her want desperately to become his welcomed guest. It felt like the right place to heal, explore and meditate, like a hidden and remote monastery, inviting and quiet in its pleasant obscurity.

As she intuited, the evening brought long, soft, never-ending kisses from Ray. He came into his kitchen where Lucky sat on a barstool. Chicken breasts were lined neatly on a baking sheet on the counter; rice steamed on the stove. Several guests Lucky hadn't met yet were sitting on the deck overlooking Honolulu drinking cold beer and laughing.

"Some white wine?" he offered. She didn't answer; she didn't seem to hear. He had come from the shower, still wet. She was bowled over by his partial nakedness, by his invitation to be at his home, by being there at all.

"I'm sorry, Ray," she laughed. "Anything. I'm feeling slightly distracted." He stood facing her, towel wrapped around his loins, legs spread apart in a broad stance, his wet hair slicked down. She absorbed his maleness, forgetting the children and the guests outside, letting the two of them experience a rarefied moment together in that room.

He told her he had never imagined kissing her. She blurted without thinking, "Oh, my God. I'm insulted."

"No, no, it's that. I like all of you so much, your family. I think you are very attractive people. It never occurred to me I'd be kissing you tonight."

He was smaller, slighter than she had imagined. His hair was as baby soft as his skin. She caressed his hair and face with gentle fingers. His mouth was the most beautiful she had ever seen, his smile, relaxed, sweet, and unpretentious. He had a long neck, and his shoulders sloped downward smoothly like a snake's instead of paralleling the ground. His body was very beautiful. She thought of Bullet's body that was heavier, stronger and more forceful.

After everyone had left, Ray and Lucky stood kissing in the misty rain. Lucky's opened truck door also stood as a stiff wedge between them. The kisses were sweet. Lucky waited breathlessly for him to take her back into his house to his bed, but he did not. Married for so many years led her to respond to his simple kiss as the green light to make love. His step-by-step action took her aback; it was a little like high school. Sensing this coolness, though overheated by the kisses, she stopped.

"Goodnight," she said and flopped into her car seat. Then, she had to admit, "I can't drive yet." Her strength came half-heartedly back. They talked. The kissing began again. She lost a pearl earring somewhere on his driveway.

Bullet would never let a lady wait to make love. As their youthful winter's train pulled into the French/Italian border at Ventimiglia for a customs check before going on to the Italian Riviera, the conductor had announced a train strike. All passengers had to de-board the train, as there would be no train travel in Italy that day or perhaps for many days to come.

In the January cold of 1967, suitcases, museum mementoes, and passports in mittened hands, they had searched the tiny gray train stop for a hotel. Bullet had decided to see Rome with her. Together, they found the only hotel. The proprietor told them there was only one room left due to so many stranded travelers. There was a bathroom, but it was down the hall to be shared with everyone else.

Before agreeing to stay, Lucky went upstairs to inspect the room. Bully followed. It had a huge double feather bed, piled high with white comforters. A small daybed stood next to the wall by the door. She looked at Bully to see if the arrangement would be acceptable. He had that moral, platonic student look on his face.

"You can have the big bed," he said politely. They took the room.

Lucky was wakened in the morning by the tapping of Bully's stretched fingers on her shoulders. He was reaching as far as he could from his bed to hers.

"Can I come over there?" he asked.

"No. You can't."

"Why not? I'm not comfortable in this *itty bitty* bed."

"Too bad."

Not getting the response he wanted from Lucky, he added, "I'm cold."

"Go back to sleep," she said.

Suddenly, he pulled hard, digging his fingers into her shoulder, shrinking the distance between their beds. He lunged on top of her and squirreled under the covers, kissing her, his stiffened member ardently seeking the warmth of her crotch.

Lucky rather liked the kiss and succumbed to the intrusion. She hoped manners and her underwear would shield her from uninvited intercourse.

Bully thrust and shoved.

"No," she told him, trying to raise her knees up.

"No," she repeated more forcefully.

"No," she yelled as she squeezed her hands under his shoulders and pushed up as hard as she could. His mouth covered hers, muffling her protests.

He panted sugary, "Come on, come on, come on..."s trying to lick her "No's" away. She continued to protest. He held her hands tightly by the wrists and caressed each palm. His semen-frosted member, like a knowing third hand, edged her panties aside. Adroitly, it slipped itself in like a soft-spoken captain on the battlefield of rape.

35

IN HEAT

A child cried from a passing car, "Hello, doggie" as Lucky walked Hula Girl in sunny morning light to the park, reminding Lucky of when she interacted with all animals, birds, and plants as a child. *When did I cease? When did I forget that affinity?* Rarely did sane adults talk to the plants, trees, and rocks. Now Lucky looked for faces on orchids, love on beams of light.

She packed pots all morning for shipping to neighbor island galleries, fielded phone calls, stopped to see Ray in his parking lot en route to UPS. Ray didn't let her come up to his office for fear people would gossip, claiming to be protective of her.

"One of us has to be mature. One of us has to be responsible," he said. "And, I want to look out for you."

They flirted, eating melon on the shipping dock at noon, discussing canoe racing from Maui, reconfiguring his house plans, deep aquamarine water below their dangling feet. Boyish Ray, his shirt slightly opened at the collar, girlish Lucky in ponytail, white ruffled cowgirl shirt, all ninety-six pounds of her in Ande's borrowed jeans.

Her girls loved stories of her romance. They were disbelieving at first, hearing Lucky say, as they got into separate cars one morning to go to school, "Kissy, Kissy, Yim, Yam, Yum," which was family code for 'getting some.'

Ande and Marianna looked at each other in astonishment, whooped, "AAAAAyyyyyyhhhlllllllllaaaaaaa," and slapped their hands together in a high five. Everyone felt loose. Spring was in the air with family whipped cream fights and wrestling matches. The four Pulaskis emerged from the dark and turbulent winter.

Lucky never wanted to look back.

Nico asked, "Hey, Mom, why doncha marry Ray? I'd like Ray for my dad."

At a friend's wedding on the other side of the island, she envisioned herself being married, toasted and roasted. Her children needed a man, a pace setter, pal, disciplinarian. She needed a man, a mate, a friend.

Ray was kinder than she remembered people could be. Maybe she needed that kindness so much that she brought it out in him. He lived with grace. His home was neat and organized. His architectural project was well planned. Ray was also respectful of Hawai'ian traditions, artifacts, places, and people.

"I think you're a wonderful, whole human being and possibly the kindest man I've ever met."

"Thanks. I feel under-educated. I never went on to graduate or business school. I had to help my dad. I'm getting a late start now," Ray responded. "I have a lot of regrets over the way I've handled his business. What I really want to do in life is become an interior designer. Not a faggy one," he quipped, "but a good one. I'm also starting a landscaping business, and

I've signed up for a night accounting class. I see you, Lucky, on a level above me, intellectually. We're different, very different."

This remark triggered terror in Lucky, reminding her of Bullet's parting refrain: "We're different, Lucky, very different."

She and Ray walked arms around waists, her fingers probing the skin beneath his shirt, through the tropical forest toward a neighbor's house further up the ravine, as Kula, his golden retriever, forged ahead. They stopped for long embraces. They walked in rhythm. Sporadic rain wet their hair and shoulders. Taking shelter in his tractor shed, they looked at the farm equipment and talked about landscaping and mondo grass and buckets for glazes. Long-standing kisses melted her. Feeling his height, his slimness, and the fineness of their bodies held together, Lucky almost swooned.

Ray's dark hair was tousled; he wore a white sweatshirt, his eyes were brown and his face was tan, even in the moon's light. He had biker's narrow, lean hips and a tiny, flat butt. They stared long into each other's eyes, warm smiles gently lifting their mouths. The two of them were perched on that rare plateau of his like night herons, nestled between the ridges, the wind passing, Honolulu half asleep below.

"I'm enjoying this process of getting to know you," Ray murmured. "I want to make love to you, Lucky, for hours."

"Oh, Ray, yes. I want you to enter my life. I would like so much for you to make love to me."

"Not now, though," he said. "I won't sleep with you, Lucky, make love with you, until you are legally free and settled. I want you to be able to say with integrity, 'I've done nothing wrong and been only the good wife.'" Her hope slipped a beat, chastised.

"Don't get me wrong," he continued. "I'd like to make love to you for hours and hours, but when the time is right. I don't want to be a wedge that Bullet can use against you. One of us has to be mature here, and I want to take care of you and protect you."

The erection beneath his khakis pulled them taut and cleanly molded into the space between her clothed legs. The knowledge it was there, full and hardened, wanting her, calmed her, gave her courage for a future night and took the edge off the immediacy of her famine. To find love again, to embark upon the whole discovery process of loving another, to be given a second, and possibly better, chance at life was an unexpected delight. *Oh, this man.*

She sat at his deck picnic table in the rainy darkness, happy and downcast simultaneously, appreciating his concern, humbled by her hot loins carrying her too far again, fearful she might be pressuring him, sensing he hated pressure, this man who moved in his own time to his own rhythm. The heavy weight between her legs, like a plaster cast dragging at her for the past ten days, changed to a bearable ache, reminding her of his concern.

Thanks for pulling me from the wreckage of my life, for being my savior. Like a phoenix, she was rising reborn from the ashes of destruction. She experienced an air of unreality like a prisoner must have upon being released from his cell, the regimentation and prison ordeal ended, unable at first to believe he was truly free, free to live as he chose. That sense of unreality manifested, because her two-week-old love story was as illusory as a romance novel from the grocery checkout rack. The unbelievable part was that she was cast as the beautiful heroine, the newly beloved. She felt more like the voyeur, the moviegoer or reader, watching the scenes unfold, rather than the main character acting them out.

"Lucky," Ray asked, "would you be willing to spend some more time helping with my house? Planning some of the spaces and decorating? I mean, in addition to the tile work I've commissioned you to do in the kitchen and baths?"

"No."

"You wouldn't?"

"Of course not," she teased.

"That means you will?"

"Yes," she laughed.

36

ARRESTED IN NEGATIVE SPACE

She drove home at nearly midnight. She approached the new resort exit and overpass, driving in the fast lane, truck set on cruise control at fifty-five miles per hour. A car was parked in front of the overpass buttresses in the median area facing her, which she thought odd, a big blousy old American make, bronze or rusty gold with its lights off. It suddenly lurched forward straight at her. She jammed her brakes and moved to the right lane.

The bronze car fishtailed onto the highway into a screeching "U" turn. Its headlights came on. Speeding up, it pulled behind her. The driver of the bronze car initiated a game of cat and mouse. If she slowed, he slowed. If she changed lanes, he passed only to slow in front of her. This stretch of freeway was pitch-black and devoid of cars. After five or six miles of this ridiculous game, looking in her rear view mirror, she saw blue police lights flickering. She was uncertain if the car behind her was the game player or the driver of a bona fide police car.

Afraid, she proceeded cautiously into Nanakuli, looking for a shoulder lane or a safe spot to stop. She didn't want to stop in the dark. Maybe the *Circle K*, she thought, or, maybe even the police station in Wai'anae eight miles further.

At the Haleakala Avenue intersection, a roadblock had been set up. As she stopped for it, three police officers charged toward her.

"We're uniformed officers of the police," they yelled, waving flashlights. "Get out of your car."

Lucky rolled down her window.

"Hi. What's going on?"

"Get out of the car. We set this road block up to catch you."

"Me?" she asked, bewildered.

"Have you been drinking?" the cop screamed. "I think you've been drinking."

"No, I have not been drinking. I'm trying to get home to my children."

"Oh," said the officer, "you left children alone at home, and you're out on the freeway? That's child-neglect, lady."

She replied, "My children are not small, and they are not alone."

"What were you doing in town? Why are you out so late at night?"

"Working."

"Oh, you work?" the cop sneered.

"Yes. I'm an artist, and I had a show opening." She didn't need to explain herself, but she decided to use a soft touch with the local police. "A car has been tailing me on the highway freaking me out."

The old *cat and mouse* bronze car pulled up with a blue police light askew on its roof. A tall man jumped out of it, buckling his belt and tucking his shirt in.

"I'm arresting you," he shouted running toward her. "You're under arrest."

"That's the nut who was tailing me," Lucky said. *He must have stopped to dress and pretend he was on duty.* The officer, who accused her of drinking, ordered her to get out of the car. She released her safety belt, opened the door and stood in the center of the blocked highway.

"I'm very sorry for any trouble. I hope you understand that I was too scared to stop out there in the dark."

"Get over there," the officer gestured for her to move a short distance toward the back of her truck.

"Take off your rings." She was wearing an opal on the left hand and a jade on the right.

"Pull the sleeves of your jacket down to the wrists, so the cuffs won't hurt." Stunned, she didn't resist the handcuffs.

"We're gonna strip search you."

"What?" she gasped. "Are you serious? Out here on the highway? Why? What have I done?"

Another officer interrupted, asking to see her driver's license. With hands cuffed, she awkwardly crawled into the truck cab, got her wallet and handed it to him. The other officer deposited her rings into the change part of her wallet.

"I want to see your no-fault card."

Still handcuffed, she crawled across the front seat to reach the glove compartment. She could feel their eyes on her buttocks and got the sickening sense she was their evening's entertainment. She retrieved her package containing the no-fault card. The officer removed it.

"Put the package back in the car," he ordered. She complied and felt their eyes follow her backside again.

"Would you please listen to me?" she asked when she stood back on the pavement. "That man," she pointed to the half dressed police officer, "scared me. I was a witness in that terrible Pearl City case. You know, that seventeen-year-old girl who got abducted, raped, and murdered from the bus stop there? The girl got into a fake police car, remember? I spent four hours down at the Wai'anae police station with Crime-Stoppers rendering descriptions of the assailant and his vehicle. The roads aren't safe for single women drivers. Especially at night. You know that. The papers tell us that."

"Tell it to the judge, lady. You are under arrest. We're taking you to the station."

"What reason do you have to arrest me?" No one answered. "What about my truck?"

"It stays here."

"But, how will I get it home? Can't I drive it to the police station?"

"Negative." An officer drove her truck with its parking brake still engaged off the highway, leaving it in the heart of vandals' paradise.

The officer who had handcuffed her, a short, stocky, youthful Asian Filipino, put her in the back seat of the official police car. She was old enough to be his mother. There was no safety belt. He followed another police car from Haleakala Avenue to the Wai'anae police station, possibly eight miles, speeding at sixty-five miles per hour in zones clearly marked twenty-five to thirty-five. Her driver actually went the distance in the center lane, cutting into on-coming traffic, sliding Lucky across the cheap vinyl seat, jarring his criminal baggage dangerously close to a bruised and untimely death.

Siren still screaming in a grand finale, he cut off an oncoming motorist when he jerked left into the station's parking lot and burned rubber acridly in a sudden halt.

He opened the car door and pushed her roughly into the station where five male officers loitered. She recognized one as a jogging partner of a detective friend who passed her house every morning. But he didn't acknowledge her when she said, "Hello" at the station. Her driver unlocked the handcuffs.

"Go to the back room," he ordered. Lucky hesitated. The driver took her by the elbow down a long, darkened corridor to an empty room and closed a heavy door behind them. Only the two of them were in the room.

"Strip," he commanded.

"What?"

"Strip everything off. We're gonna strip search you."

"What for?"

"Procedure," he replied.

"What procedure? I want to talk to your commanding officer."

"After this procedure."

"No. Now."

She walked bravely toward the door. He blocked the way, grabbing her. She put up her arms, elbows bent, hands palm out between face and shoulder area, defensively.

"Don't you touch me," she ordered coldly, deadly serious.

The half-dressed arresting officer entered at that moment. The two officers eyed each other and mouthed police jargon. The closed air in the room filled with their sexual aggression.

"The prisoner will not cooperate."

"Would you please explain your 'procedure' to me?" Lucky asked, sitting down, feeling safer in a chair.

"We're going to book you."

"What does that mean?" Silence. "What have I done? I don't even know why you are holding me. I haven't broken a law."

The driver sat down in front of the typewriter.

"Don't I get a phone call? Can't I talk to someone before you start all this paper-work?"

"No. You get one phone call, after this procedure. Put your hands on the table. Remove your rings."

"You removed them out on the highway, remember?"

"Take off your jewelry then. Take off your earrings." She did so, slowly, and laid them on the table. "Take off your necklace."

"I cannot release the clasp."

The arresting officer pulled up her hair and yanked on the necklace, a gold chain. Lucky grabbed at her throat.

"Hey. What is the point here? Why do I have to take off my necklace? Don't I post bail and go home? You're not keeping me here." The officer who was typing appeared to think for a moment.

"Oh. You're gonna post bail?"

"Well, sure. Isn't that the proper 'procedure'?"

The arresting officer walked out. The driver at the type-writer gathered her earrings into her wallet.

"They might get broken," she warned. "Would you please put them in my makeup bag?"

He counted her money and small change, filled out a white personal effects form, and asked her to sign it. He saw her watch and asked her to remove it. She laid it on the table. He typed out the trivia at taxpayer's expense in triplicate: name, address, education. The arresting officer returned, sat on the table and ogled her.

"Bail," he smirked, "is set at seventy-five dollars: twenty-five for failing to stop for a police officer and fifty for speeding." She had not been speeding, but she was not about to argue.

"May I have my wallet to write a check?"

"No. Cash only."

"I have twenty-five in cash in my wallet. Could you hold that, and I'll leave my credit cards, go home, get the other fifty and bring it back to the station?"

"No. You have to have cash."

"It's now one o'clock in the morning. No place is open. To get cash means I'll have to wake my children to borrow from their piggy banks or stay here until morning."

"That's your problem, lady."

"When do I get my phone call?"

"Here," he pushed a telephone toward her, then dialed her house himself, noting down her number on a separate scrap of paper.

"Marianna," she whispered, embarrassed when her daughter picked up. "Mom's in trouble. I've been arrested, and I'm down at the Wai'anae police station. I need you to go into my money or Ande's and bring fifty dollars for bail money, right now. Can you please do that?"

"Okay. Yeah, Mom. See ya."

Lucky noted that the arresting officer's name was Jimenez. He had a pink plastic piggy attached to a pencil in his shirt pocket. He was Filipino with possibly some Chinese, unusually tall, over six two, thin stiletto mustache, exceedingly large hands, absolutely dead eyes. Jimenez put on surgical gloves and inked a surface.

"Come here. I'm gonna take your prints."

Lucky had thought her ordeal was over.

"Why?"

"Because failing to stop for me is a felony."

Pig, she thought for all the good it did her.

"I have to get your prints."

"When did you decide to arrest me?"

"I knew I was going to arrest you the minute you didn't pull over."

"But why, after you saw me? I mean I'm only a small woman, alone."

He tries to waylay women driving alone at night, and even now he's jacked up on testosterone.

"You had a radio," she continued. "You could have found out if I was dangerous, if the car was stolen, whatever you stop people for. You know I wasn't speeding. I told you that I was too scared to stop out in the dark. So, why have you arrested me?"

He proceeded with the inking. *Oinking?* She wanted to kill him. Lucky was stressed: the confusion created when the mind overrode the body's basic desire to choke the living shit out of an asshole who desperately deserved it.

"Relax, just relax, relax your fingers, look away, sometimes that helps." He took four sets of prints, cleaned her fingers, and seated her in a chair to take a frontal mug shot.

"Look straight into the camera." Click. "Sit back in the chair." Click." A side view." Click.

"What happens now?"

"You get a court date."

"What happens then?"

"You appear in court."

"What happens to my bail money?"

"If the judge lets you off, you get it back."

"What about my 'record'?"

"You can get it expunged."

"What does that mean?"

"It means it gets erased."

"You mean, all these prints and photos get destroyed, and I do not have any trace of a criminal record?"

His *grunt* indicated *yes*. She followed him to the front desk where the officer filled out more paper work.

Lucky asked, "Who is the officer in charge?"

"Him, Sergeant Furokawa." *Not Major's old nemesis at a time like this,* she thought. She waited while the sergeant finished whatever he was doing. He handed her two white bail slips.

"Sergeant Furokawa, how do you do? I'm Emily Pulaski."

"Yeah. You're the *ha'ole* with the donkey."

"I would like to say something to you. I think my arrest was unnecessary. Officer Jimenez didn't take into account that I was simply a woman driving alone at night, not some armed, dangerous, or drugged-out felon."

"You can tell that to the court, Ma'am. I think your daughter is here. You'd better go."

Lucky had a hard time sleeping.

She suspected that the arresting officer had not been on duty at all when he terrified her with his aberrant behavior, driving his car with its headlights off, no identifying blue light, pulling a "U" turn on the freeway in front of her. *What if he had followed Marianna?* She hated to think what might have happened to a naive young girl. Or, what routinely must happen to women less articulate or affluent than she.

Monday she was depressed, felt violated, and wondered if she'd been punished for spending time with Ray, the sensuousness of their Sunday night arrested by the terrible ordeal with the police. Wednesday she retained a criminal lawyer, who prepared her defense strategy and a possible civil suit against the city for police misconduct.

She joked in a pidgin note to Ray:

To Sergeant Medeiros from Your Lucky Prisoner:

> *Evah since dat night at da police station, I keep tin-kin' a you. When you called, it wuz so nice. Den I knew you was tinkin' a me, too.*

> *Do you got any da kine empty cells where I could stay for lil' while? Bread and water is okay wid me. Someday I like try your portagee bean soup....*

She met Ray for lunch by the waterfront near the *Oceania Floating Restaurant.* He brought Irish Cream coffees from the Coffee Works, a Greek salad full of marinated mushrooms and Kalamata black olives, and *ahi* tuna sandwiches. Eating under a *hau* tree, they spoke of the monthly patterns he designed for surf shorts. His designs for May were sailing canoes, a woman with tray of fruits on her head, catches of fish, and *kapa.*

He mentioned he wanted to add Japanese flavor to his house. She loaned him her bamboo catalogs from Kyoto. Memories flooded of Bullet not even looking at the catalogs or photos after her trip, showing no interest in what had excited her. She'd never shared her Kyoto experience with anyone. Suddenly, Ray said the word, and it came alive for her again: how she wanted to make a bamboo garden gate into a bed frame, for instance, loving the designs and materials, bamboo and black string.

Ray left her with another bouquet of gardenias tied in a green ti leaf. At night its fragrance intoxicated her as it wafted across the dining table, exuding a sultriness from its thick, white, lusciously white petals, pure yet seductive. She loved these tropical gardenias with a scent that swung into her nostrils, causing them to flare and distend in vibrant anticipation of love. She could have come over that fragrance, Ray forever twined with gardenias in her senses.

Thursday he arrived for coffee at the gallery. He touched Lucky's black silk stockings on the ankle just above her red suede heels.

"Oh Ray, Ray, Ray, you make me laugh."

Ray played Sergeant Medeiros: "Eh, sistah, you rattle my cage."

"Ray, you know, your new house needs to be plumbed for a bidet or, at least, a hand-held shower for your female guests."

"What about one squirt gun?" he suggested. "All need is one hook. Straight shootah, you know."

"Like one *mastah blastah*?"

Lucky laughed so hard she had to reshape her face muscles by hand in order to talk. What a relief, what a joy to laugh and be silly again. She was reminded of days in Spain falling in love with Bullet, looking for the breakfast *rosquillas*, sugar donuts, sold in carts, or playing gin rummy in Italy when all they did was laugh.

She was free falling, letting go, not knowing where, how, or when she'd land. When she anticipated seeing him or hearing from him, her stomach dropped ahead of her about fifty feet down some elevator shaft, her body descending behind it. *Alice* down the rabbit hole, "I'm faaaalllllliiinnnnggg."

She thought she didn't want to be "swept away" by some man or love affair. She was forging a different trail for her life, her career, and her spirituality. She did not want to get sidetracked or lost, sliding blindly into another downhill relationship. But, when with this man, she was excited, intrigued, fascinated. He was never the same: often boyish, but when manly, mysterious.

A week after vascular surgery for varicose veins in her legs, she went to Ray's office to pick up fabric to cover her old rattan chairs. Lucky updated him on her police case. At home, she cut cushions from old pads stored in rafters, which she spied while drinking morning coffee sitting on the deck stairs. She finished wrapping the cane chairs with rush and decided to stain them with *Watco* Danish.

Lucky worked in her studio after days of procrastinating. She wanted to create a series wherein there was a "ray." The feeling for the entire series was to be light: shafts, rays, beams; the colors: yellows, golds, corals, crimsons, white. This was very different work for her. She made seven forms, all non-functional. Her practical mind clicked in: *Will they sell? Don't put too much effort into something that won't sell.* Not sure if she liked them or if they worked, but she did manage to execute the ideas that had been formulating in her mind.

She abandoned handles and lids. She created doorways, windows, entries and passages. Empty spaces interested her, devoid of clay. She made a clay form, removed some clay to detour the eye to see the void, the emptiness, the hollow. She let the eye focus on emptiness. And, therein she discovered something new: Negative Space.

She thought of it as space where experience had savaged a section of the heart, chewed and spit it out, leaving a pit where the living flesh once was. *The wounded walked naked, like sponges, holes apparent like mine, riddled by the caustic acid of experience.*

The space carved out also became an invitation, hinting of an entry or passage, a glimpse of new realms to be explored; perhaps promises, perhaps shadows. She thought she'd change her pottery to whites and high-fires, small forms of delicacy and simplicity. Although she loved her medium, raku's, wildness, she had wearied of the blackness and impracticality.

It was almost eleven at night. No call from Ray who canoe sailed the next day from Maui to O'ahu. She didn't know what to do. She had been hoping to sleep over at his house. Without a call she didn't feel comfortable going into town with such an expectation. She entertained the idea of putting the newly refurbished chairs on his deck as a surprise. She also thought of picking up salmon steaks, potatoes, and greens to make a nice, simple dinner. But, she had to pull back, do her clay, not push ahead.

Her period coming on made her blue. *Oh please, don't let me be hurt by Mr. Hope, not hurt again.* She trotted Hula Girl to the Maili end of the beach where the sunset held its own bit of melancholia. Broiled embers seemed to pierce the sky. She sat on an ivory slab of coral. The water caught her attention.

The tide pools were perfectly calm, mirroring the reddened sky. Every so often a wave *whooshed* under the reef. Directly in front, the blowhole corresponded by spewing a geyser of water close to her face; camera-like, it forced a close-up shot of perfectly focused and separated water drops.

At the edge of the sea, the water looked ruffled. Tiny waves, hundreds of them, looked like the wind was making the water laugh and show its dimples. The sky, too, soon was affected by the wind where fashionable clouds in barbershop cuts strutted sporting hues of hot pink and purpled magenta.

The sun, golden yellow and peach, pink and coral and red, warmly outstretched its rays. The sun, the soul of the sunset, bearer of light, that distant orb, that fiery circle, was the source of energy, of turning and beginnings. Did the water beneath the sun's ingested light have a like soul of its own? Wet and dark, endless, beginningless, the ocean: where lay its source, she wondered. Was it a drowned soul, perhaps? Or, not one, but countless, submerged souls adrift beneath the tide circling a homeless earth?

Ray brought her a phonograph. She had a hard time fathoming someone liking her enough to bring a gift. She had re-done the two chairs in rush, silk, and suede and had given them to him. It had felt natural. Now Ray had gifted her, teaching her to receive.

Early morning around six she watered front and back yards, washing the studio and carport down. Then, she mowed lawns after Nico and Ben raked the leaves. Next, she rearranged furniture and pottery. She dusted and wiped everything down, arranged Ray's beautiful pink and lime heliconias, "sexy pinks" from Maui and orange birds of paradise from Manoa, elegantly in her tall blue raku floor vase in the living room.

At Fujimura's, she bought ingredients for cannelloni and cooked all afternoon: eggplant relish, chicken cannelloni, Manoa lettuce with arugula salad, mango ice cream, espresso with lemon peel. She even let Ande and Marianna drink a share of *Mouton Cadet* Bordeaux at dinner as they teased Ray.

"It's a good thing you're here for dinner," Marianna said, "otherwise, we'd starve. My mom only cooks for men."

He enjoyed the meal, offered to do the dishes several times, and was so charming Lucky almost forgot to show him the "Ray Series" drying in the studio.

He liked the series but commented that the rays on the edges looked like barbed wire. He suggested some softer angles and ridges, something more refined. They talked a long time about matching kitchen sink colors for his house, the green beam-warpage, and his dissatisfaction with the contractor.

Passion burned behind his eyes with fresh memory of the previous night when she had lain across his bed. Lucky liked to wear teddies, little peach silky things. He had placed a large pottery bowl filled with at least twenty gardenias on the table near her head, handed her a chilled glass of white wine and a coconut frond basket of blue corn chips. *Kitaro* played on his tape deck. Everything felt very special. "Very special" were Ray's favorite words for people and places. She remembered the slight pain in pleasure, new for her, when he had twirled her nipples. His passionate glint excited her, making the pit of her stomach fall. Her vagina, in a constant state of arousal, pulsed with involuntary contractions, wanting to hold him inside. She had entered a phase of slow burning, intensifying desire, not quite the unendurable heat wave she experienced earlier.

A certain darkness, a certain unexplored mystery, lured her to him. He was a different kind of man, a different sensuality, and different masculinity, more subtle, more profound than Bullet's openly macho, direct sexuality. Ray had patience. He waited.

Lucky dreamed of World War I. She was in a French foxhole or trench near Verdun. Pre-dawn. No color, only filtered gray light. It had been raining, and the muddy, denuded ground was very wet and slick. She stood chest deep in the trench, looking toward the German line. Tense. Alert. There were long, countless rows of empty trenches furrowing the ground ahead of her. Battle ready. No one else was there. Suddenly, she realized that she had dug all those trenches in front of her. All by herself. Dug one after the other. She was tired of repeating herself over and over, the only soldier on the battlefield.

There wasn't an enemy. Wearing a metal helmet, she was waging the war alone, digging entrenchments, protecting herself. She woke up laughing.

37

BLOWING HOT AND COLD

Lucky spent most of the night awake in her new lingerie as a born-again virgin in Ray's bed. He was steadfast in refusing to make love. He touched her naked limbs and rubbed her back. He allowed her to caress him, to massage him with oil, to mouth, tongue, and kiss him. He caressed her for long periods of time, bit and sucked her breasts as she moaned with desire. He had an immense, thunderous actually, erection, which never seemed to need release. He wouldn't let himself go. She didn't think her mouth could open wide enough to encompass him. Then he stopped, leaving her on that high plateau untouched, unentered. She felt let down, a little ashamed, and mildly confused.

She was highly conscious of but not embarrassed by her body. She knew she was slim, skinny actually. Her thighs still had cellulite, and her skin was aged by the sun. She survived the thwarted lovemaking without comment. It was disappointing.

She got up in the night and sat on the floor looking out over sleeping Honolulu, wondering if she should go home. He slept, snoring softly.

Shoot. Bullet and she used to make love like crazy, and she thought everything was fine. Maybe she was looking for the ready stud service Bullet used to provide. Perhaps she needed to look again at Ray, at the respect and kindness he offered. Perhaps they were worth a lot more than hot kisses and momentary passion.

I probably should look at my needs and reassess. Otherwise, I may get a repeat of the same old unhappy situation. Patterns were interesting, easy to recognize in her friends' lives; difficult, if not impossible, in her own. She had to talk to herself, had to tell herself that she was worthy of a wonderful man like Ray, had to tell herself it was okay to let good things happen, that she deserved them, since she almost expected rejection.

After doing sit-ups and yoga stretches in the morning, they waited outside for her girls to come. They pulled up in "Pale Rider," and Ray took them all on a hike to the volcanic crater bog four miles up the ridge behind his house.

The forest was full of unusual birds whose songs they heard but could not see. The wind rustled up periodically; *likolehua* stood in stark scarlet silhouette against the morning sky and fast moving clouds. The forest was full of wind noises being hushed by thick carpets of moldering leaves and spongy lime-green mosses, studded with tiny, beige capped toadstools. Strawberry *guava*, stag horn ferns, Australian tree ferns, eucalyptus, mango and *koa* trees lined the narrow trail up the Koolaus. Their legs got badly scraped by the ferns and dingle berry branches. Ande swabbed her calves and knees in mud as they hiked, looking aboriginal. Marianna was in a foul mood, typical of her these days, which embarrassed Lucky.

Alone together at the bog, Ray counseled, "Lucky, you give so much, maybe too much, to your children. Maybe they don't appreciate it or need it. You have your own life, too. You have to live your own life."

"Her anger is driving me nuts, Ray. She breaks all the rules. We're in a nasty power play."

"Marianna has to realize she's part of a family. You can't farm her out to Cherry or to her grandparents. She has to face living with you and following your rules. Kids need to act out."

"I hope you're right. Her anger frightens me."

"When my parents broke up, I was only in the seventh grade. I drove a car through a loading dock wall right into the lower school cafeteria."

"Oh, my god," Lucky gasped with a laugh.

"She'll be okay, Lucky," he reassured. Lucky hiked back silently ruminating on the potency of Marianna's anger.

"The pottery firing at Kualoa is this weekend. You are coming out, aren't you, Ray?" she asked. "The potluck is Saturday and at midnight I'll be firing your *Ray Series*. You can see me in my fire suit," she teased.

"Is it as good as your birthday suit?" he quipped back. "Sounds very special. I have a tent. I might like to come. Hey, did I tell you I'm getting a golden retriever puppy on Sunday? So, Sunday might be out."

Lots of energy from a good night's sleep, her first in many months, enabled Lucky to accomplish chores. She was reviving. She had slept in that beautiful man's bed, where he wanted her to be. He made her feel okay about herself, accepted, helped her live again.

"You must be in love. You are radiating light," observed Cherry.

"Well, maybe. Maybe. Yes, I am getting lighter all the time, glad you notice."

Erlichtda. She felt honeybees buzzing in a halo of light round her head, like a whiff of Tom Robbins' *Jitterbug Perfume.* Lucky flashed on the ticket price in ancient Egypt to enter Heaven where a feather sat on one side of the scale and the heart of the deceased on the other. The goal was to end life with a heart lighter than that feather.

Cherry spent an hour with her, reaffirming blue-edged white light to ward off evil, blue and green light for wisdom and clarity. They also did a reading. The card Lucky pulled blindly from the deck to represent herself was The Sun, represented by a joyful young child astride a white horse with sunflowers and a banner waving triumphantly behind.

"You are to come into great good luck and a change of fortune and prosperity," Cherry predicted.

For her divorce, Lucky pulled The Wheel of Fortune; for the significant other, Bullet, in her love life, she drew the nightmare Nine of Swords card, the same card she had drawn for herself nine months before. Cherry said he, too, was awakening from a guilt-induced nightmare. Cherry pointed out, "Bullet's black energy will drain your sunshine away if you align with him."

The card for Ray was the Two of Swords, which were crossed, and he was blindfolded, upside down. "He's stuck, suffering from an inner conflict. He's unable to break free or make a decision. It's a gray card for a transitional relationship, which may go on for two years. You must be careful not to let your energy be drained away by it, Lucky."

The bright yellow card for her future showed an unknown lover, an arbor above and cups below, a couple in harmonious embrace watching children playing. "This is the true relationship, coming soon. Drawing the card upside down means that individual is working out some confusion in his own life right now, and when it's cleared up, he'll appear. He's dark and under six feet tall. You will experience unbelievable happiness and prosperity in this union. Fear will hold you back from growth and change. The quicker you release fear, the faster you will grow and move toward your destiny," she advised.

Temperance, a healing card, a balancing of life's lessons, was her life card. "Your aura and spirit are strong and lit," Cherry said, gathering the three arcana cards together, The Wheel of Fortune, The Sun, and Temperance.

Lucky picked an animal shaman to protect and guide her again for a period of time. Cherry held it in her hand unturned. "Are you certain that this is the card you want? Are you certain?"

"Yes, yes, it is." Cherry turned it over: it was the Snake again, the snake, protecting Lucky. The first time she had drawn it in the fall, it had frightened her. The viper was cold, poisonous. She had grown to respect it as a deadly protector, grateful for its strength, protecting her young. Like the snake, she had shed her skin and been reborn. Drawing it a second time, she laughed. Okay, she acknowledged she still needed protection.

Ray arrived at Kualoa after four to see the pottery firings. Heather and Cherry knocked their knees together, exhaled breath, and hand motioned blow jobs in approval of him, all giggles and excited huzzahs.

"He was my neighbor when I lived in Kahala fifteen years ago," Heather exclaimed in surprised recognition. "He was single, a surfer and gorgeous."

"Lucky," Ray said to her quietly after being introduced around, "I have another commitment and cannot stay. I came out to tell you myself."

Oh Ray, how can you? I made this series for you. How many people get art made for them? And, you're not staying to see it fired? She was silent and stoic. She walked him to his truck, not wanting him to go.

"I brought this for you." He handed her yellow ginger, wrapped in ti, warm from the parked cab's heat in the afternoon sun. Fragrance, as always, knocked her out. She would never again inhale gardenia blossoms' cool lush succulence or the tropical fragrance of these ginger without thinking of him. They looked a long, shimmering time into each other's eyes.

"Lucky, you look so sad." Her eyes brimmed as she kissed him where he sat in his green pickup.

"I wanted you to be here with me tonight."

"There will be other times to fire and glaze," he rationalized. She knew there would not. He backed out.

The Koolaus loomed behind his retreat in rugged sheerness. Kualoa beckoned her on the other side with blue calm. Lucky pulled down her dark glasses and rested on a hillock near the parking lot to gather herself while her kids played touch football. *No strings. No ties. No obligations. No expectations.* She vowed to never plan times together. She hated to be sad from unmet expectations. Then, she laid on a mat in the privacy of her purple tent and let down disappointed tears.

She found a free kiln and fired from midnight to three a.m. Afterward, she took a pre-dawn walk. At the land end of the beach, a pit smoldered. She headed toward the embers and, in the shadows, saw a figure. Heather's buddy from Maui, Teddy Bear Ha sat by his fire, Kaneohe's lights in the distance, glimmering orange across the blackened bay. She sat down next to him where they whispered secrets, histories, and longings into the night air.

"I talk better when I'm working with my hands," he said shyly. "Would you like a foot massage?"

"Sure." She shifted her weight on the sand as she pulled off her high-topped *Reeboks*.

"I love clay for shaping and expressing, and I love massage for healing and knowing," he told her. His hands felt sure, gentle, and strong, filling her with relaxing warmth. He spoke of his infant daughter's recent death from liver disease, of the gift she had given him of unconditional love. His heartache, his life turning gray, then colorless upon her death and his divorce from her mother.

In his dream one night, his dead child's eyes glowed iridescent, and her skin ruffled like owl's feathers. A woman, nurse or angel, came to smooth her feathers and take her away, perhaps back to God.

Working their magic, his hands traveled from Lucky's legs to her back. He told her to let her mind go, to listen to her body while he loosened her muscles. "Work on letting go and you will find your authentic self."

When Teddy touched points for her lungs: the scapula, the sternum, shoulders, front and back, memories ambushed her. The kitchen of her childhood at Edna and Jack's house appeared with its yellow counter tiles, curling red linoleum table tops, ancient Westinghouse fridge in constant need of defrosting; the counter covered in layers of newspaper with the day's garbage pyramided on top where it stewed above the silver drawer, beneath the cupboard of dishes: a unique garbage sandwich of Edna's making.

Lucky saw black edges around the room, around all the rooms of that house, black edges of grief, of night, of darkness. Suddenly, she saw each room of the house as a torture chamber. The kitchen, where the *Hershey* bars were stored above the broom closet filled with paddles for meting out punishment. The kitchen, where cream of turkey or cream of celery were cooked *ad nauseam* and spooned onto toasted white *Wonder* bread pulled from its balloon bedecked plastic wrapper and thrust onto the children's plates. The kitchen, where her parents fought, where her mother slapped Emily across the face for refusing to eat one of Edna's leftover dishes. She caught Emily's cheek, ripping it open with her diamond wedding ring. The office, where the rocking chair sat, an object of comfort, but used before dinner when Jack got home and Edna filled him in on the children's wrong doings for the day. A rocking chair for whippings. The storeroom with its freezer full of used milk cartons stuffed with duck or quail along with several five-gallon brown ice cream cartons of Jack's favorite, maple nut. The storeroom was also stacked with discarded 2x4's, which Jack used. He liked to beat his daughters on their bared bottoms, if the standard whipping hadn't been enough. Emily's bedroom, later Linney and Jackie's, with the bunk beds where she had received unchaste kisses and reams of guilt for her childish sins. Her middle-school bedroom where she had sobbed into its lavender plastered walls while her parents fought. The middle-school bedroom where she tried to maintain her self-esteem when Edna or Nana had coerced her to wear dresses too sheer for decency for Easter or some other occasion, which humiliated her pre-pubescent self. The covered *lanai* where she heard, oh, how she wished she'd never heard, Laura's shame, the secret story of their father's penetration.

Loss of innocence, loss of sweetness, loss of childhood. She wanted to scream. She wanted to scream and scream and scream. She wanted to go back to the time she looked at comic books and loved the images before learning to read had ruined that joy, lost it forever. She remembered the dark green living room with its red sofa, a room where so much pathetic furniture was battered further during parental fights. It was her nightmare house where there had not been one safe room.

Lucky had a vision during the massage. Her lungs were holding Bullet. He leapt out of her left lung tiny and adult and naked except for a red satin devil's cloak, his feet swathed in flames. Bullet, the root of her pain. And, then came their wedding day, sunny and lovely, Lucky sporting a pert pixie haircut and ivory linen, ducking through the redwoods, smiling. But, it wasn't she, it wasn't the true Emily, for the authentic Emily hadn't wanted to marry. Her wedding day had begun many years of trying to please others, the Pulaskis in particular.

Oh dear. Wrong turns. She had taken too many wrong turns on the road map of her life.

Less than two-year-old Ande appeared in Lucky's reverie, curling blonde hair and chubby *opu* stuffed into a blue and white striped bathing suit, Marianna somewhere behind her but blurry. Ande, the reason Lucky had stayed married after learning of Bullet's betrayal with Lei. Lucky forced herself to stay in a lie of a marriage, so her little girls would have a daddy.

Arms around each other's waists, the massage over, Lucky and Teddy walked back to her firing area and took out the cooled pots, her rays. They joined Heather and Cherry, to polish off an immense bottle of sake in the dawn, loosely discussing art and pots. They laughed hysterically when Heather posed as a statue, covering her privates with gardenia leaves, proclaiming, "I am a statue of the god of love, known to the ancients as Ray Dope." Ray *Dope*? Lucky peed her pants racing Heather through the park, laughing hysterically, to the rest rooms as the other campers rose, greeted the morning, and brushed their teeth.

She took what felt like an hour-long pee and laughed at herself.

She asked Heather in the adjacent stall, "Are you entering any of your pots for jurying?"

"Good God, no. It's bad enough to be rejected by men. I don't want my pots rejected, too." Heather was unsure if love would ever come her way. She said, "You know, Lucky, I have recurrent sensations of drowning. There is no life preserver in sight. I'm just bobbing for air and drowning."

Lucky prepared a *poi* supper for her book club discussion of *Change We Must*. On square monkey pod plates lined with freshly cut banana leaves, she placed chicken long rice and *aku limu poke*. A huge hand-carved pig board was piled with *kalua* pig from the imu and steamed *laulau* wrapped in ti. Pink protea and red ginger graced the table. She worked all day cleaning, cooking, shopping, and organizing, outdoing her usual self in spectacular presentation and preparation.

Cherry said, "What a wonderful book club meeting. I think we should let you do it more often. I like a small group. Thank you so much. And, thank you, too, for all the wonderful things you brought me for my birthday. I entrusted the stone to Joe this weekend, because he's in a fishing tournament. He's actually carrying it in his pocket. When can you and Ray come to dinner? Let me know."

"Why don't you and Joe come to Ray's for a picnic?"

Lucky mentally replayed Ray's caresses, kisses, the length of his erection beneath the denim over and over in her mind as she drove to his place taking the leftover *poi* supper as a picnic. Her body pulsed with rapture on a floating, harmonious, eternal song of desire. Ray had already grabbed a sandwich after the canoe races. He put her food in the fridge. He didn't even ask if she had eaten.

"What about Cherry and Joe?" she asked, already chilled by the windy rain. She asked for a sweater.

"They called that something came up," he said. "Someone, one criminal, tried to rape me," Ray needled. Lucky didn't understand why he was drawing out her humiliation. She felt too vulnerable to take his joking humorously.

"I'm not a criminal. And, I went 'rehab' and 'was completely rehabilitate'," she countered. *What woman wants to be told she's a rapist for desiring a man?*

Doubts beset her: *Is he 'using' me to do his tiles and planning to dump me when the house is done?* His aloofness depressed her. She suspected the snake's cold-bloodedness resided at Ray's core.

At home, Lucky found Marianna distraught.

"Mom, I've messed up big and gotten busted."

"What happened?"

"I wanted to stay in town to goof around with Birdie, Darryl, and some other guys. I called Fujimura's twice and lied to get out of working."

"Oh no. You didn't?"

"Nobody would have found out. But, Dad took Nico, Ben, and Ande to Fujimura's for plate lunch after the surf meet, expecting to see me. But, of course, I wasn't there. Oka, my supervisor, told Dad that I was at a surf meet and had won third place."

"Is that what you told Oka?"

"Yeah, one of the lies. Then Dad had to go and say, 'Marianna wasn't in a surf meet today.'"

"Marianna, you're going to have to apologize to your supervisor," Lucky said, "and hope that you keep your job."

"Can't you call them for me?"

"No," Lucky said.

They bickered over her situation in the garage for about an hour. Marianna abruptly ended the conversation, screaming, "Bitch I hate you," and ran into the house, slamming doors, rattling the glass. Even Hula Girl looked up, alarmed.

"Abrasive, needy little brat," Lucky retorted under her breath, frustrated. *Getting divorced is bad enough, having to deal with teenage lip is worse. Why does it have to be so hard? Why can't it get easier for us, God? Please, please, make things easier. Why has Marianna become so outrageously rude and violent? Where is this streak of anger and meanness coming from?*

Marianna, guilt ridden and humiliated, crept upstairs in the night and sat on the edge of Lucky's bed. Lucky felt her weight and turned over.

"Mom, Mom," Marianna whispered. "I want you to know I'll never lie again." Lucky reached out to touch the small of her daughter's back.

"That's good, sweetheart."

The following Saturday, Nico took first in his heat body boarding at the *T&C* meet in town. He had to return to compete in the finals on Sunday, which was Father's Day. Bullet acted like his normal mega-selfish self, insisting Lucky drive Nico to it, so he could stay home with Rex. Lucky wanted to say, *Well, Rex could care less if he ever sees you.*

Instead she said, "It's Father's Day, and Nico is your son. You take him surfing. You and his grandfather."

"Queenie isn't feeling well. And, Dad needs me over there."

"Well, I have work to do," Lucky protested. "I have to go with Marianna to Fujimura's to be sure she still has a job."

Lucky set up with a tent on Father's Day and spread out lunch. Nico caught three waves in his heat body boarding. Queenie walked across the sand from the parking lot and sat down.

"How are you feeling?" Lucky asked, surprised to see her there.

"Pretty weak, but I thought the sun would do me good. I might not have many more chances to see the children surf."

Bullet showed up. He paddled out on his surfboard to push Nico along. Bullet shoved for the fourth wave, which Nico missed. Nico was crying when he returned to shore. Bullet had upset Nico, by throwing off his concentration telling him what to do out in the water. Nico took last place in the heat and didn't advance.

"Look," Lucky fumed, "Bullet has never won a contest in his life, but look at him telling Nico how to do it. Nico was doing fine all on his own."

Queenie blabbed Lucky's comments to Bullet, who in turn, bullied Nico.

"Nico, did I make you lose? Did I, huh? Speak up, boy." Bullet the Boss, ordered the kids to get up and give Gramma a better seat, one of Lucky's seats, not anything he had thought to bring for his ill mother.

"I never invited you to the beach, Bullet," Lucky shouted. "You told me I had to drive, that you couldn't come. Yet, here you are anyway, here to bother Nico. Shame on you, ordering us around." She wanted to spit blood.

The next two days Bull deliberately invaded Lucky's privacy, residence, and space. He didn't stay confined to the painting studio with his disruptions and *Lord of the Manor* attitude. He watered and raked the yards where he no longer belonged. He didn't belong there. She tried to escape and cool down in the shower. He even interrupted her there, crossing the boundaries of propriety, entering the bathroom, showing no respect.

He yelled into her shower stall, "Hey! About that art supply bill you pinned to my easel: forget trying to get money out of me. And, I won't pay for studio electricity or water, either."

She could not live under these conditions. She thought she'd move back to town, find an apartment or house, get out and start a new life. She had to.

Her lawyer, Thomas Ayck, had been calling Bullet for weeks and finally reached him at Fannie's apartment.

"Lucky and I might be reconciling," Bullet lied to him. "We might not need your services."

"Are you?" Thomas called Lucky to ask.

"No."

"Okay, I wanted to be sure," Thomas said, promising to mail her a copy of the property settlement in the current decree.

"I want Bullet kept away from me."

"I can't keep him away from you, Lucky, without a TRO, unless he threatens you with violence, or there's a history of it. Sorry. The way things are going, let Bullet pop Marianna or you a good one, and he'll go to jail for a long time."

"Great," she said, wondering why she was paying for this 'legal' advice.

All she did was work, talk, think about the divorce proceedings, and long for love. Lucky felt like sands were swirling in confusion up to knee level, obscuring her path. Days and moods swung high or low. She was either anchored or awash. She wanted it over.

꧂

It musta been love
But it's over now
It musta been love
but it's gone like
the water flows
Like the wind blows
Leave your whisper on my pillow
Leave the winter on the floor

Roxette, Theme from *Pretty Woman*

Addicted to Late Night Radio, her breathing stuffed with mucous, she coughed and sputtered. She blew her nose on her studio apron till it was soaked. *Only I care,* she wept, *only me. Keeper, guardian, perpetuator of memories. Of what was. Of what isn't.*

Wine. Beer. Beer. Again. She was drinking. Solitary. Long days and nights in the studio. She didn't call anyone, didn't want repercussions of anyone feeling sorry for her or saying, "Oh, she's been drinking."

Despite the alcohol, she made two magnificent, really magnificent Samurai teapots. She named them *Weeping Samurai*, not because of them but because of her, the artist who was weeping.

She liked working alone and making discoveries as an artist, knowing the discoveries were uniquely hers. Excited, she wobbled around drying work on ware tables in the back studio. Forms a-gogo. *Zabuton* pillows, footed boxes, dragonfly teapots. *Grass Shacks, Samurai Warriors, Secret Rays. Mini Hapi Coat Teas* with landscape feet, tiny *Torii Gate Teas* seated atop mountains of clay rays reaching for the sun.

Working with a new, heavily grogged clay body, she tested, making tiles, wall pieces, and two medium teapots; tested for strength, cracking, warping, and drying. She over-fired a bisque and hoped she could salvage it through glazing. Bumping a large teapot spout for the second time with her head, she finally broke it. *Some things just need breaking*, she admitted.

Lucky looked at her cracked and damaged work from the last bisque. Instead of throwing them on the scrap heap, she decided to use these cracked pots. She titled them *Wounded Warriors* and *Survivors*. She glazed them anew and fired them again. The ware was doubly traumatized by the fire, its suffering forged onto the surface and into the body. Phoenix-like, it rose anew. Though fragmented, she fused broken parts with fiberglass and resin.

She was able to sleep through many nights, staying in bed till seven-thirty, eight, nine a.m., beginning to catch up on sleep and rest, feeling she was "normalizing" after one full year of "traumatizing". From October to May she had been able to sleep only one to two hours before waking. At last, she could sleep, refresh, and restore herself.

"Mom," Ande said, "Dad wants to know where you are. He wants to take you to the movies with us tonight for your wedding anniversary."

Ande was so excited that the soles of her rubber *Convers* squeaked as her heels rose up and down off the floor.

"You go and have fun, darling."

"Come on, Mom. Please."

"Do you even imagine I'd go?" Lucky asked, "or that it would be a treat for me?"

"I guess not," Ande replied, crestfallen.

38

ZIPPED

Lucky followed one of her Little Red Birds. He *chirruped* flitting from side yard to back studio, bananas to sea grape seeming to keep tabs on her all day.

Each night she prayed, *"Infinite Spirit, open the way for great abundance. Make us irresistible magnets for all that belongs to us by divine right."*

"Buddha, Mom," Marianna shouted across the newly mown grass at the waterfall in Nuuanu. Lucky squatted, meditating beneath a *hau* tree out of the rain. She was collecting light and bathed each of the children, Ray, and even Bullet (though she asked his image to recede very quickly) in golden light. She pictured light as a waterfall rinsing over them. Ray was Leonardo's renaissance man, diamond-faceted, white light radiating from him.

Seated in the lotus position, she imagined filling her spinal column with crystals of light, some small, some enormous. All of a sudden, God came over and dumped a full wheelbarrow of them into her. She engorged, bloated, and floated into space, arms and legs outspread with crystal fat, bobbing like some *Macy's* Thanksgiving Day Parade balloon. She contained this overstuffing of light by zipping herself, her body, with a big, wetsuit body glove zipper. Returning to the ground, her size returned to normal with her "secret stuffing" safe inside.

She spent time with Marianna. They took long walks or sat at the dining table, talking about the family, sex, relationships, work, college, and the future.

Darryl, Marianna's first boyfriend, was asleep on a futon downstairs.

"No hanky-panky, my girl," Lucky clearly instructed. "No lying down on the futon together, okay? Darryl gets the futon; you get your room. Understood?"

"It's a deal, Mom. Thanks for letting him sleep over."

Later that night, hearing scuffling sounds, Lucky looked over the landing rail. There they were, lying down together, giggling, making out, entwined on the futon.

Do we speak the same language, she wondered, but said nothing.

Ray and Lucky accepted an invitation from Cherry and Joe to have dinner at *Sergio's Italian Ristorante.* As Lucky dressed, Ray decided he didn't want to go.

"Am I not reading your signals right, Ray? Are you trying to tell me you don't want to go out with me?"

"Don't be crazy, Lucky. I am tired. I'll be having an early morning, setting up a first aid station for the marathon, and I am fighting a cold." She called Cherry and cancelled.

A week later she sat outside *Dances with Wolves* with Ande until four-thirty, sure Ray wouldn't show, sure he'd gone to the

North Shore to surf, sure he'd stand her up, steeling herself against disappointment. He came dashing around the corner, scolding her for not telling him which theatre, lost in Waikiki. She was flung into instant good humor, glad to see him.

Touching him and not being touched, they stood in line for his ticket. Ande and she had bought theirs half-an-hour earlier. Rushing into the theatre as the previews began to find Ande, whose arms were full of popcorn, waiting for them along the darkened aisle. The gunshots in *Dolby* stereo made Lucky jump twenty times. The killings made her cover her eyes, cringing and squirming in her seat. The pratfalls made her laugh; the love scenes made her hot. Throughout the film, Ray never looked her way.

They went for Mexican food. He teased Ande during dinner, hugged her good-bye, totally at ease, and left. In the parking lot, Lucky opened her car door.

Ande said, "So, what, Mom, no kiss?"

"Be quiet, Ande, or I'll cry."

Ray was a young puppy, wet behind the ears. It was one of those days she felt older and wiser, with more layers to her existence and experience. She had baked macadamia-apricot-raisin-oatmeal cookies for him as they planned to meet when she closed the gallery that night. He surprised her by coming to the gallery far too early for their date, dashing their evening plans.

She looked out the window. She wanted to speak, to say, *Ray, love me. Make time for us to be together.* But, she was silent, a lump blocking her words. She sensed he was wary, careful and guarded, like quarry not wanting to be ensnared.

"Felicia called," he said. "She's miserable and regretting her actions. She begged me to come back."

"How do you feel?" Lucky asked, no detectable panic showing in her voice.

"I've lost the feeling I've had for her in my heart. It's sad and hard. It's a really good relationship that went sour. She's in a lot of pain. And, I feel really badly about it. I told her if she came back, we might break up again and what then?"

Their breakup was only four months old. If Ray wanted Felicia back, Lucky would be happy for them and glad for the zest Ray had added to her own life. *But if I get more involved with him, I won't feel like that.*

"Well, I'm sorry, Lucky. I can't make our date," he said. "Next time you're going to be in town, let me know," he added. He was shy, like a deer that would bolt into the forest, if she was too bold, if she moved suddenly or too soon.

"I have to sit the raku show on Friday. I shall be in town then," she said.

"Okay. Let's see about Friday," he said, elusive.

"We seem to have the 'Five minute, Gotta go' relationship," Lucky remarked. He turned to leave.

"By the way," she said, veiling her hurt in smiles and a weak attempt at humor, "here are some cookies and bread from the Wolfeson Bake Shoppe. I brought presents for your dogs in my truck."

"I don't usually go empty-handed," he said, embarrassed, shifting around. She watched him, waiting.

"Well, Ray, you call me when you get your priorities worked out." He sort of shook his head, smiled wanly, and left.

A meanness, a crankiness born of Ray's silence invaded her mood as she checked her watch throughout the day, listening for the phone to ring, aware that one day's loneliness could be erased by the next day's phone call. She was cranky to her kids: shouting, yelling commands, sassy, high strung, over-wrought with tension, trying to second-guess him. *Is he busy? Is Felicia there? Will he return to her? Is he giving me space to clear my divorce?*

Do my work? Are we going too fast? What happened? Did I invade his space? Pressure him? Was I too aggressive? Or, is he stupid?

Ande said Lucky was crazy.

"Mom, you saw him two days ago. It's only two days."

For Lucky, it was an eternity and a broken promise. She felt stood up and let down. She clock watched waiting for his calls, which didn't come. She waited, conscious of each passing moment, until finally the minutes ticked into too late, and she knew the opportunity for that day had ended.

Letting the wind pass through her legs, swaying like a man, she loitered on her deck. Then kissing, French kissing in her kitchen, a poster, a goddamned poster on her refrigerator door, of *Kanaka Clothing*, Ray, Ray's company. So lonely, so desperate, she'd kiss a goddamned poster on the refrigerator door, because it represented the man she desired.

Maybe God spares me from myself on these insecure days. Ray doesn't call, because my wrong attitude might spoil things. But then, if he did call, I wouldn't have a wrong attitude.

He had said in his casual and friendly way, "Come up and meet my puppy." But, there wasn't a "when" attached; she was unwilling to go without a specific invitation. What if he had someone else there? She didn't want to impose on him, she, the accused rapist. She felt sensitive about that. She could not handle the joke. It had prowled around her mind for days scratching, leaving little rivulets of pain.

She got pissed when he didn't return her calls. She occasionally wondered if he was seeing someone else. And, really, none of it mattered.

If Ray's inattention caused her pain, tears, insecurity, as it did now, she wanted to forget it. She bid adieu to the calling of her heart. *One step forward, two steps back.* Cherry was right. She had told Lucky to go slowly, to guard her rear.

"If he's a known heart-breaker, avoid him," Cherry had counseled.

She had been living, waking, sleeping, and breathing Hope for two months now. She had clung to that first month of fun with Ray, fed off it like a vampire of loneliness, and refused to waken to the reality that the man had lost interest in her. One delirious fast-moving month; the second spent curbside watching joy recede into the distance, she'd gone from growing pains to going pains.

She entered a period of lethargy, unable to work effectively, adrift in erotic cloudscapes, seeking to restore the "years the locusts had eaten" to her life.

I am making myself unhappy mooning over Ray, wishing my life would align with his, failing to live my own life in the meantime. Mean time. What a word. I have to shake myself out of this bovine mooning.

Transition. Everything seemed to be in transition. Going from one phase to the next, never sure when or whether she had arrived, or where precisely she was.

39

A BOULDER

S he lay at the beach in the late afternoon summer sun, unraveling her hair from its high bun to doze. She swam to let the water cool and revitalize. Diving under four large waves, she let the fifth carry her toward shore, let herself blend with the sun's heat, the beach, the sea.

She sat on her towel reading *Spiritual Healing*. Looking up, squinting at the turquoise-green sea swells, she watched the whitewash shoving the rocky rubble up the shore. She saw herself as the rock, the rugged coral boulder at the edge of the fluxing tide, resolute in its solidity. The sea washed over it, eroding and re-shaping it with the regularity and dispassion of the waves, one strong and forceful, the next mild and soft, each bearing corrosive power. Wave after wave, the rock stood there, strong, mute, and seemingly imperturbable, yet changing in minute but ongoing ways.

She supposed the soul was like this rock by the sea, altered by the force of nature. It had moods, changing energy, beyond human understanding.

The sky, ever-present, changing from light to dark, dark to light, filled with weather and time. And, like the sky, the soul cleared and clouded over. It could blow hot or cold, windy trades or doldrums calm. Souls were to her like clouds of every variety, traveling on different stratospheres, some thin and wispy, some cream puffs, some gray and shapeless, some coalesced into a dark bank of fog. Others higher had their edges deckled sunset bronze, pink- fringed inside the last pure blue of daylight.

All her life she had known she needed the sea. Perhaps not only for peace, but also to have time to see inward, to be soulful in a way she couldn't in the country confines of Fruto, or the city tension of San Francisco, or among too many people, or too much civilization. Cherry, her astrologer, found no element of water in Lucky's fiery chart.

Maybe she was attracted to Ray for his "water" side. He was liquid, soothing, gentle, and tender. She liked the care he gave his dog, Kula, and the new pup, his reassurance, his steady stream of love.

Her physical desire for Ray and loneliness clouded her from herself. She had to get back to center to understand her happiness did not depend on another person, to stop creating plans and expectations for a lover to fulfill, because when he failed to perform, disappointment and disillusionment pierced her. She realized that the best spot to dwell was in the stillness within.

Physician, heal thyself, she whispered.

She had a vision of many, many empty pews in a gothic European cathedral. Lucky knelt alone in the middle of the empty pews surrounded by space. To the left was an immense organ with huge enameled pipes, white with gilded edges. She prayed, her palms pressed together, raising her arms slowly in front of her face and above her head. *Dear God, help me, guide me.*

A blue "ghost" filtered down, ethereal, hooded, like an animated wisp of blue smoke. It was the Holy Ghost, God, the Holy Spirit--and He took her hand, pulling her up. They began to boogie to hard erotic music, music like *Enigma*'s; the music was not coming from the organ, but rather from life all around. In that cathedral, God and Lucky were full of life, dancing without a word.

Perhaps her attitude was coming nearer to its proper state of grace.

The rock at the beach was much more exposed when she saw it during her daily stroll. A large portion formerly covered with sand was exposed, jutting out prone, back toward the shore. She liked seeing that rock, feeling its permanence, observing the environment alter around it.

Ray had stayed sweetly on her mind. She felt both doomed and faithful. His silence was stretching into forever. She concentrated on radiating warm red-colored heat and passionate love through her belly on a jet stream across the sky to envelop and permeate him.

Phone rang; it was Ray. The long silence was broken.

The universe must have been responding, because many men came to her. Lucky and neighbor, Rod Moore, went on a date to the Bolshoi. She had sewn a tiny little black velvet dress; he had bought new clothes. He picked her up in his Mercedes; they dined at *Philip Paolo's* on calamari and seafood, drinking Vouveray wine. After the ballet, they headed to Restaurant Row for the singles-scene and dessert. They behaved like understudies, rehearsing, waiting in the wings for their chance to play at being the leading lovers. A perfect gentleman, Rod made no moves to touch her. And that made her happy. Could she beat that? One man's touch she craved, the other's she shunned.

Oh, it should have been so easy to love, to open up and relax, like shaking out a beach towel, lying down on the sand and laughing with the wind blowing, and sunshine warming, and someone wearing red, and it was easy. Everybody was happy.

"Hey, I pick you." And, you paired up and forgot all the fussing, accepted one another, made love, ate, kept each other company, and that was it.

Instead, the way it seemed to work was with a lot of shuffling and sidestepping, fear and anxiety, conflict and desire.

Rod dropped his shyness.

"I've wanted you ever since I was fifteen, Lucky. You are the kindest, most wonderful woman I've ever met. Hope is hope, but Moore is more," he joked self-consciously.

"Oh, Rod, I know you love me, and I thank you. But, I'm not the one for you. You need someone younger. You're tired of being single. Don't worry, the right person will show up soon." Rod looked embarrassed. They drank wine and talked of other things.

"Rod, do you know what your destiny is?"

"What's that?" he asked, not grasping what she meant.

40

THE VISIT

Edna arrived at Lucky's doorstep from a nightmarish UNESCO mission to India. Edna reeled from the enormity of its population boom, the immediate need for birth control, and jet lag. The visit was one of those rare occasions when she actually looked at one of her children instead solving some looming global problem. She chatted to Lucky with an absolute outpouring of love. Edna described her in-flight thoughts during those long airplane hours spanning half the globe. She expressed her love and pride in Lucky's accomplishments and in Lucky's tremendous potential to do more.

"Pay no never mind to Fannie or to Bullet. They're unimportant, irrelevant. What's relevant is you, your new time, new creativity. Use your imagination, Lucky. It's the greatest friend you've got. You've always had it. It's the Irish in you, that free-floating, soaring, air element, the spark, the humor. Fly, my girl, in mind and spirit. Now's your time."

Edna laughed, "Don't keep those clay feet of yours stuck in the mud."

The trip to see Lucky and the grandkids had cost Edna over two thousand dollars. She had enough money tucked away from her retirement and rental incomes to cover it comfortably, but a childhood spent penniless in the Depression taxed any joy in extravagance. Worse, her purse got stolen from the rental car at Makaha Beach, along with her return ticket, cash, and camera.

"How can you live in a place with so much crime, Lucky? They even stole my beach towel. Not even an old lady is safe here. Now that you're free of Bullet, why don't you get out of this god-forsaken place and come home? What are you doing with your life anyway?"

"Trying to raise my kids, Mom, in their home and with their friends, where they are comfortable. I want to provide whatever security and continuity I can in their lives, especially as we go through this change." They shared a bottle of Beaujolais at dinner.

Edna repeated in drunken frustration, "Lucky, are you going to fritter the rest of your life away on this flea speck of an island in the middle of nowhere?"

Yep. That'd be the whole reason I'm sittin' here stretchin' my ass, Lucky thought, *fritterin'.* Edna tried her best to kick-start Lucky into Edna's notion of Lucky's life, ignoring the obvious fact that Lucky was raising three kids and creating art.

Edna stayed the week visiting Lucky by day and sleeping at a luxury resort by night. She much preferred to sit beside the chlorinated pool than to swim in the sea.

By way of a backhanded compliment, she told Lucky, "The roar of the waves at your place sounds like the echo of the freeway traffic I hear from my house."

After a few days, she complained that the grandchildren looked far too much like Bullet to be of interest to her, too blonde and athletic; she, too red-cheeked, dark haired, and boozy Irish to look related.

Marianna and Ande had never liked the dollies Edna brought when they were younger or the tea parties she coaxed them to play. They choose boogie boards and bikes over board games and toys. Now that they were teenagers, they acted bored around her and refused to laugh at her puns. Edna accused Nico of having a one-word vocabulary, "surf."

"Your boy is as articulate as Bullet," Edna remarked and rolled her eyes.

When the week was up, they hugged, and Lucky told Edna many times, sincerely, "I love you, Mom. I want to thank you for being my Mom, for 'being there,' for loving and supporting me and for boosting my courage."

Maybe hearing her daughter's words of love made the two thousand dollars the hotel cost her, the stolen purse, and her disappointment in the heat and sand and grandchildren worthwhile. Lucky hoped so.

She leaned a wet cheek on her hands at the airport railing, her head tilted sideways, where the moon reflected in her eye. The moon looked misshapen; the side of its head had been lopped off, briefly illumining dark clouds around it. She thanked this moon, as though a spokesman for all things divine, she thanked this moon for her mom, missing her while she had been there, relieved by her parting, Lucky asked for Edna's safekeeping, blessing the goodness she knew lay concealed deep in Edna's heart. The clouds drifted, obscuring the light, darkening the sky as Lucky wiped her eyes to watch the *Continental* and *United* jets jockey for departure.

41

MAJOR

Lucky whacked banana leaves and put up new rain awnings, reorganized studios, and unloaded bisque kilns, having created new ware: *Hawai'ian Fish Hales* and *Japanese Barns.* She loved seeing a body of her work, especially if it held humor, strength, mystery, antiquity, and something slightly Hawai'ian or Asian.

Nico sat shirtless in her studio carving an *ulua* fish onto a slim paddle for her to use to decorate clay. Ande produced fifty pillows and forty-three baskets as Lucky's paid studio assistant. Ande created little grass shack scenes in clay, selling her own work, little pillows and boxes, under Lucky's name at the galleries, too.

"Mom, I feel so sorry for Dad. His trailer is smaller than our bathroom. His bed is shorter than Nico."

"Well, Ande, your dad chooses to live there; he can afford an apartment or something nicer."

"Uh, Mom. Dad wants me to come live with him." Lucky was taken completely by surprise.

"What? He's asked you?" Ande nodded. "What do you want to do, Ande?"

"Well, I love you, Mommy. But, Dad needs me. He's really lonesome."

"Honey," Lucky said, "he works nights and lives in that trailer out in the middle of nowhere with Major. It's not safe for a young girl. What would you do all by yourself from after school until midnight?"

"I don't know. I've already packed my clothes. Dad's stopping by for me, Mom."

Lucky let Ande learn for herself whether her father could take care of her or not.

On the weekend, on her first day at Bullet's, Ande went outside the trailer to greet Major, bringing him a treat of half a box of *Cocoa Crispies*. He laid his ears flat to his skull, rolled his upper lip up and his lower lip down like reversing window shades to reveal parallel horseshoes of flat donkey teeth, and inhaled deeply. Then, on the exhale, he brayed the classic song of the *Kona* "nightingale," *a* wheezing *heehaw heehaw heehaw*.

Ande held out the cereal. Major was wary, suspicious that Ande would steal the very cereal she was offering.

He reared up and struck her with his front hoof on the left side of her head before she could back out of reach. She lost balance, and Major rushed her. He stumbled on impact and fell on top of her. Ande was knocked unconscious. Her head was bleeding. Two hours later, Bullet received a call at the office.

"Dad, can you come get me?" Ande asked very softly.

"You know I'm at work. I've told you not to bother me here."

"I'm hurt, Dad. Major fell on me. My ribs really hurt. It's hard to breathe. I got a big cut that won't stop bleeding on my head. Can you take me to Kaiser? I don't want to tell Mom."

"I can't leave work, Ande. I'm sorry you got hurt. Call your Mom. She'll take you to the doctor."

Ande needed eight stitches to close the gash over her eye, a tetanus shot, and painkillers for three cracked ribs. She had a mild concussion, which needed to be monitored. She wouldn't be able to dance *hula* or body-board for a couple of months. She'd have to miss the next week of school.

"I'm going to call the Humane Society to impound that damned donkey," Lucky swore, livid, once she knew Ande would be okay.

"No, Mom. Don't do that. Dad would kill you," Ande protested. "It's my fault, too. I wasn't watching Major carefully enough."

"If a Doberman had attacked you, Ande, I would have the animal put to sleep, and I would sue its owner. What's the difference if it's a donkey that happens to be vicious and can't be controlled? That your dad is the owner?"

"Dad can't kill Major," Ande said, and then smiled. "Dad did offer to make him into jerk meat, though."

"Nobody in his or her right mind would eat that ass," Lucky muttered.

"But I told him not to," Ande continued. "It was my fault. I should have carried a big stick and put the cereal down before I called him."

Lucky tucked in the blanket. When Ande got out of the hospital, she didn't mention living with her father again.

Cerulean, the Pacific rose in wide, deep surfing waves. Edged by purple sunlit bougainvillea, the brown summer-crisped mountains descended in three dry lumps to the sea.

Rex and Queenie's house was almost obscured by green naupaka and palms; Lucky's house was indistinguishable along
the coast. Everything looked diminished. The elements
dominated, as always. The sea, the sky, and the land. The
living, mere moveable specks on a timeless shore. Thinking
cleansed Lucky, like cloud puffs that scrubbed the sky, *Ajax*
of the spirit, an *SOS* pad scoured her soul blue.

Her phone rang.

"Hello. Hello? Hello?" Some heavy breathing preceded a
deep male voice.

"I see you, eh? I see your dottas down the beach. I gonna
fock you. I gonna fock you an' your dottas up the ass."

Lucky would like to think it was a random crank caller.
But, it was the fifth call that week. She told the kids not to
answer the phone anymore. They screened all calls with the
message machine.

"Eh, I stay watching you. You nevah come home las' night.
I still like fock you."

Lucky called the police. An officer stopped by to give her
an official police whistle.

"What's this for?"

"When you get a dirty call, you blow the whistle as loud as
you can into the phone. I guarantee he'll never call again."

Despite whistles by every phone, the calls continued.

"Eh, whea you wuz las' night? Your car stay home. I stay
inside da house. You nevah come home, you bitch."

She saved four hours of terrifying messages on tape and
delivered them to the police, who finally had enough evidence
to tap her line.

She returned from taking Queenie to the radiologist's
and running errands in Honolulu to find her house had been
broken into. The TV was gone, as were the stereo, the girls'

Hawai'ian gold heirloom jewelry, Nico's *sega-genesis* games, three bikes, five boogie boards, and Lucky's compressor. The police dusted for fingerprints. Bullet arrived.

"Do you want to come in?" Lucky asked.

"I'll come in if I damned well please. I don't need an invitation from you."

He wanted to take one of Lucky's pots to use as a funeral urn for a relative of Pearl's who had died.

"You can't have that unless you pay for it," Lucky said.

"Well, everything here's half mine, now, isn't it?" he snapped. "What're ya gonna do? Call the cops again? Shove any payment up your fuckin' asshole."

Queenie was there. Trying not get caught in the crossfire, she had crept quietly into the girls' room. Lucky placed the pot Bullet wanted with its lid shaped like a wave on the ground outside her front gate. She felt her pulse racing and spleen swelling; her rage jittered like caffeine through her veins. Ignoring both Bullet and Queenie, she went out back to do laundry. When she finished, he was still there, muttering a barrage of obscenities. She cleaned the kitchen, then escaped upstairs.

I hate him. I hate him. All her love had turned to hatred. He was impossible to deal with, battle-armed with old anger. She felt miles away from that relationship, the old her, the old him. It jolted her to feel its aliveness.

Bullet asked for the umpteenth time if his students could come and paint.

"It is not a negotiable subject," she told him.

"I don't understand why they can't come."

"You've had plenty of time to organize your classes elsewhere," Lucky stated.

"I thought you'd change your mind."

"I haven't."

The kids were on spring break. Marianna was ill with a cold, a frog in her throat.

"How's about a kiss, Marianna," he asked.

"I'm sick, Dad."

He almost whacked her when she refused. Ande and Nico still responded to his love. But, Marianna's affection was blocked. She hated Bullet's exit from her life and resented Fannie's entrance.

"I've got so much anger in me, Mom. I know I shouldn't do dumb stuff like painting those nasty words on my walls, but I get so mad, I explode."

"Maybe we should get you a punching bag. Just think, you could draw faces on it, Marianna, even add wigs for whomever you want to punch. And, you could hit it as often and as hard as you like without getting into trouble with anybody."

"Mom, I saw Dad down the road. He says he's coming back tonight," Ande announced, coming in from a bike ride. "He says he forgot to get his *Kamakura* painting, because Marianna was being mean to him."

Lucky left a message on his machine. "Tonight is not a good time to come over."

"Fuck you," he said when he heard it. "I'm coming to get my painting and that's that."

Marianna took off despite her cold, driving Ande and Nico to *hula* and soccer practice. Ten minutes later, Bullet walked in and took his painting off the wall. All Lucky could do was toy with the impulse to trip him or throw something at him.

Once alone, she grabbed a knife off the magnetic rack in the kitchen and walked resolutely back to his painting studio. She felt reckless, profane, and ready to desecrate something she'd held sacred.

First, she struck the mini version of *Kamakura*. She liked that piece; it was a shame to cut it, but she'd always remember it. Next, she stabbed one she hated, the *Paris* piece. *Screw it. Screw him. Screw his art.* She slashed his *goddamned* paintings, ripping and throwing the strips of painted canvas out the front windows. It was easy.

She gathered up the shreds intending to stuff them into the toilet. But, there was far too much to flush. Instead, she gathered her metal garbage bins by the road and loaded them with the canvas strips. She went back into his studio, where she kicked and stomped the wooden stretcher bars from the paintings till the frames gave way. She piled the wood into the cans as well. She took her portable two hundred BTU burner from her raku kiln and with her propane torch set the torn paintings ablaze. Black smoke and blue tipped flames leapt from the cans, which spewed toxins from the oil paint into the air.

She took down the photos of Bullet from the walls in the house, going up and down a footstool muttering, "I hate you." She scraped off the eternal cockroach eggs, which clung to the backs of the wood frames with a yardstick, venting her spleen like a nutty bag lady, throwing the photos into the fire as well.

She watched the flames until they died away. Tired, she sank onto the sofa and looked at the bare walls in her house. She hadn't really enjoyed the ablution or her recklessness. But, his paintings were gone. It meant there was nothing left of him in the home, and nothing left in the studio to bring income.

Please release me from this relationship. I want to be free of this man.

She recalled daily lessons from *The Course in Miracles.* *"Nothing in this room has any meaning"* or *"nothing in this room has any meaning except the meaning I give it."*

⟋

Bullet and Francine broke up. At least, that was the word according to Ande.

"What happened?" Lucky asked, driving to Gigi's in town.

"I think you and Dad should pay me for every time you talk about the divorce. I'd make a lot of money."

"Sure," nodded Lucky.

"Dad is sleeping over at Gramma's, because he and Francine broke up, and she's staying in the house."

"Really?"

"She dumped him. He asked me if I thought you'd let him sleep at home."

"What did you say?"

"Not a chance in a million trillion, Dad."

"Good, Ande. Thanks," Lucky said.

Bullet stopped by in his wide-load, suburban housewife's red van with Nico and his gang of friends to pick up sheets for a camp-out. He called Lucky over to the van, nice like, to talk. She knew his style and waved him away.

Bullet yelled, "I'm at the lowest point in my life, you know. I've lost the children. I want the house, so I can be in a natural setting when the kids come home, and we can visit."

"You want the house?" Lucky yelled back. "Forget it. I don't want your phone calls, your demands, or your presence in my home. Three times you've broken in. The cleaning lady caught you like a common thief. You pushed in the doors and ransacked the house. Taking things. *Whatevah.*"

"*Whatevah* yourself, bitch. It's all mine anyway."

❧

Ray stood outside his car at his office looking vital and handsome. A big grin spread across his face as Lucky tooted at him from her truck.

"Eh, tita, howzit?"

"Hey, I just called you. They said you were in a meeting."

"Whatcha doin?"

"Got some time?"

"About five minutes. I've got to be at *Ralph Lauren's* at twelve. You got time?"

"Yeah, about twenty minutes. I've got to meet Ande at school."

"Oh, book day?"

"No, picking her up from an overnight She's got a scholarship job meeting. Then I'm going to get beautiful."

"Well, that shouldn't take long."

"See ya," she smiled.

At *Paul Brown's*, she had her hair highlighted blonder, cut blunt at the shoulders. She looked in the mirror. There she was: blue eyes, pearls, wispy bangs, tight jeans, and red plaid shirt, cute.

She returned home to find her doors swinging open in the breeze and all the living room furniture gone.

On the answer machine, a male voice growled, "Tonight. I coming tonight fo' kill you. You and your fockin' kids."

Ray had wine, Vietnamese rolls and sprouts waiting when she arrived with the kids.

"Thank you so much, Ray, for letting us come. I didn't know whom else to call. I am so scared." They ate and played with the dogs. They inspected progress at his building site where kitchen cupboards and the fireplace were newly installed. They laid futons out for the kids to sleep.

"Who's doing this, Lucky?"

"I don't know. The police say they can trace the source of the calls. I guess I'll find out pretty soon."

"Do you think it's whoever's ripping off your house?"

"I don't know. I'm clueless. There have been twenty-one break-ins so far. I feel like hanging a big banner from the deck that says, 'Don't bother: it's all gone' My *State Farm* insurance agent won't renew my coverage, because I'm a 'poor risk'."

"Maybe you need to get a security system."

"Are you volunteering?"

"There's not much I can do from here in town," he answered. "But, I'll call a security company and get someone in touch with you."

"Okay. Sounds like a good idea."

"Maybe you should get a guard dog: a Dobie or a Rottweiler."

"Maybe. Or, maybe a bodyguard. My assistant, Frankie, is pretty big. He's looking for a place to stay."

Switching gears, she blurted without thinking, "My neighbor, Rod, you met him, proposed to me." Ray looked at her, surprised.

"Marriage, you know? I told him I wanted to be friends; I couldn't be his lover. I told him he deserves a young woman who would have his children and see him as a knight on a white horse."

"Hmmmm. Sounds good to me, too. Being your lover would be hard, Lucky. The kids," he said, nodding toward them. "You have a complicated life. You're two steps ahead of me," he added, kissing her twice before going up to his other house to sleep.

"I'll always be your friend, though, Lucky."

42

VERTIGO

Next day silence filled the car. She thought about timing; life was timing. No radio love songs played as she drove to face the nameless terrorist.

Lucky called classified ads to find a fully trained attack dog. She settled on a very hyper, muscular and chocolate-colored Weimaraner/Doberman mix they named Bosco.

Frankie agreed to act as bodyguard to the whole family. He took the downstairs bedroom off the kitchen and planned to housesit while Lucky flew with the kids to Maui for a 'working vacation' at a five-star resort where she had been hired as a "show and tell" artist to enhance the guests' experience. She was excited about the all-expense paid trip. She packed eight cartons of pottery and workshop supplies, ironed and packed clothes until midnight.

In the midst of readying for an early morning departure, Ray called. He wanted to come along. Lucky agreed happily. Bullet walked in. He gave the kids twenties and handed her an extra twenty.

"Marianna, howz about a kiss?"

"I don't think so."

"Hey, I just gave you a twenny for your trip."

"I didn't ask you for it."

He said, "I gave you a bike, too, the other day."

"Mom did," she corrected.

"I want credit for it. I want love for it. The least you can do is kiss me. I've wasted a lot of years of my life on you."

"You're an asshole, Dad."

They were in the living room where Frankie was putting his bags down. Lucky was still on the phone with Ray when she saw Bullet hold Marianna by the shoulder and slap her hard across the face. Marianna broke loose and ran to Lucky, who hung up the phone fast. Frankie was stunned motionless.

"I hate you," Marianna wailed.

"This house is full of hate," Bullet roared, catching her arm. Lucky wedged her body between Bullet and Marianna to try to prevent him from hurting her more. But, he hit Marianna in the face again as he gripped her arm. It was happening so fast. Marianna fell, hitting her head on the dining table; Bullet stood over her.

Lucky got between them again, screaming, "Leave her alone."

Marianna scrambled on all fours to her room where she slammed her louvered door. Bullet shoved Lucky aside to follow Marianna.

Lucky dialed 911. "Come quick. My husband is beating my daughter."

Bullet ripped the receiver out of her hand and knocked the phone off the wall, as he charged out the kitchen door. Hula Girl wouldn't stop barking. Lucky's adrenaline pumped.

"The police are here, Mom," Ande said fifteen minutes later. Lucky met them at the gate.

"We traced the phone call and came to help."

"Thank you. He's gone now."

"Do you want to pursue the matter?"

"Oh? No," she said, looking down the street. "I guess it's all right now," she added without even checking on Marianna.

It was not all right. Ande was in the bathroom, crying. Marianna had punched her, part of the old pecking order. *You hurt me, then I'll hurt someone weaker.* Both girls now had bloody noses. They lay down on tile floor in the bathroom holding toilet paper to their faces, miserable. Nico, a wildness invading him, yelled and annoyed everyone. He didn't know what to do.

Lucky wanted to get out. They raced to the airport only to find their flight delayed by two hours. They sat on wooden benches outside the small interisland terminal, stewing, the morning humidity adding to their discomfort.

Lucky had to tell someone what had happened. She called Queenie. Queenie normally fed on gossip. But, she had no reaction whatsoever to the juicy news of her son bloodying her granddaughter. Instead, she accused Lucky of turning the children against them.

"The children didn't call to wish us a 'Happy Anniversary'," Queenie whined.

"What?" Lucky asked. The nerve of Queenie to accuse the kids of hurting her feelings. "Did any of your kids or grandkids: Meg, Bobbie, or Walt call for your anniversary?"

"Well, Patti's kids are busy with their own lives and live far away. Your kids are right here."

"Yes," Lucky said, "Ande and Nico were home sick on your anniversary, and Marianna was working, remember? We didn't want to give you germs. I came to your house, and I thought I made it clear the gifts were from the kids and me. I delivered a pot and champagne. What more did you expect? I did not forget your anniversary."

"That's not the same," myopic Queenie wheedled. "Your open marriage encouraged Bullet to have sex elsewhere," she announced and hung up.

Open marriage? Where did she come up with that notion? Is this how Bullet justifies himself to his parents? And, they believe it?

Lucky suspected her in-laws were beginning to make a "blood is thicker than water" case to close ranks with their son. She repeated calming prayers as their plane finally took off.

Once settled at the resort on Maui, she discovered a copy of her bio had been placed in every guest's room. It mentioned Bullet and his share in her work. She had forgotten to tell the staff that she was divorcing. This bio was embarrassing.

The children were beastly. While Lucky talked business at the *Hana Ranch Trading Co.*, for no apparent reason Marianna bashed Nico's head against the Mexican tile floor in the room, causing multiple head bruises and splitting his lip.

"Fuck you," he screamed, crying and struggling against her.

"Fuck you, ya little brat," she yelled back. Nico stayed upset, tearful, and disconsolate most of the afternoon. Marianna vociferously blamed him for the fight. Ande mediated. Lucky recognized the pecking order. Bullet hit Marianna, Marianna hit Ande; Marianna hit Nico.

Next morning, they took a horseback ride, cantering over coastal ranch lands on the greenest grass ever grazed, Maunakea viewed at fourteen thousand feet across the deeply chopped blue channel. Midday was spent in a glaze-firing workshop with guests at Hamoa Beach. Lucky got chilled and felt a cold coming on. She took a hot shower, drank tea, and popped a *Contac*. She prepared to join Ray for dinner wearing a navy silk tank and jacket, pearls and white slacks, heels, and a crimson rose in her hair.

"Ray, you can't be thirty-seven," Marianna challenged. "You act like such a kid."

Ray slept on a sofa; the kids slept in the master suite, and Lucky slept on the rollaway. Talk about being a kid.

She and Ray rode bikes on trails through Kipahulu looking for gardens. They found an old friend of Ray's who was building a house, discovered a beach *heiau* with fresh water pools. They swam laps in the wellness pool, ate breakfast on the hotel *lanai*, photographed many parts of the newly remodeled hotel: its lights, furnishings, roof, garden fences. Ray even lined up an account for his company to design the staff uniforms before he returned to O'ahu.

Lucky drove with the kids in a rented *Toyota* wagon in pre-dawn dark up densely eucalyptus lined roads, seeking a sunrise at Haleakala. Somehow she got lost, taking wrong roads and turns, reaching dead ends. The gas tank's orange "empty" light flashed as they reached the two mile marker of the thirty-odd mile drive up the flanks of the volcano. Not willing to risk running out of gas before reaching the summit, she descended to find a gas station. None were open before six-thirty a.m., neither Ching's nor Gramma's in Kula. Well after dawn, Calasa's Shell opened.

Still, they made the ascent. Lucky's hands, stiffened knuckle-white, gripped the wheel in a ferocious struggle with vertigo, her nerves shattering as she steeled herself to the centerline, not to succumb to the lure of the cliff's edge. Finally, at almost ten thousand feet, right below the summit, she stopped at a parking lot, dizzy. She held tightly to the railing at the lookout point.

Awed, they were absolutely awed by the might and enormity of the crater. A landscape eighteen miles long splayed out below their eyes. The drop off was swift, dramatic, and much steeper than she'd remembered. Looking across the summit at tiny figures traversing Sliding Sands trail, she recalled her eagerness for the descent fifteen years ago, in sharp contrast to her current fear.

They hiked to a silversword spot, and then descended to the switchbacks, winding down a horse and mule trail through misting clouds. In the crater, she saw a boulder flanked by ferns bearing green and red fronds, then the mists, trapping sunlight, swirled to obscure it. She dawdled, photographing plants and rocks, invoking the divine. The mists cleared a bit to reveal the path.

Two hours later and only halfway down, they stopped for peach nectar, apples, gum, and trail mix.

"Do we have to go all the way?" the kids whined. She decided to forgo exploring the crater floor and its lava tubes. They ascended. It was a good plan, as Nico's shoe came off due to a blister, and Ande's knees gave out near the top.

43

LAYING BARE

Lucky had counted the days for the two o'clock appointment to go over Ray's kitchen tile design and then dine
with Cherry and Joe. She bathed, oiled, went braless
under a silk shirt, donned pearls, gold turtle earrings, sported
a new hair color and cut, wore her *Levi*'s tight with a thin red
leather belt.

Ande noticed, "You look nice, Mom."

She took a vegetarian lasagna, mangoes and a lemon.

And, Ray? He'd forgotten she was coming. He owed her
money, which she didn't mention. He had a friend over and
was bathing his dogs when she pulled up. He didn't even look
up to greet her. She put the lasagna in his fridge and left the
mangoes on counter. She towel dried his new puppy, Pua, while
he finished Kula. Bored, she measured his kitchen. He came
in with his friend, Walton, and they discussed the tile project.
Finally, Walton left, but three more showed up. Ray got beer
and made guacamole. Meanwhile, Lucky waited down at the
new house, quietly petting Pua, who sat in her lap.

"I have to cancel our dinner date," Cherry phoned around five. "I got food poisoning and slept all day. Sorry."

After the neighbors went, Lucky and Ray talked till dark his floor plan, about where to place his bed, where to set his bathroom door. Shivering and hungry, they went to his old house. He put her lasagna in the oven. They drank wine, waited for the lasagna, and made garlic bagels. She read magazines while he returned phone calls and showered.

They enjoyed one another's company over dinner. She massaged his back, tucked him in, and kissed his cheek goodnight. He lay motionless, rising only to turn on the outside light for her. That was it. Ray had been hot in May, but he was cold now.

In her mind's ear, Lucky could hear Nico asking as a joke, "Is he a fag, Mom?"

Nico, wearing his *Kanaka Clothing* fish shirt, well-worn *Renn and Stimpie* hat on his head, spent the morning sitting on the living room floor drawing what he termed an 'unreal' breaking wave with magic marker on his new stinger boogie board's bottom.

Nico's principal called. It was a Saturday.

"Mrs. Pulaski, Nico was crying at school yesterday. I called him into my office for a chat. Did he mention it to you? I asked why he was crying. Nico told me, 'My dad was calling me bad names.' What names did your dad call you, I asked. 'Little Fucker. Asshole. Little Shit.' "Those are not nice names for anybody to call anyone," I told him. "I gave him a *Kleenex* and told him I was sorry he was having a hard time. I tried to reach Mr. Pulaski by phone but only left a message to call me to arrange for a conference. I thought you should know."

⚘

"Is this my masseuse?" Ray asked on the phone. Lucky hesitated before answering. *When do people really tell other people their feelings,* she wondered? *Or, do they let them drift away, letting time stretch them, like rubber bands, which snap into oblivion?* She took the plunge.

"Ray, you washed your dog instead of greeting me when I came over. You treat me like I'm 'one of the boys'. Each time I leave your house, I am crying."

"It's hard for me, too. I don't want to lead you on, or hurt you, or let you down."

"You are hurting me. I want to be your friend, but I'm a woman, and you act blind to that fact."

"I have to turn it off and be completely cold. It's a difficult situation."

"You've been good to me. Lord knows, my personal life is not exactly appealing. Yet, you've become my friend. I am grateful for that."

"That's why I'm calling. I want to thank you for being kind, for the massage and lasagna and house tiles. I hadn't planned on Walton being there, or the others dropping by. I wasn't getting done the work I needed to do. My dogs were two weeks overdue for baths..."

"Do we live on two different planets? I couldn't tell if you even remembered I was coming," she interrupted him. "Sorry. I'm sorry to be crabby. I don't want to make you defensive."

"Well, don't be crabby," he said.

"Ray, I haven't been intimate or felt close to anyone in years. I feel awkward."

Ray was at work. She could hear people talking in his office. "You're not free to talk; I'm running late for my gallery. By the way, you owe me money."

"Hey, I had the receipt book on the counter to go over with you."

No doubt I've blown it completely with that man. Another casualty of my dementia. Me, the kids, Bullet, the in-laws, friends, Ray. Oh God. Save me.

She raku-fired at ten-thirty at night. A blue/black sky filled with puffy clouds was lit by a ripened slice of cantaloupe moon that looked like it had been set afloat on the darkened blue dish of the sea. The night air felt so warm, she could wear her bathing suit, cooled by a slight offshore wind. She waited with Frankie between firings as the ware heated up. Her energy was unfocused. She was not pleased with earlier glaze choices, and the early firing results showed she had pulled the ware too soon. She was aware that though these were some of her best forms, they were being "lessened" by the glazing and poor firing.

Back breaking work, those arduous hours hot-gloving pots from the kiln. Frankie helped. She relied on him to lift the kiln rings off with her and put lids over the flames leaping from the reduction cans, even though she could handle the ware alone. She climbed on a ladder to bend and pick up the tallest work. Dangerous, she lifted out several four-foot high, seventy-five pound slab pots at twenty-two hundred degrees Fahrenheit with steel mesh mittens. Without any breakage, she managed to get the pots into the reduction cans. She praised the mittens, the fire suit, God.

Diligently, she plugged on, patient, firing, waiting, and looking. Her energy had fled during the day to legal problems and other issues. At least, she thought, the house hadn't been robbed since Frankie moved in. Bosco was a bit of a pest. He had developed a predilection for laundry, pulling it off the line and dragging it across the yard. She retrieved Marianna's missing *Christian Dior* bra from the front lawn. She found one of Nico's socks in a pile of poop. That dumb dog had actually eaten it.

Forty minutes later she checked the cooling pots. They were miraculously intact but under-fired with the glaze all bubbled inside and pooching out of spouts in webbed, foamy globules. They would have to be redone. Again, she fired.

Finally, she pulled off her fire suit hood, saw her face reflected in the window, red-purple like a boiled lobster as heated blood pumped through her veins like drum beats. Her body was wet, steam-bathed inside her firefighters' silver jacket. Three days later, she continued to choke on the smoke inhaled from her smoldering reduction cans.

44

UNPALATABLE

Thursday night while Lucky attended a craft council board meeting, Bullet came to the house.

"Hey, Marianna, why don't you say the *F* word to me," he baited, "so I can hit you again?" She called the police. He left, but he called twice to see if the police had come.

Bully called Lucky at her gallery in Honolulu the next day.

"I'm thinking about getting joint counseling with Marianna. Would that be possible?"

Lucky gave him the number for Kaiser's psychiatric department. Bullet called her back. *Why don't I let the answer machine screen my calls?*

"I've gotten the divorce papers, Lucky, and there are things I don't agree with: the fifty percent ownership of my paintings, the furniture, and...."

Lucky interrupted, "Don't start."

Thomas Ayck waved the manila envelope containing the Temporary Restraining Order in front of her. She hadn't wanted to take a hard line as the past, the dusty specter of her adversarial parents engaged in battle, haunted the present.

"You know, Lucky, this means war?" Thomas asked.

"Yes, Thomas, I do. I've BEEN in a war. It was just undeclared. I'm through with being a pushover and a doormat. Bullet has to know his limits."

"Lucky, you've been nice," Thomas Ayck reminded her. "But now, with this, Bullet could become very, very dangerous," Thomas warned.

"Bullet beat up Marianna before we went to Maui," Lucky replied. "I took pictures. He continues to break into my house. Marianna is getting run over. You don't want me to come crying when Bullet kills one of the kids or me, do you?"

"If there is so much as a hint of violence, grab the kids and get out of there fast. Stay away from his parents. Remember, they had him first. He learned his behavior somewhere," surmised Thomas. Then he added, "I need a payment for my legal services to date of seven thousand dollars."

"I'll pay you, Thomas. I want a divorce. I want that in my hands before I pay you."

"Well, Lucky, we've written twelve different decrees. We've certainly done our work."

"Yes, Thomas, you have. But, am I divorced?"

She hand delivered the TRO to her old buddies at the Wai'anae Police Station for immediate service on Bullet.

"Hey, Mrs. Pulaski, we've gotten confirmation on two numbers for that mystery caller."

"You know who's making the threatening calls?"

"Well, we don't know who, but do these numbers mean anything to you?" The sergeant handed her a sheet listing every call made to her number with the time, duration of call, and

date. At home, she checked it against the times she'd logged in the obscene calls on her calendar. The first number was a mystery. The operator verified it as belonging to Kalani, the drug dealer. Lucky was totally confounded. The other number she recognized: it belonged to Francine.

She called her wealthy brother, Jackie, who lived in Idaho.

"Jackie, I've got to get out of here. Bully is threatening to kill me. He's even hired somebody to call me with obscenities and death threats. I don't have any money. I need to rent a new place, pay legal bills, and get a new studio away from Bully. Please, Jackie, can you give me some money? I really need help."

"Sorry, Em. I'm broke due to my house building overruns. I can't help you now. I can't make your life for you, either," Jackie told her.

"I'm not asking you to make my life for me. I am asking for help."

"If you have to flip burgers at *McDonald's*, flip burgers," Jackie recommended.

She called Edna, who was sick with a cold and was so sympathetic to the divorce woes, that Lucky hadn't the heart to worry or beg her for money.

The strain exhausted her. Her calves, gritty with white clay, cramped from standing too long. She looked for herself in the mirror, checking to see if she still existed. Okay: still there, still here, still her.

Bosco was whining, turning in circles of discomfort. A stringy bowel movement dangled from his rectum. She pulled on the greenish sludge and disgorged Ande's missing bathing suit.

She propped her forehead up on a bottle of *Sharp's* non-alcoholic beer, the mouth of the bottle pushing hard into the furrow above her eyes. Sorrow whacked her in the face like a wet washcloth, and tears rolled down either side of the bottle. She drank *Sharp's*, because she feared alcohol. She would love to drink. But, it was more dangerous than a year ago. Sixteen months of this never-ending divorce had worn down her reserves.

"Put yourself number one and clean up your life," her therapist told her. "You are the kind of woman any man would want to have." It took her a moment to let that thought sink in.

"Thank you." Six months ago she probably would have said, "Really?"

"Now is not the time for Ray" the therapist advised. "It's time to end your marriage. Be mean. Anyone who's found fault with twelve divorce decrees will never be satisfied, is clinging to the marriage, and is not letting go. Think only of yourself and your children.

She returned home from an ultimately boring day sitting the gallery to find her mail missing from the box. An envelope bearing Ray's *Kanaka Clothing* logo lay ripped open on the dining table. Her blood pressure soared. A check for five hundred dollars and a letter lay there, too.

"So, who's been opening Mom's mail?" she shouted. "Was your dad here while I was gone?" Nico came forward.

"Oh. Sorry, Mom. I thought it was a letter from my sponsor."

"Did your dad read it?"

"No. He brought in the mail, though."

"Ande, Marianna, Nico. Listen you guys. Your dad isn't supposed to come in here anymore. I know it's hard. But, since he hit Marianna, he's not allowed to come past the gate. Okay?" Her blood boiled at the thought of Bullet invading her privacy, opening her mail, and coming into her house again. The immediate sweetness of hearing from Ray soured.

351

"Girls, I don't want you going to town this weekend, because something might come up for me, and I might need you to baby-sit Nico."

"Can't Frankie do it?" asked Ande who wanted to sleep over at Gigi's.

"Oh, who are you going to fuck, Mom?" asked Marianna.

"Good grief," yelled Lucky. "What a way to talk to your mother. Aaaaarrggh. Maybe it's time for a rules review around here, like manners, jobs, expectations and responsibilities? Huh?" The kids disappeared into their rooms.

Hula Girl licked Lucky's arm as she picked up Ray's note. He wrote,

> *You've got to put on your protective armor, Lucky. Get ready for this fight. Be tough. He's dealt you some bad blows. You deserve better. You've done a good job raising those kids. It's easy for me to say 'cause I sit here on my mountain far away, and I don't have any kids. But, I think you're doing the right thing, and you've gotta hang tough.*

Rallying behind Bullet, Queenie called to cancel the eightieth birthday brunch Lucky was throwing in her honor at the *Halekulani*.

"It's not palatable to me," Queenie said. "I can't eat with you and the children." The irony was not lost on Lucky, the one who had been throwing up for months, losing twenty-five pounds over the unpalatable, nauseating actions of Queenie's son.

"I am not feeling well," Queenie added. "The doctors want me to start another round of chemo. Rex won't admit I'm sick for fear of losing me. Bullet wants me to stay away from doctors altogether and drink aloe, which he thinks is a cure-all."

Lucky felt curiously detached from their conversation. Perhaps she had anticipated this outcome. It failed to surprise her. Queenie had brought worry to a state of near perfection over the years. She was a pro. She had internalized the pain of her son's marital demise, growing a cancer in herself.

"Queenie, I think you are making a big mistake. It's a mistake to get involved in this divorce or choose sides. It's between Bullet and me. Not you. It's making you sick. I love you. I bet you've forgotten you wished Bullet had AIDS, that he was dead. Now that Francine's out of the picture and your 'little boy' has returned home, he's in the right, and no matter what, we're in the wrong. Queenie, I called you and asked you twice for help," Lucky accused, hot tears scalding her lips. "He hurt Marianna. That is a fact. And, you, you won't hear it."

Queenie murmured, "I know it must be hard on you."

"I'm sure life isn't the same for you either without our little family to dote on and worry over. Can't you acknowledge your pain and disappointment?"

Queenie let the phone go dead.

"I know it must be hard on you, too," Lucky whispered, putting the receiver down.

Rex leafed through the *Yellow Pages* under divorce attorneys the following morning and dialed the lawyer with the largest ad to represent Bullet.

Bullet tried to set up visitation with the kids.

"You can't contact the kids," Lucky told him. "The TRO requires that you arrange visitation through me."

"You're insane. I can call or see the kids anytime. I am the children's father."

"Call a lawyer."

She felt hooked up to a one-way intravenous machine the wrong way. Nothing flowed into her while all of her blood was sucked out.

She hated the Pulaskis, hated them for their strings and power trips; she hated being poor and unable to leave.

She prowled the house, planning new locks on the doors to keep Bullet from coming inside. She imagined fleeing with the kids.

Lucky's month, October, marked her forty-fourth birthday and another heat wave. It was not a wave generated by Ray. She hovered, ready, waiting, as though a surveyor preparing to plumb some unknown depths, over passion strong within her, waiting to express itself. She felt this power, indescribable, something akin to the surging of the sea, pressing to release her fully into herself.

A fire opal glittered coral, yellow, green, and blue out of its rocky whiteness on her left hand. She sensed The Wheel of Fortune had begun to turn. She hoped that prosperity, newness, change, and happiness were close.

She was sat at the beach, wet with coconut oil in the midday sun, completely content. Steady ocean waves broke into white foam from sapphire water over black reef rocks and up the beige sand incline. The sound of the sea breeze sang in her ears along with the crescendo splash of the waves.

I want my next marriage to embody the spirit of water caressing land. Waves from deep water flooded the reef. Quietly the reef reciprocated, returning the water to the diminished sea. The waters and waves flowed rhythmically: one powerful, the next gentle ebbing and flowing almost imperceptibly across the reef.

Her rock was very exposed, most of the seaweed scoured away by the abrasive sand. *This is probably the most wonderful birthday yet,* she thought. She was free, living in a place of beauty, graced by healthy, loving children and many friends, established in her career, becoming who she was meant to be.

She had looked like "one grad" at her show opening, up to her chin in *lei*: mostly ginger (Ray, of course) and *pikake* (six strands from Rod), gorgeous *ola'a beauty* purple garlands from Heather on Maui, roses from Cherry, *ilima-pikake* from Frankie. Flanked all evening by David Warfield, her new attorney and the most intelligent man she'd met to date, and Ray, who invited her to dinner afterwards. She gave the kids twenty dollars to get ice cream for their dinner, shades of W.C. Fields, and asked Marianna to drive everybody home.

Marianna quipped, "I'd rather eat *Bubbie's* ice cream than your food any day, Mom."

Ray was sitting at a tiny table for two when Lucky walked in, its white tablecloth offset by a single peach rose. Lucky was taken by being there with him, realizing her dream. A bit tipsy on reception wine, she kissed him three times on the mouth before she sat down. The poor guy was trapped behind the table unable to move. She sang, *"Love, love me, do, and say you'll be true, oh, please, please love me, dooooooo. Yeah,"* dancing to her chair.

First morning she'd had to herself in a long time. She was not engaging in any chores even though plenty needed to be done: the broken clothesline was full of wet laundry, half of which Bosco had dragged out to the front lawn and chewed, packing boxes and materials from galleries loitered by the front entry, inside boxes full of unsold pots needed display; laundry was folded on the living room floor, not yet put away.

Instead, she had brewed herself a pot of macadamia-vanilla Kona coffee, considered walking Hula Girl and exercising, but the malaise and letdown from weeks of intensive and exhaustive work overtook the health program. She returned to prone position on her bed.

She wondered if she had embarrassed Ray at the restaurant the other night. She still could not loosen him from her thoughts.

A mysterious letter arrived. "Lucky 4 M & A". *Who could this be from?*

Inside, Outrigger Canoe Club applications. She unfolded a fifty-dollar bill, what for? Delightfully surprised, she read:

Lucky, I'll sponsor the girls only if they're good to their Mom. Please use the fifty to buy us both tickets to Cherry's Auction at Iolani Palace. Okay? ...Ray

She was giddy. She dreamed, dozing the day away, lingering in bed. In the late afternoon, she got out a piece of fabric from his company and sewed a *mu'u mu'u* to wear to the auction. She felt old-fashioned, sewing for a date.

In the studio, she created his tile kitchen mural, a land and seascape of the islands. When scoring the tile backs, she got inspired and wrote blessings in the moist clay: *Bounty, Prosperity, Abundance, Joy, Health, Love, Hope, Passion, Faith, Peace, Grace.* Her 'secret' gift would be adhered in mortar to his home.

"How about if I come up early tomorrow, around seven, Ray, to drop off some mangoes and have coffee?"

"I'd like that," he said.

In the morning, she ran into him on the road.

"I'm on my way to a rough water swim. Sorry, I forgot about you. The house is open. You can leave the mangoes on the table." She shook her head, unnerved, and laughed as she sat stopped behind the steering wheel. *He almost got away.*

"How was Coronado?"

"Oh, I saw Felicia in Coronado. We had a wonderful four or so days together. We got along so well. She's a wonderful person." Lucky came unglued. *When I love someone, I'm so stupid.* No wonder he hadn't called for five days after his return from the mainland. *Why then has he made two dates with me?*

Her lingering desire was humiliating. She sat on Ray's carpet looking at boat ads from the thirties he'd collected in California. The *mu'u* she'd sewn from his fabric kept slipping off her shoulder, and she was sorry she hadn't worn a bra.

She gathered up her purse, bag, and keys. He gave her three quick lip pecks. She put everything back down.

She swallowed pride down her throat past the heartache lodged there and said very quietly, "Ray, I really like you, and for a very long time I've wanted to express that to you. The only way I know how is to kiss you."

Without stepping off the threshold to his house, he leaned down. She stood at a much lower level on the deck. He kissed her the most glorious, warm, delicious kiss.

She hugged him like a child, since their heights are all crazy: he up on that threshold, she down on the deck. She walked cautiously down the darkened staircase and through the foliage of wet ginger to her truck.

"Drive careful," he shouted from the doorway. *His house is too exposed,* she thought, *there is too much wind.* It was too easy to get lost or blown away there where the weather was so changeable.

She was not crying; the gasping came a little further down the road, small choking sounds barely audible over the radio. All the way to Wai'anae, she repeated the gasping, choking, crying. She dwelt in double limbo: not knowing doodle squat about her divorce, not knowing doodle squat about love. This on-again off-again jerked her heart like a yo-yo on a string.

Cherry was right. Ray's color gray was a drain on her sun. This unfulfilled, unrequited love was exhausting.

If he weren't so good looking, she might have been free of her obsession. If he had been ugly then his neglect might have turned her off. *He never should have had an erection*, she thought. It had been driving her crazy for five months.

Singing while shaving her legs in the shower, "I need a MAN, man, man oh man, I need a MAN, man, man man oh man I need a MAN man, man oh man oh man. Not a Boy, oy, oy, oy-e y, Not a Boy-oy, boy oy oy oy Not a..."

She dressed in bright red Christmas satin lace panties and old-fashioned saloon-style bra. Her nipples were sagging, a rude reminder that she was completely forty-four. She gyrated and sang in front of her bathroom mirror. She turned on all the lights and held a small hand mirror, trying to see all her moves from behind. Appraising her aging body, she hoped it was not completely disgusting, looking for a glimmer of hope in its moves that she was still desirable.

She wished the mirror could reflect her soul instead of her body. Her soul felt young and vital. Her body had a history, not of weather but of meteor storms, eons of suckling and birthing, light years of chocolates forming asteroid fields of pure cellulite. *Why does it have to show? Jeez.* The sins of excess and extravagance, of age and a little fun, were sagging, gravity pulling all her sins a little lower.

She sat half nude on the john, leaning over her knees, thinking, lingering after a pee. She thought she looked like Rodin's *The Thinker.* Then she pulled on her super-tight Lycra jumpsuit, and with thumbs under each armpit, flipped her nipples up, so the Lycra wouldn't reveal their droop: the tongue out-of-mouth, half-laughing, "together" look. *Older women flip their nipples up*, she chuckled.

She went to Ray's house in pouring midday rain to deliver the first increment of kitchen tiles. He was meeting his architect at one to go over the furniture order from Bali. Walton's tan *Mazda* truck was parked on Ray's newly poured concrete drive-way. She thought it was Walton, a genuinely nice fellow with a spiritual outlook on life, coming down the stairs, but it was Ray, shirtless.

Happy to see him, she ran into his arms, giving him a big hug. He bent to kiss her; she averted her face, going solely for the hug. She needed to pee.

"I have to use your bathroom at the old house before I can be sociable."

"A friend of mine is up there," he yelled after her. It was raining harder as Lucky dashed up the concrete driveway and over the roadway to keep her birthday shoes from getting muddy in the newly landscaped yard. At Ray's old house, she had to pass through the darkened bedroom to get to the bath-room. The bed was very rumpled, and wrapped in the sheets, a blonde girl slept.

"Excuse me, I need to use the bathroom," Lucky managed to make her tongue say. She slid the bathroom door closed, absorbing the shock. *It's one o'clock in the afternoon and a girl's in Ray's bed.* No toilet paper. Ray's funny handwriting was on the empty roller, "Ayaaaaahhh."

"Is there any toilet paper?" Lucky called, wakening the blonde.

"Use a paper towel."

Opening the bathroom door, Lucky asked, "Who are you?"

The blonde sleepily rolled over, "Denise."

"What are you doing here?"

"I'm waiting for Ray. We're going surfing on the North Shore at two, but he says he has to do some work on his house."

"Are you his girlfriend?"

"No. His surfing buddy."

"If you're not his girlfriend, what are you doing in his bed at one in the afternoon?" Lucky asked again.

"Who're you?" the girl asked.

"Lucky."

"Oh, really? That was my old dog's name," the blonde exclaimed, scoring really big points. Lucky shut the bathroom door and peed. Betrayal and the insult of aging percolated through her system. Ray walked across the muddy landscaping carrying a roll of toilet paper in his hand.

"Lucky, you need this?" he shouted.

"No," she yelled back, already on the deck. "I never use the stuff."

"Oh, five dollah bill, eh?" She shook her head in disbelief at the situation she'd fallen into and walked back on the concrete drive to the new house. Ray stayed with the girl. Lucky saw them talking briefly as he adjusted a surfboard on his truck. In the new house, she examined Walton's grout job on the Mexican tiles. It was abominable. She determined she couldn't do any work on the kitchen, upset as she was.

"Would you believe there's a beautiful girl in Ray's bed?"

"There is?" Walton smiled. "A beautiful one?"

"Yes, there's a beautiful girl in Ray's bed. I can't believe it. Well, I can't work here today. I guess I'll be going. I don't think Ray is going to like my tiles anyway."

"Oh, he took a look at a couple of them and loved the ocean colors."

"Well, I've got to get out of here."

"Peace be in your heart," Walton wished her.

"Oh yeah," Lucky laughed, running quickly down the stairs to her truck, "I'll hold that thought."

I don't need any more unmade beds in my life, she thought as she drove away. She looked a few times in the rear view mirror to see if Ray was following, but he wasn't. She got gas in Manoa. She didn't cry. She gasped a little. She didn't listen to the radio.

By night, the sky had broken down, and rain was spilling in noisy torrents on the eaves, pooling and puddling on the asphalt below, going nowhere in particular.

She called Cherry.

"Suspend any judgments. You'll hear from him."

She called Heather.

"I told you all along, Lucky, there was something abnormal about his behavior. He's manipulative and controlling. You better take a long look at the men in your life to determine what kind of man you want in your future."

She called Edna.

"Oh, Emily, I'm sorry."

She called Laura, who wasn't home. She called Jackie, who had big news of his own. He had sold Wolfeson Outfitters for $100,000,000 to Japanese investors.

"Em, I feel like I've cut off my arms and my legs, and oh yeah, it hurts like hell. But, I like the terms of the deal. They'll pay me in yearly increments for the rest of my life. And, when I'm dead, they'll still be paying into a trust I've set up for my heirs, if I ever have kids. It's a clever little package, if I say so myself."

Lucky did not pay proper heed to the selling of the family business. She wasn't a beneficiary anyway.

She was into a crying jag and bawled, "Jackie, I can't have anyone like Ray in my life again. I have to be able to trust the person and have that person fully want me and take care of me."

"Lots of men use a girl like that Denise, or whatever her name was. Psychologically, she may mean nothing to him. He may truly like you. You may be too much for him, or he's waiting for you to get clear. I'm really sorry you got hurt, Lucky. He can still be a good friend, so don't criticize him or lay a heavy trip on him.

"Listen, Em, sorry, but I'm on the run now. Wanting to hear that the divorce is behind you, and Mr. Rights are hounding and humping you."

Another Christmas season approached. Lucky drank rum and *7-Up* on ice, wearing a pink knit ski cap to keep pneumonia at bay, seated on a metal stool in the open air studio's wetness making samurai teapots with delicate spouts, squeezed handles, exquisite, time consuming. Ande helped, making thirty-eight cylindrical vases.

The air was so wet that the clay didn't dry a bit, melting to the touch. Lucky was glad for Ande's company: sensitive, humorous, and conciliatory.

Lucky thought: *Please, dear God, never make me work this hard again. I love clay, but I don't want to HAVE to work in the rain, chilled, under deadlines, worried about my health, and my family's welfare.*

She contracted pneumonia nonetheless. *I am like a pool of water after a violent storm. Between pain, codeine, guilt over work not done, and bed, I am not my usual self. But this resting self is learning patience. I have to stop, to slow down and wait this illness out.*

The anti-inflammatory medicine gave her hideous headaches, shooting vertical pains from her eyes to the top of her head. She was sleepless for days. Relief came at last by a change in medications. Codeine made her calm enough to sleep to end the storm of nervous energy.

45

MORE THANKSGIVING

Marianna ironed, protesting all the while, the white linen tablecloth, its few holes apparent.

"Why do I have to iron, when I'm not going to eat turkey anyway?"

Lucky reflected on the elegance of twenty previous Thanksgiving dinners: those glorious November sunsets with shrimp cocktails on the lawn, before-dinner drinks, when they were 'family.' This year Queenie was hospitalized, the chemo taking its legendary toll. Rex was beside himself in pre-mourning anxiety.

Rex brought over some red cabbage, green beans, and yams for Lucky to prepare. She gave him a pumpkin cheesecake and promised leftovers tomorrow. He wore his misery like a straight jacket. No meal would be shared this year.

The new life the kids and she were forging was full of unexpected idiocy and laughter. She pushed her red hot kiln out of a sudden downpour too late: the kiln blew all the power out of the house, leaving them with raw turkey and half cooked pies at three-thirty in the afternoon. Emergency repairs came from Wade Charger, the electrician who had called earlier that day to wish them a happy Thanksgiving, chancing to say he'd be eating at Rod's.

Finally, she and the kids ate a scorched turkey at nine p.m., cooked at five hundred degrees for two hours after Charger had replaced the fuse box. Lucky sat down to a table set with mauve candles in hurricanes, pink and rose ginger in a raku vase, the kids still garbed casually in wet bathing suits from a day playing in the rain. Nico and Ande lit their Woolworth seasonal turkey and Indian candles, burning the turkey butts and Indian heads in ritual torture, *Freddy Kreuger*-ing the bodies with hot wax, laughing maniacally all the while.

As the meal progressed, all decorum was lost. Lucky let them pick at the bird with their hands. She pulled off wings and sections of breast, tossing them through the air to the kids. They whooped and hollered like Indians at a war party.

"Gobble, gobble, gobble, the turkey is in trouble," they sang in unison. Nico and Ande swung their drumsticks high overhead like tomahawks, and then dive-bombed them directly into the gravy bowl. Only Marianna avoided the turkey, nibbling instead on green beans and yams. They all ate pie and mousse.

Nico burped, blueberries staining his lips, pronouncing, "It's the best Thanksgiving ever."

46

MARIANNA

Fourteen months had passed since Lucky filed for divorce. She owed Thomas eleven thousand dollars in legal fees. She was calm, as only a long period of unrelieved stress and anxiety can induce. She had kept the restraining order in effect. But she was also troubled by Marianna's hostility and anger, which now extended to everyone.

Lucky also wanted to get a new truck. The banks had refused her loan application. Then a loan miraculously came through in time for Marianna's seventeenth birthday. Lucky took Marianna on a mystery-shopping spree. Together they picked out a brand new white *Mazda* pick-up. At the last moment, Lucky ordered customized plates, which read FAITH. But, Marianna didn't seem particularly excited about the truck.

She was budding into womanhood angrily. She was ashamed of things she'd done. She especially didn't want to talk to her mother about boys or sex. She had lots of secrets on her mind. And, she wanted them kept secret. Lucky worried that Marianna wasn't using birth control and wanted her to practice safe sex.

"Marianna," Lucky said after dinner, "come outside." They sat on the stair landing under the old sea grape tree. "I love you, honey. I'm worried about you. What is wrong? Why are you so mad all the time?"

Marianna answered, "I don't like you, Mom, for starters. You're a blabbermouth. You don't keep anything to yourself. You make me sick, dating younger guys like Ray. Talking about your love life. All you care about are appearances: how you dress, how skinny you are, how young, how cute your kids are, like we were toys or something, how the table is set, how great the food looks. Yuck. It's sickening. Besides, you don't know how to cook right," she continued. "You don't cook healthy, vegetarian meals. You won't let me do the things I want to do. Sometimes you're really nice, like buying me the *Mustang* and now the *Mazda*. But, mostly, you try to run my life. You want me to be perfect, like you, and I'm not."

"I'm far from perfect, Marianna."

"I can never be like you, Mom."

"I wouldn't want you to be. Don't you know that? You are uniquely you."

"I hate it when you drink."

"Oh. Are you remembering me and *beer: thirty*?"

"Yeah. Drinking when you start to fix dinner at five-thirty every day. Yeah, yeah. It's not in the past tense, Mom."

"Yes, it is. I have cut beer out of my diet."

"Well, if you don't drink, I'm glad, Mom. It was a bummer. You'd get so mad, you'd hit Ande or me right in the face, and we'd get bloody noses."

"I did not. When? It wasn't like that. It happened once, I think. Yes. And, I am so sorry. It was the tension. There was so much tension in the house. I was tired all the time. The drive to school in town. Your dad's constant nagging. By the time I had to cook dinner, I had to have a beer," she paused, "to unwind. Otherwise, I knew my blood sugar would be so low, I'd be a snapper head for real," Lucky confessed, rationalizing her behavior.

"So, I remember: around five-thirty you'd grab your first beer from the fridge. If dad and his friends had drunk them all, you'd start screaming and raid the money bowl and run to *Long's* for a quart of *Asahi*."

"That bad, huh?" Lucky winced.

"I'm glad if you don't do that anymore, Mom." They sat quietly for a while.

"I don't really know why I'm so angry; I just am. My feelings are so strong. After Dad left, I felt you and I were equals. I had no dad to ask permission to do things. I didn't feel I needed your permission; you were too weak. I thought I could do what I wanted."

"I didn't let you do what you wanted."

"You're such a push-over. I don't respect you. Don't you get it, Mom? I don't respect you. I am angry with you for not saving me. I am angry with you for not doing anything. I am angry with you for staying home and not going out and meeting new people and doing things with your life. My anger grows and grows. I am mad at Nico for talking to Birdie about Darryl. You know, he told her about Darryl sleeping over. That's private, Mom. It's my personal life."

"Are you a little disappointed in sex?" Lucky asked.

Marianna blushed, "There you go again, Mom, asking things you shouldn't." After a while, Marianna pursed her lips and remarked casually, "You know, Mom, I think that holding hands is more intimate."

"Do you blame me for the divorce, for losing your dad?"

"No. I am mad at Dad. He never talks to me. He's never apologized for siding with Francine at the beach or for hitting me. He's never even said he's sorry for punching me this summer. How can he say, 'Hi, How are you?' and never talk about how I really am? He's a hypocrite. And, and… Why doesn't he love me anymore, Mom?"

Before Lucky could answer, Marianna added, "The thing that hurts me the most is how could anyone hurt my mother? The person I love best in the whole world? How could anyone hurt you, Mom?"

Lucky was taken by surprise.

"I am so angry at Dad for lying to you and not taking you out to dinner and calling you a fat ass and not being nice for so long, for treating my mom like garbage."

Lucky was unable to respond.

"Dad's immoral, Mom. I can't understand why Gramma loves him and not me. I can't understand how Gramma and Grampa can forget about me and not care anymore." She began to cry. "Nobody in this family loves me anymore."

"I do, Marianna. I love you so much," Lucky said, holding her. "Remember when you were little, and you'd ask, *how much do you love me?* And I would answer, spreading my arms wide: *I love you wider than the whole wide world.* Then I'd point down and say, *I love you deeper than the deep blue sea.* And then I'd point up and say, *I love you higher than the sky, that's how much I love you, and I love you even more.* I'm sorry. I hate everything that's happened. I wish Queenie had room in her heart for you and your dad, both. I feel, Marianna, that your dad leaving me is actually a gift. I have gotten a second chance, and I feel reborn. I don't know if you can understand this, because you have never been a wife. And, God, I am so sorry your dad is being so awful to you. I suppose God wouldn't have given me the responsibility of raising you kids alone if it wasn't best for us all. We all would have suffered if your dad and I had stayed together. Just like old Chubby: loving too much and getting kicked for it."

"Do you think I should talk to Dad?"

"Oh, brother. Your dad is confused. I don't know. Talking to him now might not get you the love you miss or any answers. Maybe later on would be better when you can become close again."

47

DEAD DOG

A gust of wind at the annual "Christmas in the Park" craft fair shattered Lucky's best pots. The gust flung the display drape over the delicate handles of her *Samurai Teas*, pulling them off their pedestals into a thundering torrent of ceramic shards. Six weeks of her life broken, wasted, those late nights working till two, lonely, stressed, crying, fearful of debt, all gone in a puff of wind.

Losing these pots caused terrible pain. Her heart felt like the railroad spike she dreamt of using on Fannie had been pounded into her own, then wrenched out of her body, stretched, and staked to the ground.

Lucky still had to install Ray's tiles despite her disillusionment. She took Ande with her in the heavy rain, scared, not wanting to make a mistake that would ruin his kitchen. Some tiles were too small; some were too big. Many needed to be re-cut with her wet diamond blade. She got depressed about the tiles not interlocking precisely in the pattern she designed.

Ray said he was going to a Christmas party. Lucky saw a blonde like Denise pull up to the house and wait, playing with Pua. Lucky assumed she'd come for Ray. But, a *ha'ole* man from the rented house got into her car, and they drove away. A few moments later, Ray tapped on the kitchen door to say good-bye.

When he left, she focused on the installation. She adhered three sections, matching grout lines to glaze colors. And, wow, smasheroo: they were really beautiful. What she had created wrapping around his kitchen was a bird's eye view of the islands.

When Lucky and Ande had cleaned up to leave, she found the light on in her truck, its door ajar, a box of chocolate truffles in her *Kleenex* box with a note, along with a big bunch of pink and red ginger soaking in a dog dish of water in the rear bed. "Merry Christmas, Love, Ray."

Lucky let Bullet and his parents come for Christmas breakfast and present opening. Queenie looked very frail. Lucky wanted a peaceful time with them on this day. Without tension, she listened to her exes talking around the table after breakfast, glad they were no longer her family; their talk and history were trivial. Bullet's one and only college football touchdown had been relived at family get-togethers and holidays for twenty years.

"I was playing tight end, kids. I was fast, a real mover on the field. Whenever I got the ball, the cheerleaders would yell, 'He's faster than a speeding bullet' Yep. That's right. Your dad was a real mover on the field," he repeated with pride.

Rex interjected his own version of how he named his son. Rex liked to think he named Richard, "Bullet," after the single leave encounter he spent in bed with Queenie toward the end of the war, World War II.

He laughed, smugly nudging her, "I was a real straight shooter, huh, Queenie? That's all it took. One shot. When I got home from the Pacific, there was our little *Bullet*."

They retold the myriad cross-country moves during Rex's career as a pilot, Queenie tittering like a schoolgirl at the memories. It was peaceful; Lucky survived. *That was the last one I'll ever do,* she determined. *My life will be different next year.*

For Christmas dinner, she cooked an elaborate seafood Creole especially for Marianna, baked chicken in feta cheese for Ande and Nico, pomelo salad, beans, pasta, baguette, blueberry pie, and bouche de noel for everyone. She laid an elegant table with a new damask cloth, plaid wool mats, silver service, and fresh holly imported from the mainland surrounded the Christmas crèche candle carousel.

Ray came late bearing sweatshirts wrapped in beach mats for Marianna, Ande, and Nico.

"One of those is for your mom," he said.

One for me? He's brought me a sweatshirt for Christmas? Nico ambushed him at the kitchen door with a spray of water from his new *mastah blastah* squirt gun, accompanied by the staccato *ratta tat* of a machine gun. Ray looked annoyed.

"Sorry to be late, Lucky," he said. "It's been a rough day. Someone shot Kula this morning."

"What?" Lucky gasped. "Is she all right?"

"She's dead."

"Oh no, Ray. Excuse me. Nico, would you knock off the squirt gun, please?"

"Sorry, Ma. Sorry, Ray."

"Who would shoot Kula?" Lucky asked, dropping her hot pads on the counter and going to Ray. "Who would shoot a dog? I mean, who's out with a shotgun on Christmas morning anyway?"

"I don't know, Lucky. My neighbor at the coral house at the bend in the road found her. She called me. Kula wandered down the hill, I guess. She collapsed on her front porch, dying. My pup, little Pua, must have followed her down, because she was yiping and licking her."

"Did you hear anything? Did anybody hear shots?"

"I didn't, Lucky. I was on an early bike ride." He looked dejected. "She was a real good dog. She was arthritic and loyal. She was my best friend." *Kula*, Hawai'ian for gold, all that was most precious, Ray's beloved Kula, a golden retriever of fourteen age-thickened years, ex-surfer pal and beach buddy, shot dead by some unknown assailant on the privacy of his six forested acres.

Lucky tried to comfort him, but he was unresponsive. His coldness hurt. He ate and played half-heartedly with the rambunctious kids. Nico got calls from friends to compare toys, and Marianna got a call from Darryl.

After dinner Lucky invited Ray to watch the surf at the beach in front of the house, the place she walked for meditation. She needed to relax after the strain of the Christmas push, and she looked forward to some time for herself with him.

"No thanks, Lucky. I am tired, and I want to go home. Check on the puppy. Long drive, you know."

"Yes, I do know. I've been doing it for eighteen years." Out by his truck, he gave her a very brief kiss on the mouth. Her hopes, whatever they were, her non-expectations, whatever they weren't, dashed. The letdown she felt was phenomenal.

She went back inside the gate as the wind was blowing hard. She turned around. She walked to the beach after all, barefoot in the cold and wet, wearing Chinese red silk pants, white silk shirt, and her Christmas shawl. She sat on a rock facing the darkening storm, holding her head in her hands.

"Give me nothing," she muttered to the night. "Nothing is better than the insult of a *sweatshirt*. Give me perfume, give me panties, give me jewelry. Give me something for ME, something personal. But don't, don't give me a goddamned sweatshirt."

Nico had given her a green crystal on a silver chain. She remembered the day he stuffed fifty dollars into his T-shirt pocket and walked into the mall to shop for her.

Going home, Lucky washed the salt off the upstairs deck windows at nine-thirty at night while the children slept on mats under the Christmas lights twinkling on the railing.

Ray did not call to thank her for the knock-your-socks-off Christmas dinner or the gifts of saffron bread, book, platter, and thousand-dollar teapot. Lucky was keeping score. She blamed him for her own generosity.

Mr. Hope, her current lesson in life, cold, manipulative, frightened by intimacy, baited her and disappeared. She responded by burning with sexual desire, pretending the attraction could bring her a genuinely satisfying relationship. She wanted to enter his heart, removing the distance between them. He would not let her near. In fact, he ran from her approach.

hi mom you did not expect me to be writing to you i wanted to tell you to get a life

the other day and today all i heard you doing was talking to your friends about you and ray

mom you think that he is in love with you

well let me tell you one thing

he is not

all he wants to be is your friend all he needs from you is your friendship. nothing more nothing less

i know that when you guys started out he gave you a little more than you expected you wanted that little something to last

but it did not

ray is confused he does not know what he wants but one thing i can see for sure is that he does not want you for a lover he is your friend if he does not call you for a week, don't be i don't see heather calling you every day

another thing that has been bothering me is the way you have been acting i want to tell you some thing about you

you are the most conceited person i know all you say and think about is you you say how you are so beautiful and skinny mom you are too skinny you look gross all that is on your body is skin, no muscles it is flab that hangs off your legs

mom, to break the news to you, you are 44 years old you may be better looking than most people your age but that's only to your age

and you don't know why ray won't go out with you mom he is looking for someone young and who can have his children someone he can spend his whole life with not just part of it also some one who does not have emotional problems like you

i swear mom you don't have to cry about every little thing like ray not giving you an expensive christmas present you should just be happy that he gave you something man

don't take life so seriously you only have one time to live so make the best of it be thankful for what you have you have a life three kids a house a dog a business and people who love you and take care of you that is most important mom you have to make life worth living

mom you have to be happy with yourself and that is all live life as best you can don't make it a living hell for you and others around you i hope you get better love ande

Post-Christmas Blues. Her kids didn't listen to her. She sat, knees up, on the kitchen floor, facing a corner of the stove, weeping. She figured she looked mentally ill.

Lucky asked Dr. Dousch how to deal with loneliness.

"Keep busy. Put that side of your life on hold."

"Ray gave me a sweatshirt for Christmas. I can't shake my outrage over it."

"It's deeply intimate of him to put your ceramics in his house, Lucky, on his walls, to live with. At this time, you are too vulnerable, and your choices in men might be very wrong. When you're ready, the right man will definitely appear."

"Why am I hooked on physical sex as proof of love?"

"Next time we meet, let's take a look at your father, at the men in your life, and your need for their approval," he suggested.

The little red birds were driving her crazy. They woke her every morning with their twitter twitter chirruping, letting her know that promised happiness was out there. She had thought the bird was Ray. Her hope. Then she had thought it was her happiness. Now she understood it was her psychic lunacy.

She saw the red birds everywhere, even on neighbor islands. On Maui, at a business lunch in Kihei at a restaurant, installing a new piece on the Big Island in Waimea, at Malaekahana's long beach, hopping right behind Jackie on the roots of a tree as they caught up on personal histories, in the thickly leafed boughs of the sea grape tree outside her kitchen door when neighbor Rod came over. Always, the bright red, orange beaked male, chirruping insistently, as she craned her neck upward, straining to see his feathered body as confirmation to her ears' report. *Why, why, why are you here? Why are you reminding me of promises unkept?*

"Lucky, you bought rejection from Bullet and have been wearing it with Ray," Rod told her at dinner one night. "Even I knew who Bull was fucking. Dark hair? Out back in your studio? Yeah. I knew it. She's the one. And, I knew about your assistant, the one from Japan he fucked before her."

"You did? Did lots of people know?"

"Oh, Lucky. Why not buy acceptance of yourself? Accept Lucky and the wonder and remarkableness of Lucky. Get into her. Stop channeling energy into other people and relationships. Stop eternally playing out the Bullet rejection."

48

TABOO

D r. Dousch told Lucky her relationship to her father had resulted in emotional paralysis, which belly flopped her back into her childhood heart. There she found a girl seduced by her dad's promise of love, gifts, and misplaced sexuality.

As a ten-year old, forewarned by tales of his incestuous lust for Laura, Lucky had fled his embrace, frightened by his advances. It was heady stuff, to know she was sought in place of her mother. Juicy, too, too juicy for a child. Damaging and worse when later Big Jack abandoned them all.

"Maybe I chose men to love who are twisted and worldly," Lucky guessed, "who treat me like my father did, promising me the moon and stars, only to tell me I'll have to design my own rocket to get them."

"You may be right," Dr. Dousch affirmed.

"Maybe I expect the men I love to disappear into outer space as well," she half-heartedly joked.

Lucky had never grieved when Jack left. Due to the terms of the divorce and custody rights, she never saw her father in any context beyond adversarial, never knew him in a growing up, getting through adolescence kind of way.

Lucky knew he loved her; that was never an issue. He loved her the wrong way.

"What was an issue for me, Dr. Dousch, was that the love I felt for my father was powerless, powerless to control his violent outbursts against my mother and sister, powerless to control his sexual proclivity, powerless to make him a decent person."

"Did you expect your love to change him?"

"Yes, I wanted my love to be a viable force: respected, helpful, conciliatory, healing. I grew up believing: if I'm good enough, my goodness can transform the Beast...like Beauty's did."

"What a fairy tale," Dr. Dousch said. "The grim reality was your goodness was defenseless in the face of his savage brutality to the women in your family. You might think you rebelled against the weapons he used: money deliberately withheld, abusive sex, and brute physical intimidation. But look who you chose for a husband."

"I wanted to grow up fast. I didn't want to be a helpless kid. I was impatient to be an adult, because adults had power."

How many years have I wasted in abhorrence and deep embarrassment over my father, she wondered?

"Did you ever play out your rage?"

"No."

"Perhaps part of your heart got stuck, ranting, in that crevasse of defenseless childhood."

Edna's diminished family had to survive. Lucky survived. *Survival* seemed to be a key word for her experience. Many challenges filled those days: Edna's three-year divorce epic, tinged by fear and hatred, moving from the small town's vicious gossip to the anonymity of the big city, leaving childhood friends, starting over.

Lucky could look back and see how she was shaped, why she inadvertently got hooked by men who were cold and controlling, men who set impossible standards, which she could never satisfy yet found sexually exciting. Why did she imagine her love would change them?

When she grew up and was ready for sexual intercourse, she thought all the true fruits of love formerly out of reach would be hers. Promises would be fulfilled. She would not only catch, but also own, the brass ring for life's carousel. In her marriage, she had let sex substitute for all the kinds of love denied to her. If the sex was there, in an otherwise intolerable relationship, so was Lucky. Screwing Bully three times a day was like a recreational drug; it was her love substitute. Not getting the nurturing love she needed, she accepted sexual activity in its place.

"Fantasize, Lucky," Dr. Dousch advised. "Pick the forbidden fruit. It will free you from its bondage."

During the weeks between appointments, she tried. She played out the incest by fantasizing screwing Big Jack. She imagined orgasms. This final piece seemed oddly to complete the puzzle of her own erotic dynamic, allowing her to understand the control imposed on her life by her father's taboo groping. She determined not to let any other man control her through lust, money, or power again.

She had to learn that sexual attention was not love. She began to unchain herself link by link from the shackles of emotional enslavement and a past that bound her.

49

KULA

Lucky was on Maui at her dear friend, Heather's protea farm, situated five thousand feet up the slopes of Haleakala where the air was crisp and fragrant, the colors clean and vibrant. Kula rode the slopes of Haleakala like a well-softened bandanna in God's hip pocket. Being there with the island world crisply laid out below her gaze, Lucky knew she sat astride the back of something far greater than she, greater than any ordinary mountain, for *Haleakala*, a once powerful and long dormant crater, was the *house of the sun*, a center of Hawai'ian spirituality.

From the deck, she looked at the rolling green and gold pastures, interrupted sporadically by tall eucalyptus windbreaks and barbed wire fences, which cascaded down the bib of the volcano to the cane fields near the sea.

A sugar refinery spewed its white smoke far in the flattened distance. To the west curved the graceful arch of Kihei, where tiny white boats moored in the glassy blue water; to the right stood the green and impenetrable West Maui Mountains, and beyond them the island of Lana'i rose brown and low from the sea. To the north, Moloka'i nudged, edging behind the cliffs of Waihe'e. Way to the south, Kaho'olawe and Molokini islands lifted red and umber from the cobalt channel in pristine clarity from this Up-country vantage.

The Pacific framed both sides of her peripheral vision in its vast blueness, so distant the sun reflected off its mirrored surface. At this altitude, Lucky stood taller than the West Maui Mountains, across the flat isthmus planted in highways, pineapple, scruff, and cane. Eucalyptus surrounded the cottage and barn like a horseshoe, the cattle freely roaming the open range above.

A bird, *Was it a hawk?* glided over the sloping pasture to her right. She held her gaze on its flight. It was an owl, *pueo*, bird of the goddess of wisdom, Athena. It banked and flew low to the hill, gliding toward Lucky. She saw the yellowed whiteness of its face and belly, its round, hooded eyes when it turned; an owl hunting at high noon, a night creature out in the brightness of day. She was mystified by this bird's presence. A creature both from this natural world and from the invisible realm, the owl came like an omen, a sign, something sacred, beyond her grasp, to be noted and respected.

Nestled in this horseshoe were acres of exotic protea from South Africa and Australia, the large, rangy bushes were cousins of the macadamia, with triumphant blooms, sometimes a foot across, luminescent velvet-soft pinks or deep-reds fringed in black. Kings, queens, duchesses, they were named, no two blooms alike, chartreuse minks, silver tree. Some banksia foliage was diamond shaped as though pruned with pinking shears to look like rickrack, other blooms appeared to be made from crocheted red plastic telephone cable into pincushions from the planet Mars.

ARABELLA ARK

Lucky walked through rows upon row of these bushes towering ten to thirty feet above her head, fuller with their ornamentation of blooms and foliage than the best mink decorated San Francisco *I. Magnin* Christmas trees she remembered from childhood. She didn't realize at first that she had burst into song. She sang to the flowers: *You are so beautiful, to me, can't you see?* She caressed their petals. She would have been mute, except that she was crooning her love song, gently, softly, amazed, to these velvet coated beauties.

She stood on the cottage's deck overlooking the noonness of everything, her eyes slightly weak. She had drawn several fabric designs for Ray's textile company, having woken in Heather's gingham bed with images fresh in her mind, frustrated at having left her camera at home, unable to document precisely the blossoms, seedpods, and foliage. Instead, she took mental photos, memorizing nature's patterns as inspiration.

She had gotten an idea to enter business with Ray: glazing protea and foliage decals in Hawai'iana patterns on her ceramics with his coordinated fabrics as tablecloths, sheets and towels embroidered with maile borders and protea centers.

She didn't want to invite Ray over or to interrupt her privacy and her peace. She coveted this focus, drinking tea made from bottled water, as the well water was impure, and stoking the fire to keep the chill away, as intense hours of work passed. The smell of eucalyptus was in the air as was the smoke from her fire, pungent, sweet, mountainous, and distinctly Up-country. The farm was quiet, so quiet that she could hear the birds chat like neighbors, and the wind whisper intimations of a gentler future.

In the evening as the sun set, a veil of mist gently obscured the isthmus, islands, and sea below. The tips of the mountains peeked their chocolate heads like truffles into the ever-pinking dusk, and the eucalyptus cast black silhouettes against the almost whitened sky. The blue was worn from the day, fading away like bleached denim.

She planted both feet firmly on the ground, the high and fertile Kula ground, acknowledging the antiquity of the Jurassic tree fern at her left shoulder, breathed deeply and fully of the moist air and, without thinking or planning, began to vibrate and hum *AUM*. She hadn't hummed, thought, or chanted *AUM* for over twenty bygone hippie years. Her third finger on each hand curled to meet the thumb forming perfect circles. She stood her ground, vibrating and *AUM*-ing.

An echo resounded, a clear response, from the other side of the eucalyptus closer to the dying sun. A cow lowed, sounding like her. She *AUM*-ed again. And, catching her breath, she heard the bovine echo. The lone cow and she continued *AUM*-ing and lowing while the sun, fiery coal red, submerged into the clouded sea. Coolness and dark fell upon her. And, this, this was Kula, pure gold.

It was a blue moon. December 31st, the last day of the year. A blue moon didn't occur very often. It was the thirteenth full moon of the year, the second full moon for the month of December. It was said to bring added lunacy to the planet. The moon aligned directly opposite the sun, with the earth in the middle as a sandwich to create a condition known as *syzygy*. This moon, like a ripe pumpkin, did not really appear blue. It was soon dissected by a cloud and split into orange segments that appeared like two glowing steer horns in the night sky.

She gloried in this time. She was grateful to have been set free, to begin anew. She was alone, deeply contented, rich, and warm as the coals in her nightly fire. Happy to be herself, happy to be in Heather's cottage, cozy, creative, alone, unbelievably alone. The telephone beside her could connect immediately to her children, sister, brother, mother, Cherry, or Ray's answer machine. Connected or alone, her choice.

Why did she feel un-alone? She kept company with the cattle, the birds, the lone owl or pheasants under brush, the flowers, the wind, the world below. She stepped outside to hear isolated firecrackers explode in anticipation of the New Year. She beheld the island world from this distance. Perched there was like being in a small plane scudding over the land. Everything was smaller, everything was vaster, and everything was in perspective, the human problems lessening to insignificance.

On New Year's Day, she called Ray. He was home, unusual on a Sunday morning. He thanked her for Christmas, saying he had tried to reach her at home and at the gallery.

"How're ya doing, Ray?"

"All right. Fine, I guess."

"I'm on Maui. It's beautiful. It's God's country. And, Ray, the protea on the farm are gorgeous, inspiring."

"I'd love to see them."

"Are you free? Would you like to come over?"

"Well, no," he paused. "Thanks, but it wouldn't work out," he paused again. "Felicia came in yesterday."

"Who?"

"Felicia. My ex."

"Oh. To Honolulu?"

"Yep."

"Where is she staying?"

"With me."

Lucky rambled about the cold and her fire and all the fleas. Ray added, "She loves your tiles."

Finally, Lucky said goodbye.

PART THREE

THE HOMECOMING

50

WRECKAGE

A midwinter hurricane assailed the islands. Lucky loaded the kids, Hula Girl, Bosco, Suds, food, fresh water, clothes, sleeping bags, tent, lantern, radio, money, art slides, passports and birth certificates into her truck and drove deep into the Wai'anae Valley to wait out the winds.

Her beach house survived, although most of its downstairs windows were broken and bit of roof dangled from its western exposure. The floors lurked under ten inches of sand, reef fish, and seaweed as the stench of a dead eel rotted the air. Civil Defense and the state were busy restoring roads, phone, and power lines. There was no electricity or manpower to help Lucky clean up. Not a word from Bullet or Rex, not even to ask if the children were all right.

She and the kids put in back-wrenching hours shoveling sand. It took two full days of wheel barreling before a swath was cut through the wet sand from the driveway to the kitchen. They were exhausted. The stove and refrigerator were ruined by their unexpected salt-water bath. As was her old truck, its engine flooded by tidal waters during their floating escape down the sea-inundated street the night of the storm, not to mention the complete destruction of her studio, equipment, and art.

The flood insurance company sent a representative to process her claim a week after the phone system got restored. He scheduled the next day to photograph the damage and take stock of the situation, recording the value of each damaged or missing item. Lucky had lost five kilns. She had a big exhibition scheduled for early March, which had been her prime prospect for income. She needed the insurance money immediately to get new kilns and make her studio operational again.

And, so, Peppard Strong arrived, red birds behind either shoulder. He was a tall man, well over six-five, freckled and virile, limbs covered by soft red fur. He brought a pair of tall teenage boys with him.

"I thought you could use some extra hands. These are my sons, Kelty and Sean," he said.

Surprised, she readily accepted their offer of help. After they documented the damage, took photographs, and cleaned, she made peanut butter and jelly sandwiches, "camp food," which they ate with warm sodas, as there would be no cold food until the insurance money came through for a new fridge. Two days later, Peppard returned holding an insurance check for twenty seven thousand dollars.

"I thought I'd better deliver it myself, as the post office is still messed up by the hurricane, and *FEDEX* and *UPS* are overburdened these days."

Lucky couldn't believe it. The money kept her family going for the next several months as, despite her desperate burst of creativity, nothing sold at her March exhibit.

Peppard began to ask Lucky out for dinners in the city. He was single; his wife had died six years earlier in a car accident, leaving him with the two sons to raise. He had spent some time after her death in shock, sailing the coasts of Central and South America, only settling in Hawai'i the previous December. He and the boys lived on a yacht in the Ala Wai boat harbor.

That little red cardinal chirped outside her window as she woke. When she opened the kitchen door to start the day, he and his chubby brown mate were swinging on the branches of the sea grape tree right in front of her. She knew the day would bring love.

She had had a dream. In it, she had come upon Peppard in a garden near a pond somewhere on the mainland, where he bent on hands and knees digging in bulbs, narcissus for the spring. They were much older in her dream, in their early seventies and living somewhere cold on the mainland. In the dream, he was wearing the red tartan flannel shirt she'd given him that winter, pants held taut by tawny leather braces, legs wet and stained with the grasses and mud, the whites of his socks barely peeping above his boots.

She didn't say anything, watching him work in the stillness. Then she laid her left hand gently upon his back as he maintained the rhythm of his labours. She rested her torso atop him a moment before letting her right hand slip under his midriff where it deftly unlatched the buttons of his trousers one by one. He was not alarmed by her presence. She languidly rolled onto her own back, acquiescing to the damp of the soon to be fecund ground. Fingertips edging under the soft fall of his hair, her hands met again in a delicate embrace around his neck. On exhalation, the air in his lungs met the world with chuckled surprise.

In this dream of hers, he entered her in the same manner he handled his trowel to dig into the wet earth, cleanly and with purpose. It was a strange sight, this mid-February sowing. For they were newly in love and fully dressed, he a grandfather with silver hair and she well past her seventieth birthday. Yet in the damp chill light of a winter's morning, together they planted a new bulb for spring.

Of course, knowing herself, Lucky wanted to become smaller than a little doll, so she might enter the deep purple and magenta auricle of Peppard's heart to abide deep in his chest in a perfect kind of love. She bought new white silk pajamas from *Victoria's Secret* and some lacy underwear. She released her fears and insecurity, as she had learned to do and concentrated on her ability to succeed. She realized that she had the power and dominion to choose what was right for herself, yet she tingled with *Anticipation*.

In late April, her phone rang.

"Mom, it's me, Ande. We've had a car wreck. We're okay, but ya gotta come."

"Where are you?"

"Down in Maili by the Hawai'ian food stand. Hurry up, Mom. Marianna's going nuts."

The new *Mazda* was almost cut in half from the front bumper to the windshield by a trailer hitch on the rear of the semi Marianna had been following. She didn't see the semi stop and rolled right into it. Fortunately, the after-school traffic was inching along between the dozens of intersections in Nanakuli, and Marianna had only been going about five miles per hour.

Lucky held each of the girls, kissing them, asking them if they were all right. Waiting for the police, they sweated in the relentless late April heat rising from the shadeless asphalt parking lot next to the highway, polluted by exhaust fumes. Lucky bought shave-ice.

"Well, girls, how did school go today?" she asked, handing them their flavors.

"It was shitty, as always," Marianna exploded, biting into the cold, cherry red head of her shave-ice.

"At least there's good news for you at home, Marianna. You got two college acceptance letters today, one from University of California and one from San Diego University. They say you need to maintain your spring semester grades. Isn't that great?"

Marianna wanted to bolt, but her truck was wrecked, home was six sweltering miles away, and the shave-ice was dripping sticky red sugar water like blood down her arm.

"Yeah. Great," she said. "So great it sucks. I got my SAT results today. I only got 520 verbal and 460 math. Monsieur Beaumont says I'm losing my 'A' in French. I hate you, Mom. And, I hate school. I don't want to go to fucking college."

The police arrived to gather data on the accident. The *Mazda* got towed back to the dealership. Lucky was silent on the drive home.

Marianna spent the weekend in town at Birdie's house and cut school on Monday. She called Lucky that evening to announce she was sleeping over at Birdie's again.

"No, you're not," Lucky told her. "You're catching the bus home. Now." Three hours later Marianna showed up sullen and not worth talking to. Lucky left her alone.

Peppard's son, Kelty, had suffered Hodgkin's disease when he was thirteen, and it resurfaced. The bone marrow transplant he had gotten at that time had put it in remission. Kelty woke during the night in a pool of blood. It was oozing through his pores onto the sheets. His screams woke Peppard, who carried him downstairs and took him by cab to Saint Francis Hospital.

"Lucky," he called. "It's my boy, Kelty. We've spent the night at the hospital. He's in bad shape. He's resting now and is under observation."

Lucky spent the afternoon playing poker with Kelty and Sean on the hospital sheets. She sensed how much Kelty needed to be held, reassured by touch and hugs, this boy without a mother. She massaged his feet, his legs, and his head.

She smelled a foulness she guessed to be the scent of death on his breath. It frightened her. Peppard told her a blood-filtering machine was being flown in from New York. The surgeon scheduled Kelty's spleen for removal the next day at four.

Why, why, she thought, *is the rug always getting pulled out from under me?* She already wanted to marry Peppard. He hadn't asked yet. But, he was the kindest man she'd met and of such a high caliber that her neck was stiff from looking up. She wanted to wake up in the morning with this man beside her. She wanted to explore the tenderness and beauty of making love with him. She wanted to know the security of his embrace. She wanted to sail Hawai'i's blue green seas, slide down her waterfalls, hike her valleys and mountains, to smell the green and wet, to ride horses sensing the ranch lands beneath, to share pets and plants, become man and wife.

Her feelings, feelings of immense comfort and compatibility, created that most tender sense of belonging, of finally coming home. He was someone she could love, perhaps for the first time in her life, unconditionally.

Marianna skipped school on Tuesday and Wednesday. Kelty remained in the hospital, recovering from the surgery. Peppard was stressed. Teenybopper Ande lived on the phone. Her friend, Gigi, had moved to the mainland.

Ande was talking to her on the phone that early Thursday evening when Lucky dropped Nico off at the beach to surf while she went to aerobics. They stopped at Fujimura's for lettuce, oranges, *Haagen Dazs* bars, and milk on the way home, making them later than usual. Ande was still talking on the phone when they returned. It was getting dark, but the house lights were off.

"Where's Marianna?" Lucky asked, carrying a grocery bag into the kitchen and flipping on the lights.

"She went to the beach."

"What beach? The loaner is parked outside."

"Our beach. Mom, can't you see I'm on a phone call?"

"How long's she been there?" Lucky persisted.

"She went over right after you left and told me not to bother her."

Lucky dropped the groceries and ran across the park to the beach. Suddenly, Ande hung up the phone. Her face turned gray. As Lucky ran up the dune, Ande following her.

Lucky saw a man at the far end of the beach, walking away. *Oh, no. Let Marianna be all right.* Her eyes scanned the shore faster than her legs could plod through the deep sand. A body, Marianna's body, was washing in and out of the shore break, along with shell and coral rubble.

"Marianna," Lucky screamed.

She waded into the water in her shoes and grabbed her daughter's arm. It was limp. Her elbow joint, wrists and ankles were cut with jagged gauges, drowned bits of skin and muscle tissue, dangled loosely. Lucky sank into the water. She embraced her daughter, praying for life, hoping she could hear Lucky's hushed and desperate words.

"I love you, Marianna. I love you. It's Mom. You'll be all right."

She staggered to her feet and tried to drag her daughter's soaked and resistant body a few feet up the incline. Marianna was too heavy. Lucky rolled her over and bending to the ground, hoisted her waterlogged girl onto her back like a gunnysack. She fell to her knees.

"Come on, Marianna," Lucky begged. "You've got to help me. You're too heavy. Stand up and move. Come on. Help me."

Marianna's eyelids flickered; her eyeballs rolled back into her head. She gagged.

"Ande, run. Call 911. Get an ambulance." Lucky crawled slowly across the sand on all fours with Marianna slumped over her back. Nico ran up to them.

"Mom! Mom!" he cried, his mouth pulled down to his chin, his face white with fear.

"Nico," Lucky panted. "Call your dad, at his house or Grampa's. Get him over here."

Ande returned, and together they dragged Marianna home across the park and slid her into the shower where she lay crumpled on its tile floor. Lucky turned on the hot water, which sprayed over Marianna. All Lucky could think was to warm, clean, and dry her, and then get her into dry clothes before the ambulance arrived. *Those hospital emergency rooms are cold,* Lucky knew.

"Mom," Marianna whispered, "I can't breathe."

"What did you do, Marianna?"

"Pills, Mom. I took pills," she wheezed.

"What pills?"

"There's a bag on the reef."

"Nico," Lucky screamed at her terrified little boy, "go to the reef and find a paper bag. It's got the pills Marianna took."

Two paramedics burst into the bathroom, pulled Marianna out of the shower, and strapped her dripping wet to a gurney. Lucky hadn't even heard them arrive, despite the blare of their siren. Bullet parked next to their ambulance, where neighbors had gathered in curious groups.

Nico retrieved the bag. It was full of empty *Tylenol* bottles, *Contac* wrappers, and a codeine container prescribed for Lucky's last pneumonia. One paramedic called the information to the ER doctors while the other two lifted Marianna's gurney into the ambulance. Lucky climbed in the rear to ride beside the gurney.

"You'll have to sit in front, ma'am."

"No. I want to ride by my daughter."

"Sorry. We have to pump her stomach. You can't be back here."

The siren wailed, and the red warning light gyrated. Lucky gripped the cold vinyl seat with both hands, turning her head often to the back, straining for every sound and motion. Beside her concern for any signs from Marianna, Lucky also felt embarrassed, humiliated, by this new family tragedy made into a public spectacle. Strangers, strangers drove them. *Was this the road to hell,* she wondered? She gritted her teeth, steeling herself for death, sitting stiffly erect on what seemed like the endless thirty-mile ride to the hospital, where a different wait began.

Several hours later, an ER doctor signaled her to come in from the waiting room, where Bullet waited as well.

"Your daughter will be all right," the doctor said. "She was about three minutes away from total shutdown. She took enough *Tylenol* and codeine to stop her breathing for good. Luckily, there's caffeine in *Contac*. That's what saved her life."

"Can I see her?" Lucky asked.

"Right this way. Most of the cuts cleaned up pretty well. Good thing she fell in the ocean. The cold water stopped more serious bleeding. Why would a pretty girl like your daughter want to die?" he asked as they passed down a corridor. Lucky could not answer.

Marianna was hooked up to a respirator, intravenous tubes wove in and out of her arms, and bandages covered stitches on the appendages bearing the deepest cuts. Bullet and Lucky each took one of her hands.

"Mom. Dad. I died, you know," she said very slowly as though still under water. "I was being pulled through this long tunnel. It felt delicious to be pulled. There was someone at the end. And, a light."

Lucky's heart, like Marianna's voice after each word, seemed to stop after each beat, running if at all on slow motion.

"I love you, Marianna. I love you so much," she said, feeling such a need for gentleness. "How do you feel?"

"Real tired, Mom."

Lucky slept on the floor next to Marianna's hospital bed for the next five days. She used the wheelchair access toilet stalls every hour. They afforded the only privacy she could find in the hospital. She prayed there. She was on her knees so often, she asked Frankie to bring the kneepads she used for tiling floors. She had long since forgotten about Peppard Strong, not questioned why he hadn't called.

"Mom," Ande said when Lucky finally returned home, "Kelty died, you know."

Lucky set up family counseling both in the hospital and when Marianna was released with therapists in the private sector. Dr. Dousch recommended a Dr. Korek, a psychiatrist who specialized in teenage problems. He immediately prescribed *Prozac* for Marianna. A social worker from Unity Church was also engaged to help. Professionals abounded to analyze their family life and point the way to Marianna's recovery.

Marianna came out of a rehab hospital three weeks after her suicide attempt. Lucky drove to Makaha with her to pick up Ande and Nico. Marianna was sitting in the back of the truck. Bullet was sitting at the beach on a bench under the hala tree. He signaled Lucky to wait. He sauntered up to the truck.

"Hey, kiddo," he said to Marianna. "Good to see ya. I love you so much, *BeeBee*." *BeeBee* was the name Bullet had called her from infancy, *BeeBee* for *Baby Bullet*.

Marianna listened. She did not look at Bullet, but she did absorb his words.

"I'll always be here for you, honey," he added. "Can I have a kiss?"

"No, Dad. I don't feel like it," she whispered, still fragile from her ordeal.

"Fuck you, then" he exploded and slapped the side of the truck. As he walked off, he shouted to her over his shoulder, "You'll never get better."

51

MORE FOOD FOR THOUGHT

The summer proved quite remarkable in ending cycles. Lucky won her felony suit against the police. She paid her debt to her divorce attorney, Thomas Ayck, after he made important changes in the settlement, which had taken three years to negotiate. She took Bully back to court twice for unpaid child support.

She received unexpected emotional and financial support from Edna as the rusted doors to love and communication squeaked open between them. Lucky encouraged her sister, Laura, to get counseling, years overdue, to heal from Jack's abuse. Lucky cleaned and painted her house with Ande's help, inside and out.

The social worker from Unity uncovered part of the problems plaguing Marianna. One part was food. One part was control.

"What did Marianna feel she could control in her world, a world that had spun out of order into chaos with her parents' divorce?" the social worker asked Lucky.

Eating, the social worker suggested was the answer. "Marianna could control what did and did not go into her body. Her eating disorders involved deprivation and starving, bingeing and disgorging. These partners in crime are labeled anorexia and bulimia."

"Are you saying Marianna has anorexia or bulimia?"

"Yes. Look at her body. She' s thin and doesn't get her period. Do you ever see her eat with the family? Doesn't she always say she's already eaten, when she really hasn't or has binged and vomited? She is chemically imbalanced, and it is the imbalance, which creates her mood swings, depression, and amenorrhea. Anorexics and bulimics are often high achievers and perfectionists like your daughter."

Lucky and Marianna began also to see the psychiatrist, Dr. Korek

"The disorder has apparently been part of her life for some time," Dr. Korek surmised. "Not getting proper nutrition contributed to the irrational thinking, which led to her suicide attempt. Marianna tells me her pattern is to starve, then when her self-control fails, to binge on junk food for a quick sugar high. Feeling guilty for the caloric rush, she forces herself afterwards to vomit. Being a runner, she also runs beyond her limits to burn off calories and enjoy the high she experiences with the release of endorphins. The chemical imbalance in her body allows her emotions to rage out of control, almost identical to a mental illness, or to at least to mask as one. The blood and urine work I ordered confirms an imbalance in her electrolytes."

"How did this happen?" Lucky asked, feeling threatened and responsible. "I don't understand. I am a good cook! Nutritious meals are a priority with me!" Lucky was shocked that she had not noticed, food preparation and enjoyment being such an integral part of her world. She had thought letting Marianna become a vegetarian was safe.

"Marianna's world blew up when your marriage failed," the therapist informed her. "She couldn't control the changes. The only thing she felt she had control over was her own body."

Lucky's thoughts veered to Jackie, how controlling food was his only line of defense as a child against Edna and Big Jack's craziness. And Laura, how she grew fat to protect herself from Jack or any other intrusion.

"Hence, Marianna's obsession with her body and fitness," Dr. Korek went on. "Intense physical training for track and cross country. And food. What she put into her body. And, what she threw out of it. Her father may have placed too much importance on physical appearance. Marianna told me he hated fat women and that he wouldn't let her Auntie Laura visit because she was overweight. And, he disliked her grand-mother, Edna, who also was fat. Is that true?"

"Yes," Lucky admitted. "I was afraid to get fat myself, for fear he wouldn't love me. In fact, he used to say, 'If you were ten pounds thinner, Lucky, I could really love you.' I guess Marianna must have heard that a lot when she was growing up."

"Marianna tells me you lost a lot of weight yourself when your husband left."

"Yes. Yes, I did."

"You also vomited?"

"Yes, but it was from disgust at my husband's betrayal."

"Marianna also tells me you are vain. She complains that you run after younger men instead of focusing on the family. She thinks you are starved for love like she is. She tells me she doesn't feel she can be loved unless she looks a certain way, fits a certain standard."

"What do you suggest I do? Not date?"

"Of course, you should date and lead an adult life. What you can do is stop referring to body size, for starters. Stop your own focus on your body and your appearance. Be a role model for her."

"I thought I was."

"You were, you are, but in quite the wrong way. You can turn it around if you try. You need to stop talking about how people look. Don't pay compliments like, 'Don't you look pretty today.' Don't point out that fat person, or that girl with long legs, or that good-looking guy."

"I won't have anything to say if I can't talk about food, and if I can't comment on what I see as beauty or ugliness. I'll have to change my view of the world and what I say about it," Lucky admitted.

"That's right. You'll have to change, Mrs. Pulaski. Focus on behavior, not on appearance. Point to positive behavior rather than achievements, because they are another problem area in this illness."

"What do you mean?"

"Anorexics and bulimics are perfectionists. They are compulsive, competitive, and controlling. They are workaholics and over-achievers. You don't want to encourage the best in anything: grades, sports, music, or contests. Forget winning first place or being number one. Encourage learning for learning's sake, exercising for pleasure, kindness to animals. Encourage the care of a pet. Give her a dog, a cat, a horse. Something she can love and focus her attention on instead of herself. A creature that needs her."

"We have a lot of pets."

"Give her one of her own."

"I have. Hula Girl is her Shar Pei."

"That's good. I am glad. My advice is for you to focus on positive behaviors not achievements. Do you see the difference, Mrs. Pulaski?"

Lucky nodded assent.

Dr. Korek assessed, "Marianna wishes her old world and family would come back. She seems unwilling to accept that life changes and goes on in new patterns. She does not have the skills or tools to handle loss. The loss of your family overwhelms her. She cannot handle the intensity of her feelings. On top of that, she tells me her father has hit her on several occasions."

"Yes, he has."

"She also tells me you refused to protect her. And, she said you tried to hit her, too."

A new blanket of shame silenced Lucky.

"Marianna has powerful and adverse reactions to both her father's and your new relationships with other people, Mrs. Pulaski," Dr. Korek continued.

"You mean, my current relationship with Peppard?"

"Yes, and others before him. And, your ex-husband's liaison with Fanny. The possibility of new step-brothers and sisters, outsiders intruding in her world, spells a topsy-turvy world, spinning further out of her control."

"Are you saying Marianna is trying to manipulate the family by attempting suicide? Forcing us to do what she wants?" Lucky asked, upset at the idea of being held hostage by her daughter's immaturity and jealousy. Nor did Lucky want to live in the 'crisis' situations Marianna's eating disorder and emotional imbalance created.

Dr. Korek answered, "The eating disorder is the tip of the iceberg. Your daughter made a very serious attempt to kill herself. She not only took poison, but she cut herself, and she threw herself into the ocean when you were not at home to come to her rescue. She didn't want to be rescued. Do you understand that? She didn't leave a note. She didn't warn you. Your daughter wanted to die. Do you understand?"

Lucky looked at him bleakly at a loss for how to respond.

"What makes you think right now that she wants to live?" the therapist pursued.

Again, Lucky could not answer.

"No one tries to kill herself that hard without a good reason, Mrs. Pulaski."

In a joint counseling session, Dr. Korek asked Marianna and Ande if their dad or any other man had ever touched them sexually.

Ande said, "No way. Not my dad."

Marianna hedged, skirting around *yes* and *no* furtively, and finally said she couldn't remember *exactly*.

Dr. Korek picked up on this clue of uncertainty. He told Lucky that Marianna might be harboring a secret, perhaps of sexual abuse, and that perhaps she was overwhelmed by shame.

"Secrets are events left unspoken and unexamined. They fester in isolation in the psyche creating shame, like pus growing in an unclean wound. Feelings of shame are deadly to the human heart," he told her, "and they can kill the soul."

Into Lucky's lap fell this new possible accusation of molestation, the nightmare of incest returning to haunt her life.

She became wracked by anxiety. She felt blind. Her breathing became wrenched by sobs, disappointed in how her best efforts as a woman, a wife, and a mother had failed. She felt sullied by her association with Bullet.

How could she not have seen her daughter's pain?

She wanted to learn the truth. Had Bully abused Marianna or not? Lucky hunted through the closets of her memory but didn't pull anything suspicious from storage there. She wondered if the accusation was Marianna's girlhood fantasy of father-as-first-lover? Perhaps it was her angry way of hitting back at him for breaking up the family?

To Lucky, it was as if all the dirt that came out in the wash of three generations had been thrown into a dryer, characters and relationships tumbling in a time continuum of changing configurations. Patterns of abuse recycling, as different players tried on each other's garb. Marianna's suicide attempt reshaped her sister, Linney's, suicide years earlier. Her victimization was a hand-me-down from big sister, Laura. The hospitalizations and relationships shrank and stretched into new colors, shapes, and sizes to become the same threads of abuse weaving in and out, unraveling and snagging over time, making damaged goods of their entire lineage.

The marriages as competitive partnerships: Wolfeson's Wilderness Outfitters and Pulaski's Art Studios, where the wives were yoked oxen, enslaved workaholics. The divorces, Edna and Lucky's, tied up in years of litigation. The violence wreaked by the men, Bully and Big Jack. The physical and emotional violations of the defenseless children. The passivity and the blindness of the women. Edna should have protected her daughters, Laura, Lucky, and Linney along with herself from Big Jack; Lucky should have protected Marianna from Bully. Daughters like Laura and Marianna who ran to their mothers' defense received near mortal wounds. Others, like Ande and the Emily of old, suffered helplessly in the wings.

If Marianna believed, truly or falsely, that she had been abused and manifested such a grave illness as a result, to affect a cure, Lucky decided her role was not to take sides but rather to simply support her daughter.

Marianna got admitted as a freshman to Berkeley on a track scholarship. She enjoyed the graduation parties that had spread out over the summer, and excitement abounded that autumn as she packed for college. Lucky hoped distance from the family, and new friends would open Marianna's world enough to distract her from her problems and bulimia. They toured the Berkeley campus together, attended orientation meetings, signed her up for classes, and spent time with her roommates. Gramma Edna lived close to the campus where Marianna could visit her easily, if she wanted. Lucky felt reasonably reassured this would be a good move for Marianna.

But, when Marianna returned home for the Christmas holiday, she looked dreadful. Her face and neck were puffy. She did not look thin, even though her weight was down from one hundred seventeen pounds to ninety-four pounds.

She moved like a sleepwalker. She disappeared with the truck for days at a time saying she wanted to spend time with her friends. She skipped her appointments to see Dr. Korek, threw up the *Prozac*, and grew ever more insolent the few moments she spent at home.

Lucky got a call from Birdie's mother. "I know you well enough to say this, Lucky. And, I love you, and I love your kids. So, I am sorry. I have to tell you that Marianna does not want to be at home. She's fine here with us. But, I think you should know she is suicidal again. I found her face down in our pool, dead drunk, this morning. God knows how long she'd been there. She's all right. Don't worry. Dr. Korek is one of our neighbors. He came over. Like I said, she's all right. If anything else happens, I'll call him again. Are you okay with that?"

"No, I am not okay with that. Keep her there. Don't let her go anywhere. Thank you, thank you so much for calling me and helping. See you as soon as I get there. Don't tell her I am coming."

Lucky drove to Honolulu and picked up Marianna, who was completely listless and compliant. She didn't have the strength to move or to function. Lucky saw her daughter certainly was not going to recover from bulimia on an outpatient basis, which meant seeing a doctor for twenty minutes a day, and being left unmonitored for the remaining twenty-three hours and forty minutes when she could binge and vomit to her heart's content. Her health had deteriorated, and Lucky realized Marianna required hospitalization not the university.

Honolulu had drug rehabilitation programs, alcohol abuse programs, and psychiatric wards. What Lucky found out was that Honolulu didn't have any in-hospital eating-disorder treatment programs, despite the growing statistic that one in every four women nation-wide suffered from this illness, an illness that had proven too often to be fatal.

Through Dr. Korek, Lucky found a care facility on the mainland, the *Remuda Ranch Center for Anorexia, Bulimia, and Related Disorders*, which came with a fancy price tag of twenty thousand dollars a month not covered by insurance. The health care community did not consider eating disorders diseases.

Fortunately, Jackie, health-conscious as always, acknowledged the severity of Marianna's illness. Having sought therapy for himself in the past, he recognized himself as the "King of Control" and saw in his niece a budding "Queen." He pulled through with the cash to get her admitted.

"Em," he said to Lucky, "I think your daughter is going to die. I'm not giving you this money to save her. I am giving it to you because when she dies, I don't want you to blame me for not helping."

Lucky didn't know how she'd convince Marianna to get on the plane. The flight was a red-eye leaving Honolulu close to midnight. Ande would stay with Cherry; Nico would stay with Ben while Lucky and Marianna were gone. She packed for herself and Marianna. When she was ready to leave, she found Marianna sitting on the bedroom floor, face, neck, arms and legs swollen with fluids, eyes half-lidded. Lucky squatted beside her and spoke in a low tone.

"Marianna. I love you. You are dying. I want you to come with me. Please. I am going to save your life."

She expected the usual explosive fight.

Instead, Marianna whispered, "Okay, Mom."

They flew into Phoenix and spent the night in a motel near the airport. In the morning, Lucky didn't bother with breakfast. She rented a car and drove to the Remuda Ranch in dawn light.

Marianna had to be lifted from the car and helped up the path to the entry. She slumped over on the waiting room bench as though spineless and lay semi-comatose while Lucky registered. An orderly rushed out with a gurney, put Marianna on it, and the next thing Lucky knew, Marianna had been hooked up to several IV solutions.

The attending nurse quietly said, "A few hours later, Mrs. Pulaski, and we would have called an ambulance. She is in the worst shape of any patient we've admitted."

Lucky filled out pages of medical and personal information. Jackie had wired the deposit and first month's fee.

"Marianna wanted me to mention to you that she prefers a vegetarian diet."

"Mrs. Pulaski, we cure our patients of their eating disorders," the nurse explained. "We do not recognize vegan, vegetarian, non dairy, gluten free, macrobiotic, raw, or any other diet as healthy or in the best interest of our clients. We teach them what foods are healthy and to eat them. Period. You may go now. She's in good hands here. We'll see you at the required family therapy weekend in four weeks. Remember, every family member over the age of twelve must attend. That includes her father."

"Dr. Graham," Lucky said on the phone weeks later, "I understand Marianna's

father is required to attend the family therapy session."

"That's correct."

"It is important that you understand my goal in coming to Remuda Ranch is to heal my daughter. It is not to open the door to more emotional and physical assaults from my ex-husband. Can you guarantee our safety? Can you guarantee confidentiality?"

Dr. Graham replied, "Your well-being is our concern, Mrs. Pulaski. Our staff will be sensitive to your safety. We are aware of the gravity of Marianna's allegations of sexual abuse. Be well advised that Marianna exhibits the symptoms of a disease your whole family suffers. It is called 'Addiction.' While it is our job to actively treat her, please be aware that you all have contributed to her illness."

"Addiction? Addiction to what?"

"From what Marianna tells me, alcohol, drugs, work, sex, coffee, chocolate, exercise, fitness, and fad diets might start off the list of addictions found in your household."

"Addictions?" she questioned, "in my household?"

Thomas Ayck served Bullet an order to pay for Marianna's medical costs and hospitalization.

"I'll give you one day to drop this lawsuit, Lucky, or Pandora's box will open and maybe even the house will be sold. You will be the cause of the destruction of the whole family," Bullet raged to her on the phone.

"I am clear in what I want. The lawsuit speaks for itself. Any further discussion, you can have with my lawyer."

"Lucky, I'm a lot of things, but I'm NOT a child molester."

"I am a lot of things, too, Bullet, but I'm NOT rich. I can't pay for damage you have caused. You hurt Marianna; you pay for it."

52

BLESSING IN DISGUISE

Lucky set new boundaries. She moved the children out of her upstairs bedroom back into their own rooms and lives. She got a new puppy to surprise Marianna when she returned from the treatment center. She opened room in her heart and her house for love. Knowing Peppard had changed her.

"Aren't you afraid, Lucky?" Peppard asked as she prepared for the trip back to Remuda for the family therapy session. "Afraid Marianna will die?"

Lucky didn't speak for a long while.

"You must never ask me that again, Peppard," she finally told him. "Even when there seems to be no apparent good in a situation, I can look for and discover it," she said. "I live on faith that good will come of every situation, even if it appears to be desperately black. I met you on the heels of a hurricane, didn't I?'

"Yes, yes, you did," Peppard admitted.

"I have to be hope-filled, or I cannot carry my children and myself forward. So, to answer your question: of course, Marianna will recover. To answer your other question: No, I am not scared. This is an opportunity for me to help her get better."

"Well, I'm terrified."

"Don't say that, Peppard," she interrupted, turning to him.

"No 'good,' as you put it, has come out of my situation. Kelty didn't make it," he said flatly. She pulled his head to her lips and kissed him on each closed and freckled eyelid.

"I know. I know. I am so sorry," she whispered. "So sorry."

"Haaaag," Queenie yelled as loudly as her cancerous body allowed. She was suffering, even now as she was about to die, from female pride in youth and beauty, *yut and beaute,*'she used to quip. "An old hag," she called herself.

Queenie had decided not to leave anything to her grand-children: no letters, no will, even though she'd had six months to take care of *her last wishes.* Queenie was limited by lack of imagination and spine.

Queenie's friend, Dottie, whispered, "They don't speak well of you, Lucky dear. They are self-centered people. And, their daughters are riddled with petty jealousies, you always being so close to Queenie. You have served her as a decent daughter-in-law. I love Queenie, lord knows why, and I am sorry to see her go like this. But, I can say it must be enough to turn you batty to have been surrounded by emotional cripples all these years."

Lucky thought about Queenie who had been blessed with a long life and financial ease. Why had she never asked why her granddaughter tried to commit suicide? Never asked why Marianna had been hospitalized in Arizona for five months? Never asked why Marianna refused to come home now?

Lucky hated that she still loved Queenie.

Lucky was sipping sweetened espresso at home on Marianna's birthday when Queenie's ashes were carried out to sea in a koa canoe festooned with dozens of yellow plumeria lei. Bullet paddled, while Rex, holding one of Lucky's pottery urns containing the dust of his wife, sat stoic and bereft on the stiff center seat. Ande and Nico swam along side the canoe in the tranquil shallows in water so clear the coral heads and tropical fish were clearly visible below. Boxer, Big Al, and Rod were among the many paddling mourners dotting the turquoise water above the reef at Maili.

The family court judge ruled against Lucky in the lawsuit. Bully did not have to pay half of Marianna's medical bills.

"As Marianna Pulaski had attained the age of eighteen, making her a responsible adult, at the time of admission to Remuda Ranch Treatment Center, this court finds the defendant, Richard Pulaski, not responsible for the medical bills incurred by his daughter."

"But, Your Honor," Thomas Ayck sputtered, "if he's not responsible..."

Almost four years of repressed pain and anger slapped Lucky in the face, as the judge exited the chamber without a second glance. Beneath a veneer of good clothes and civility, rage and disgust engulfed Lucky at this new miscarriage of justice.

In the courtroom, she had recounted their lengthy divorce, the cost to the children, and the trauma to Marianna, including her suicide attempt, illness and hospitalizations.

*He fathered her and injured her but is not financially responsible?
And, by omission, I am?* She wanted the judge to make Bully pay,
the only way she could think to punish him. She had wanted
formal acknowledgment of Bully's responsibility.

In losing, she felt dirtied, and life itself was sordid, ugly
and unfair.

53

SHUT

Lucky walked in the shallow the reef pools in early evening with Hula Girl. The bare, whispered edge of a new moon made her think of Peppard as the twilight gave way to darkness. Peppard had disappeared. He had shut down after Kelty died and was gone when she returned from taking Marianna to the mainland.

Lucky opened her latest exhibition in Honolulu under the worst rain deluge in forty years. A handful of clients washed in as the thousand invited drily stayed away. At about two o'clock she canceled the musicians, opened one bottle of wine instead of twelve, and looked down the empty marble hallway to the escalator bank hoping to spot late arrivals.

Such an unpredictable grab-bag of people showed up; names riding her mailing list for twenty years; flotsam and jetsam from her career in art. Charles Black, the first designer she'd ever sold a pot to, came, reintroducing himself. They had met after she had given birth to Ande and thought she knew how to sell art. Back then Lucky had called ten designers for appointments to show Bullet's paintings. She had hauled his largest pieces to their offices. She had to climb a narrow flight of stairs two stories to see Charles Black. He loved one of the pieces, bought it, came to a few backyard sales, and disappeared only to emerge out of the storm at this exhibition.

Lucky dribbled home from her opening where forty people came and no work had sold. She had enough wine and sliced Brie, summer sausage and baguette to feed what she'd hoped would be a hungry art world. She didn't weep until she got midway home at her latest bout of bad luck, having almost no one show up for her opening, disappointment sneaking up from behind.

At home, shielded under a roof of dripping water and windows pounded by the wind's vertical onslaught, she watched *CNN* News. *Sotheby's* and *Christie's* auction houses announced the sale of the Havemeyer collection: Degas, Rembrandts, Monets on the block. Hundreds of people were shown milling about the galleries. The female auctioneer looked like a Picasso herself: one small brown eye, one large blue eye set lopsided in her skull. "America's economy is stronger than ever. The stock market is at its highest level. Americans are eager to buy art. We expect to make three hundred and ninety million dollars on the auction of these works," she predicted.

"You might as well kill me now, Ande," Lucky announced. "My work will be worth a lot more when I'm dead. I don't think Degas and Monet were rich in their lifetimes. And look, *CNN* says the Degas bronze went to an anonymous bidder for a record twelve million dollars."

She was in the hardest profession in the world: art.

Marianna remained hospitalized. The new puppy Lucky had gotten for her fell sick and died. The vet called it, "a failure to thrive." She dug its grave on a knoll above the beach and planted one of Ande's palms next to it. Rod helped bury the puppy, then treated her to a day at the spa to relax, and took her to a restaurant that night.

It was hard for her to fully grasp time: Peppard was in Europe eleven hours ahead, experiencing dusk when she was in Hawai'i at the day's dawn. Yet, despite the elapse of time and the vast distance, she thought they saw last evening's moon together. She had laughed aloud when she looked up and there, in a brilliance of blue shone a slim curved scimitar of a moon, a smile, really, flanked by a jeweled star.

She didn't know how to deal with the disappointment of their lost opportunity.

She could not rise in the morning. She returned to bed after Ande and Nico went to school, seeking her bed as comfort and refuge throughout the day. She slept long hours in a lingering malaise.

She spent empty days remembering isolated moments of touching and kissing, reliving the moments endlessly, like playbacks on a VHS tape, each moment in vivid color and detail, preserved on celluloid, sealed in a loop, to play over and over, forward and backward while nothing else happened in her life, waiting for her daughter to heal.

The countless points of pain in her back astounded Lucky. Touching her body was to locate one small pocket of pain after another. Ande massaged her in the morning. *How can I carry all this torment within me day after day?*

Lucky laid in her bed, semi-comatose, lost for long hours, addicted to memories and carnivorous dreams, obsessed by a desire to lasso Peppard. Her memories turned into present day phantoms, haunting and binding her to melancholia.

She mused, *Perhaps we ought to be Native American Indians and give each other names. For I think of you as Man-in-the-Cloud, Man-in-the Mist, and Purring Lion. I have never experienced such tenderness as that first night with you, Peppard. To be held so long, caressed and stroked by your fingertips ceaselessly, kissed and touched. You touched my cheek, my hair, and my arms so lightly I could only faintly feel it, but you were always there, never stopping. I only realize in retrospect how tender and truly loving you were. It was the most beautiful night I have ever spent.*

I sensed we were clouds, we two, ephemeral and white and semi-transparent, and we were merging and passing quite through one another, yet not changing shape or direction. You were borne on one air current and I on another. But, as we touched, as we held one another so tightly, I didn't feel mass-skin-flesh-sweat, but rather, I felt air, open and freely floating, the kind of merging and shifting that only clouds can do on the winds of the sky.

How beautiful you were, speaking of form and substance. Your body is one of the most masculine, mature, and fit figures I've seen; it also was the most tender, gentle, caring. You loved me in a feminine way, caring, nurturing, sweet, and unexpected.

I must have thanked God fifty times by now and plan to go on thanking Him for bringing me this remarkable experience of you.

Your curling red body hair, radiant and thick on your arms, felt like a delightful air mattress, buffering me, cushioning us. When you pressed your chest to my back, I called you the Man-in-the-Mist, for that cushion of hair was like some fine mountain waterfall mist, once again, separating my skin from yours, but making our contact ever more gentle and special.

Your sighs: sigh and moan and delight, long absence of pleasure, all mingled in one sound, the passion and strength of a lion's roar, subdued into a relaxed, pre-nap purr. You, Peppard, are a Purring Lion at my gate.

She reread Peppard's letter again: "I've been doing a lot of thinking. You're the kindest, most loving and generous woman

I've ever met. But, I cannot help you, Lucky. I cannot even help myself right now."

She felt left in the dust, nothing happening, her life on empty.

She undressed and watched herself in the mirror. She congratulated herself on being slender. She liked her small breasts. They made her feel tender and delicate. She also liked her very hard abdomen. She apologized to her saddlebag thighs. She turned and twisted in the mirror to peek at her rear cellulite situation, which never appeared to improve. She sighed and improvised some good thoughts to those parts of her body she wished were svelte and seventeen. She laid down on her bed, clearly a single woman's. She had her *Daily Word* missile on the left side along with her glasses, an angel book, and the novel of the day. No man had slept there in a long time. A vibrator resided under the pillow as did some *Giorgio Red* body lotion.

For the eight monastic months since Peppard had left, she had taken no pleasure until now. Sex surely wasn't only the body. Her womb awakened to shadows and memories. It wiped the year's sleep away and drew back the covers of hurt and protectiveness. Shuddering, singing, and praising the great indefinable sensation of prolonged and long-overdue release, it pulsated out into the universe, passing through heaven and beyond, her body simultaneously locked into grief, into aloneness, into memories of men, babies, and profoundly etched love with a boundless shudder. Her womb seemed to yell with her, crying, reminding her that it took two, not her alone, but her with love, a lover, a man, to love it.

Her lips swung into a smile and her head flung back onto its crown on the quilt, as the familiar dark shadow slowly passed once again over her mind and heart. She wailed and sobbed, as rhythmically and uncontrollably as she'd climaxed, for the crime to her heart; the reality of being alone; the sadness of love without a mate as she lay alone on the bed at midday, sun shining down on the whitened sands outside her deck and the breeze chopping up the indigo swells below.

"Going to bed on Valentine's Day and crying frequently are the hallmarks of depression," Cherry declared. "You need help. Again."

"Literature supports the notion of love sickness, you know," Lucky countered. "I'm suffering from unrequited love."

"Take drugs, get some antidepressants, take the edge off the obsessiveness and get afloat in normalcy," Cherry advised.

"I don't want to take drugs. Anyway, I don't want to zone out on tranquilizers or mood enhancers."

"But Lucky, you give away your power, all your power, by coveting men. The Peppard situation is hopeless. Besides, it's out of your control."

Lucky hid from herself, wishing fervently not to be discovered in disarray. Her nails were torn and chewed, pieces of skin hanging in ripped fragments from her fingertips and cuticles. Tense, her mouth pulled her face in downward spirals, layered with worn folds. She wanted a way out of the pain.

She lived like an automaton, carried on an electrified beltway, not choosing a direction of her own accord or desire. She didn't want to know what gnawed at her. She could not look at herself. No more mirrors. Not now. She denied herself, completely, while Marianna was gone.

Lucky resumed therapy. Dr. Dousch utilized EMDR, the Eye Movement Desensitization Rhythm technique, to unravel the miscues from her childhood.

Lucky, feeling like she'd had surgery, stayed in bed for five days afterwards.

"I feel like my insides got ripped out," she told her brother, Jackie. "I feel like I left my body from my knees to my throat hanging on a barbed wire fence somewhere and went driving down the road without it."

"How's Marianna?" he asked. He had been footing the bills for several months of expensive care.

"They don't let me talk to her," Lucky answered. "They did say she has moved into their third level, which means she is sharing an apartment on the grounds with other recovering bulimics. I guess that is good news."

Lucky got over the intense bouts of vertigo she'd suffered on freeway overpasses, on the Pali highway, up the slopes of Haleakala to the crater. Vertigo had blocked her creativity, masked her fear of failure as an artist, perhaps as a woman, and as a mother.

She got the courage to write Peppard:

I think being honest and direct is the only way I can communicate with you. I miss you very much.

She called his office to find out his flight arrival time wanting to greet Peppard by surprise at the airport. His secretary told her he was due from San Francisco on Delta's ten o'clock flight. She dressed in a black silk shirt, leather pants and boots. She carefully printed a sign to hold by the gate, "Limo for Peppard Strong." She chilled wine and put two glasses in an ice chest. Ande asked where she was going.

"Nooooo, Mom, not a good plan."

Lucky called Cherry.

"Oh, no. Don't do it. Big mistake. The man knows you're out there. Are you ready to humiliate yourself further?"

"I'm feeling strong, like a gambler, a risk taker. People like surprises and other people doing nice things for them."

"What if he's mad? What if he doesn't like it? Are you ready for that? What if he is not alone and has a woman with him?"

"You mean not to do what is in my heart to do for fear of rejection?"

"What if he sees you, not as a positive, happy and beautiful woman coming to be sweet to him, but as a lonely and desperate divorcee who can't take good-bye for an answer and keeps popping up in his life?"

Abandoning her plan, Lucky realized she was the one who had shut down, not Peppard. She had been the one unnerved.

As before, a vast loneliness propelled and agitated Lucky, creating an itch in places too deep to scratch. As the tide of her being receded out to sea, a massive, deep sensation lodged in her mouth, jaw, neck, chest, lungs, heart, and diaphragm. It was the yearning to be loved.

The older she got, the more terrified that there wouldn't be enough time left for her to live, that she would never experience a true love, which she desired beyond anything else except her children's good health. She could not imagine life, all the years ahead, without love or passion.

She visualized windows on the soles of her feet. She mentally traced her skeletal armature. She imagined the earth, seeing its armature inside mountains, ridges as the bones that support the earth's crust. Its mountains had caves, openings, and hollows mirroring her pelvis. A source of extraordinary energy passed through the windows and into her.

Phrases from T. S. Eliot's "The Hollow Men" trickled through her memory: "We are the hollow men....Shape without form, shade without colour....gesture without motion..."

She started work in her studio with the notion of hollowness. Patterns metamorphosed in her work from *thresholds* to *passages*. Utilizing negative space, she dug, creating *wombs, caverns, burial caves, tombs,* giving rise to a concept of *barrenness.* She understood the seemingly impossible duality of *hollowness* and *fecundity* cohabiting the female core.

It seemed to her, physically anyway, that women were hollow. Men were not. Men were penetrators, equipped to enter any opening. Their spiritual emptiness could not be compared to a woman's. Women carried a vessel of emptiness within like a metaphor, every day.

She was aware of her own profound hollowness, aware of the tremendous energy required to participate in life as her own malaise bespoke it: the inertia felt prior to movement in the studio. How readily depression blanketed her energy to block her.

The constant in life was change as nothing stayed the same in the physical world. Stasis or paralysis spelled death and decay. She wondered if everything, seen and unseen, changed? *Were there relationships that stayed constant? What did a promise become when it was broken? Did it have a name?*

God sort of opened a path. Her house hadn't been cleaned in three weeks or more when Lucky received a call from Peppard. She spent Friday cleaning, scrubbing the shower with SOS, wiping stairs, weed whacking the front yard. Then she rode her bike to Pokai Bay where she saw Boxer with the sailing canoes. They chatted for a while. He pointed out Peppard's sail, his red boat moored in the harbor.

Peppard knelt on the deck mending the jib. Lucky swam out, climbed quietly aboard, and touched him lightly on the shoulder.

He turned and, looking up from under the brim of a cotton hat, said so sweetly, "Oh, Lucky. Lucky. Well, hello, Lucky." But, he didn't stop what he was doing. Embarrassed, she turned her attention to greet Sean, who was working by the prow.

"You've gotten so tall," was all she could say.

That evening when Nico came home from Makaha Beach, Peppard, Sean, and the canoe crew were standing around in the front yard. Lucky fixed them chicken pasta, an enormous salad, and garlic bread. Peppard boiled breadfruit along with taro Ande had grown.

Lucky relished having the house filled with male energy again. *How devoid it's been, sexless and boring,* she thought. To have the table set for nine, a big meal, happy stories, the man she loved seated beside her. Heaven, if only for a moment.

Peppard looked much older, leaner and drawn out. His eyes looked sunken and lashless, his skin was raw from the sun and aging; his hair had grown thinner and was receding; his lips were pursed tight. She questioned her fixation, wondering if the real Peppard measured up to her old fantasy.

Then, the little hum of their beings began to pervade the atmosphere. She found herself in the old comfort zone where they kept talking, kept brushing each other in a sort of rapture, enfolded in the contentment of souls meeting once again. It was comfortable, so very comfortable. There was a rhythm and magnetism to it. She showed him the latest pieces in her studio, the distressed temples. He didn't show much interest. He did tell Sean about her fire suit; perhaps he had paid attention at some point to what she did. He touched her often, embracing her on the beach, coming behind her at the dingy and tweaking her waist.

"Knowing you and not having you made another burden for me to carry," Peppard told her, "though my wife and son's deaths are heavier burdens."

"I thought knowing each other was a gift," Lucky answered, "a beautiful gift. My times with you were spectacular. I'm greedy. I want more. I've missed you."

"I think of you every time I take a shower, looking at the tiles you made me."

Lucky laughed, "That is my revenge."

In the morning, he confided that he hadn't slept well, that he'd tossed and turned upstairs in her bed where she had not been as she had slept chastely outside in the hammock where she cried for a while. It was ironic to finally get him into her bed when she couldn't be there, because his son and crew were also sleeping over at her house.

Peppard said he kept remembering the last time he'd been there, its sweetness. She was glad putting him in her bed did pull up the memories, a little more revenge for her year of lonely nights.

"I really cared for you," he admitted by way of explanation, "we were sleeping together, weren't we?" *Nice of him to remember.* "I was doing a great deal of soul-searching at that time and couldn't see a future for us."

"I couldn't imagine the future then either," Lucky confessed. "My life was changing so fast. One day I had three kids, the next, one almost died. Your Kelty did die. My Marianna got well."

"Oh, Lucky, I'm glad. When I didn't see her here, I was afraid to ask."

"That's okay. But pretty soon, Peppard, when Ande goes off to college, I'll just have one kid, Nico, at home."

"It's feels strange to have only Sean. Not to have Kelty around."

"I am very sorry, Peppard."

"I'm doing all right."

"Are you involved with anyone?" she asked, her face soft and sweet like a sixteen-year-old's first valentine.

"Why do you ask?"

She sensed he was not going to rock the boat of his life. He probably feared losing someone else he loved. He was going to maintain the status quo. It was easiest and safest for him to be alone. She took a deep breath.

"Because I still care and," she admitted, "time hasn't changed anything." She walked a little further out on the limb, vulnerable. "I never stopped caring for you, Peppard. It was Kelty's death and nothing to do with me that I know of that turned your emotions off."

"Ironically, the answer to your question is yes, I have met someone, Lucky. Someone very nice. I met her the day I felt I could see you again. I've been dating her for three months. We're getting married. I..."

54

GRADUATION

Marianna wanted to see Ande graduate from high school in Honolulu, and Ande wanted her to come. For the two years since her hospitalization, Marianna had lived on the mainland, still angry. She remained angry at Lucky for not moving away from the family house in Hawai'i. She remained angry with Ande and Nico for having a relationship with Bullet, when they knew he had abused her. She felt betrayed and dishonored by them.

Ande wanted Bullet to watch her graduate as well, creating a new conflict for Lucky to navigate.

"Marianna, you will make a trip home one day," Lucky called to say, "and you should, and I want you to, but, not yet."

Marianna had held Lucky in tight bondage of guilt and anger with her multiple suicide attempts. Afraid to speak her truth for fear of hurting her daughter, Lucky had kowtowed.

"Returning to Hawai'i for the first time after all the mending you've done will be charged. I can't control where your dad is or what he does. Seeing the house, the family, the beaches, friends, and relatives will bring up lots of feelings. You've been hurt too many times to ask for it now."

"It's not fair. Why do I have to be the victim again, Mom? I couldn't come when Queenie died. Now I'm not supposed to come see Ande graduate, because of Dad?"

"You're right," Lucky said. "It's very unfair. And, the unfairness is, he's the jerk who should stay away. Look, I'm sorry, Marianna, if you think I'm not confident in your recovery. It's not that. I want you to make the trip when there's less risk. That's my preference. I have seen your dad out of control too many times, and I haven't been able to protect you."

Marianna's plane landed close to midnight. Nico, Ande, Cherry, Birdie, Darryl, Ben, and Lucky encircled and draped her with fragrant lei as she stepped through the arrival gate. Everybody shrieked; their tears floated on reunion laughter. Lucky photographed all the happy faces.

After graduation and a week of soaking in friends and sun had passed, Lucky and Marianna were alone together at home. Lucky held Marianna carefully by both shoulders and looked quietly into her eyes.

"I want to apologize to you, Marianna," Lucky said. "I want to ask your forgiveness. I am sorry for my failings as a mother. I am sorry for the times I behaved immaturely. I am sorry for the times I was out of control."

They cried.

"I am very sorry you were abused. I never, ever thought of it or suspected it. I'm sorry I wasn't there to protect you. I didn't know."

Marianna began to squirm in discomfort.

"I can't tell you the personal horror I feel, Marianna, to have a collapsed marriage and a tormented daughter. The twelve years I was struggling with my failing marriage were the twelve years you were growing up. I think I've been cursed with blindness not seeing what must have been going on around me."

Marianna found it difficult to listen to Lucky justify herself.

"The times when I was still married to your father, and he hurt you by hitting and yelling, remember the time you were vacuuming and couldn't hear him calling you? I interfered and tried to get you to safety. I was at risk, too, you know."

Marianna eyed her coolly.

"I failed, okay? I failed, Marianna. And, here we are. You hurt. A rift between us. Please understand. I love you."

Lucky paused.

"My parents' divorce taught me that each of us needs parents, no matter how bad they are. We need love and affirmation and understanding. Vengefulness hurts; kids get hurt in divorces."

"You're right about that, Mom."

"Bitterness doesn't work. Hate makes us crazy. I'm relearning that lesson the hard way."

"Oh, you think you've learned it?" Marianna asked, looking away. Lucky went on.

"I read books about people who never knew their parents and spend their lives searching for them or wondering what they're like or why they don't want them or what they're doing. Whether we live with our parents or not, they shape us: present or absent, good or bad, in fundamental ways. Of course, it's worse when a parent has aberrant behavior, because the child suffers more."

"I think it's worse if the other parent loves the sick parent more than she loves the kid," Marianna accused. "I wonder

why there have to be people in our lives who hurt us so much?
Like: you say you love me. But, you hurt me, Mom."

"I never intended to hurt you. I'm sorry. So sorry. Maybe
that's the distinction. I hurt you out of blindness. That's not
the same as deliberately hurting you, is it?"

"Well then, all I can say is, you sure were blind, Mom. You
never wanted to see what was really happening."

"I turned a blind eye to ugliness, to cruelty. I couldn't bear
to admit it was part of my world. But, refusing to see denied
reality, denied myself and denied you."

"You need a chiropractor for your soul, Mom."

Lucky laughed.

"We are individuals who have come into this life to learn
lessons in our own way. Each of us has unique experiences.
Mine are not yours. Yours are not Ande's. Ande's are not Nico's.
Nico's are not yours. Even though Bullet and I are parents to
you, Ande, and Nico, each of you has a different perception and
experience of us. The thing is, each of us has 'selective' memories. I remember one thing; you remember another. We each
have different needs, different desires. We perceive the same
events differently. Ande and Nico know Bullet has abused you.
Don't you think knowing their own father has hurt you, hurts
them? But, they also have their personal experiences of Bullet
and are making their own relationships with him, which they
have to do to be healthy and whole. They are not betraying you
or being disloyal to you by letting him be part of their lives."

Marianna turned away to blow her nose.

"I know it hurts you. They love you. They understand your
situation. And, they still see him. Whether we live in China,
Europe, California, or here, in Bullet's presence or absence, in
life or in death, they still will be dealing with their relationship
to him. I won't cloud them with vindictiveness and hatred."

Marianna's face reddened as Lucky went on.

"Gramma Edna made a big mistake in cutting me off from Grampa Jack. That's why I let Ande and Nico see Bullet."

"Oh, yeah, Mom, you're not vindictive or hateful at all. Right. You are the most self-centered person I know. You can turn everything around to be about you. You, you, you."

"I have nothing more to do with your dad," Lucky protested. "I have taken him to court three times since the divorce was final, and by now he has, I pray, learned not to mess with me. Okay. I admit it. I carry rage. He betrayed me, and everything I hold sacred, and he hurt my kids. And, yes, I've tried to punish him for it. He defiled my world."

"You let me do your fighting, you mean."

"I know. I'm sorry. I fight my own battles now," Lucky sighed. "I want this legacy of pain to end. I want to understand the past. And, I want a positive present."

"Do you know how scared I felt when you abandoned me at Remuda?" Marianna interjected. "I hated you then more than ever."

"Wow. That must have been a lot of hate."

"Mom, don't make fun of me. I'm serious."

"Sorry. I know how scared and abandoned you must have felt, right? It was the worst time for me, too. You were so sick, and I had to leave you, not just anywhere, but four thousand miles away on the mainland. I screamed all the way back to Hawai'i."

Marianna nodded, her face reflecting the terror she'd felt left alone at the hospital. Then she said carefully, looking her mother fully in the face for the first time, "But it really marked a new beginning for me, Mom. It made me conscious of my eating and of my pain. It made me look at myself. And, it made me change."

"You are an inspiration, Marianna. And, it's a challenge for me to do the same. To change. You're a very brave girl." Lucky touched Marianna's cheek. "I want you to know how dearly I love you."

She embraced her daughter, who folded into her arms. "We have talked so often about you coming home, like for Christmas the last two years, but I knew you felt too vulnerable. But, you're here at last. I am proud of you."

"Mom, did you ever forgive Big Jack for leaving? Or, for hurting Auntie Laura?"

"No, I never did. I don't think I can. Should I think about it?"

"It's probably a good idea. I wonder all the time," Marianna added, "if I can forgive Dad."

Lucky felt quietly content. Her lips were fuller and softer than since the days of childbirth, when she was always reborn herself. She smiled, feeling loose and refreshed.

She let little things inform each day and took pleasure in them: a nice breeze, a phone call, the sunshine, and going about her business of mothering, cleaning, potting, and befriending in a calm and regular sort of way. While working, she listened to audiotapes of novels, science, and self-help. She didn't fuss as much over her appearance. She had abandoned dinner parties altogether. And, she took her kids to Moloka'i on a small vacation.

She was beginning, like a novice, to understand that men need not fill the longing of her soul, though hollowness there occasionally echoed the need for male affirmation. She didn't feel the bite of the old hunger as keenly, and she seldom used sex to dull its itch. Her art helped heal the wound and scratched her soul enough. Her attitude was transforming.

She didn't want more lovers to soothe the edges of her addiction to love. They were the symbol of need, of her itch, of a quest for attainment. She wanted to find out what life offered a woman emancipated. She hoped, with a healthier attitude, pain and memories need not unclothe the body of her days.

She abandoned her crusade of self-righteousness, leaving the vigilante side of herself in the dust along the traveled road of her life with its punished and frayed baggage. She embarked on a journey of patience, trust, and suspended judgments.

She traveled picnic basket in hand, sitting down now and then under a shady tree for a little snack. No big, fancy meals to cook, no table to set. A handful or two of raisins, some *m&ms*, a couple of olives: for her, soul food enough.

She felt an air of excitement. Marianna was doing well on the mainland, working on a university degree in art, holding a steady job, enjoying a decent boyfriend, moving into a new apartment at summer's end. Ande would begin her freshman year at a local college in the fall. Nico would enter high school. Her family was growing up.

And, without the demands of family or crises, Lucky had more and more solitary time. The last of the dogs, Bosco, the ravenous laundry eater, had died. She didn't need to shop or cook as much, since many nights no one was home for dinner. She ate half a leftover grilled cheese sandwich after watching the last fiber of sunset disappear from the horizon. She was glad she didn't get a puppy. Not again.

PART FOUR

AFTERSHOCK

55

THE PRICE

Nico hung himself from a chandelier in the dining room.

The winter sea, swollen, perilous, surged darkly, mouth agape, gnashing the shore, biting the sand where Lucky stood nearly naked in a thin bathing suit, wet in the morning wind. She had entered her fifties, breasts no longer resisting the earth's pull, eyes straining over the waves, looking for her son, a son who wasn't there, at least not quite yet. His ashes were in her car, contained in a jar on the passenger seat, lid tight-fitted against the wind, needing protection against its howling, soon enough to be cast onto the waves.

She longed to be that wind, as free to shriek her fury through the sky, to release the salt water of her blood, to shower it back upon that primal sea. But, free she was not; she was bound and numbed by loss, paralyzed, because her child, her beloved son, was dead.

How did she find herself still there, isolated on a windswept shore in the midst of the great Pacific, her womb wrenched loose as though ripped and fed upon by grief-starved sharks? The funeral service had finished behind her. Bleeding, she was bleeding, from orifices long dry as though cellular memory was weeping with her. Her blood was thick and sticky between her legs. She was hemorrhaging. It was not frenzied sharks gnawing at her insides; it was a miscarriage. She had failed her children. And one had died. Lucky felt tormented as though crucified. But she was neither a saint nor a child of God. She was a sinner.

At the hospital, motionless, she had held his feet. She had looked down the length of him, foot to head, willing him to live. When the nurse or doctor or orderly, she could not remember which, pronounced him dead, her breasts began to leak, leak milk, wetting her shirt.

She was fifty-four, for chrissake. Her son was twenty-one, plus a week. He was her youngest. She hadn't nursed a baby in twenty years. Even so, defying reason, following nature, her breasts had flowed in that cold hospital holding room trying to nourish, trying to revive, that poor boy she loved so much. She stood rigid, as a memory from childhood Bible school flooded her mind: *Saint Paul's Letter to the Galatians,* where he wrote, "I bear on my body the marks of Jesus."

Stigmata, she knew, were bodily marks, sores, or sensations of pain in locations corresponding to the crucifixion wounds of Jesus Christ, such as the hands and feet or a gash in the side. But, to a womb, to breasts? No mention of Mary's suffering, no mention that Lucky could remember of any physical marks of suffering showing upon Mary's body on the loss of her son.

Individuals displaying stigmata were often described as ecstatics. At the time of receiving the stigmata, ecstatics were overwhelmed with emotions. Stigmata might be hysterical, linked to dietary constriction by self-starvation, dissociative mental states and self-mutilation, usually in the context of a religious belief. Anorexia nervosa cases often displayed self-mutilation similar to stigmata as part of a ritualistic, obsessive-compulsive disorder. A relationship between starvation and self-mutilation had been reported amongst prisoners of war and during famines. But, Lucky was hardly an ecstatic. She had only been a prisoner of grief a few days, not long enough to qualify for starvation, even though neither she nor Marianna had eaten since Nico's death.

She wondered what these sensations or signs from her body meant. Christian suffering seemed obsolete; she found images of crucifixes neither helpful nor comforting. Yet, she continued to bleed. She knew forms of stigmata included tears of blood, sweating blood, and wounds from scourging with recurring bleeding that stopped only to restart later. Some stigmatic's wounds did not appear to clot, staying fresh yet uninfected. This blood was said to have a pleasant, perfumed odour, known as the *Odour of Sanctity*.

A nurse speaking, speaking to Lucky, repeated a question, jerking her out of her reverie.

"What?" Lucky asked, not taking her gaze from her son's face.

Again, the nurse said, "Your son's an organ donor. It says so on his driver's license."

Lucky didn't understand why she was being told this now, when he was lying there in front of her stiff, his neck held in a brace, his mouth propped open with a foreign apparatus, there, where he needed her strength, her love, her full attention to bring him back to life.

The nurse persisted. "He's an organ donor. If you want to give his eyes, you must do it now, within a half an hour of death."

Death? Is he dead?

Bullet, removed from her life by ten years, was there as were Nico's sisters. They stood together in the clinical chill, this long-broken family, unbelieving, dazed and shaken.

Nico had been their golden boy, a boy of light, of love. As a child and a teen, he had never fought, never struck, never uttered a hurtful word. Any argument, he could turn to laughter. Once, shortly after obtaining his driver's license, a car stopped abruptly in front of his on the highway. He jammed on the brakes but not quickly enough to prevent tapping the bumper of the other car. A woman jumped out of the passenger side and began to scream.

Nico was a tow-headed *ha'ole*, or white boy, living in a community of native Hawai'ians, Filipinos, varied offspring of Chinese and Japanese plantation workers, as well as *hapa,* chop suey, or "mixed plate"; in other words, people from multiple heritages. The woman was "mixed plate," which on this day was overshadowed by the crystal meth pumping through her veins.

"Honey, honey! Kill da focka!" she screamed, fury erupting from every pore.

From the driver's side, Honey appeared. Eyes glazed and circling, higher than high on crystal meth, he replied, "Okay. I gonna beat da livin' shit outta dis motha focka!" He pounded on the hood of Nico's car. Coming closer, he pounded on the windshield.

Nico got out, asking, "Are you okay? Anybody hurt? I'm sorry I bumped your car." Looking down at the bumper of the other car, he could see no damage. Not even a scratch.

"Kill da focka!" the woman repeated. "He jess one *ha'ole* we nevah need. Kill 'em!"

The man looked at Nico. Then the man rolled his gaze down to the bumper. He couldn't focus.

Nico got out his license and insurance. Then, he pulled up his shirt and pointed to his heart. "If you want to shoot me, do it quick, okay? We're holding up traffic. And shoot right here," he added, tapping his chest.

The man turned away shaking his head, saying, "Ah, das aw-right. I let you go dis time, lil focka."

Nico came into the house with tears freely flowing down his face. Lucky had rarely seen him cry.

"What happened?" she asked.

"I hit a car, Ma, but everyone's okay. No damage."

"Oh. Good. Why are you crying?"

"Oh, Ma, they were hateful," he said. "They didn't know me; I didn't hurt them or their car, but they wanted to hurt me just because I am white. Seeing that kind of anger and mean-ness makes me sad. I knew they were on meth, so I tried to turn it around and make 'em laugh."

Only now that he was gone did his family recognize what a gentle, kindly soul he had been with a uniquely unblemished record.

At his service, a stranger, a homeless man, took the microphone. He recalled that every morning Nico had rid-den with a baguette in his back pocket on the city bus on its two-hour journey to the university. A baguette? Yes, a baguette, which he broke and shared with anyone who was hungry on the bus.

A local kid took the mike and told about his shoes. Nico's athletic shoes had been a source of irritation to Lucky. He lost the expensive *Nikes* and *Pumas* she bought him on a regular basis, coming home bare-footed from the skate park or the beach where he routinely surfed in the late afternoons.

"Where are your shoes?" she would ask in the morning when she saw him put on slippers for school.

"Oh, sorry, Ma. I musta lost them."

The boy at the funeral told how many of the local kids from welfare families, including himself, had come to the skate park barefooted and risked mutilating their feet as they rode their boards or had walked the hot asphalt highway shoeless to the beach. Nico would say, handing over his footwear, "Here, take these. Keep 'em if they fit."

He did the same with beach towels, boogie boards, and surf shorts, generous to a fault, oblivious to the expense he was causing.

The surf was running high. A thousand people lined the shore waiting on this brusque December morning before Christmas to bid Nico a final farewell. The canoes could not safely venture out yet to spread his ashes at sea. At least five hundred friends vied for places in dozens of canoes or stood with their surfboards at the ready to paddle out if and when the conch was finally blown. Those mourners choosing to remain on shore held cameras and fragrant *lei*.

Lucky didn't care that the world could see her naked. She was stripped bare, exposed, her identity lost. Her life was not what it had been; her expectations of the future were also erased. She had no son to share laughter, no facial muscles willing to form a smile, no son left to protect, no heart left to beat, no life left to live. She felt like a pariah to be barred from any future camaraderie of mothers who shared child rearing wisdom or swapped kid stories. Son-less, after all, Lucky might carry bad luck.

Through the wind, the roar of Jet Ski engines bursting to life cut through the morbidity of her thoughts. A lifeguard tapped her on the shoulder respectfully, wrapped a towel around her, and signaled her to mount the ski behind him. There were four large and shiny Jet Skis lined side by side in the shallows. Behind each was tethered a bully board large enough to hold two people. The skis' powerful engines revved in a fury, rearing up, eager to dash forth like the four horsemen of the apocalypse.

There was a White one, a Red one, a Black one, and a Pale one: Conquest, War, Famine, and Death, as described in Revelations. Perhaps their riders looked more like four replicas of *Darth Vader*, their towels like his cape flapping at their sides. Whatever they were, these bounding coursers charged with taking her son to a watery grave, appeared ominous and deadly, chilling her the more.

Her daughters lay belly down on different boards, tightly gripping the sides. Marianna on the Black horse, Famine; Ande on the Red, War; and their father, Bullet, on White, Conquest, ironically becoming a conquistador of sorts. Holding the lifeguard around the waist, Lucky stood up on the Pale Jet Ski, Death, the symbolism not lost on her. They launched into the water in unison, the girls' long golden tresses ribboning out like horses' manes in the wind, white water surging over their hips and down their thighs, salt spray blowing high and wild off their faces.

They rode the top of the water in silence under the cursed roar of the engines. One hundred yards. Two. Three. About half a mile out, the Jet Skis circled and came to an idling halt. The sea calmed, and the wind died. Next came the canoes, then surfers, and lastly the swimmers. When all were gathered, Lucky rose to her feet, rocking with the swells. Standing on the White Jet Ski like the conquistador he once longed to be, Bullet held the urn, not trusting Lucky to carry it on the turbulent ride.

He lifted Nico's ashes high above his head, swaying sideways with the motion of the sea. He began to sing, "Hurray for Nico! Hurray at last!"

"Oh, no!" Lucky gasped as she recognized the tune. The song was a rowdy Hawai'ian drinking song she had heard thousands of times yelled uproariously from drunken and stoned lips late at night under the *hala* trees at the beach or under the metal roof covering the family *lanai*. Bully was singing this obscene song at her son's funeral. Were they to be the last words heard over his watery grave?

To her horror, Bully continued, "Hurray for Nico, he's a horse's ass! He's a horse's *okole!*" which means "ass" in Hawai'ian.

Outraged, Lucky waved her arms to the assembled crowd, doing jumping jacks as well to get their attention, which caused the Jet Ski to roll wildly. She cried slowly against the wind, articulating one word at a time, "My-son-was-a-gift-from-God!"

No one could hear or make out her words. Without further ceremony, Bullet opened the jar and dumped Nico's ashes into the sea where they fell in a solid lump. Lucky leapt as far from the Pale Jet Ski as she could and swam into the mass before it dispersed. She showered herself in him, in what was left, of her boy.

She did not come up. In fact, she could not come up. The canoes above her were being jostled to and fro by the tidal surge. Each time she tried to rise, a shifting canoe bumped the top of her head, trapping her beneath. As her breath ran short, she thought, *Just as well. I may as well join Nico.*

A lifeguard's face appeared underwater hanging upside down from the ski. He extended his hand toward her. She took it and was pulled free. Free. What a cruel joke. She was not free. She was pulled from the water, that was all.

A small pod of spinner dolphins surfaced in the center of the circle. One held something in its mouth. It was, of all things, its calf. The pod dove and surfaced over and over, as though asking for help. She could see the calf was partially supported, unmoving, on its mother's back. The pod seemed to push the mother dolphin and calf toward the canoes. No one knew what to do, watching in silence. After several circles around the group, the mother dolphin rolled her eyes and, in front of Lucky, let the dead calf go. It sank, leaving a pale pinkish glow, which quickly dimmed beneath the weight of the dark water.

The wind picked up; the dolphins dove away; the swells reappeared, and the congregation surfed, swam, or paddled to shore.

Back at the beach, Marianna asked, "Ma, could you believe those dolphins? That was so sad. Everybody was blown away. I've never even seen dolphins here before, and then they came, I think, for poor Nico."

Lucky didn't say anything.

"Ma, what were you doing out there?" Ande asked. "I thought you had gone crazy, jumping up and down and yelling. I was sure you were going to fall off the Jet Ski!"

"Did you hear your father?" Lucky whispered. "It was disgusting! He sang that horrible barroom song in front of everybody when we were supposed to be blessing your brother on his journey. I couldn't believe it. How could anyone be so crude? Heather was supposed to lead us in *Silent Night*."

"What happened when you jumped in? You took a long time to come up," Marianna asked.

"Oh. Yes. Well, I guess I wanted to join your brother."

There had been holiness, a perceptible and measurable holiness, in the small viewing room at the funeral home a few days earlier. Nico had lain on a gurney under starched white sheets. She had let them take his heart, the organ donor people. She didn't want them, the organ donor staff, to touch her son. But, they had pleaded their case.

"We use the heart for women who cannot survive their pregnancy," they explained. "We give the valves and stem to newborns who would otherwise perish."

How could she say no? They wanted the rest of him, too.

"What?" she asked. "What else do you take?"

"We strip the veins from the muscles; we harvest the organs…" Lucky cut the speaker off.

"Enough. I cannot hear anymore. My answer is, "No. I gave you his eyes, and you may take his heart. That is all."

Oscar Wilde's fairy tale, *The Happy Prince*, played through her mind; she had so loved the story as a child, reading it to her own children when the time came. Wilde wrote of a gilded statue of a prince and a swallow that built her nest at its feet. "Swallow, Swallow, little Swallow," the Prince would say, looking out over his city, "Pluck out my sapphire eye and take it to the poor seamstress; take my ruby to the student in the garret far away; take my gold to the match girl freezing on the street." And, the swallow would. After many such gifts, the Prince was stripped to bare metal and looked quite shabby without his gold leaf, naked in his under layer of lead. The swallow had flown on these errands instead of to warmer lands for the winter.

> *"It is not to Egypt that I am going," said the Swallow. "I am going to the House of Death. Death is the brother of Sleep, is he not?" And he kissed the Happy Prince on the lips, and fell down dead at his feet. At that moment, a curious crack sounded inside the statue, as if something had broken. The fact is that the leaden heart had snapped right in two. It certainly was a dreadfully hard frost. What a strange thing!" said the overseer of the workmen at the foundry. "This broken lead heart will*

not melt in the furnace. We must throw it away." They
threw it on a dust-heap where the dead Swallow was also
lying. "Bring me the two most precious things in the city,"
said God to one of His Angels; and the Angel brought
Him the leaden heart and the dead bird. "You have
rightly chosen," said God, "for in my garden of Paradise
this little bird shall sing for evermore, and in my city of
gold the Happy Prince shall praise me."

"Oh, Nico," Lucky sighed. "You gave so much of yourself. Now even I have taken your broken heart and given it away."

She went outside the viewing room for a cup of water. Back inside, she asked God to bless it, to make it holy. She sprinkled droplets of it onto her son.

She looked carefully at him. His hair had grown. It was darker. She took a clipping. His eyes seemed sunken, but of course, they were gone. His nails were longer and unclipped.

She felt a special presence. It wasn't that her son was there; he was not; his spirit had clearly departed. Yet, the room filled with sorrow and goodness, shoulder to shoulder, resting tolerably, amiably even, on each other.

She pulled down the sheet covering him. The mortuary had dressed him in a new white *Hanes* tee shirt. She had to look. She had to pull down the shirt to look at his chest, to look for the incision.

It was there but not on the left side where the heart was located but rather on the right. She was confused. She tucked her wonder in the back of her mind for perusal on another day. On this day, she needed to say goodbye to her son.

"I love you, my darling," she whispered. "I love you. You were the best. The most wonderful son I could have had. You brought me joy and light and laughter every single day of your life. Thank you. Thank you."

In Peter Paul Rubens' painting, *Pieta*, Mary looked beseechingly toward Heaven as she cradled the dead Christ on her lap. That look of Mary's mirrored Lucky's incredulity.

"Why, God?" it openly accused. "Oh, why? Why? Why have you taken a soul of such beauty?" it seemed to ask.

Lucky was beside herself, sobbing, moaning, and choking talking to God. "He was a rose, a yellow rose. A bloom in the sun. A brilliant daffodil. And, You, You, God, You are the beast in the garden! You ripped him out! You tore up the flower-bed! Like a mighty, unfeeling bulldozer, You've destroyed him! Why? I am asking You, why?"

For Christ's sake, she thought, *I don't even believe in God, do I? Why am I talking to Him?* But she went on.

"I begged you for a son! I prayed everyday! Finally, you brought me this beautiful and pure boy. I named him in Your honor: Nico Samuel, *His name is God.* How could You do this? How?"

Fred Holland Day, at the turn of the twentieth century, created over two hundred and fifty sepia images of himself as the Christ, portraits that sometimes created an uproar when they were shown publicly. Lucky remembered weeping on seeing his haunting images as she and Marianna looked through an enormous book documenting the history of photography, a Christmas gift one year from Nico to his sister.

The first three photographic self-portraits by Fred Holland Day as the Christ, starved and wearing a beard, read:

"Father, Forgive them. They know not what they do."

The latter four photographic self-portraits read:

"Today thou shalt be with me in Paradise. Woman, behold thy son. Son, thy mother. My God, my God. Why hast thou forsaken me? I thirst. Into thy hands I commend my spirit. It is finished."

On the radio, Lucky heard *NPR* report a story on the cost of the human heart. An inmate on death row at San Quentin penitentiary wanted a heart transplant and petitioned the courts for state provided medical care. The cost of a new heart amounted to over a million dollars, which would be charged to the taxpayers in California. Another story came on the radio about a crematorium in Georgia that failed to cremate the bodies in an effort to save money and flung them instead in a rubbish heap out back of the facility.

Lucky learned shortly after Nico's death that his corneas had been successfully transplanted and two formerly blind people could see. She had not heard what had become of his heart.

She called the organ donors asking them who the recipient had been. They said they would need to check their records. They told her it might take some time as no one normally inquired. A few days passed. Then they called to say no one in Hawai'i had needed Nico's heart, so it had been shipped to an organ holding center in Georgia, where it had been lost.

"Lost?" Lucky asked. "How can you lose a human heart?"

"We're sorry," was all they said.

Lucky searched the web for an organ holding facility in Georgia. Maybe there was such a place, like the Center for Disease Control. But, she couldn't find anything. She searched the entire United States. Nothing. Then, she understood, horrified. Her son's heart must have been sold, a black market heart no different from a black market baby. There were people in desperate need and those greedy enough to exploit them to profit from a much-needed organ.

She felt her own heart constrict as if erecting bars to lock itself as a prisoner into her life sentence, a cell of grief.

Lucky's sense of time began to alter. She did not realize she was being initiated into a different life with new perspectives. A passage for her through the "veil" was being torn open.

In those last weeks of Nico's life, he had tried to tell her the impossible: that he was inexplicably dying, that he was called by a force not recognized on earth, that he was made of energy, not matter. She hadn't understood then. But, the veil was lifting. Was it the heightened emotions of grief; was it the shock of insight? Like playing with a *Rubik's cube*, she tried to fit together the hours, minutes, experiences of his last days.

Nico had called her in London to wish her a happy fifty-fourth birthday. She loved his exuberance. They laughed a long time. "I'll call you when I get to San Francisco next week, sweetheart," she promised as they hung up.

She had been working and teaching in London for months, returning to Hawai'i over the summer only to complete a commission, then flying back to London for the fall term. She was coming home for Thanksgiving. Ande was working and Marianna was in graduate school in the islands. It was to be a family reunion they all anticipated with joy. Her partner, her lover, Juan was traveling with her. He was not a favorite of her children, but she hoped he would impress them positively over time. He was not from Hawai'i; he was not a surfer. He was an international banker, quite formal in a stiff and outdated, upper class way, but he was also cosmopolitan, brilliant, and wealthy. He treated Lucky well and added a measure of elegance to her life.

After a dinner in Japan Town in San Francisco and checking into their hotel, she called home. Nico said, "Mom. I'm sick, you know."

"No. I don't know. What is wrong?"

"I can't stop throwing up."

"How long has this been going on?"

"A week, Ma. And, I can't sleep."

"Oh, no. Poor you! Did you go to Kaiser?"

"Yeah. Bonnie went with me."

"Well, what did the doctor say?"

"Nothing."

"What do you mean, 'nothing'?"

"He said nothing was wrong. Maybe stress."

"No, that's not right. What tests did he do?"

"Nothing, Ma."

"What? You told him you were continuously throwing up, and you couldn't sleep? And, he didn't order any tests? No lab work?"

"Nothing."

"Did you also tell him about that coral cut on your ankle that hasn't healed?"

"I forgot."

"Honestly, no blood or *shi shi* tests? Nothing?"

"Sorry, Ma. No tests."

"Honey, are you well enough to pick up Juan and me at the airport tomorrow? We come in on United at noon. If not, we can rent a car."

"Yeah. Sure. I'll be there."

"Okay, my love. Get some sleep. Be well. I adore you. I am so sorry you are not feeling well. I wish you'd told me sooner. We'll take care of this. See you tomorrow!"

"Yeah. Sorry, Ma. See ya."

At the airport, Nico looked ashen. His deeply tanned skin was gray. This tall, broad shouldered, blond surfer whose blue eyes matched the sea on a sun glistened day looked exhausted, weak, and sallow. As they got into the car, Juan complained from the back seat, "What's wrong with this kid? He didn't pick up our bags or even bother to open the trunk!"

"Juan! For heavens sake! He is ill! It's amazing he even picked us up. We should go straight to the hospital."

"Oh, no. Let's go home first. I am feeling jet-lagged."

Nico drove them the hour's drive to her beach home. As it was a Sunday, she waited until the next day to take him to the doctor's in Honolulu.

At Kaiser, the family practitioner told them there was nothing wrong.

"Wait," Lucky said as he turned away. "How can you tell me there is nothing wrong? My son is twenty years old. He is a senior in college. He is a math tutor. And, he can't stop throwing up. Don't you tell me there is nothing wrong! You have not run any tests! You didn't even look at his ankle where even I can see an infection. Look at that red line up his leg! How can you say that?"

"I think it is stress," remarked the physician.

"You think what is stress?"

"Make an appointment with behavioral medicine."

"What, may I ask, is behavioral medicine?"

"Psychiatrics."

"Give me a break. My kid is throwing up, unable to sleep, has an infection in his leg, and you tell me to take him to see a shrink? Take a blood sample. Order a urine test. Prescribe some antibiotics. Then, we'll see about a shrink."

The doctor left the room. They made an appointment, a very future appointment, with the behavior medicine department. They did run lab tests.

Nico complained of back pain. They got x-rays. The osteopath was Korean and in addition to speaking a stilted English, his bedside manner was abrasive. He was all business. He put Nico's spinal x-rays on the light box. What Lucky saw surprised her.

"You must have the wrong patient's x-rays," she said. "Did you bring the Hunchback of Notre Dame's? These x-rays look like an old man's spine or a cripple's."

"Yes," replied the osteopath. Looking at Nico, he asked, "Can you still urinate?"

"Yes," said Nico.

"Hmm. You won't be able to much longer. Your lower four vertebrae," the osteopath said, pointing to the x-ray on the left in the light box, "are compressing. You will stop being able to urinate or defecate within a few weeks. That is when the paralysis will set in."

"What paralysis?" asked Lucky.

"Your son will be paralyzed from the waist down."

"What?" she gasped.

"Your son has advanced scoliosis," the osteopath explained, tapping down each vertebra in the x-ray with a wooden pointer. "The vertebrae are crushing down on each other like pieces of cheesecake."

The spine in the x-ray looked like a dishcloth, which had been wrung out and slung over the back of a kitchen chair.

"My god!" Lucky said. Turning to Nico, she asked, "Is that why you only have surf rash on your right side? Your ribs are twisting to the back?"

Nico looked stunned and shrugged quizzically.

Lucky said to the doctor, "I thought only girls got scoliosis."

"Yes. It is not common in males. It is hereditary, however."

Lucky's sister, Linney, did spinal exercises when she was around ten or eleven. Yes, Lucky remembers, having forgotten about the scoliosis. And Nana, her Nana had that classic "dowager's hump."

"What can we do?"

"Nothing. Wait."

"What about a surgery?"

"No. Less than a fifty-fifty chance. We might knick the cord and irreversibly paralyze him ourselves."

Nico did not comment. He did not ask questions. At home, he went into his room and lay down.

"Nico, honey," Lucky said kneeling beside him, "this doctor could be very mistaken. I don't trust Kaiser when it comes to important issues like this. Don't worry. Please. Don't freak out. I'll make some calls and find the best osteopath here or on the mainland."

Nico's health deteriorated, along with his spirit. He continued his classes at university; he continued tutoring at Chaminade University. He continued to live alternately at the dorm and at home on weekends. But, he stopped surfing. He stopped seeing Bonnie.

"Don't you like her anymore, honey?" Lucky asked.

"Oh, yeah, Ma. I love her. But, I don't want her to see me like this."

"But honey, she knows you are sick. She's seen you vomiting and went with you to Kaiser the first time."

"Nyah, Ma. Not now. Maybe later."

He sat at the computer for hours. Not keyboarding. Staring. He said the screen went blank on October 12th, the week he got sick, and he had been unable to see anything on it since. That was six weeks ago.

She went to lunch at the Outrigger, where her girlfriends gave her a belated birthday party. She told them something was wrong with Nico but she could not figure out what.

When she got home in the late afternoon, Juan was furious. He attacked her.

"Look what I found under your bed! Love letters! You hide your old lovers under your bed!"

She stared at Juan. Nico was sitting in her bedroom with his back to them staring at the blank computer screen.

"Nico, darling, are you okay?"

"Yeah, Ma."

"I am sorry, Nico, that you are going to hear what I am about to say," she said and turned on Juan. "How dare you? I leave my home and you spend the day snooping around my house?"

"Look at these letters and photos," he sputtered.

"Not your business! Do not say another word. You have no right. You are not entitled to any questions or any answers. You are a snoop and a thief, and perhaps this is a good time for you to pack your bag and go right back to England."

Kaiser called to cancel the appointment with the behavior department, rescheduling for several weeks hence. She demanded an appointment with someone, anyone.

"My son cannot sleep. Do you hear me? He is in crisis. Help. Help us!"

"Well, ma'am, you can go to the emergency room."

They did. The on-call doctor happened to be one of Lucky's hiking buddies, Amy, who had coached Nico's soccer team when he was six. After examining him, she told Lucky, "Your son is having an existential crisis."

"What the hell are you talking about?"

"There is nothing we can do for him. It's not physical. It's his spirit."

"Order a CAT scan, will you? He has scoliosis. We had blood and urine work done. Are the results in his chart?"

"No, there is nothing here," Amy replied, leafing through Nico's chart, confirming Lucky's mistrust of Kaiser's preventive health "care."

"I don't buy your analysis," Lucky continued. "My son is in love, has his first major surf competition in a few days, and is a regent's fellow at the university. He has picked up some virus and needs medical help. Some insensitive osteopath tells us that due to his diagnosis of scoliosis, Nico is going to lose the ability to urinate, defecate, and walk. Wow. Sorry, Amy, but fuck your existential crisis bullshit and help him, for Christ's sake. How about a prescription for sleeping pills for starters? And some antibiotics for his infection?"

Existential crisis? While she was in London, Nico had attended summer school, wanting to graduate early. He took creative writing and existentialism, two classes he'd not had time for in the regular year due to his heavy course load of math and physics. He loved Jack Kerouac's *On the Road* and could not get enough of Albert Camus. He had read aloud sections of *The Plague* and *The Stranger* to her on the phone.

"Ma, Ma, I get it. I mean, Camus is saying there's no meaning, no abstract, absolute meaning or value in life. But, we are our brother's keepers. Get it? What we are here to do is take care of each other, right?"

Camus touted the idea that the absence of religious belief can simultaneously be accompanied by a longing for "salvation and meaning." Camus showed the dualisms of happiness and sadness, dark and light, life and death. He emphasized that happiness is fleeting and the human condition is one of mortality, which can, if allowed, create a greater appreciation for life and happiness.

"Look, Ma, as I see it, Camus investigated our experience of the Absurd. He asked how we live with it. Our life must have meaning for us to value it, right? If we accept that life has no meaning and therefore no value, should we kill ourselves?"

"No. Let me say that again. No, Nico," Lucky interrupted. "I think Camus pointed out that there is no more meaning in death than there is in life. And, suicide evades the problem.

I say, at least I say the way I have chosen to see life, is that we entertain death and the absurd simultaneously, while never agreeing to their terms."

"What the hell does that mean, Ma?"

⚬

Lucky was furious. She called every doctor, therapist, psychologist, specialist, and social worker she knew or had heard of.

"What? Your son has gone twenty-nine days without sleep?" Dr. Korek asked. "The CIA uses sleep deprivation to torture people! You get unhinged. Going without sleep for even three days is known to kill people."

When they finally got to see the behavioral medicine doctors, Dr. Dousch said, "I am ordering your son a prescription for *Risperdal* and *clonazepam*."

The cocktail. To drink or not to drink became the question.

They held a family meeting at the hospital: Bullet, Marianna, Ande, Nico, Lucky, and the doctors. A month into his illness and a month without sleep or proper food, Nico checked off all the boxes for depression.

"*Risperdal* is an antipsychotic medication. It is an 'atypical antipsychotic'. It works by changing the effects of chemicals in the brain," Dr. Dousch told them.

"Why would Nico need to take that? He is not psychotic!" Marianna exclaimed.

The doctor replied, "Clearly, Marianna, your brother is depressed. *Risperdal* is a first line drug used to treat schizophrenia and symptoms of bipolar disorder or manic depression. It is also used in autistic children to treat symptoms of irritability."

"Nico is not bipolar!" Marianna cried. "Nor is he autistic. And, now, I am the one who is irritable!"

"Mom, let's get outta here," Ande said, standing up. "These shrinks don't know what they are doing. They don't know Nico, and they are trying to force an arsenal of goofy pills on him. If he's not goofy now, he sure will be if he takes them."

"Not necessarily, Ande," intervened Marianna. "I've taken *Prozac* for seven years. It evens out my moods and keeps me from hurting myself." She turned her attention to Nico. "Neeks, do you feel like hurting yourself or dying?"

"You've gotta be kidding me," he whispered. "No way. I just can't sleep. I can't focus. I feel like I'm losing my mind."

Lucky knew psychiatric practices often failed patients, particularly young adults. Her sister, Linney, had been a prime example.

"We have a significant travesty being done in this country with how the diagnosis is being made and the meds are being administered," admitted Dr.Korek, their old psychiatrist. "I think it's an abnegation of trust. Doctors are saying, 'Just take the meds to see if they help.' But whom are the drugs tested on before FDA approval? And how many tests are discarded that do not support the results the drug companies want? And when a drug is finally approved, no one, no agency keeps track of the results. In the clinical trials, perhaps no one committed suicide while on the drug. But once it is released to the general population? No tracking, no data, no nothing. The public needs to say this buckshot approach to mental health is totally unacceptable. They need to walk out. You can walk out now, Nico, if you want, and simply ignore us. We don't know enough about the brain to tell you what to decide for your health."

"Why do you insist Nico has a mental or emotional problem? I think there is a physical cause. I keep asking and you keep ignoring me," Lucky said.

Dr. Dousch chimed in. "I hear what Dr. Korek is saying, and I am not ignoring you now, Ms. Pulaski. But, please bear with me. I want you, Nico, to try a cocktail of *Risperdal* and *Clonazepam*. Let me explain. *Clonazepam* is a benzodiazepine drug having anxiolytic, anticonvulsant, muscle relaxant, sedative, and hypnotic properties. It has been found effective in treating anxiety disorders, migraines, panic attacks, mania, and parasomnia. I am quite sure it will relax you, and then you will be able to sleep."

"I don't want any drugs," Nico said quietly.

"These drugs have a clean track record," Dr. Dousch promised.

"Don't they make patients more susceptible to suicidal thoughts?" Lucky asked.

"Sometimes. When they kick in after about six weeks, the patient can feel stronger and often that is the most dangerous time, as the patient has enough energy to end his own life. All you can do is to monitor him carefully. What he needs is sleep and these drugs are the only sure way he will get it."

"You are talking about depression. Fine. I want to know about Nico's spinal scoliosis. I want to know about his leg infection. No one has addressed those problems. I want to rule out any physical causes for his sleeplessness and vomiting. So. How are we supposed to proceed?"

At home, Nico did appear depressed. He did not speak about his back pain, but Lucky noticed he spent longer and longer periods of time in the bathroom. He laid in bed but failed to sleep. She tried to convince him to try the pills. He had no interest in books or television. He did not want to venture outside. He refused to see his friends, saying he was embarrassed for them to see him when he wasn't the life of the party. He did not call Bonnie. Lucky felt sorry for the girl, certain she must feel jilted and confused by his silence. Lucky spent most of her time on the phone trying to find more suitable doctors and secure appointments to cure his sleeplessness, the vomiting, the depression, the scoliosis, and the leg wound that refused to heal. She wanted to get out of this helpless hell, to leave these uncaring doctors and re-scheduled-for-later appointments. They were not getting help; they were not getting answers. They were getting ineptitude.

A year earlier in a burst of maternal generosity, Edna had bought a home for Lucky on another island, a beautiful home on a cliff above the sea flanked by gardens and waterfalls. Edna was not wealthy and her gift came as a complete surprise. Juan and Lucky had taken a holiday to see Haleakala, the dormant volcano on top of Maui. They visited friends on the Hana Coast, hiked the bamboo forest, swam in the Seven Sacred Pools at Ohe'o, and fallen more deeply in love. She photographed him in the gardens on an historical estate there, sending some prints later to her mother, who began trembling with excitement when she received them.

"I dreamt of this estate when I was about five years old!" she exclaimed to Lucky on the phone from San Francisco. "I never knew where it was. But, it was this place, this place in your photos, with green grass terraces tumbling down the hillsides, the cobalt blue of the sea, the bright sun. I was swinging from that avocado tree in the front yard facing the ocean on a little wooden swing, kicking my legs to go higher and higher and laughing."

Lucky was astounded by Edna's gift and wondered what it would be like to live quietly on the back of this dormant volcano at the edge of the sea.

Lucky had hated living in her marital home after the divorce from Bullet, but she could not afford to move. The home was itself lovely but unfortunately was located in an area of extreme

poverty, considered the "armpit" of O'ahu. It was on the leeward side, which was arid, the rocky earth filled with prickly
pears and sharp thorned kiawe scruff. Residents who migrated
there had found cheap housing and poor schools compared to
the rest of O'ahu. The area was reputed historically to be filled
with thieves and parolees, and even a century later, tourists
were advised to stay away. Most who came were surfers, Bullet
among them, intrepid in their search for giant waves. The western beaches were long, golden tongues licking a coast often
slapped by a slobbering backwash. In the winter months, huge
waves almost seemed to upchuck along the shore.

Lucky got Nico up for a walk. Down the street stretched
Maili beach, a beach whose waves he had ridden since he was
a toddler, first on a boogie board, then, as he got older, on
a short surfboard. He made doing aerials and spinners look
easy. As a ten year old, he had won a national boogie board
championship held in Southern California and gotten an article in *Sports Illustrated Junior* with an endorsement from *Capri
Sun* drinks. He might as well have been born in the water like
a playful spinner dolphin, Lucky often chuckled, for he spent
more time in the ocean than on land.

Nico did not want to go. She cajoled him and prevailed.
When they got to Maili Beach Park, he wanted to stay on the
grass, not cross the sand to the water. Lucky went ahead. As she
put her bare foot into the shore break, he grabbed her elbow
and pulled her three steps back.

"No, Ma. It's dangerous. Don't go near the water."

She saw a sincere look of fear freeze on his face. "Why,
Nico..."

"Come on, Ma," he cut her off. "We're going home now."
She was shocked. She looked at the sea; it was flat, the day
calm. She looked back at Nico, who looked terrified. He was
scheduled to compete in his first pro surfing meet in five days.

"People drown every day, Ma," he urged her to understand.

She didn't argue. She let it go, walking home with him, knowing she faced a crisis she did not understand.

Nico laid down in his room. She brought in a stack of books. She opened James Michener's *Hawai'i* and read aloud the preface describing the origins of their beautiful volcanic islands, how the wind, birds, and the seas brought seeds, how the islands flourished as a natural and unspoiled paradise. She continued to read to him every day as they waited for appointments with medical specialists from mid October through early December. Homer's *Odyssey*. She opened coffee table books filled with splendid photographs of the world's most beautiful places, animals in their habitats, people in foreign lands. She tried to refill Nico's mind with life, beauty, history, art, and civilizations. She even read the string theory of physics from Brian Greene's *The Elegant Universe* aloud in those weeks.

Suspended above his bed, a paper version he'd made of the solar system slowly turned. On his wall hung a large map of the cosmos; distances between our solar system and others were neatly calculated; planets, moons, suns, stars circled elliptically. Before taking a leave of absence due to his ill health from the university, he studied astrophysics.

He had pasted photos of his closest friends on various stars.

"Why are Ben and Abe's photos on those stars?" she asked as she sat down beside him one afternoon.

"I think we have been friends forever. You know what forever means, Ma?"

"Tell me what you mean by forever," she replied.

"Well, you just sorta know. I know Ben and Abe inside and out. I know you. Even if you weren't my mom, I'd know you and love you. I would love you forever. I have loved you forever, always. Do you get what I mean?"

"Sort of," she smiled.

"What I've learned is the dynamics of physics like falling apples and rotating galaxies is embodied *within* the unchanging configuration space. Space is not *frozen* like a cryonics patient suspended in liquid nitrogen. It is not motionless as an isolated system while the rest of the universe goes on without it. Space is *timeless*; time exists only *within* it. To talk about time, you have to talk about relations *inside* the configuration space."

Lucky looked a bit lost.

"Mom," Nico stressed, "we have always belonged together. Always. You have to learn to recognize people without their earth jackets, without our faces and bodies to help. It's like you have to see into their hearts. Like goodness. You just know if someone is good or bad."

"You mean like intuition or a gut feeling?"

"Sorta. I mean, there really is good, Ma, and there really is evil."

"Oh?"

"Yeah. I see it. I know right away when I meet people what they are about. Like, if they are here to help or to harm."

"I thought you liked everybody."

"It's not that, Ma. My job is to be a good guy and like everybody. But, it doesn't mean I don't recognize what some people are up to. That's why I cry a lot."

"Oh, honey, I know you are sad…"

Nico cut her off. "No, Ma. You don't understand. I am not SAD sad. I am helpless."

"Helpless?"

"Look at me. I am weak. I can't think. All my power is leaking out."

She put out her hand, laying it on top of one of his in a gesture of comfort. A brilliant light shot out of his left eye like a laser pointer, going from his eye straight to the back of her hand in a continuous line of infrared radioactive isotope green. She jumped up. Without a word, she ran from his room, out the back bathroom door to a far corner of the garden, hiding herself in a clump of bamboo. She was shaking all over.

What had happened? Tears streamed from her eyes. She was not hallucinating. She saw what she saw. A brilliant green line of light emitted from her son's eye to the back of her hand as hers covered his. Even a low-powered green laser was visible at night through *Rayleigh* scattering from air molecules and was used by astronomers to easily point out stars and constellations. This light had been high-powered and clearly visible in the day. She felt undone. She tried to figure it out.

A bright green light had emitted from her beloved son's eye to focus on the center of her hand. Okay. It might have happened in a science fiction movie, in an alien take over or some such, but not in her home, not from her son, not in her realm of experience. Like the stigmata, suddenly appearing, unearthly, yet real, this green light had appeared. Ah, she realized: it had centered precisely where the spikes would have been driven to hold Christ's hands to the cross.

She went back inside but not to Nico's room. She busied herself in the kitchen as cooking usually calmed her. She peeled and cut eight Granny Smith apples and rolled crust for a pie. She hoped he was taking a nap.

In her studio around four p.m., she was working on several four-foot long clay slabs to construct a temple. She had a commission from Queen's hospital to make temples that could be mounted in niches on the waiting room wall of a new radiation wing they were building. The art consultant had told her that the hospital administrators wanted to create a soothing and contemplative atmosphere for patients and their families. Her temples, reminiscent of Daitokuji in Kyoto where Zen Buddhism originated, gave the right feeling.

Nico came out.

"Ma, I'm leaving."

"What?" she wiped her hands on her apron and walked to him. His hands were empty; his feet were bare. There was no duffel bag or backpack on him.

"I'm leaving," he repeated quietly.

"What are you saying?" Instinctively, she knew. He was telling her that he was dying, that he didn't know what was wrong, he didn't know why he was dying but he was.

Then, she saw it. From his left shoulder, near the collarbone, there rose a small gray puff, almost a mushroom shape transparent as smoke and smaller than a tiny paper bag. She lunged. With both hands cupped over it, she pushed it down, pushed the delicate, little gray puff back into his body. Then she held him, clasped him to her, held him so tightly neither of them could move, she on tiptoe coming closer to his six foot height.

"You are staying right here!" she commanded. Not knowing why or with time to plan, she added, "You are going to be a man, a father. You are going to do the human thing. You'll have a career. You'll fall in love; you'll have a family of your own. You are fine. You are just fine."

He pulled slightly away from her grip and gave her a funny little look. A tiny smile toyed with his mouth. He looked at her with the saddest eyes she had ever seen. Then, he turned and walked back into the house.

She booked flights to take them to her new house in Hana.

"I cannot keep waiting for these stupid doctors and tests and appointments. Staying on O'ahu is not doing Nico any good," she told Ande and Marianna. "We're going to Maui. I think he'll feel better being away from all the pressure here. Did I tell you, he took a leave of absence from the university?"

"Is he that bad?" Marianna asked.

"I think so. We moved his things out of the dorm on Tuesday as well. It was my first time there. Did you know his apartment was on the ninth floor? When we got out of the elevator, it was open air on both sides of the landing."

"I know. I helped Nico move in. Maybe I shouldn't tell you this, Ma, but I used to go up there a lot this summer when you were in England to hang out with him."

"What's wrong with that?"

"Listen. Before you came back from London, I went up. When the elevator door opened, Nico was there. Not there, but sitting on the railing with his legs over the side, like he was about to push off. You know. Kill himself. Drop the nine stories down."

"My god! Why didn't you tell me?"

"Oh, Ma. How many times have I tried to kill myself? A lot more than you will ever know. I wasn't about to rat on my brother. It's private. Personal. We have free will, you know, and a person doesn't have to be crazy not to want to live anymore. Living is a choice. Sometimes a bad one."

Back in the December of 1989, dismal black and gray winter storms besieged O'ahu. The loft bedroom Lucky had as her own held two futons and a sofa bed where her three children huddled for comfort. Bullet had left in June. She filed for divorce in October. The rains and their accompanying thunder ravaged the roof where the skylight revealed the onslaught through the night. Under his cotton duvet, nine-year-old Nico quietly wept and moaned. He had swollen glands and mild flu.

"Mom," he called. "Am I going to die?"

"No, my little lamb," Lucky soothed. "It's just a bit of the flu. You'll feel better in a few days."

"No, I won't."

"Why do you say that?"

"Because. Dad is gone, and he won't come back."

Nico never mentioned his father's departure to her again over the next twelve years. Then, a month before his death, he spoke to Bullet and Lucky who were seated at the dining room table in the family home, together after so many years of animosity, their sole purpose to help their son regain his health.

Bullet had asked, thinking of the loss of his mother, Queenie, to cancer, "Nico, have you ever lost anyone you really, really loved?"

Nico looked at his father for a long time and rose from the table.

"No duh, Dad."

"Gramma Queenie, right?"

"No, Dad. You."

"Well, I'm here right now, Bub."

"No, Dad. It was a long time ago. A long time."

How many valves shut off in the heart before it is completely broken? Lucky wondered.

There was the day Nico's best friend told him he wasn't his best friend. Nico could hardly breathe. He had been playing at Ben's house. Ben's mother had gotten pretty involved with the born again crowd. Gramma Edna always asked, "What was wrong with them? Weren't they born right the first time?" Ben's mother's lover was the grand pooh bah of censors. He told her what she could and couldn't wear, what she could and couldn't say, where she could and couldn't go. He did the same to her son, Ben, who had a gang of neighborhood boys over playing that day out back in addition to nine-year-old Nico.

Nico and Ben had played together every day since they met at a Halloween preschool costume party when they were three. Nico had dressed as a shark in blue satin; Ben wore green as a tyrannosaurus rex. They were a match made in heaven.

Ben's dad was Japanese, not a waterman, and didn't take him to the beach. Nico and his sisters lived at the beach where they learned to surf before they could skip, jump, or run. Water was Nico's medium. As a five year old, he entertained the tourists with shore break back flips and somersaults, which he happily taught Ben. Together they spent hours in the water.

They also loved to eat shave-ice at the beach. Red cherry *Malolo* syrup was their favorite, running down their salty chins as they grinned like sunny cherub vampires after a particularly good feed.

Something must have been bugging Ben that particular day, and he was ready to snap, needing to be the grand pooh bah of something himself. So, when Nico claimed his status as best friend, Ben shot him down.

"No yer not! I got lotsa friends I like bettern you!"

Then there had been the moment he was made aware of race and differences on the first day of kindergarten. Nico had looked bewildered when Lucky picked him up.

"How do you like school, honey?" Lucky asked, placing him on the child seat of her bicycle. He and his sisters had been preschool "dropouts," finding preschool dreary and dull compared to mornings spent with mom. At home, they painted, played piano, cared for dozens of pets, enjoyed play group, listened to stories, danced, rode bicycle, jumped endlessly on the trampoline, or swam and played in the tide pools outside the front door. There was so much to do in the fresh air and sunshine. At preschool, children cried and were rough. Long *hanabattas*, pidgin for green boogers, hung from their noses, the "aunties" or *kupuna* yelled, the toys were tattered, and mornings were not sweet. Lucky was concerned about his reaction to kindergarten.

"The kids call me 'Grandfather Hair,'" he told her.

"Grandfather Hair?" she repeated. "Oh," she laughed with sudden understanding. "You have blond hair, and your classmates have black hair. Maybe they have only seen white blond hair on old men! Maybe you are the first boy, *ha'ole* boy, they have met! It's okay, honey, you'll be friends."

But, he wasn't happy at school and cried everyday. She scheduled a meeting with his teacher.

"He's a wonderful child," Mrs. Kanemitsu said. "He gets along well with everyone. He's no trouble at all. And, he is so bright!"

"I don't understand, then, why he is so unhappy."

"I am surprised to hear it," the teacher said. "Every morning after attendance, I seat him at that table," she said, pointing to a round table off in a windowless corner of the classroom. "I give him his work. He never needs my help or attention."

"You mean he sits at that table alone all day?"

"Yes. He's no trouble at all."

"Of course, he's no trouble! But, look what you are doing! He feels as though he is being punished!"

"The other children are so rambunctious," Mrs. Kanemitsu defended. "I have thirty-three very naughty children in this class, and it takes all my effort to keep them in order!"

Lucky began looking for private schools that afternoon.

There weren't many choices on the rural coast near their home. Those choices were the religious hangers-on from missionary days. Her choice was between the Baptist School and the Fundamentalist School. The Baptists ran the preschool, which ruled them out immediately. The Fundamentalist school required parents to sign a document promising that they believed in God and the Devil. Oh my. Lucky couldn't do that. She complained to a local Japanese friend about it.

"Oh," advised the friend, "we're Buddhists, but we signed. No other choice, eh?"

The principal drew charts of concentric circles in chalk on the blackboard. The innermost circle was the child, next the family, then Wai'anae, then O'ahu, then Hawai'i, next the United States, then Earth, then the universe, then God surrounding all. He talked to the students about their role in the order of things, where their allegiance lay, who they were. Above all was God. Whether Lucky subscribed to this hierarchy was unimportant; the school ingrained it in Nico, where he learned to be profoundly respectful.

Nico felt happy there, cherished, in fact. Each Monday the students were assigned a *Bible* verse to memorize and recite by heart on Friday. Nico excelled. By the sixth grade, his memory was so honed that he could recite the Gettysburg Address, the Declaration of Independence, and dialogue from feature length films.

But, betrayals of faith like the loss of his dad and the loss of Ben hit Nico in that year, 1989. Two years later a worse betrayal occurred: the near loss of his beloved big sister, Marianna, when, after school one April day in her junior year, she saw her parents' divorce decree had arrived in the mail. Instead of life and family, she chose poison and self-burial at sea.

There were times when Lucky's eyes were closed. She had to keep them closed, her hands pressed over them. She screamed, breathlessly. She hiccupped. She cried, horrified. Why? Memory, her memory and what it contained.

Oh, say the memory of a hanging. Outside her house. In the dark. Yes, it was dark. So very dark. Except for the headlights from her truck shining on the beach. Rather, shining on the *hau* tree in front of the beach. Her headlights were shining on dangling legs. Another car's headlights. Whose? The police, but she didn't know that yet. Her son, her eighteen year old, naïve, sweet son had swung open the wooden gates to her compound, when she saw in her rear view mirror, legs. Legs dangling. From a tree. And she stopped, halted, and pulled on the brake. Jumped out, yelled, and grabbed her son. Together, they dashed into the park. My god. My god. A man, a boy, someone, was hanging, dangling from the tree. She pulled his legs. And, she screamed. And, her son ran to get hedge trimmers and a ladder. As he climbed the ladder to cut the rope, a cop pushed him aside and yanked or cut or pulled the body down. And it, the body, he, the person, was dead. Stiff, so stiff he bounced whole as he hit the ground. Turning away, Lucky and Nico went home.

They didn't want to know. The horror. Who, who was it? No one knew. They went to bed. Next day, next morning, they asked. Who? What? What happened? Who was that? They would never forget. Nico would never forget. The legs caught dangling in the headlights at ten o'clock at night. Gray pants, running shoes, swaying a bit to the left, then a bit, only slightly, to the right. Bare movement, barely moving. But dead.

Lucky stood under a thick rope net filled with head sized boulders. One rock at a time slipped out of the net to conk her. The single rock would not kill her, like the whole net full dumping on her head would, but it caused some damage and quite a bit of pain. It was as if the net held all her grief, which was far too great to experience at once, needing to be meted out over time like the slow drip of Chinese water torture.

$$\wp$$

And so, a rock dropped, and she remembered her daughter. As Lucky closed her eyes, the memory of Marianna's shattered body in the funeral home surfaced from the repressed folds of Lucky's psyche, Marianna dead of a fall into anorexia a year after Nico's funeral.

Lucky got up and walked the moonless garden trying to escape the horror of the loss. Yet, she needed to wrap her mind around her daughter; Lucky needed to understand Marianna. But, as usual, Lucky came up empty and helpless, able only to remember Marianna's babyhood and precious time with Ande before Nico was born.

How serious and darling and precocious Marianna had been. How every night she fell asleep in a hammock as Lucky sang "Swing Low Sweet Chariot" or "Hush Little Baby, Don't You Cry..." And once asleep, Marianna would be tucked snugly into her crib. How horrible beyond words Lucky felt to have her children self-destruct.

Impressions took hold. Her daughter. Marianna awash at sixteen. Her lithe body in the water, in the shore break. Lucky had sent that boy, her son, that impressionable boy, Nico, barely nine then, to fetch the paper bag Marianna said she had dropped on the reef above the tide pools, the paper bag of pills and poisons and god knows what Lucky's daughter, her precious, precocious poetess daughter whispered she had dropped there, whispered as Lucky held Marianna's soaked and barely breathing body in her arms, Marianna had taken, eaten, ingested, because she no longer wanted to live, this baby, this first born, this newborn, this sixteen year old kissed too few times, this blissfully nubile daughter, laid on a gurney defying the orderlies who were trying to save her life, who were lifting her into an ambulance with its blaring red emergency warnings, who needed to see the bag's contents to learn what she had taken to end her life, as if cutting all the arteries in her ankles and knees and elbows and wrists was not enough and thrown herself into the deep end of the sea was not enough, and drunk all the poisons a household could contain, as if all that horror would not impress a young mind, a young heart, a young brother that death might be preferable to this sunnied life by the shore of this tropical now tranquil sea.

Twenty-nine, yes, Marianna outlived her first suicide attempt to live to be twenty-nine, lived only to be lying thirteen years later on a sheeted gurney in an air-conditioned funeral parlor viewing room. She was covered lightly by a peach silk teddy and white robe, as her body was too broken to be dressed. Twenty-one stories she had dropped.

"Mom," she had announced before Nico's funeral. "I am going to honor Nico by not eating for thirty days."

"I don't think that's wise," Lucky had said, fearing the return of Marianna's dormant anorexia but too dazed by Nico's death to focus.

"I need to find him, Mom. I need to find Nico. I'm his big sister. I should have taken better care of him. I should have seen how sad he was. I feel guilty, responsible. He needs me now. Nico is not the crazy one! I am! I wanted to die. Not Nico! Not my brother, not my butterfly, not my Nico."

"He's gone, honey."

"I am cutting off my hair, Joan of Arc style," Ande decided, "and giving it to the ocean where we put his ashes. I want some of me to go with him."

Marianna and Lucky agreed to barber. The next morning standing on the shoreline, the three mourning women cut their hair and swam half a mile out, letting their loosened locks disperse into the deep.

Marianna was all about white. Her skin, the way she saw things, her inner light. When she'd talk about her wedding, everything had to be white: the dress, the cake, the flowers, everything white and pure and perfect, like she.

For the wedding, she wanted to wear strand upon strand of white, pearl-like jasmine strung into *lei,* their fragrance emanating through the air as she walked down the aisle.

Marianna had been slow. Not slow as in stupid, rather slow in a special way. She waited until she was ready and then did what she needed or wanted to do with precision and perfection. Like learning to walk.

Marianna had not been quite ten months old when Lucky took her to a neighbor kid's first birthday party. All the other babies were a little older and able to toddle, walk, or even run around. Marianna didn't move a muscle at that party. For three hours, she sat still and watched, blue eyes wide open, lids barely blinking, taking it all in. She sat so still, one of the other mothers asked Lucky sweetly, "Oh, Honey, is your little girl retarded?"

When the party ended, Lucky lifted Marianna up to carry her home. As soon as Marianna saw her own front yard, she wriggled out of Lucky's arms and stood up. Marianna steadied herself, and then walked straight across the lawn without tee-tering or toppling all the way to the front door.

Her anger was white, too.

Marianna was going to marry Dude. She had stolen him from her best friend, Birdie. It was part of Marianna's watching habit. Her love thefts started in high school. She watched her best friends dating, got familiar by association with their boyfriends, and suddenly, she'd glom on to the guy, stealing him away.

Dude and Birdie had been together for seven years when Marianna made her move. Dude was older, a trust fund baby who didn't have to work. He either stayed home all day shaping surfboards, adding rooms to his house, downloading music on his computer, or he went out on the ocean, surfing, fishing, diving, photographing. He was pretty cute. Even Ande said she wished he wasn't already Birdie's boyfriend.

Marianna had stopped eating when her world turned from white to black. It had blackened during the divorce, regaining a gray tone for some years after therapy and before she and Dude fell in love. Birdie was doing research on the mainland and didn't realize her place was being usurped. Dude wanted children and made Marianna promise to eat: if she ate, he would marry her. But, Marianna's world darkened again when Nico died. Her urge to self-destruct became greater than her urge to procreate. She broke off with Dude, confessed the affair to Birdie, and embarked on a liquid diet of pure alcohol as her life rotated void of color.

Her paintings, her photographs, her poetry turned black. Obsessed with black horses, she painted and wrote about one, the black horse of the apocalypse, which brought famine to mankind.

Marianna stood five feet eight inches tall and weighed eighty-two pounds. Starving herself, living in her university studio away from family and friends, creating piece after dark piece, she began cutting. Herself. Small incisions on her arms, legs, labia. Wanting to hurt. Wanting to see if she could feel physically the pain, the terrible, relentless, tormenting pain she felt in her heart. People. She cut people out of her life: Dude, Ande, Lucky, Birdie, friends, and colleagues. Marianna found ways to fight, ignore, or lose anyone she had ever loved. Lucky wouldn't hear from her for months at a time.

Marianna swam every day for hours as though being so long in the ocean she would find her brother. Or at least his remains. Or perhaps she herself would just dissolve. And never have to return.

She was showering at the natatorium after such a swim when a small child approached.

"You look scary, like one skeleton. Why?" the boy asked.

"My brother died, and I am really, really sad," she answered.

Alone with Marianna's corpse in the crematorium viewing room, Lucky melted paraffin from the candle she'd brought. She placed a thin, warm layer of wax between her own lips to seal them like Marianna's were sealed.

Silence, that was Lucky's vow, silence.

Her mind flickered like a dagger point over a flame of revenge as it had on and off during the years since her divorce. To relax her mind and appease her heart, she took idle pleasure in planning Bullet's death, as if he alone had killed her children, as if he alone was responsible. It was no different for her now a second of their children was dead. What had he done to Marianna? Had he done anything beyond being himself, just as Lucky had been herself, both flawed?

When Lucky took the sack of Marianna's ashes down to the edge of the sea, she was alone. She quietly dropped her daughter by fistfuls into the water.

"Sleep with those angels, my darling girl, those angels who cherish moonlit pagodas, those angels who sleep on crescent pillows, those angels who heard your cries," Lucky whispered into the sea, which was thrashing below the cliffs as if grasping at Marianna's remains with its salty airborne brine.

Did Marianna stand a chance on the tides of time? Lucky wondered. *Had Marianna been reborn as Linney the broken, had she lived her life as Laura the victim, had she ever freely lived as Marianna? Was she destined to die in this lifetime of sadness after the loss of family?*

Twenty-nine years before on a similar shore, Lucky had stood for an invocation, her new infant daughter in her arms, both squinting against the morning light. That other sea had been calm. Lucky had looked at the tidal pool, at her baby girl, at her bronzed husband as he lit a match and held it to the dried umbilicus. Lucky looked beyond the white clouds, through the blue sky, and beseeched God to protect her baby. She looked through the blue of the water and asked the sea to be safe for her child, as they lived by the edge of the sea and she knew her daughter would grow to play in its pools and swim in its depths. Lucky and Bullet offered the burnt umbilicus as a sacrifice to nature and dipped their baby's head into the water for a blessing.

A holy blessing. Now it was Marianna's whole body that was burned. It was the remains of her once whole body that Lucky threw into the brine. Marianna had become the sacrifice.

hey moms

*thank you so much for a wonderful extended birthday i really
enjoyed my first days of being 28 thank you for all the gifts and
great foods*

*i am also so sorry we get futtless with each other and sometime have
this tendency to hurt each other's feelings i truly love you tons and
also pray that our relationship can be easy sometimes i wonder why
it feels like it gets so hard sometimes i feel a lot of pressure from both
you and dad pressure to do well pressure to make you happy to give
you guys enough love since i am the last kid standing it is really
hard sometimes and i think that pressure in me comes out nasty
anyway it is no excuse for making the mama feel mistreated and
abused so i am sorry i love you tons and tons*

i can't wait for you to come and see my new hale

whee

*thanks again for all the prezzies especially the beautiful dishes love
them*

smooches

ande

Lucky normally found having a conversation with Ande,
who refused to offer an inch of herself, about as productive as
pulling hen's teeth. Lucky sat, pliers in hand, asking question
after question. She could hear Ande's impatience and disin-
terest on the other end of the line. Then, came the almost
breathless, inevitable, "Gotta go, Mom" and she'd be gone.
Sometimes Lucky cried so hard, her tears seared bright red
streaks down her cheeks.

It was too fraught with emotion for Ande to talk about anything to do with family. She had made a few negative comments
about Nico after he died, like "he was such a big crybaby," to
which Lucky took offense, or referring to Marianna as "a liar,"
as though to deny the validity of her experience. Neither could

bear to have an argument over their different perspectives on the family. They were very different people with very different versions of a shared past. Lucky might hate it, but that was the way it was.

Lucky tried to "walk in Ande's shoes" to imagine or understand how she felt since the family had diminished.

Ande had found Nico. He had been standing in the dining room on his way from his bedroom to the bathroom. She had seen him through the glass; that entry side of the house was a long corridor of glass. She'd come home early to grab her long board and ride some waves with her father. Finding the kitchen door locked, she had called,

"Nico, hey! Open the door!"

He hadn't moved. She had yelled again, and still he hadn't moved or turned. She grabbed a key from the shoebox outside, unlocked the kitchen door, and went into the dining room, yelling, "Hey" when she saw the rope. Around his neck. Oh god. His feet were on the floor, a pool of urine around them. Lucky's pottery stool brought in from her studio was toppled on its side.

"Dad! Dad! Come quick!"

Bullet sauntered, then ran down the concrete corridor, rushed into the dining room and pulled the rope, which didn't give way. Ande grabbed shears and cut it. She threw herself on top of Nico and began blowing into his lungs.

Later, much later, Ande wrote in her journal:

"The Amazon couldn't save him. My brother. I couldn't save him. The light of my mother's life. My sister and I were like candles in the wind: blown out once Nico was born. I grew up jealous. Why couldn't I be the special one? I clung to Marianna; I clung to my dad. I pushed my mother away. I couldn't stand that I thought she loved my brother more.

My brother hung himself from the beam over the dining table. My sister threw herself off the roof of a Waikiki hotel. Twenty-two floors she

fell. She landed next to the pool. My mother spends her time wanting to kill my dad. My dad stays busy fucking anything female that walks. I am the last kid standing.

I am not sure what to do with myself. Am I supposed to kill myself, too? Am I supposed to bob like some kind of soggy refuse on the sea of sorrow that spreads between my parents, the two floating basket cases? Am I supposed to try to make nice and mend what cannot be mended? I often think I should end their misery and kill them both. Ha ha. The big problem is I love them.

I am the middle kid; correction: I was the middle kid. The Oreo white crème center. Marianna and Nico held me up. Without them at my sides, the question begs, can I stand on my own?

And now, wow, only my floating nutcase parents flank me. That's what I'd call a depression cookie. They don't offer support. My folks hate each other so much, I get pulled apart every day, and when my center flops out, they don't even seem to notice.

I get cranky, which makes me mad, because I used to be happy. In fact, my middle name is Happy. Ande Happy Pulaski. Marianna gave me that name when I was born. She was two. Dad brought her to the hospital and said, "Today is your baby sister's birthday." Marianna said, "Happy! Happy! Happy!" It stuck. She was my best friend.

Two things worry me: God and the gene pool, the gene pool a bit more because it's what I have to live with. The existence and concept of God are too mercurial for me to think about in my average waking moment. For the most part, I relegate Him to the back burner. I mean, He's always there to blame or to beg from when I'm particularly angry or needy. He sure must have had his back turned when Nico and Marianna's lights went out, unless He was the one who flipped the switch.

I guess I am angry with God, if He exists, because, if He planned this, He's a lot meaner than I thought.

But, the gene pool: it makes me suspicious. I don't play chess, but if I did, I'd be in big trouble. I can't see any moves. Forward, backwards, sideways, diagonal. If I go back, that's the past, and it's eaten my brother and sister alive, not to mention numerous other relatives. If I go forward, yikes, that's the great unknown. Love? Marriage? Family of my own? What if I screw up the way my parents and grandparents did and have kids who kill themselves?

What if I carry the genes for depression and obsession and compulsion and addiction and masochism and god knows what else might be helixed together in my sweet little throbbing ovaries, which whine at me day and night with their biological time clock ticking to the hormonal tune of nest nest nest!

I'm twenty-eight. My mother calls me her green-eyed, blonde-haired Amazon. I suppose Mom means I am a "modern" Amazon. I rock climb, mountain climb, kite surf, wind surf, surf surf, run marathons, compete in triathlons, engage in marathon sex. Those are some of the things I do do. What I don't do is drink or drugs. I also don't talk about my family. Especially I don't talk about Nico or Marianna and never to Mom.

Not because it would hurt her. Hurt and sorrow are her middle names. Not really. She thrives on talking about them. Her voice goes all quavery, and she tears up. Intimacy is the password to my mother's ready salon of little horrors. I can't stand it.

She is also the Queen of Questions, asking, like, "How are you doing, Ande?"

Silence.

"You know, you can talk to God. You can talk to Marianna and Nico, too. I do. I know they are out there somewhere."

Silence.

"Do you pray, honey?"

Silence.

"I wanted to tell you about a bereavement group that's starting..."

"That's okay, Ma," I say, cutting her off. "I gotta go now."

My mother sees what happened her way and thinks that's the way it's written in stone. But, it's not. She doesn't know the half of it.

Markers: the times Lucky knew her life had shifted, perhaps not by her hand, but shifted nonetheless, into another gear. The time she became invisible: post menopausal, not looked at by the checkout clerks, no backward glances as she walked down the street, no construction worker whistles, and the shock of realization that the reflection in the store window glare was hers, that wrinkled and somewhat sour looking old woman. Oh god. *She is me.*

Markers: too stiff at sixty to enroll in that fun looking yoga class she taught when she was twenty-four.

She had stories too hard to tell. Incest, regret, guilt. Apologetic, *Mea culpa* stories.

Her daughter cried rape. Rod had called to tell Lucky.

"They took Marianna away in an ambulance."

"Why? When?" Lucky asked.

"Just now. Bullet is out in the street with the cops. She was yelling rape. Most of the neighborhood came out to the street. Looked to me like Bullet cut his lip, and he has scratch marks down his chest."

"Marianna was yelling rape?"

"Yeah. Sorry, Lucky."

"Where are they taking Marianna?"

"They must be going to the hospital."

Lucky flew to Honolulu to help and to ask the results of the rape test. The soonest she could get there was the following day. But Marianna was not hospitalized. She was locked up. It took Lucky several phone calls to locate her. Marianna was not in a jail. She had been taken to a psych ward. *Why, when she needed to be in a hospital?*

"Too late," they told Lucky at the admissions desk of the psych ward. "No rape test was done."

"Why not?"

"Too late," they said.

"Why was she brought here?"

"The medics said she was hysterical."

"And no rape test was done?" Lucky asked again. "It has not been twenty-four hours since my daughter was admitted."

"Too late," they said.

"No, it's the law. It's her right," Lucky insisted. "Marianna says she was raped. Listen to her. I can hear her. She is still saying it. Turn around. Hear her shouting at us through the glass in the middle of the room?"

"She is delusional," they said.

"Her father," Lucky said, "my neighbor said. Did you see his lip, split? Did you see his chest, raked? Marianna is screaming, she is crying, she is saying she's been hurt."

"Delusional," they repeated and repeated and repeated.

Her baby, her daughter, crazy, distraught, delusional? What kind of hospital was this?

Lucky was growing stale, smelling stale. She reminded herself of linens too long stored in her grandfather's cupboards: unused, mildly mildewed, yellowing like her teeth.

She hit her dog. She had gotten Seer after Nico died. Seer wouldn't release the ball. She held his head with one hand and punched the side of his muzzle, which was firmly clenched on the ball with the other and screamed, "Drop it, damn it, drop it. Bad dog. Drop the ball, god damn it."

She had lost her mind.

She did let the cat sit on her lap and eat some beef jerky while she watched a film. It was a violent film. She could not watch CNN any longer. *They should call it the horror station, maker of bad dreams and stomach aches,* she thought.

She sat at sixty in front of the TV as though she had already become her eighty five year old mother, Edna, who had grown used to lying abed day and night gleaning all her life's info from the tube. Lucky was gaining lard on her own ass. She might as well have preserved herself in a pickling jar in hopes of becoming some future culinary delight.

Her cat was seventeen and incontinent. He liked to sit on her wide lap at night while she watched *Netflix*. The other night she had showered and donned a chenille bathrobe. The cat moaned his new, old man, cat moan, and she lifted him onto her lap. He settled in, began purring, directing her hand to his head, and unleashed a horrific blast of diarrhea down the front of her robe.

Heather called it entering their period of decrepitude. Lucky called it pathetic.

Time. What to do with it? So little left. Yet each day stretched emptily, nothing filling the hours. No children, lover, or adventure. Oh, there were lawns begging mowing, tables begging dusting, dishes begging washing, beds begging making. But they did not make a life. Tasks and chores were like meals, to be done, to be eaten. But, they did not make a life. They were the slices of bread that housed the sandwich filling. The filling was the stuff of life. And, try as she might, wish as she might, she could not replace the filling for hers.

In California, Edna whimpered in her bed, moaned, cried for breath, barked commands, and was a bitch. She was not going gently. She was not forgiving; she was not kind. It was her cruelty, her blatant and pervasive cruelty that astounded Lucky, stopped her breath, and choked her with shame and sorrow.

Lucky had asked Edna before she died to tell Laura that she loved her and that she was sorry for the past, words that Laura had needed to hear from her mother since she was twelve years old and Jack had violated her.

Edna replied, "I can't stand her. She's like some lousy dog, piddling on my leg."

The words her mother spoke were too cruel for Lucky to stomach.

Making a grimace, Edna continued, "She bothers me. I just don't like her." How sad, how infinitesimally sad and tired she made Lucky.

"Mom, are you going to spend your entire life crucifying your own children? Is there not one ounce of mercy or empathy for Laura in your heart?"

Lucky could not accept that even in her deathbed, Edna refused to love her first born, Laura. Lucky resolved to lie to her sister, hoping to release her from years of pain and guilt. Lucky buried Edna's truth before she buried her.

Lucky called Laura and told her that Edna wanted her forgiveness.

Laura sobbed, "At last!"

Night after night, Lucky listened to Edna choke on phlegm during the death vigil Lucky held, awake as a watchdog on the pull out sofa bed in the living room where large brown beams striated its ceiling horizontally. They looked like a broiler rack. Lucky lay beneath them feeling as if her own blood was being boiled away. She felt entirely dispirited by her mother whose desperate cling to life seemed undignified.

"Get on with it!" Lucky wanted to shout. "What is the point in lingering? Why be so afraid of dying?"

Days before, during a rally back from the dead, Edna told Lucky over and over,

"Oh, Em, I am happy. I am having one of the best times of my life."

"You are?" Lucky asked.

"Yes!"

"Why?"

"You are with me. You are right here. I am the queen bee, the center of attention, reigning from my bed. Look at all my visitors. You even got Jackie to come."

"Yes. I am glad he came and showed you pictures of his kids."

Edna interrupted making a grimace, "He sure looks old. Why, oh jeez, why couldn't he have come sooner?"

"Oh, Mom..."

"Look, look at all my flowers and chocolates. Look at my caregivers and all the new Hospice workers. They pay attention and that makes me glad."

"What about Laura? Don't you want to see her?"

Laura stood half in and half out of the doorway. It had been almost forty years: thirty-nine years, eleven months, and a smattering of days, since Lucky had stood in Edna's bedroom, Lucky against the windows, her back to the panorama of the bay, Laura in the doorway screaming.

Lucky stood there, lost in a crack of time, remembering the angry voices and the venom of hatred dripping from the words spoken, shouted, so many years ago, the same hatred that drove Linney to fling herself from the Golden Gate bridge, that drove Jackie away, that drove Laura crazy. The words hadn't been important or memorable. It had been their mean-hearted tone that was deadly. That had been the August Jackie was ten and away with big Jack. That was the August Edna called Lucky on the phone to say fourteen-year-old Linney was seeing snakes in mirrors. That was the August Laura would scream and kick Lucky in the shins with the full force of her frustrated and fat, two hundred and thirty pound frame. That was the August Linney got locked up in an insane asylum, as Edna and Jack fought yet again over her custody, dragging their broken family roughshod along a ragged legal road where no one came away unbloodied.

Edna reclined as dowager ogress on her high four-poster bed. Linney was noticeably absent, long dead. But, Lucky was there, remembering. And, it was happening again. Edna and Laura were going at it, fangs bared. Nothing had changed. Yet, everything had, because Linney was dead, as were two of Lucky's children. A new generation had come unraveled.

Lucky could not understand. She could not understand how people, the people she had loved, could take such pleasure from systematically and deliberately hurting each other, how they could survive their own wickedness. She couldn't believe that nothing had changed, the dynamic between Edna and Laura, in all these years, these years of sorrow and loss, remained as the two uncooperative, yoked rhinoceroses jostled against one another.

By month's end, it was evident that Edna was not going gently into her goodnight despite the prediction of her palliative care doctor. She was raging, voracious to stay in her fight for life, refusing the morphine that made her nap, forcing herself to stay awake for thirty-six hours at a time.

"Why don't you rest, Mom?" Lucky asked, rearranging Edna's pillows.

"I might not wake up," Edna replied. It had been nine days since Hospice decided to deny Edna food or water, allowing Lucky only sponges to mop Edna's mouth to assuage her thirst.

"Mom, are you so afraid to die?" Lucky asked.

"Yeah," Edna nodded. She could no longer open her eyes, but her hearing remained acute, and she spoke or grimaced when she could summon the strength.

"Well, are you afraid of death hurting, or are you afraid of the afterlife, if there is one?"

"You're so damned stupid," Edna slowly enunciated, rolling her head slightly to the side. "I hate this pain, and I am going straight to hell."

"Because of your mom?"

Edna tried to nod as tears slid through the yellowed crust on her lids and down the folds of her cheeks.

"Oh, Mom," Lucky sighed. "You had to. She begged, right? You told me she was in terrible pain and begged for the morphine to end it."

"I miss her, Em. I've always missed my mom. I killed her. I had to. She wanted me to. I could never go to church again. I hated those priests."

Edna seemed to lapse into sleep when she suddenly added, "You keep that morphine away from me."

"I think death must be like going to sleep and not waking up again," Lucky said. "I don't think it hurts, Mom. Maybe we dream another dream; maybe we don't dream at all. Maybe we go on, and we just leave our bodies behind. I'd like to think that."

In this infernal wait, Lucky was hearing too many conversations in her head. She called to her children, alive and dead. She told them she loved them. She had never asked for their forgiveness, as that was beyond asking. She asked them to come near; she told them she missed them. She looked for Linney. She was so, so sorry. She did ask Linney to forgive her.

Lucky hadn't saved anyone. Was it her job? Linney had begged Lucky to save her many times. Lucky had walked away, flown away, turned her back, and hung up phones, always promising "later."

She had tried to save Nico and Marianna. They had had enough. They had wanted out. Lucky tried to let Edna know it was okay to go, but she wanted to stay.

The coffin was black, lacquered, and conical. It looked like a hellishly sleek art-deco dream. Edna lay inside, nestled on the cream tufted silk, quiet at last; her face wore the same twisted smirk it had carried in life. She was quiet, a corpse in a black and white casket. Laura took the first turn to say goodbye. She practically danced a jig to the coffin, looked inside and giggled. Lucky requested privacy, and Laura left the room in a huff.

Lucky gazed a long time at her mother before she apologized. Lucky was sorry, sorry for so much not of her own doing. She was sorry there had not been enough love or understanding in her mother's life. She was sorry that she had not had sufficient patience to kindly entertain her mother's demands or to be the truly sympathetic daughter her mother deserved. She was sorry her mother had been given the task of a mercy killing of her own mother. Lucky was sorry for Edna's subsequent depressions, her loss of faith, her post-partum blues, her choice of Jack for her husband. She was sorry Edna covered her vulnerability and pain with such an abrasive manner that it made it hard to get close or be comfortable around her.

"I love you, Mom. You know that. I really and truly love you. It was just so hard. Everything. I am sorry." And, after a lengthy sigh and a few moments' passage, her left hand holding the casket lid, Lucky added, "I really love you, Mom. Thank you. Thank you for being my Mom."

She carefully closed the casket. She placed on top an elegant spray of pure white tulips, in the center, a single rose of deepest red. And, on it alone, droplets of dew. Not dew. They were her tears. They looked like diamonds. Trickling down, they pooled into the furled velvet petals of the solitary red, red rose.

Months after Edna's passing, Lucky began working in her studio on a theme of transformation. It had begun as a tiny flicker in her mind when she had burned Bully's paintings. She had changed along with the paintings; she had burned away her dependence on him. Later, and to her horror, she'd had to cremate Nico.

When she buzzed at the entrance to the coroner's office, she was startled by the sterility of the building. It was three stories of concrete, glass, and metal. The buzzer echoed off an interior wall somewhere above. Then the door unlatched with a click. She went inside and climbed the industrial metal staircase suspended against a wall, each of her footsteps clanging. Nothing was on the walls except a drab coat of gray paint. She had come there to sign forms. Her son's death had been unattended. The county required an autopsy, which meant strangers would cut on her son, examine her beautiful boy, violate his privacy. What for? He was dead. An autopsy would not bring him back. She was there to sign forms to release his corpse from such an intrusion.

The mezzanine landing was quite empty except for a cheap vinyl couch. There was a glassed reception window on the right, an alcove in the center, and a door marked "coroner" on the left. In the alcove, a large Plexiglas case dominated the entry to the morgue itself. In the case was the largest raku pot Lucky had ever made.

Her pot. *How could it get here?* She heard someone screaming. She heard someone wailing. The door to the coroner's office flew open, and she was lifted up from where she had fallen to the ground, disoriented and sobbing.

"Why is my pot here?" She screamed at the staff, suddenly angry. "Who brought it here? Is this some cosmic joke?"

"Ma'am, Ma'am," the receptionist asked, "what is wrong? How can I help you?"

"That's my pot," Lucky said. "Right there. I am the artist. I made it. I want to know why is it here?" Lucky remembered making the piece years before. It was a large masculine torso reminiscent of a Samurai warrior but more regal. It was colored tarnished green and black, like the skin of a slightly rotted fig. Where medals might have been placed over a western general's chest, she had torn the clay and tinted it a matte maroon like dried blood over a heart. And atop the neck of the piece, she had placed a clay helmet. It looked like a figure from feudal Japan, not the Shogun nor the Samurai. She had titled it, Daimyo, Guardian of the Realm."

"The county brought it just yesterday," the receptionist said. "We've never had art here before. Why has it upset you?"

Lucky had sold many pieces to the state and the county during her career. They were placed in public places; some were in legislative offices, some in libraries. Most she did not keep track of.

"My son, my son is here. That's why I came." Lucky steadied herself. "I am Mrs. Pulaski. I came to sign release papers."

And then it made sense. She, Lucky, had symbolically been present through her art in the morgue, she, the mother, to watch over her children as they passed through its portals into the next realm.

Lucky did not believe Nico's spirit had been destroyed when his youthful body was changed to ash and smoke. And, then there had been Marianna. The flicker of a theme of transformation turned to a flame. After Edna's funeral, that flame burst into a conscious fire.

Lucky had always used fire in her work to transform the clay from white porcelain to smoke imbued raku and to transform the copper in her glazes from oxidation greens to reduction reds. Yet she had never deeply considered the other changes fire made. The fuels for her kilns were gas, dung, and wood. Now Lucky thought about the wood and how it transformed itself in the fire.

A tree was a living plant. It was cut, dried, and burned to heat and change her clay, to vitrify it chemically into rock. As the wood burned away, it turned into ash and smoke. The smoke dissipated in the air becoming invisible to the naked eye, yet its elements of hydrogen, carbon, and oxygen were ever-present. It did not matter if she could no longer see the tree, nor the wood, nor the fire, nor the smoke. The original elements still existed in the universe. That matter could neither be created nor destroyed was a cornerstone of physics.

She liked transferring this principle to her lost children, to her loved ones, the idea that they could neither be created nor destroyed. When they were born, they had been called into being by love. When they died, their bodies had been burned. Even though the ovens at the crematorium used radiant heat and gave off no smoke, Lucky had sat outside the building on a curb to wait as her children's bodies were transformed from flesh to ash. And maybe, she hoped, it was also true that their souls, their eternal souls, could neither be created nor destroyed.

In her clay work, she began leaving walls unfinished. Instead of a six-sided box, she left out a side, even pulling it into a fragmentation of itself. When she glazed, she deliberately left portions of the piece unglazed or sponged the glaze away. She made boxes with an animal emerging from the base as though a geometric shape was suddenly morphing into an organic shape. In this way, she began using her forms to make suggestions of something else coming into focus, quite different from the original shape.

If she had learned anything, it was that the invisible and the intangible were more real than what she saw in the physical world. *Look at communication,* she thought. *Wireless. Imagine that. Look at love,* she thought. *Invisible. Imagine that. Look at thought itself, invisible. Even the imagination was invisible.*

Her imagined pots could be physically manifested with real clay in her real studio. Her dreams of motherhood, she had manifested through love, marriage, sex, and childbearing. And, death, it turned out, by taking her loved ones, wore arms that "lifted the veil" from her eyes. Death had allowed her to see, like a Tiresias or a Cassandra, into the world or worlds beyond this one. Death had raised the shade on eternity allowing her a glimpse, perhaps, of hope.

She thought of Marianna's question, "Mom, did you ever forgive Big Jack for leaving?" It didn't matter now. She wondered if Marianna had forgiven Bullet for leaving the family or hurting her before she had died. Marianna had in the end wanted forgiveness for herself, for being the one who left them. Her suicide note had said, "Mom, I am so sorry. Dad, I am so sorry. Ande, I am so sorry."

There is a horror to loss, Lucky thought, *like it belonged to someone else. It was a news story; it was alien; it was foreign.* It could not be hers. Her loss. And then she remembered that it was. Her children were gone, dead. And, she had been in grief for years. She realized, she remembered, that she was alive. That their deaths were not hers. Even though they felt like hers. Somehow she had survived, if such a word fit, and she didn't want to. That was part, a small part, of the horror of loss.

Her children's lives had been eviscerated by sadness. Neither Marianna nor Nico had been mentally ill or evil. They had been sad. It was as simple and as devastating as that.

One morning, listening to Book Two of *The Hunger Games* with its theme of survival at her round glass dining table with its view across the endless Pacific Ocean, a demitasse of coffee steaming to one side, a soft coral rose unfurling in Edna's maroon Chinese cloisonné vase in front of her, and to the left, a blue and white porcelain bowl of steel cut oats melting its bright butter into flax oil, Lucky realized it might have been perfect. What? Everything. The day. Her mood. Life. As it was. Everything might have been perfect.

She was dressed for yoga in black tights, white tee shirt, magenta tunic, lotus pendant, a pearl in each lobe. Dark chocolate dipped Turkish apricots were drying on the travertine counter. She had found the dried apricots in Edna's belongings, which Lucky had packed nearly two years ago when her mother had died and which had arrived at Lucky's doorstep the other day in a crate of furnishings and memorabilia finally taken out of storage and shipped to the islands. Lucky had melted dark chocolate in the microwave before dipping the apricots and packaging these treats for her beloved three-year-old granddaughter. What fun to introduce Ande's little Ku'i to their succulence along with a cup of tea in one of Edna's treasured China cups as part of their first tea party.

Lucky's golden retriever, Seer, suffering old age and doggie Alzheimer's, panted and wagged his love rhythmically, his tail hitting the screen door while he patiently watched Lucky in the dining room. Birds sang above the thrum of the morning rain on the metal roof, their song lilting despite the heavy grey mist. Thick low-slung clouds obscured most of the verdant hills and stands of green bamboo fronting her view of the coastline.

Lucky sat quite still, calmly seated on a floral dining chair, conscious of her place on this tiny island in the middle of the vast Pacific. The island, like Lucky, was isolated. Her large tea temples flanked each corner of the dining room like sentries guarding the view beyond. Years, years ago, when she was ending her marriage, she had thirsted for both beauty and protection. She had created these serene clay fortresses to calm her fears and give her courage.

Little could she have known how much would be lost: two children, a life, an identity, a husband, a home, and a career. Nor how much would be gained: a home in the garden of Eden, grandchildren, new friends, an alignment with divinity, a life of the mind and spirit, love. Here she sat, surrounded by beauty and serenity on an island floating in a sea of chaos, listening to literature, looking at art, seeing the world, imagining the universe, pondering eternity. She wondered if she had salvaged enough of her heart to go on.

It seemed to be about transformation, life that is. As an artist, she continued to create beauty from clay, molding lumps of it into shimmering temples, transforming torn negative spaces into intriguing hollows, continuing to create the series, *Vehicles of Transport,* she had begun when she met Ray. The only path to atonement or redemption or salvation she had found over her years of loss and guilt was in creating beauty.

In the evening, a new moon peeked over the horizon in the last quieting moments of dusk. The sky was glazed a deep blue like one of her porcelain boats, tinged by a fringe of salmon light against the silhouetted hills and blackened furls of the palms. The dying clouds thinned into ghostly, shadow-like wings seeming to flutter across a heaven of navy. And the wind's song ruffled the evening air like the feathers beneath the sleepy twitters of birds ascending their nests.

Gently stroking Seer's golden head, Lucky watched the sky darken before the whispering white crescent of the rising moon brightened it again. Then the evening star began to shine like the *Hope Diamond* in front of the vast cosmos. Without doubt, she thought, gazing over the sea and sky, her loved ones were there, lighting the way.

THE END

ACKNOWLEDGEMENTS

To three brave proof readers who are loyal friends, my thanks
for your unstinting help, time, criticism, and insights:

Cheryl Joseph, Kayleen Polichetti, Sherry Kline

To artist Barbara Chu for the use of her print on the cover,
my gratitude

To my wonderful children for enriching my life:
Aloha 'oe

ABOUT THE AUTHOR

Arabella Ark, who has never harmed a dog, by the way, lives in the Hawai'ian Islands. She received a Master's degree in Directing from University of California at Berkeley and worked in theatre, film and news journalism. Love, always serendipitous, has often come through the backdoor of her heart, unexpectedly. Children, pets, family, lovers, the sea, the sunset, the islands, and art arrived to play. And there, she made them welcome, even if they slammed the door behind them.

Made in the USA
Charleston, SC
22 January 2015